Award-winning author Summer Faye pens fun, contemporary romances. Internationally published, with books translated into more than a dozen languages, she is a two-time winner of the *RT Book Reviews* Reviewers' Choice Award and winner of the CataRomance Reviewers' Choice Award. Now living her dream, she resides with her very patient husband and Writer Kitty. When she's not plotting out her next romance you can find her with a mug of tea and a book. Learn more at jenniferfaye.com.

Justine Lewis writes uplifting, heart-warming contemporary romances. She lives in Australia with her hero husband, two teenagers and an outgoing puppy. When she isn't writing she loves to walk her dog in the bush near her house, attempt to keep her garden alive, and search for the perfect frock. She loves hearing from readers and you can visit her at justinelewis.com.

Also by Jennifer Faye

Princesses of Rydiania miniseries

His Accidentally Pregnant Princess

Greek Paradise Escape miniseries

It Started with a Royal Kiss
Second Chance with the Bridesmaid

Also by Justine Lewis

Billionaire's Snowbound Marriage Reunion
Fiji Escape with Her Boss

Discover more at millsandboon.co.uk.

ROYAL MUM FOR THE DUKE'S DAUGHTER

JENNIFER FAYE

BACK IN THE GREEK TYCOON'S WORLD

JUSTINE LEWIS

MILLS & BOON

First published in Great Britain 2023
by Mills & Boon, an imprint of HarperCollins*Publishers* Ltd,
1 London Bridge Street, London, SE1 9GF

www.harpercollins.co.uk

HarperCollins*Publishers*, Macken House, 39/40 Mayor Street Upper,
Dublin 1, D01 C9W8, Ireland

Royal Mum for the Duke's Daughter © 2023 Jennifer F. Stroka

Back in the Greek Tycoon's World © 2023 Justine Lewis

ISBN: 978-0-263-30649-1

07/23

This book is produced from independently certified FSC™ paper
to ensure responsible forest management.
For more information visit: www.harpercollins.co.uk/green.

Printed and Bound in the UK using 100% Renewable Electricity
at CPI Group (UK) Ltd, Croydon, CR0 4YY

ROYAL MUM FOR THE DUKE'S DAUGHTER

JENNIFER FAYE

MILLS & BOON

CHAPTER ONE

ONE FOOT IN front of the other.

It had been Rez Baráth, the Duke of Kaspar's, mantra for the past year. Some days were easier than others. Today was one of the better ones. His fourteen-month-old daughter, Evi, had just taken her first steps.

And though he'd been such a proud papa in the moment, it was when he instinctually thought of telling Enora that her absence from their lives seared through him like a sword straight to his heart. In the past year of grieving his wife's death, he'd started to forget the little details, like the sound of her voice and her contagious laugh.

There were other times when he'd have to pull up a photo of Enora on his phone in order to remember her smile and the way it made her eyes twinkle. Guilt would assail him. How could he let those details grow fuzzy? What was wrong with him?

A moment was all it took for the gravity of one man's careless action to destroy Rez's perfect family. And now it was up to him to take the jagged pieces of their life and reframe it in order to recreate a family for his daughter.

He could never replace his wife in their daughter's life. Enora was so organized and seemed to instinctively know exactly what their baby daughter needed.

He was quite certain he was making an utter mess of

everything. But he refused to give up. He had to keep putting one foot in front of the other and hope he didn't do too much damage.

He was sitting on the floor in the study as the sunlight streamed in through the large windows. Evi was next to him on the floor with her toys. She'd pick up one wooden block, put it to her rosy lips and then toss it aside. It would appear she didn't appreciate the taste of wood.

He'd learned the hard way that it didn't matter how many times he told her not to put things in her mouth, it didn't stop her. Now he just made sure anything within reach was appropriate to be drooled on.

Evi turned her head and smiled at him. He saw his wife in their daughter's smile. His heart swelled with love. Enora would live on through their daughter.

In the next heartbeat, he worried that he didn't know what was best for Evi. Perhaps he should marry again for Evi's sake. His little girl needed a mother to help guide her in ways he couldn't even imagine. But he just wasn't ready to make such a big commitment.

Instead, he'd immersed himself in his life as a single parent, hoping he could somehow be enough for Evi. He'd even taken a leave of absence from his law firm. But if he didn't return to the office soon, his leave would turn into a resignation.

The funny thing was that when Enora had first mentioned having a family, he hadn't been sure he wanted to be a father. He couldn't envision himself sitting around playing games and doing the middle-of-the-night feedings. And now he couldn't imagine his life without Evi in it. She was the most precious gift that Enora had given him. And he would be eternally grateful that she had known this was right for the both of them.

But he was torn between his responsibilities for Evi and his desire to return to the office. As much as he loved his daughter, he longed for some adult conversation and something to challenge his mind. He had nannies to look after Evi, but with his long hours, he wouldn't see much of Evi. He knew it wasn't what Enora would have wanted for their daughter. Guilt settled on him for wanting to be somewhere else. Because Evi was now the center of his life and she needed him more than ever now that she didn't have a mother.

Buzz-buzz.

It startled him. His phone didn't ring much because he'd pushed most everyone away after his wife's death. The first thing that came to mind was that something was wrong.

When he removed the phone from his pocket, he expected to see his mother's name on the caller ID. But instead it was Princess Beatrix. Why in the world would she want to speak to him?

And then he sighed. How could he have forgotten about the wedding? Her brother's royal wedding. And if his memory was correct, it was in a couple of weeks. He knew he should be more on top of these things since he was the best man. But when Istvan had asked him to stand up for him, Rez had told him that with being a single parent he wasn't the best choice. Istvan had insisted he totally understood. Istvan assured him that he just wanted his childhood best friend there with him on his big day.

Rez pressed the phone to his ear. "What may I do for you, Your Royal Highness?"

"Rez, you know you can just call me Beatrix."

The sound of her gentle voice swept him back in time to a point where they were young and carefree. He missed those days and he found himself missing the Princess too. He highly doubted she'd called to catch-up on life. Although it wouldn't hurt to extend the conversation just a little.

"It's been a while since we really talked and I wasn't sure how you would feel about me taking such liberties. After all, I seem to remember you getting upset with me for calling you—"

"Stop. I remember," she said dryly.

Her seriousness only egged him on. "So then you don't want me to call you Bizzy-Bea?"

"Definitely not." Her voice held no sense of humor. "How about we go with Beatrix?"

Beatrix was almost as bad as Your Highness. It was so proper and the Beatrix he remembered used to be all smiles and giggles. She'd been full of sunshine and rainbows. She'd been the little sister of his best friend and too young for him back then, but he always knew she'd one day grow into a beautiful woman.

But there was a part of him that wanted the carefree girl of their youth back because he could use some sunshine in his life. "Or Bea."

There was a noted pause on the other end of the phone. He imagined her pursing her lips together as she tapped her foot. The image made him smile—something he didn't do unless in the presence of his daughter.

Bea expelled an exasperated sigh. "Or Beatrix."

It was so good to speak to her. He let out a laugh. He couldn't help it. When had Bizzy-Bea grown up to be so serious? And then he realized it really had been too long since he'd felt the elation of a genuine laugh. When Enora had died, his happiness had been buried with her.

Laughter had been sucked into a vacuum and lost in the darkness.

"Rez, the reason I called is because the wedding is in trouble."

"What?" His amusement was long forgotten. "What's going on?"

"You're probably the only person in Rydiania that hasn't read the gossip." When his phone buzzed, she said, "I've sent you the link."

He lowered his phone and put it on speakerphone before he looked at the link. "I don't know why anyone cares what the *Duchess Tales* has to say. They're forever making up nonsense."

"It's more than that this time. Read it."

He clicked on the link and began to read.

Princess-to-Be Banished!

He read the headline again. Beneath the all-caps headline was a photo of Indigo, Istvan's fiancée. Rez was confused. Someone had made a big mistake. Indigo was about to be welcomed into the royal family with open arms.

This royal watcher has some big news for all of you. I have it from an excellent source that Prince Istvan's intended bride is the daughter of a thief, who stole from the crown years ago. The thief, along with his family, was banished not only from the royal court but also from the entire country of Rydiania.

You've heard it here first. This duchess has sworn to

keep you up on the latest with the royal family and I am doing just that.

You might ask how something like this could have happened. Well, you aren't alone. I assure you, I am hard at work on securing the nitty-gritty details on how this fiasco could have happened.

Did Indigo deceive our lusciously handsome prince? Or was the Prince hoping to carry off this illegal affair in public, hoping us royal watchers wouldn't catch on?

Surely poor Prince Istvan has been duped by the conniving princess-to-be, who wasn't even supposed to be in this country. Did she really think that by using her mother's maiden name she would get away with this level of deception?

Keep reading, my lovely watchers, as I will share the details as they unfold.

This was outrageous! Preposterous. And perhaps a bit worrisome.

"The palace should go after the Duchess for slander and defamation." Anger pulsed through his veins. "The case should be announced loud and clear as a warning so no one else tries the same thing."

"I don't know. It would be up to the King and Queen. Anyway I need, erm… We need you to come and stay at the palace. I think it's going to take all of us to keep this wedding on track."

The palace was a few hours south of his country estate. It was too far for him to conveniently commute back and forth with the hope of spending quality time with Evi. If he was to help, he'd need to stay at the palace. He hadn't left his home since his wife died. And yet he felt compelled by the great debt he owed Istvan.

He took the phone off speaker and pressed it to his ear. "You really think me coming there will help?"

"I do. You didn't see Indigo's face when she first saw those headlines. She was utterly crushed. And you know how much my parents hate scandal."

Was he ready to reenter society? His presence at the palace would be exactly that. There would be paparazzi lurking at the gate keeping track of the comings and goings of palace guests. The thought of dealing with the press knotted up his gut.

He never left his estate these days. He stayed at home with his daughter, but he was also deeply indebted to the Prince. If it wasn't for Istvan, he wouldn't even have his little girl. The Prince had saved his baby daughter's life.

He owed his best friend more than he could ever repay. He owed him his life because if anything had happened to Evi... He drew his thoughts up short. He refused to imagine a life without his sweet, adorable Evi in it. It was tortuous enough having lost his wife.

He'd never forget what his friend had done risking his own life. And that was why he was still here having this conversation with Bea. A conversation he didn't want to have. But a debt he was driven to repay. He'd sworn if Istvan ever needed him, he would be there for him—even if the repayment ended up being a steep one.

It was with the greatest hesitation that he said, "I'll come, but I need to bring Evi and her nanny. I can't be away from my daughter for any great length of time."

"I understand. Please bring them."

"All right. I'll be there tomorrow."

"Couldn't you come sooner?" There was a note of desperation in her voice.

"As in today?"

"Oh, yes. That would be perfect. Thank you." She ended the call.

He couldn't believe Bea had convinced him to go to the palace. He had no idea how he could help the situation. He supposed he could lend a shoulder for Istvan to lean on.

Still, going to the palace, where he would have to be sociable. He didn't do social these days. Perhaps remaining within the palace walls and away from the press wouldn't be so bad. It was for his best friend, who would do the same for him.

CHAPTER TWO

THE PALACE WAS ABUZZ.

And not in a good way.

The bride and groom were at odds. Beatrix wanted to help them, but she didn't know what she could do to rectify this awful situation. She was used to being the peacemaker in the family, but she was out of her element when the threat came from outside the palace walls.

At the moment, she was the only bridesmaid in Rydiania. The other two bridesmaids were in Greece on a little resort island called Ludus. It's where Indigo used to work. As for the groomsmen, Istvan had picked three of his childhood friends. One was out of the country until the eve of the wedding. Another was with his wife who was due to give birth to their first child any day now. So that left her and Rez to do what they could to help Istvan and Indigo. But how?

Her thoughts turned to the Queen. Her mother was the one who protected the family and the royal name. Her mother had dedicated her life to doing whatever was necessary to protect the royal family. It used to bother Beatrix the way her mother would manipulate people and circumstances to make the palace shine, but perhaps in this particular instance her mother's skills were exactly what they needed. She worried that even the Queen might not be wily enough to right what had gone so drastically wrong.

Indigo had just called off the wedding before fleeing the palace with Istvan in pursuit. Beatrix hoped they were able to work things out. If it wasn't for that gossip site, they'd still be happily preparing for their wedding.

Beatrix rushed down the grand staircase to update the Queen on the bride and groom's departure, but before she reached the bottom step, Rez walked in the door. She came to an immediate halt a few steps from the bottom. The breath caught in her lungs. Rez grew increasingly handsome with every passing year.

When she was a teenager, she'd had the biggest crush on him. Of course, he'd been five years older than her and her older brother's best friend. Rez had never looked at her as anything but a little sister. Looking back on those times, she was mortified at the way she'd mooned over him.

Ever since he'd announced his engagement, she'd kept her distance from him, lest her brother tease her for her childhood crush. Why did her brother have to have a memory like an elephant?

Rez was tall, even taller than Istvan. He was certainly a man to be reckoned with, but as she recalled he didn't have a temper unless provoked. Otherwise he'd been easygoing and fun to be around.

He was also the most delicious eye candy. Rez's broad shoulders filled out the dark suit he was wearing. He had certainly bulked up since they were kids. She hadn't allowed herself to notice in the past, but now, well, he was a widower. Not that she had any intention of starting anything with him.

His dark hair was longer than he normally wore it. She'd guess he didn't get his hair trimmed all that often now that he was still spending all of his time holed up on his estate. Even though she made a point not to go out of her way to be informed about his life, it was impossible not to hear the gossip. From what she'd heard he'd all but given up on life after the tragic death of his young wife. But it was his baby daughter that kept him going.

Beatrix's heart went out to him. She couldn't even imagine all he'd gone through and now to be a single parent. She couldn't imagine what it must be like to start off co-parenting only to wake up one day and be doing it all alone. It must be quite a shock.

Her gaze met his piercing blue gaze. Her heart leaped to her throat. Had he caught her checking him out? She hoped not. If so, it would make for a very awkward start to things.

In a much slower pace, she continued down the last step to the marble floor. As she neared him, she considered giving him a brief hug and feathery kiss like old friends were prone to do. But the rigid line of his shoulders and the frown on his handsome face had her maintaining her distance.

She hoped when she spoke that her voice would sound normal. "Rez, thank you for coming."

He didn't say anything for a moment. "It's been a while since we've seen each other. You're still as beautiful as ever."

Heat bloomed in her chest and rushed to her cheeks. "Thank you. You're looking good too." Her heart pitter-pattered. She licked her dry lips. "I just wish you were here under different circumstances."

"I do too. I take it things haven't improved."

Beatrix shook her head. "It's a mess." She glanced around. "Did Evi come with you?"

"The nanny has taken her upstairs." He hesitated. "Would you like to meet her?"

Beatrix found herself caught off guard by the change in Rez's demeanor. "Perhaps it would be best to let her get settled. She must be tired after the car ride."

"Actually she slept most of the way." His eyes were guarded. "And she'd like to meet you."

Beatrix worried that he was going to continue pushing the subject of meeting his daughter. She noticed how the frown disappeared from his face whenever he mentioned his daughter. Beatrix was happy he had that special relationship.

She sometimes wondered if she would have been a good parent. As soon as the thought came to her, she pushed it away. There was no point pondering something that wasn't going to happen. It broke her heart when the doctor had told her that between the severity of her endometriosis and the surgeries that she'd never be able to carry a baby of her own.

But she'd dealt with the devastating news and made peace with her life without children. Unlike her brother and sister, she knew her life was going to be one of service. She liked—no, she loved being out among the people and shining a light on areas of life that needed assistance.

Luckily she wasn't the heir apparent—that had been her brother, Prince Istvan. However, with him stepping out of line for the crown, her older sister, Gisella, was now the Crown Princess. And so it didn't matter to the palace if Beatrix had children or not.

But seeing Rez again was bringing back all of her youthful dreams of creating a life with him—a life that had included children to carry on his lineage. Children that would resemble their handsome father.

And suddenly it was like she'd just learned the news once more that she couldn't carry a baby of her own. She felt the loss profoundly. Tears pricked the backs of her eyes. She blinked them away. A fundamental choice that had been taken from her.

"Come." Rez gestured for her to follow him. "I'll introduce you to Evi."

Beatrix didn't move. Her heart clutched in her chest. She wasn't ready for this, especially not with the man whose babies she'd once dreamed of having and now that could never be.

Rez stopped at the bottom of the steps and turned back, but before either of them could speak one of the Queen's footmen in all of his black and purple finery appeared.

He bowed. "Your Royal Highness, the Queen has requested your presence in her office." The young man turned to Rez. "The Queen has requested your attendance as well."

Beatrix expelled a gentle sigh of relief. As they started in the direction of the Queen's office, she couldn't help but feel she'd dodged a bullet.

She glanced over at Rez. But how long could she make excuses not to meet Evi before Rez suspected something? She wasn't prepared to see his sweet baby girl. It would drive home exactly what she was going to miss in life.

She worried that she wouldn't be able to keep her emotions under control. He'd push until she confessed the painful truth. And she wasn't ready to share with him that she couldn't have children. The only people that knew were her immediate family. And that's how she intended to keep it.

CHAPTER THREE

"THANK YOU FOR COMING." The Queen sat behind her large oak desk.

Beatrix couldn't help but notice the stress lines marring her mother's face making her look much older. Her mother usually took things in stride but things within the palace walls had been tumultuous lately. This latest scandal was taking a toll on everyone.

Beatrix wondered if she'd done the right thing by asking Rez to come to the palace. She hadn't thought through her plan before extending the invitation. Of course he'd want to bring his daughter. Now she worried that her emotions over her diagnosis might not be as resolved as she'd thought they were.

Just then the door opened behind her. Beatrix turned to find her sister Gisella, followed by the King. The King's eyes momentarily widened when he saw everyone congregating in the Queen's office.

Once the door was closed, all eyes turned toward the Queen, who turned to Beatrix. "You have news?"

"I do." Beatrix filled them in on the big fight between Istvan and Indigo. "And now Indigo has left the Kingdom. I think if we're going to help them we need to know the story behind the headline."

The King moved to stand next to the Queen. "It's a story we were hoping to keep under wraps because it's so painful for Indigo."

"But that's impossible now," the Queen said. "It's just a matter of time until the press knows all of the details. If only Istvan had fallen in love with someone else, the most painful page in this family's history wouldn't have to be revisited."

"This has something to do with Uncle Georgios?" Beatrix asked.

The King nodded. "Indigo's father was King Georgios's private secretary. When your uncle left Rydiania, so did his personal staff."

"You exiled his staff too?" This was the first Beatrix was hearing of this. She'd been very young when this had all happened so she had no memories of it.

"It had to be done," the Queen said. "All precautions had to be taken to ensure the future of the crown. We couldn't have powerful people with connections as well as an absolute allegiance to Georgios causing problems. After all, your father wasn't asked to step into this role. It had been thrust upon us when Georgios decided being king was too much for him and went to live on that Greek island."

"But that never included Indigo or her mother," the King said. "Now we have to hope Istvan will be able to make Indigo realize that the royal family will support her through this trying time."

"What are we going to do now?" Beatrix asked.

"Do?" Gisella looked at her. "There's nothing to do. Indigo chose to leave. We have to hope Istvan can get through to her."

Beatrix shook her head. "Not about that. We need to

keep the news of Indigo calling off the wedding and leaving the country from the paparazzi."

"I agree," the Queen said. "And with blood in the water, so to speak, the press is going to be all over this latest development."

"Hopefully Istvan can convince her to come back right away," Gisella said. "That should put to rest any rumors of the wedding being in jeopardy."

"I wish that was the case," Beatrix said, "but you didn't see Indigo when she left here. I don't think she'll be back anytime soon."

The Queen turned to the King with narrowed brows and her lips pursed. "I told you we needed to deal with her past from the start, but you caved in to her wants and thought it could all be buried."

He frowned. "Now isn't the time for throwing around the blame. What we need is a plan. And since you're so good at them, what do you suggest?"

The Queen looked directly at Beatrix. "We need a story that will tease away the press from the wedding."

The family threw around some ideas. While they talked, Beatrix glanced over at Rez. He was absolutely silent. By his blank expression, she was unable to read what he was thinking. She remembered that particular look from when they were kids. It had helped him feign innocence from childhood pranks.

But all of these years later there was something different about him. It was the pain that would periodically glimmer in his eyes when he didn't think anyone was looking. It had been more than a year since he'd lost his wife and his pain was still tangible. She wished there was something she could do to comfort him.

Just then Rez turned his head enough for his gaze to

meet hers. She was busted. Heat swirled in her chest, rushed up her neck and settled in her cheeks. For a second, their gazes locked. Then the corners of his mouth started to lift as his eyes twinkled with amusement. Was he laughing at her?

With a soft huff, she turned away. What had she been thinking to get busted staring at him? And it wasn't like she'd been ogling him because she was interested in him. She'd gotten over her childhood crush many years ago. Luckily no one else seemed to have noticed their silent exchange.

"What can we do to help?" Gisella asked, drawing Beatrix from her thoughts.

"Obviously no one can mention that Indigo and Istvan have left the palace," the King said. "We're going to imply that they are here working on some final wedding details."

"Mother," Beatrix said, "you mentioned something about distracting the press. Do you have a suggestion of how we could go about doing that?"

"What about a new romance?" the Queen suggested.

Everyone wore a look of surprise. There were a bunch of shrugs. The only problem was that none of them were in a relationship or even on the verge of one.

"Don't look at me," Gisella said. "I've got enough going on with the upcoming coronation."

"Of course, dear," the Queen said. "And we wouldn't want our soon-to-be queen involved in a fake relationship."

All of the sudden everyone turned in Beatrix's direction. Her spine stiffened. *Oh, no. No, no, no.* Surely they didn't think she was going to pretend to be in a relationship. Who was going to buy that? Everyone knew she hadn't dated anyone in the past year. And she wasn't planning to start now.

Ever since the last man she'd been involved with had proposed, she realized letting herself get that close to anyone was a mistake. She wasn't ready to be married. And there was the complication of her not being able to have a family of her own that would have to be addressed before any wedding proposal could seriously be considered.

When she'd put off her ex's marriage proposal, it had gone horribly wrong. Before she could explain to him about her infertility issues, he'd accused her of being fickle—of not knowing what she wanted. After his tirade, she'd ended things altogether. Ever since then she'd been hesitant to get seriously involved with anyone.

Her life was full with royal obligations and her pet projects. Her spare time was spent on the golf course. She loved the game, the sunshine and the challenge of beating some of the finest golfers in Europe. Did she really need anything more?

And yet it was so natural for her to step up when her family needed help. After all, she had devoted her life to one of service. But this seemed above and beyond the call of duty.

Beatrix swallowed hard. "No one is going to believe it's me. Everyone knows I'm taking a break from dating."

The Queen's eyes lit up. "That's all the more reason it'll draw the paparazzi's interest."

Beatrix shook her head. "I don't think so. There has to be another way."

As though Beatrix hadn't said a word, the Queen continued. "All we need is someone to play your love interest."

It didn't seem to matter what she said, her mother

was already set on this course of action. And as much as Beatrix wanted to help her brother and Indigo, this just seemed like a bad idea.

Beatrix watched as her family turned to Rez. She gaped. Not him. Definitely not him.

She snapped her mouth closed. Her heart raced as her breathing came in short, shallow gasps. She lowered her head and stared at the floor, hoping her family wouldn't notice that she was on the verge of a full-blown panic attack.

This couldn't be happening. Of all the people in the Kingdom, why did it have to be him? She refused to look in Rez's direction. The thought of them pretending to be a couple caused the heat to return to her cheeks. She struggled to get a hold on her panicked emotions and she was failing badly.

She concentrated on slowing her breaths by breathing in, holding her breath and then slowly expelling it. Surely Rez wouldn't agree to any of this. She took some comfort in the thought. Her racing heart rate began to slow. After all, he was still grieving for his wife. There was no way he'd want to get involved in a scheme like this.

"What do you say, Rez?" the King asked.

That wasn't fair. Who was going to turn down a direct request from the King? Beatrix's back teeth clenched as she bit back her frustration. For a moment, an awkward silence ensued.

"Are we sure this is the direction we want to go?" Rez asked very diplomatically.

The King arched a brow. "Do you have a better idea?"

Rez was quiet for a moment as though he was scrambling for a different idea. "No, sir. I just worry that the press will see through the charade."

"They won't question you two getting together. It's well-known that you grew up together. I think the public will be elated with the idea of you two dating." The Queen's direct gaze met his. "Do you feel this is something you could do to help the Prince?"

There was a distinct hesitation.

Beatrix lifted her gaze. Why wasn't he turning down the preposterous proposal? What was he waiting for? Maybe he was stunned into silence. Yes, that must be it.

"Yes, ma'am." His answer reverberated in Beatrix's mind.

No, no, no. What was he doing?

"Good. Now that it's settled," the Queen said, "my staff will work on a series of appearances for Rez and Beatrix." When Beatrix went to voice her displeasure with this arrangement, the Queen was quick to add, "Prince Istvan will be indebted to you both."

Beatrix considered doing something she'd never done as an adult by refusing the Queen's request. Although if she were to do that the King would step in and demand she do as she was told. It would also mean the Queen would take a more active role in this subterfuge. At least this way, the Queen was leaving the details up to her and Rez to work out.

As if on cue, the Queen's secretary was bid entrance to the office. She spoke softly in the Queen's ear. The Queen turned back to everyone. "I'm sorry but I must attend to another matter."

Both the King and Queen exited the office, leaving Beatrix facing her smiling sister. Beatrix inwardly groaned. Whatever Gisella had to say was best said in private— far away from Rez.

"Gisella, can you excuse us?" She implored her sister with her eyes to leave her alone with Rez.

"Just let me know if you two lovebirds need me." Gisella laughed as she walked away.

Once the door closed behind her sister, Beatrix turned to Rez. "Why do you want to do this?"

"I don't recall me ever saying I wanted to do this. Why didn't you tell your mother no?"

She reached for the first reason she could find. "Because there's protocol to follow. And you don't say no to a direct request from the Queen."

He arched a disbelieving brow. "I can't believe you follow protocol."

She frowned at him. "What's that supposed to mean?"

"It's just that I remember you as a kid speaking up and not worrying about protocol."

When she was little she did speak her mind, but what he didn't realize was that she spoke up when there was a problem within the family to resolve. She never liked to hear people she cared about in an argument. Her two sisters would argue all of the time. Gisella was the rule-follower and Cecelia was the rule-breaker. It caused a lot of distress in the family.

It was pointed out to her more than once that she was good at dealing with people. At first, she didn't believe it. As she grew older, she realized that she could talk to most anyone. And that's when she decided to dedicate her life to one of service. She loved people and wanted to help them to the best of her ability.

"That was a long time ago." Just like her crush on him was a long time ago. "If you haven't noticed, I'm not a kid any longer." But she was still a nurturer, even at her own expense.

"I've noticed."

She wasn't sure what to make of his comment. Was it just a matter of fact? Or was he implying something?

CHAPTER FOUR

HE COULDN'T BELIEVE this was happening.

Rez wasn't happy that the Queen had maneuvered him into faking a relationship with Princess Beatrix. It was the very last thing he wanted to do.

He should have never left his country estate. It was there where he could close himself off from the rest of the world. Behind closed doors, he didn't have to face the public's pitying looks or have well-meaning busybodies try to set him up on a blind date.

At home is where he should be—it's where he belonged. Not here. Not embarking upon a fake romantic relationship.

He raked his fingers through his short hair, not caring if he messed it up. "You're right. I shouldn't have agreed. I've got to go."

"Go where?"

"Home. I'm not the right person for this plan." He turned and headed toward the door.

Bea rushed around him. She stopped in front of the closed doors and pressed her hands to her curvy hips. For the first time, he really noticed how his best friend's little sister had grown up in all the right places. He swallowed hard.

"You can't go now," she said as a matter of fact.

"Of course I can."

"But you told the Queen you would do this."

"I never told her I would do it. I said I could do it… If I wanted to." He saw the worried look on her face. "Don't worry. I'm sure there's a long line of guys that would be willing to stand in as your boyfriend."

"It can't just be anyone." Her brows drew together. "Don't you understand? It has to be someone who cares deeply about Istvan and Indigo. Someone willing to do what it takes to protect their happiness."

"I understand. I'm sorry. It can't be me."

The disappointment showed on her face. She stepped aside. "I understand." Sympathy shone in her eyes. "I got so caught up in the drama that I didn't think about how hard this would be for you."

His gut knotted up. He couldn't deal with her pity. "I'm fine."

She arched a disbelieving brow. "I don't think you are."

"I said I am." His words came out with more force than he'd intended. "You know when you asked me to come here, I was only intending to comfort an old friend and give him a shoulder to lean on. I didn't expect," he waved his arms around, "all of this."

"What can I say? The Queen takes matters into her own hands and sometimes the solutions are rather elaborate."

"Surely there has to be another solution." He began to pace.

"We had everyone in the room and no one came up with a better idea." She looked at him. "Unless you have something you failed to mention to my parents."

He stopped pacing. "If I did, I would have mentioned it before."

Her hopes were quickly dashed. But she had to admit that her mother was right about one thing, the press loved a royal secret. If the fans could ferret out a secret via the press, it would be all the rage. And maybe there's a way they could use that to their advantage.

"I have an idea," Beatrix said.

He turned to her, pressed his hands to his sides and frowned. "Am I going to like it?"

"I don't think so but it's at least better than what my mother is proposing." She gestured for him to follow her. "Let's go out in the garden. It's too gloomy in here."

There was a moment or two when he didn't move, but eventually she heard him sigh. Soon after his footsteps sounded behind her. She led them out the back door, across the expansive terrace, down the steps and along the garden path.

By now Rez was beside her. "Where are we going?"

"For a walk. It's such a beautiful day and I thought the sunshine might cheer you up."

"I don't need any cheering up." His words were clipped and gruff.

She turned to him and smiled. "Am I supposed to believe you?"

He sighed again as he stopped walking. "I don't have time for a stroll in the garden. I have things to do."

"What things do you do?" She meant it honestly. She didn't know anything about Rez's life since he left court to go have a quiet life with his wife and daughter at his country estate.

"Things. You know." He glanced down at the gravel as he shifted his weight from one foot to the other. "And Evi needs me."

It sounded to her like he was making excuses to leave.

And that couldn't happen because as much as she hated her mother's idea, it was the only distraction that would have a chance to distract the paparazzi.

She began walking again. Rez was either going to join her or he was going to turn around and return to his estate.

"Would you stop walking?" His footfalls crunched over the gravel. "Just talk to me."

She ignored his grumping and let the warm rays of the sun ease the tension in her shoulders. She didn't stop until she was out of sight of the palace. The time gave her a chance to polish up her idea. She didn't have all of the ins and outs worked out but it was getting there.

Rez glanced around. "Now that we're alone, would you mind telling me your plan? And will it get us out of this fake dating?"

"Not exactly." This time she was the one to stop walking. She turned to him. "If we just date, it'll be one headline on the tabloid sites."

"What are you suggesting?"

"That we sneak around."

He shook his head. "This is sounding more involved instead of making things easier."

"No. Think about it. We won't have to really date."

"I'm confused. Are we going to have a fake relationship or not?"

"We are. But it has to be a cat-and-mouse sort of game with the press. A look here. A touch there. Just enough to get people wondering and talking. Because if they are talking about us, they won't be noticing that Istvan and Indigo aren't here."

Rez didn't look convinced. In fact, he looked as though

he was ready to bolt. How in the world was she going to convince him that this idea could actually work?

The press had taken notice of her single status. In fact, someone let it leak that she'd sworn off men for a year. So for her to break her one-year pledge of no dating after only ten months, well, it would be noted by the press.

And as awful as it might sound, a widower—a single father—entering the dating scene would be big news, especially since it had crushed a lot of hearts when Rez had married. Together, they were bound to make headline news on all of the gossip sites—especially the *Duchess Tales*.

Why was he still here?

Rez should have turned around and left as soon as he learned Istvan had departed to go after Indigo. Why hadn't he done just that? The answer instantly came to him. Bea.

Once he saw her, he'd wanted to stick around. He wanted to talk to her—to get to know her again. After he'd married, he lost contact with most of the people at court. It was like he'd stopped being one person and become another—a husband and a father.

And then he'd started to take his life for granted. He thought that Enora would always be there and Bea would always be off-limits to him. He'd never been so wrong in his life.

While Bea had been cute as a kid with her long braids that he would occasionally tug on and the innocent joy that would light up her face, as a woman she was gorgeous with her blue eyes that felt as though they could see into the deepest, darkest corners of his soul to her curvy figure that teased and taunted his imagination.

The fact he saw her that way wasn't good. Not good at all. He didn't want to be attracted to her. It wasn't right when Enora's memory was still with him.

The best thing he could do was to turn around and head home. Because pretending to be involved with Bea would be like playing with matches. One wrong move and they'd both go up in hot, burning flames of desire.

He couldn't allow that to happen. He didn't deserve to be happy again. He'd made a bunch of wrong choices and in the end, he'd lost his wife. If only he could go back in time, he would make other choices and Evi would still have her mother. It's what he wished for each night—just another chance for a do-over.

And yet the debt he owed Istvan kept him from moving. If this is what it took to help, he would do it—even if he didn't like it.

"What exactly are you suggesting?" he asked.

"That we start appearing in the same places."

"Together?"

She frowned at him. "Weren't you listening? We have to play this stealthily."

He once more raked his fingers through his hair, scattering the short strands. "And when do you want to start?"

"Right away." She paused.

"What does that mean?"

"I'm trying to think of an event for this evening, but I can't recall one. But tomorrow there's a polo match. I can go with some friends. Do you have someone you can show up with?"

Did she think he was that pathetic that he didn't have any friends? He might have holed up in his home after his wife's death for a while—for the past year, but he still had friends—even if he hadn't talked to them in a long time.

"Of course." He could call some of the guys he and Istvan palled around with. And then a better idea came to him. "What if I were to play?"

"Polo?"

"Yes." It'd been a year since he'd played but he hadn't forgotten any of it. And his team had said when he was ready to return that they would have him back.

"Do you think that's a good idea? You know. After you've been away from it for so long."

"I guess we'll find out." The more he thought about it, the more anxious he became to be back in the game.

In that moment, he realized just how much he'd withdrawn from life while he'd tried being father and mother to his little girl. The problem was that he could never be a mother to Evi. His daughter deserved a loving and devoted mother, not his attempts at being something he was not.

"Rez, did you hear me?" Bea sent him a worried look.

He had absolutely no idea what she'd said. "Of course I did."

"Good. So you'll call your friends while I work on other social engagements."

"How exactly will this work?"

"Well, for starters an anonymous source will leak to the *Duchess Tales* that you have reentered society."

He wasn't so sure how he felt about that. There was a part of him that felt guilty that he could just go on with his life while his wife's had been cut so very short. "And then?"

"Then you and I will make an appearance at the polo match. Maybe you could think about playing. Anyway I'll be excited to see you."

"And that's it? It doesn't seem very headline-worthy."

"True. Maybe we'll hug. Would that be better?"

With all of her curvy goodness, it definitely wouldn't be better. Because he was quickly finding the more he was around her, the less he thought clearly.

He swallowed hard. "It's at least something."

"We can't give them too much or else they won't be interested. We'll be a one-off headline and they won't follow us around. Remember we have to get them off the scent of Indigo and Istvan."

"Don't you ever get tired of dealing with the paparazzi?" He didn't know how she lived with it day in and day out. While he'd been at his country estate, no one had bothered with him and that's the way he liked it.

"Of course. Who wouldn't? But in this case, they will be helpful." She smiled as though proud of herself for outsmarting the press. "Anyway, after we hug and chat a little, I'll go off with my friends and you'll go with yours to watch the match."

"And that's it?" He should be able to do this. It didn't sound too terribly bad.

"Yes. At least for tomorrow. I have to check the social calendar and find out what options we have for the following day."

"So this is going to be an everyday occurrence?"

"Yes, until Istvan and Indigo return. Now we should head inside. We have arrangements to make." She turned and headed back toward the palace. When he didn't walk with her, she stopped and turned. "Aren't you coming?"

"In a moment. You go on ahead."

She nodded and continued on her way.

He needed a moment to gather his thoughts. He'd come here thinking he'd have to lend moral support to his oldest friend. Instead his friend had flown off to Greece chasing after his bride and now Rez was left dealing with his best friend's little sister—the sister who had a blatant crush on him when they were kids.

Istvan had emphatically warned him off his sister. Not that Rez would have ever made a move on Bea with her being a few years younger than him.

The problem now was with their ages no longer an issue, temptation had reared its annoying head. And as cute as Bea had been as a kid, she had blossomed into the most enticing woman. Not that he was looking for anyone to get involved with—far from it. But it didn't diminish his desire to hold her in his arms.

CHAPTER FIVE

AND SO THE royal charade was in motion.

It even had the King and Queen's blessing.

Beatrix couldn't help but be surprised that her mother had proposed this outrageous plan. Sure, the Queen could be quite cunning when necessary, but her plans didn't usually involve using her own children as decoys. This just drove home how concerned the King and Queen must be about Istvan's future and that of the royal family.

Scandals took their tolls on the Kingdom and could last decades or even centuries. To this day, her parents were still dealing with the fallout of her uncle's abdication. Ever since that monumental day, the royal family had been under the scrutiny of the press. Thankfully her mother and father were naturals at filling the position of king and queen. The people of the Kingdom loved them, but everyone was aware of how quickly public opinion could change.

Her parents were very social. They hosted foreign dignitaries at the palace on a regular basis, which was good for Rydiania's economy. The press seemed pleased with their work, until her father had been diagnosed with Parkinson's disease. And now it was time for him to slow down and take care of his health. It was the first bit of news since her uncle's abdication to rock the Kingdom.

Luckily the Kingdom loved her older brother, Istvan. And no one batted an eye at the thought of him stepping up to take over the throne. However, her brother had his own passions, including a foundation for sick children and their families. The Kingdom's charter would have forced Istvan to step away from that very important work in order to become king. And so by rejecting his birthright in order to marry the love of his life, he would still be able to do very important work for the Kingdom. That was if the wedding still took place.

Beatrix wanted to speak to her brother and see how things were going, but now wasn't the time. Beatrix and two of her friends had just arrived at the polo match. She'd known Jolan and Mari since they were kids. They were her closest friends.

As they walked toward the seating area, Beatrix focused on everything she was supposed to do that day. Because this public appearance was not one of leisure, as the Queen had been quick to remind her at breakfast.

The thought of rushing along her fake relationship with Rez was utmost in her mind. The faster it went, the sooner it'd be over. And the less risk of her getting caught up in the feelings she'd had for him all of those years ago.

But she realized that hurrying along the fake relationship was the exact wrong thing to do. She inwardly groaned. A slower approach to their romance would draw more attention—have more spies watching their every move. And then the focus would be off her brother and his intended bride, giving them time to sort things out.

Today her duty was to "accidentally" run into Rez. They were keeping it under wraps that he was staying at the palace for at least a few more days to give his public appearances more of a buzz.

"Why are you so quiet?" Mari asked.

"Yeah, you don't look happy to be here." Jolan moved to Beatrix's other side. "If you want we can set you up with someone. We know how you need some help in that department." They both laughed at their joke because Beatrix was never short on dates.

Beatrix frowned. "You two are *not* funny."

"Oh, lighten up," Jolan said. "You know that you could have your pick of dates."

"But she doesn't want to," Mari said in support. "She's what...ten months into her yearlong break from dating?"

"Yes." Beatrix nodded. "And I like it so much that I might make it two years."

"Two years?" her friends said in unison.

"I don't know why everyone is so worried about my dating life. It isn't like I'm planning to get married...at least not anytime soon."

Jolan sighed. "You know that everything your family does is headline news."

"How could I forget?" she muttered, thinking of the malicious headlines about Indigo. "Enough about me."

It was a beautiful sunny day. Thankfully women were expected to wear hats at the games. Beatrix wore a white woven hat with a yellow ribbon and a wide brim with a mesh band around the edge.

It matched her white top with a short yellow skirt. Her only problem was trying to walk in heels outdoors because she didn't like the way flats looked on her. And since she fully expected to be photographed today, she wanted to look her best.

"Oh, look, isn't that Vera and Niki?" Mari pointed to a group of people off in the distance.

"It is them. I've been trying to get a hold of Niki all week," Jolan said. "Let's go talk to them."

Beatrix wasn't ready to talk to people just yet. "You guys go ahead. I'll catch up with you later."

Her insides shivered with nerves. What if she wasn't any good at feigning surprise? What if no one noticed her with Rez? Although they had planned to meet in front of the viewing area.

Every part of this afternoon had been planned down to the finest detail. They even had a member of the palace staff calling in an anonymous tip that Rez would be attending the polo match today. Now that he was a widower and a year had passed since he lost his wife, he was once again one of the most eligible bachelors in Europe. She wondered how he felt about that title considering his circumstances.

She moved toward the edge of the field. She watched as the ponies and players moved about the field before the game. Her gaze sought out Rez. He was going to be an alternate today as a defender.

It took her a moment to find him, but at last she spotted him atop his mount. He was wearing the number three. As though he spotted her at exactly the same time, he guided his horse toward her.

A smile lifted the corners of her lips. He dismounted and approached her. He didn't smile back. In fact, he looked stressed. She was going to have to work hard to make this impromptu meeting look like a happy reunion.

"Rez, it's so good to see you." She brightened her smile, hoping he would follow suit.

He stood there stiff and unmoving. This wasn't good. Hoping to salvage the situation, she leaned forward to give him a quick hug and a feathery kiss.

To her surprise, his arm wrapped around her and held her close. Her heart pitter-pattered. For a moment, she forgot this was all for show. She forgot they were in public. She forgot they had an audience.

All she could think about was how much she enjoyed being so close to him. It would be so easy to get used to this familiarity. In that moment, she wanted him to be the Rez she remembered—quiet, thoughtful and with a gentle sense of humor. She wondered if she'd ever see that version of him again.

In her ear he whispered, "I don't know what I'm supposed to do."

She felt sorry for him. At the same time, she felt guilty for letting herself enjoy the moment. It wasn't easy to perform in front of an audience. Lucky for her, she had a lifetime of experience.

"Just smile and say something funny." She inhaled his spicy cologne mixed with the earthy scent of the barn. He smelled good. Perhaps too good.

"I'm not funny."

"You have to let me go."

"Oh, right." His arm released her.

She pulled back and immediately missed the feel of his touch. Out of the corner of her eye, she noticed people glancing in their direction. It was time to put on a good show.

She glanced to the side. A photographer had captured their moment together. Mission accomplished. She should feel good that all was going according to plan, but she was worried about Rez. This was so much more difficult for him than she'd imagined.

As she stared at the photographer, he snapped another picture. It was too late to change paths now. She would just have to help Rez any way she could think of. The game was on.

"It's so good to see you." Her gaze met his.

In a low voice, he said, "You knew I'd be here."

She let out a laugh like he'd said something really funny. Boy was he nervous. It looked like she was on her own to make this look like a fun run-in. "Rez, you forget that we're playacting. Please smile and look like you're happy to see me."

"I wish I was anywhere but here." And then he forced a barely there smile.

"There, that wasn't so bad, was it?"

When his smile broadened, it made her heart pitter-patter. Maybe this situation wasn't going to be as stressful as she'd originally imagined. Perhaps Rez realized their time together didn't have to be miserable. After all, once upon a time they had been friends—perhaps even good friends.

It was then that she noticed he wasn't looking at her. His gaze was focused over her shoulder. So if he wasn't smiling at her, whom was he smiling at?

She turned, expecting to find some beautiful young woman, but there was no one behind her. Her gaze continued searching until her gaze stumbled across a pink baby stroller.

She turned back to him. "Is Evi here?"

The smile fell from his face as he turned his attention back to her. "She is. When I spoke to some of the guys on the team, they insisted I bring her. And her nanny was eager for some sunshine."

Beatrix hadn't expected Evi to be at the game. It was so sweet that he wanted his little girl close by. The love he had for Evi was glaringly evident. She wondered what it was like to have a love so great.

"It sounds like you made the most of the day."

"Come meet her. You didn't get a chance yesterday."

Her heart stuttered. Could she do this? Up until her endometriosis diagnosis, she hadn't given much thought to having a family of her own. After all, she'd been young, marriage and babies weren't on her mind. She'd been focused on forging her own path in life and traveling.

And then in one day—one visit to the doctor—she found herself not able to have something other women took for granted—a baby of her own. At the time, she'd told herself it was no big deal, but now she realized she'd been lying to herself.

Rez stared expectantly at her, making her heart race and her palms to grow damp. She had to say something— but what? Was she ready to hold Rez's baby in her arms all the while knowing she could never have a baby of her own? And if she couldn't do this, how did she explain it to him?

"Bea?" His voice drew her from her thoughts.

Her palms grew damp. She wasn't ready for this. Not yet.

Her gaze searched the area, looking for an excuse to get out of meeting his daughter. Her focus latched on to her two friends off in the distance. They were headed in her direction.

"Maybe later," she said. "I promised Jolan and Mari that I'd meet up with them."

A distinct frown appeared on his face as her friends rushed up to her. Beatrix braced herself for the onslaught of questions because her friends knew she'd had the biggest crush on Rez in school. They used to pick on her mercilessly.

Without a word, Rez mounted his polo pony. He took off before her friends reached her side.

Mari's eyes lit up. "What were you and Rez talking about?"

"What's he doing here?" Jolan asked. "I didn't think he ever went out in public after his wife died."

Beatrix didn't respond as she walked toward their seats. She didn't want to miss this match. She was there to cheer on Rez. She hoped he'd relax and enjoy himself.

"Beatrix, say something." Mari rushed to keep up with her.

"Yes, it's Rez. This is his first time out in public since his wife passed."

"And he was hugging you." Jolan grinned at her. "Lucky you."

Beatrix frowned at her friend. "Jolan, lighten up. This is hard for him. He has to find his footing again."

"I'm sorry," Jolan said. "I hope it all works out for him."

Beatrix did too. She took the seat on the end. She knew she was supposed to circulate and talk to as many people as possible to clear up some of the misinformation about Indigo, but now that she was here, it was harder than she thought.

After feeling Rez's stress, her good mood had been dashed. It was important that he played well, but was that even a possibility after him being out of the game for so long?

She sat there and cheered him on. And to her relief, he appeared to her to play well. His team scored in the first chukka, otherwise known as period or quarter. The longer he played, the more he seemed to relax.

When she glanced around, she found she wasn't the

only one cheering on Rez. She smiled. It was good to know that a lot of other people cared about him because he needed people to help him through this tough transition into society again.

When halftime rolled around, her friends dragged her out onto the field to stomp on divots. At first, she was worried about her new shoes, but she soon gave up worrying and instead laughed as Mari and Jolan ran around stomping on clods of dirt. It was so nice to do away with royal protocols for the moment and just have a little bit of fun. And in the end, she realized her shoes would clean up just fine.

When the match was over, Rez's team won. She wanted to congratulate him, but he never came near her again. She wondered if he was mad at her for getting him into this awkward situation. She hoped not.

He didn't want to do this.

Rez left the polo field later that afternoon. He had to keep checking his rearview mirror to make sure he wasn't being followed. At one point a motorcycle followed him for a few miles and so he made a random turn. The motorcycle tailed him through the turn and he started to worry. Was this what he was going to have to put up with every time he went into public? He hoped not.

By the second quick turn, he'd lost the motorcycle. Truth be told, he wasn't even certain it was following him. He slowed down and let his mind drift a bit.

What was up with Bea dodging his offers to meet Evi? The first time he'd offered to introduce her, he understood there hadn't been time since they'd been summoned by the Queen.

However, today when he'd suggested walking over

to meet Evi, there had been a look in Bea's eyes that he wasn't able to define. Was it panic? No. Why would she be anxious about meeting his daughter? It didn't make any sense. He was missing something.

At the last minute, he made a sharp left turn. He'd been so lost in his thoughts that he'd almost missed the unmarked turnoff. Beatrix told him to come into the palace through the rear entrance, which was normally just for the staff and deliveries. They made sure to keep the press away from that entrance.

He had to stop at the gate and produce his official ID and then he was ushered onto the palace grounds. He pulled into a parking spot and then rushed inside.

He took the back steps two at a time. His daughter was supposed to be in the room next to his with the nanny on the other side of his daughter's room.

He rushed to the room and smiled when he found Evi inside. When she spotted him, she stopped playing with a teddy bear. She tossed it aside and crawled toward him. She could really move these days. It wouldn't be long until she was toddling around.

He scooped her up in his arms. "Hey, baby girl, did you have fun today?"

She said something to him but he couldn't make out her baby talk.

The nanny entered the room. The older woman with graying hair smiled when her gaze landed on Rez. "I heard her on the monitor. I didn't know you were in here."

"I just got back. Thank you for taking her to the match."

"No need to thank me. I had a lovely time."

"How are you settling in?"

Mrs. Wilson's face lit up. "It's lovely here. I had no

idea the palace was so big. I mean I know we all see the photos but they don't do this place justice."

"Is there anything you need?"

She shook her head. "They have made me very comfortable here."

He nodded. "That's good." His gaze moved to his daughter. "And you seem happy." Evi uttered some baby talk. "I agree." He had no idea what he'd agreed to but his words caused Evi to smile some more and it filled his chest with warmth.

Buzz-buzz.

He thought of ignoring his phone. There was no one in particular he wanted to speak to right now. Soon enough he'd have to let Beatrix know this charade was over. He just couldn't do it. There was a reason he never tried out for plays in school—he wasn't any good at playacting.

"I can take her for you." Mrs. Wilson held out her arms to Evi, who reached out to her.

He handed over his daughter and then retrieved his phone. He looked at the caller ID. It was Istvan. At last they'd get a chance to speak.

He pressed the phone to his ear as he made his way down the hall to his suite of rooms. "Hey. How's it going?"

"Awful. I can't believe this is happening."

Rez stepped into his room and closed the door. He was confused by Istvan's answer. "You had to have a clue the press would figure out about Indigo's past, right?"

"Yes. But I was hoping it wouldn't come out until after the wedding. And then I had hoped it would blow over quickly and they'd be on to their next story."

"So where are you?"

"On Ludus Island. Indigo has friends here and she

brought her mother to the private island to get away from the paparazzi."

"Is she speaking to you?" He was really worried about them. This was a lot for them to deal with just before their wedding.

"She is, but she's a bit of a nervous wreck. Not that I can blame her. Dealing with the press is a lot—especially for someone that's not used to it. She refuses to leave the island until this story blows over."

Rez raked his fingers through his hair. "What about the wedding? Is it still on?"

"I have every intention of marrying her, if she'll still have me."

Rez noticed how his friend didn't mention Indigo's feelings on the matter. Perhaps Beatrix's worry about the wedding wasn't overblown. "What can I do to help?"

"Honestly, I have no idea. If you could make this whole sordid mess go away, I'd be eternally grateful."

"I wish. Your mother has an idea about how to deal with the paparazzi." Rez went on to tell his friend about him fake dating his sister.

"I can't believe you agreed to something that outrageous."

"You and me both. But you know I've always got your back."

"I don't know what to say." Istvan paused. "I'm sorry you've been drawn into all of this. It means so much that you're willing to help. I hope we'll be back at the palace soon."

"I'll be here."

"You're at the palace?"

"I am. Your family insisted I stay. They even invited Evi and her nanny."

"I'd like to see Evi. It's been too long since I last saw her. I bet she's grown a lot."

"She has. Hopefully you'll be back soon and then you can visit with your goddaughter."

"Thank you for everything you're doing. I know it was a lot for you to leave your home. I want you to know how much it means to me." There was a pause. "Sorry. I've got to run."

"Talk to you later."

After they ended the call, Rez was touched by his friend's words. It was then that he accepted the inevitable—he couldn't leave the palace if there was even the slightest chance the wedding would take place. He hoped their charade ended before things escalated in their fake relationship. The image of pulling Beatrix into his arms and claiming her berry-red lips with his own teased his thoughts. He couldn't help but wonder if her kiss was as sweet as he imagined.

The direction of his thoughts startled him. He couldn't believe he'd let himself imagine kissing Beatrix. She was an old friend—nothing more.

CHAPTER SIX

HOME AT LAST.

Beatrix stepped inside the palace. She'd wanted to go home right after the polo match, but her friends wouldn't hear of it. They'd wanted to hang out. And since Beatrix hadn't driven, she was along for the ride.

She wondered if Rez had returned. Then she realized there was nothing to worry about. Rez had turned into a homebody and now with his baby daughter here, he wouldn't have a reason to go out, unless it was to continue their royal charade.

She needed to talk to him about that. He had to work on acting like he was happy to see her in public. She had a feeling he'd forgotten what it was like to flirt. Back when they were kids, he had been a total flirt—though never with her. But she didn't want to get lost in thoughts of the past now.

She rushed upstairs and headed toward Rez's suite. On the way through the hallway, she noticed the door open next to Rez's room. She wondered if he was in there.

She stopped at the doorway and looked inside. She didn't see Rez. But then her gaze landed on the white crib between the two tall windows. It was so strange to see a crib in the palace. In fact, she'd never seen a crib in the palace. She had been too young when Cecelia was born to recall it.

All of the sudden there was movement within the crib. Beatrix told herself she should just move along, but there was this curiosity to see his baby. She took a step into the room. She couldn't help but wonder if Evi favored her father, with his dark good looks.

She hesitated just inside the doorway. She didn't want to disturb the baby. After all, she knew absolutely nothing about babies. Her friends were only starting to get married. No one was having babies yet. And now that Beatrix knew she couldn't have children, she avoided babies at all costs because they reminded her of what she couldn't have. It was also part of the reason she'd decided to take a year off from dating.

She didn't want to draw someone else into her fertility issues. If things got serious, it would be asking too much of a person to deal with her diagnosis. The risk of the relationship falling apart was too great and made her all the more determined to cling to her single status.

However, she hadn't missed the way Rez lighted up when he was with his daughter. Evi was the only person who could make him truly smile. He was such a fabulous father. Rez deserved to have more children with the right woman when he was ready to move on.

She could imagine Rez with a little one pulling at his leg while he held a baby in his arms. The image pulled at the scars on her heart. An image like that would never include her.

Evi's head popped up over the side of the crib. She stood there with her dark curls and blue eyes, staring at her. Evi was absolutely adorable.

Wait. Was Evi smiling at her? She was. Warmth swelled within Beatrix's chest and radiated outward. Soon the baby's smile turned into a drooling fest, all over the crib rail.

Beatrix glanced around for the nanny. She didn't see her anywhere. In fact, there didn't seem to be anyone around.

"Goo-goo." Evi held on to the rail and then jumped. She fell back.

Beatrix's breath hitched in her throat. She instinctively rushed forward. *Please let her be okay.* She peered in the crib. Evi looked up at her and laughed.

"Thank goodness. You had me worried." As Evi stared up at her with her rosy lips lifted in a smile that plumped up her cheeks, pain arrowed into Beatrix's heart.

She would never have this experience with her own child. For so long, she'd convinced herself that she didn't want children—that she had a full life. But now she realized it wasn't the truth. Tears pricked the back of her eyes. She blinked them away.

Evi rolled over. She crawled over and once more used the rails to help her stand.

"You don't want to do that," Beatrix said. "You're going to fall again." She watched as the little girl began to jump again. "Be careful. No more jumping, okay?"

Beatrix glanced around, hoping someone would come help out. Where was Rez? She looked at Evi, who was smiling as she stood there.

"Evi, no more jumping. Okay?"

As though Evi understood only the word *jump*, the little girl began bouncing again. Beatrix's body tensed with worry. Not wanting Evi to hurt herself, Beatrix automatically reached out. Just as she was about to pick up Evi, she hesitated.

"Evi…" Rez walked into the room. He came to a stop when he saw Beatrix standing there. "Bea, I didn't expect to find you here."

"I…uh…was looking for you." Beatrix backed away from the crib. "And then Evi's door was open."

"I was in the kitchen getting her a bottle." He held up a full bottle of milk. "Thank you for checking in on her."

"Um… Yes. No problem."

"She loves to jump. She's going to have the strongest legs."

Beatrix's gaze narrowed. "How did you know she was jumping?"

He held up his other hand, which was holding a baby monitor.

"Oh." Heat warmed her cheeks. "So you heard us?"

He nodded. "I'm glad you two finally met. Please feel free to visit her anytime. She loves to be around people."

"I didn't mean to intrude on her dinner."

He set the bottle down. "You didn't. And I mean it, you're welcome to visit her whenever you want."

"Thanks."

Evi cooed. She jumped up and down, obviously excited to see her father.

"Anyway," Beatrix said. "I… I'll just be going."

She started for the door. When she passed him, he reached out and gently touched her arm. "You don't have to leave."

"I should. You, um…need time with your daughter." This situation was just too cozy. The baby was so cute.

And Rez was much too handsome. Sometimes it was tough to remember that he was a grieving widower.

Her legs moved quickly as she slipped out the door. It wasn't until she made it along the hallway and down the staircase that she took her first easy breath.

"Are you okay?"

Beatrix jumped. Pressing a hand to her chest, she turned to find Gisella standing there, giving her a puzzled look. "I'm fine."

Her sister arched a brow. "Are you sure?"

"Yes." Not really but she wasn't going to get into any of that with her older sister. "Why?"

"The way you rushed down the steps, it was like you were running from something or someone."

"Don't be silly." She attempted to sound calm and relaxed. Wanting to change the subject to anything but herself, she asked, "What are you doing here? I would have thought they'd have you holed away in a meeting."

Gisella sighed. "I escaped. There's only so much I can absorb at one time." She moved closer to Beatrix. "Can I be honest with you?"

Beatrix had no idea what Gisella was about to confess, but she had to admit she was curious. Her older sister wasn't one for confiding in people so Beatrix had no idea what to expect from her.

"Of course you can. What is it?"

"I never knew there was so much to learn to become the Sovereign. It's so much more than I ever expected." Gisella sighed again. "I better get back to it."

And with that Gisella turned on her heels and set off toward the back of the palace, leaving Beatrix alone with her thoughts. They immediately returned to Rez and Evi.

She wasn't so sure what had happened back in the nursery or why it had unnerved her so much. She just knew she needed to keep her distance.

He wasn't alone.

Rez had never seen Bea so spooked. It was like she couldn't get out of the nursery fast enough. He had no idea what had freaked her out.

He suspected it was the same thing that had gotten to him—this fake relationship. It was just too much for the both of them. He never should have agreed to it.

There had to be another way to stem off the stories about Istvan and Indigo. He'd been giving it some thought and he had some ideas. He wanted to run them by Beatrix, but when he'd stopped by her room, she hadn't been there.

It didn't help that the palace was so large a person could hide and not be found for the longest time. He had a feeling as Evi got a bit older she'd be thrilled to play hide-and-seek within the palace walls.

He'd returned to the nursery to find his baby girl standing in her crib, waiting for him to pick her up. "Aren't you sleepy yet?"

Evi jumped as though she knew exactly what he'd said.

"Sir, would you like me to take her for you?" Mrs. Wilson asked.

He was torn between staying for his favorite part of Evi's day—rocking her to sleep—or continuing to track down Bea. He'd never experienced this sort of dilemma before. Back at his estate, he didn't have distractions. He'd had all the time in the world for Evi.

He glanced up. "You don't mind?"

A smile lit up the nanny's face. "I never mind rocking such a sweet baby to sleep. Besides, I don't have much else to do here."

Perhaps this was the answer to his problem. He picked up Evi, who started to fuss because she was tired. He held her in front of him, so she could see him. "I love you, baby girl. Sleep tight." He gave his daughter a kiss on her chubby cheeks and then handed her over. "If you have any problems getting her down, message me and I'll come back."

"We'll be fine. Don't you worry."

"Thank you for everything. I really appreciate you making the trip."

"I'm honored to be here."

Rez leaned over to his daughter again. "You be good." He took one of her little hands in his own and kissed it. "And have sweet dreams."

He walked to the doorway, where he paused and glanced back. Mrs. Wilson had moved to the crib, un-doubtedly in order to change Evi into a fresh diaper and her pajamas. Knowing he wouldn't be far away, he moved on.

He made his way back to Bea's suite of rooms. He knocked but once again there was no answer.

He reached for his phone and messaged her.

Where are you? We need to talk.

Seconds ticked by as he waited for a response. The seconds turned to minutes while he paced in the hall-way. Just when he thought she wasn't going to get back to him, his phone dinged.

Do you want to meet in the library?

Yes. Heading there now.

He moved in that direction. It was on the main floor and down a hallway. Lucky for him, he'd spent a lot of time in the palace when he was growing up. Otherwise it would be so easy to get lost in a place as big as this one.

When he stepped into the library, he expected to find Bea waiting for him. It appeared he was the one waiting for her—again. While he waited for her to arrive, he practiced what he'd say to her. He'd give her a reasonable alternative to them trying to fool the paparazzi, one that didn't include him. And then he would scoop up his daughter and head home until he was needed here for the wedding. He couldn't wait to get on the road.

A couple of minutes later Bea walked in. She closed the double doors behind her. "What did you need to see me about?"

This was his chance to sell her on his plan. "We need to do something different."

"I agree."

"You do?" He was confused. He thought she was all invested in them creating a fake romance.

"Yes. I think we need to push up our timeline. Instead of waiting until Friday, we need to see each other in public tomorrow."

He shook his head. "I don't think that's the change we need."

She pressed a hand to her hip—her gently rounded hip. He swallowed hard. When had Bea gotten all of these curves? She'd definitely grown and filled out in all of the right places.

"What do you have in mind?"

"I think we need to give up this charade. I don't think anyone is interested in us."

"What makes you say that?"

"Because I didn't receive any notifications on my phone from anyone. I don't think the public cares."

"And I think we're just getting started. It was only the first day. You have to give it time. It was supposed to be subtle. It's not like you can just walk up to me and kiss me. What would be the story in that?"

He swallowed hard again. *Kiss her?* This wasn't going to happen. No way. "Since when am I supposed to kiss you?"

She frowned at him. "You don't have to sound like it is the worst thing in the world."

"That's not what I meant. It's just that it's you and me. We're not like that." They'd never been romantically linked.

Years ago, Bea had been too young for him. And then he met Enora. The timing had never been right. But now things were different. And then there was the idea that Bea could be a mother to his little girl.

The breath hitched in his throat. Had that thought really crossed his mind? It struck him with its enormity. Was he prepared to go that far to give Evi a family? He didn't have an answer to that question.

"What are we like?" Bea's voice drew him back to their conversation.

He averted his gaze. "You know."

"No, I don't know. Please tell me."

Was that a frown on her face? Why was she getting upset with him? She couldn't be any more comfortable with this arrangement than him.

He shifted his weight from one foot to the other as he tried to guess at how she envisioned their relationship. "Well, you know, you're like my little sister. Just like when we were kids."

"Kids? If you haven't noticed I've grown up, just like you."

He raked his fingers through his hair. He could see quite clearly that she was very much a woman with all of the curvy goodness that went along with it.

The problem was he didn't want to see her that way. He shouldn't see her that way. He was a widower—a single father. Romance was not on his radar. He didn't know if it would ever be something he would want again. And if he was to propose they create a family for Evi, would Bea insist on romance?

Of course, there was Istvan to consider. He would be very upset about Rez having any sort of relationship with Bea. Istvan had told him in no uncertain terms that his sisters—all three of them—were off-limits to Rez. Of course, back before Enora had entered his life, he had been known as a playboy. The love-'em-and-leave-'em type. Enora had changed all of that.

Now Bea wanted him to act like he had a lifetime ago. He didn't want to go back. He wasn't even sure he knew how to go back and be that carefree guy.

Today hadn't gone well.

Beatrix would be the first person to admit it, but that didn't mean they should give up. They were not giving up. This was much too important for them to stop now. They had to push forward.

The information from her brother was that Indigo was refusing to come back to the palace—to deal with the hurtful headlines. It was a lot for someone to take on, especially if they weren't used to having their lives dissected in the news.

It was a lot for Beatrix and she'd grown up in the spotlight. But she also knew how to use the press to her advantage. And that's exactly what they were going to do now. She just had to get Rez back on board.

"We can't stop now," she said. "Trust me. By spoon-feeding the paparazzi, it'll only make them more curious about us."

Rez didn't say anything. He looked as though he was staring off into space. He was probably thinking of some way to get out of this awkward situation.

"Rez?" When he didn't respond, she spoke louder. "Rez, did you hear me?"

"Uh… Yeah."

Ding.

He checked his phone. "It's yours."

Beatrix knew it was her phone. She'd felt it vibrate in her pocket, but she didn't want an interruption now. When Rez sent her an expectant look as her phone sounded again, she reluctantly reached for it.

It was an alert from the *Duchess Tales*. They'd just posted something. She read the title: Back in the Saddle Again…

"Bea, is something wrong?" Concern rang out in Rez's voice.

"*Duchess Tales* posted something." She pressed on the link in order to read more.

The popular site was known to post at all hours of the day or night with "breaking" news. They had sources everywhere and it was amazing the amount of information they were able to gather and at such great speed. Sometimes there was news about the royal family posted even before all of the members of the family had been notified about the matter.

"What did they say?" Interest rang out in his voice.

She read him the headline.

"I take it this article is about me?" He didn't sound impressed.

"I don't know. Let me read it."

This most devoted royal watcher has the most exciting news for all of you single ladies out there...and maybe some of you who aren't so single! *eye-wink emoji*

Ladies, ladies, be still your galloping hearts, but this royal watcher can now verify that the sexy Duke of Kaspar has gotten back on his polo pony.

There was a photo of Rez on his horse. Beatrix stared at it for a moment, unable to turn away from the image. It took her a moment to realize what was so different about him in the photo. And then she realized it was the first time since he'd returned to the palace that he looked relaxed. Even the stress lines on his face were soothed.

With concerted effort, she continued to read the post. All the while she hoped the ruse was beginning to work.

This royal follower also has a new update on the fake princess front. It appears the wannabe princess's father stole from the palace. No one knows whether it was royal jewels or just some other priceless relic, but he and his family were found out and banished from all of Rydiania. Apparently the shame was too much for him to bear because he ended his life shortly after, leaving his family to deal with the shame. Oh, my. We do reap what we sow, don't we?

Beatrix's stomach plummeted. How did they come up with these blatant lies? Did they not know what damage they do to people? For once, she was relieved that Indigo and Istvan weren't here. Hopefully they weren't checking the press either.

She was afraid to keep reading. She had no idea what other painful lies were going to be flung about and quoted as the truth. Ha! There was barely any truth to be found here and yet many of Rydiania's residents read this blog-site religiously.

And if Prince Istvan calls off his marriage to the wannabe, he'll be back on the market too. Oh, ladies, this summer is turning out to be most amazing. Dust off your slinkiest dresses and most glamorous heels, it's time to go bachelor hunting.

Beatrix huffed. Who was this royal watcher? And why were they out to ruin Istvan's happiness? If she knew who was behind the *Duchess Tales*, she would go to them and demand they write retractions. The wedding was going to happen. It had to happen because they truly loved each other. And it wasn't right for the court of public opinion to ruin it.

Though Beatrix was known to hold her tongue while

with her family, when someone came after her loved ones, she would defend them with vigor. But without a name, she was left helpless and reading these outrageous stories.

Who shall win the hearts of our two most eligible bachelors? Well, I can't tell you that. In the Duke's case, it certainly won't be Princess Beatrix.

There was a photo of her with Rez. He was frowning at her and she was frowning back. Oh, no! This wasn't good. Not good at all.

That is it for now, royal followers. Know that I am hard at work digging up the truth about Prince Istvan's status. I know you ladies want your chance to win his heart and you just might get your chance.

As for the Duke, we'll be on the lookout for him too. Now that he's out of mourning and back in the social arena, I have a feeling his social calendar is going to runneth over with invites.

Keep in touch, my lovely royal followers. I will share the details as they unfold. Until next time...xox

Beatrix turned to Rez but he apparently got tired of waiting for her to tell him what was in the post and instead he'd pulled it up on his phone.

Just then Gisella came rushing into the library. "Did you see what the Duchess wrote?"

"I just read it." Beatrix gestured to Rez with her head. "He's reading it now."

"It's getting worse." Gisella huffed. "We have to do more."

"That's just what I was telling Rez. It's too late tonight for a social function, but I know tomorrow there's a showing at the gallery in the village. They draw in a lot of big names now that the word is out that our brother is a big buyer there."

"Good idea. But how are you going to get more press coverage? They basically wrote off anything romantic between you and Rez."

"Agreed." Rez's voice held an agitated tone. "How are you going to change the narrative?"

Beatrix's mind searched for the answer to that question and came up empty. She kept coming back to her original plan, only with an escalated timeline.

She turned to her sister. "You need to speed up the palace's formal release about Indigo and her family."

"But it's royal protocol not to rush to respond to the lies in the press."

"Who cares about protocol? By the time the palace gets around to putting out a royal statement, our brother's wedding will be officially called off. Is that what you want?"

Gisella shook her head. "But they aren't going to like making an exception to the protocol."

"And they like the hurtful lies being spewed about by the Duchess?"

"You do have a point," Gisella said.

"Good. Talk to the King, have him put some people on the statement tonight. Once the public has the truth, hopefully the story will die away."

"And what about you two?" Gisella arched a brow as her gaze moved between Beatrix and Rez. "There's no way anyone is going to believe the chance of a possible romance with photos of you two frowning at each other."

"Agreed." Beatrix couldn't argue. They had to do better. "We'll work on that while you work on the formal statement."

Gisella nodded. "Getting the palace to break protocol isn't going to be as easy as you seem to think it will be."

She nodded in agreement. "Neither will faking a relationship. Now go."

Gisella huffed. "I'm going. Since when did I become the errand girl?"

"Don't think of it as an errand. Think of it as helping your brother, who is in dire need of assistance."

Gisella turned and left.

Beatrix turned to Rez. He stood there studying her with a strange look on his handsome face. "What? Is there something on my face?"

He shook his head. "I just never saw this side of you."

"What side?"

"The pushy, in-charge, don't-mess-with-me side." He sent her a smile. "Bea, you've really have grown up."

The name grated on her nerves and it didn't help when his deep chuckle followed. Her lips pressed together as her back teeth ground together. No one laughed at her, not since she was a little kid.

"This isn't a time for your amusement. We have a big problem, if you hadn't noticed."

The amusement was erased from his voice. "I've noticed. And I think we're making a big mistake if we do the same thing we did yesterday."

"I agree." When the surprise shone in his eyes, she

continued. "That's why tomorrow you actually have to look happy to see me. No frowns allowed."

"I didn't frown," he grumbled.

"Do I need to pull up the photo?"

"No, no. But you were frowning too."

"Because you were frustrating me." He had a habit of doing it, like now. "So tomorrow we have a date to meet up at the Durand Gallery."

"I still think this is a mistake."

What she heard him say was that he didn't want to pretend to be in a relationship with her. He couldn't be any more obvious. She told herself that it was because he was grieving his wife. She shouldn't take it personally, but it still hurt.

CHAPTER SEVEN

THIS WAS A waste of time.

Nothing they did was going to fix the horrid headlines.

And still Rez dressed nicely. He proceeded to drive into the village. What he hadn't expected when he arrived was the village to be so busy that he couldn't find a parking spot near the gallery. It appeared Bea hadn't been exaggerating when she said the gallery was popular.

At least the evening wouldn't be a total waste. He might even find a piece of art for his home. He wanted to surround Evi with beautiful artwork. He liked to think that's what her mother would have done but he didn't truly know.

The plan was for him to leave the palace first and allow Bea to make a grand entrance. He didn't know what she was planning but it wouldn't matter. She could wear a trash bag and she would still turn heads.

At the door stood a tall, muscular bodyguard wearing a black suit with a black shirt and tie. In his hand, he held a digital notebook. He stood between Rez and the door. Without lifting his head, the man asked, "Name?"

"The Duke of Kaspar."

Immediately the man's head lifted. His dark eyes

widened. "I'm sorry, sir. I didn't realize it was you." He pulled open the door. "Please go in."

"Have a good evening." Rez stepped into the gallery.

He had never been in here before. The gallery had a clean look with white walls and a slate-gray floor. While dozens of well-dressed people milled about with drinks in their hands, he skirted around the edge of the showroom. He did his best to ignore how people's heads turned as he passed by.

His gaze moved to the walls, which were covered with colorful canvases. It wouldn't be hard to find something here to purchase. The problem might be narrowing it down to one...or two pieces of art.

He stepped around one of the illuminated vitrines that held small hand-carved figurines. The vitrines were strategically placed throughout the large room with various works of art from jewelry to sculptures.

He walked over to a wall in order to have a closer look at an oil painting. It was a field of purple wildflowers. When he studied it, he could easily imagine being in the field with a soft breeze that carried with it the perfume of the flowers as the sunshine warmed his face. This was the type of art he wanted to stimulate Evi's imagination. He made a mental note of the painting so he could purchase it.

"Hey, Rez. It's so good to see you."

He turned around to find a woman with shoulder-length auburn hair smiling at him. He knew he should know her name, but he couldn't recall it. If Bea was here, she could discreetly let him know the woman's name.

"Hello." He tried to think of an excuse to move on.

The next thing he knew, the woman was wrapping her

arms around him. Her strong, sweet perfume wrapped around him, smothering him. Her cherry red lips pressed to his cheek.

It took him a second to detach himself. Her arms were more like octopus tentacles that didn't want to let him go. His gaze desperately searched the room for Bea. Figures, she chose tonight to be late.

"I'm so sorry about your wife." The woman spoke in a high-pitched tone. "It must be so hard raising a baby on your own."

He inwardly groaned. This was the very last conversation he wanted to have with a stranger. Not knowing what to say, he nodded his head.

"What you need is a new wife—someone to help you out with your daughter and that big house of yours." Her smile brightened.

Surely this woman, who was obviously at least ten years older than him, wasn't suggesting he was just going to up and marry her. He couldn't think of anything he wanted to do less.

"If you'll excuse me, I see someone I need to have a word with." He had no one in particular that he wanted to speak to but at this point, he would walk out and have an hour-long conversation with the bodyguard at the front door before he would stand here with this woman a minute longer.

"Rez!" Someone caught his arm.

He stopped and turned. It was a blonde. He knew her from years ago. Her name was… "Hello, Liz."

A big smile lifted her cheeks. "I didn't know you would be here tonight."

"It was a last-minute decision." And one he hadn't

personally made. Bea had insisted their appearance here would be noticed.

Speaking of the Princess, his gaze moved around the room. Where was she? Sure, they didn't want to show up at the same time, but it would be nice if they'd show up within the same hour.

Liz linked her arm with his like she had some claim on him. The move made him extremely uncomfortable. He wasn't ready to get cozy with anyone—especially someone he barely knew.

Right now, he was struggling with his new life. He needed to stay focused on doing his best for his daughter. And it would really help if Bea was here to make this evening a little easier.

"It's so good that you're here. We've really missed you. It was such a shame about your wife. I can't even imagine what it must be like with her here one minute and gone the next. Your poor little girl."

He wanted to tell the woman to shut up. His wife was not a subject to be bantered around at a social engagement. And it wasn't a subject he wanted to discuss with anyone—especially her.

Where are you, Bea?

As though his desperation had summoned her, Bea glided into the gallery. *Wow!* That's all he could think.

Bea was a knockout. He wasn't the only one to notice. A hush fell over the crowd as heads turned in her direction. As though Bea was used to being in the spotlight, she paused. Her photo was taken and then she was greeted by person after person.

Her long dark hair was down with the loose curls flowing over her shoulder. His fingers tingled with the desire

JENNIFER FAYE   73

to comb his fingers through those long locks. Her makeup was soft, just enough to highlight her natural beauty. Her lips were painted with a wine-colored gloss that drew his attention and held it a moment longer than necessary.

She wore a white lace blouse with loose flowy sleeves. The gaps in the material of the sleeves gave a teasing glimpse of her creamy white skin.

He should turn away but he couldn't move. His feet were planted to the ground. A white skirt fit snuggly against her curvy hips and ended a few centimeters above her knees.

Her blue heels made her toned legs look as though they went on forever. Rez swallowed hard. The Bea he used to know never looked this hot. He would have remembered that.

"Excuse me." He didn't wait for Liz to respond as he made his way toward Bea.

By the time he reached her side, she was surrounded by three other men. One was much too young for her. Another was much too old. And that left one other man to send him a challenging look. Rez wasn't the least bit intimidated. Even if he didn't have prior plans to meet up with Bea here, he still wouldn't have worried about gaining her attention.

After all, they were very old friends. Their friendship went back so far that he recalled her learning to ride her first bike. She'd insisted he hold on to the back of the bike so she wouldn't fall over. That memory felt like a million years ago.

Bea laughed at something the kid said to her. And all Rez could think who that he wanted her to laugh at something he said—he wanted to make her smile and put the sparkle in her eyes. As soon as the thought came to him, he stopped it.

What was he doing? He was in no position to want a woman to smile for him—to find her exceedingly attractive. He'd already had one beautiful, sweet wife and he'd let her down. He didn't deserve another chance at happiness.

Not wanting to get caught up in the painful memories, he focused on his task. He moved to Bea's side and said loud enough for the other men to overhear, "Your Highness, may I have a moment of your time?"

Bea turned her head and bestowed a warm smile on him. "The Duke of Kaspar. It's so good to see you again. Of course you can."

She said it so convincingly that for a moment he thought she was truly happy to see him. And it made his pulse pick up its pace. It took him a moment to remember that everything said between them was for show—nothing more. And that's how it should be because there was absolutely zero chance of anything real ever happening between them. He wouldn't let it happen.

He was frowning...again.

Beatrix struggled not to sigh in exasperation. What was it with Rez? Every time he saw her, he would frown. Was she that displeasing to look at?

She was late this evening because she'd taken extra care in picking out the perfect outfit to wear. She wanted something that wasn't too businesslike or too casual.

She'd really hoped she'd got the right combination, but the frown on Rez's face was having her rethink her choices—even if it was too late to do anything about it now.

Instead she turned her attention to the gallery. She'd visited it many times in the past. She loved the tranquility within these walls—today she didn't feel so tranquil.

She let Rez set the pace as they made their way through the gallery. There were many heads turning their way. Most of them were women and they were frowning. Perhaps their ruse was starting to take root. She couldn't wait to read *Duchess Tales* later that evening.

She leaned in close to Rez. "The palace's statement was released this afternoon. That's part of the reason I was late. I was reading the press coverage. So far there's no response from the Duchess."

"I haven't heard anyone mention Istvan or Indigo since I've been here so maybe the release is working and we can forget about our endeavor."

She slipped her hand in the crook of his arm. "You're much too eager to give up on our ruse. I'm beginning to think you don't like me."

He glanced her way. "You aren't serious, are you?"

She shrugged. "You certainly frown enough when I'm around."

"I do not." He frowned at her.

"Really? Because you're doing it right now."

He sighed. "Shall we look at some of the work?"

"Certainly. I love to see all of the new pieces."

And so they walked together, looking at the artwork. She left her hand in the crook of his arm, warning off some of the eager young ladies that for the moment Rez was taken. And it worked. They were given a modicum of privacy as they discussed the various pieces of art.

She was delighted to find Rez was earnestly searching for artwork for his home. This was something she could help him with. "If you like the wildflower painting, you should check out some of Indigo's work. It's just around this corner."

They made their way past a large group of people and turned the corner. Beatrix came to a sudden stop.

Rez bumped into her. "Sorry."

She stared at the empty wall. Where were Indigo's paintings? Had they all sold? Part of her was excited for her future sister-in-law. Another part of her was disappointed that she couldn't share Indi's amazing work with Rez.

Just then an older woman with short dark hair and a pleasant smile approached them. She quickly bowed to Beatrix. "Your Highness, it's so good to have you here."

"Esme, it's so good to see you." She smiled at the sweet woman. "I'd like to introduce you to the Duke of Kaspar. Rez, this is Esme Durand. She and her husband own the gallery."

"It's a pleasure to meet you," Esme said.

"Your gallery is wonderful. I intend to purchase a couple of pieces. I'm having a hard time figuring out which paintings are my favorite."

"It can be quite the challenge." Esme beamed.

"I was just about to show the Duke some of Indigo's work, but the wall where her work normally hangs is empty," Beatrix said. "Did it all sell?"

The smile fell from Esme's face. Her brows drew together as she glanced away and pursed her lips.

Beatrix grew concerned. "Esme, what is it?"

She lifted her gaze to meet Beatrix's. "We had a problem earlier this week with someone trying to vandalize the paintings. We decided to move them to the back until things settle down."

Beatrix gasped. "That's horrible."

Esme nodded. "We had to call the authorities. Some people are just so awful. I saw the release from the palace this afternoon. It should put a stop to the awful lies that have been running rampant."

"We hope so. And thank you for protecting Indigo's work. Since Rez is looking for a piece of art, I wanted to show him Indigo's work. I think she has a piece that might be just right for him."

"Certainly." Esme explained exactly where they could find the pieces.

With the aid of Esme's directions, they found the artwork in an employee's-only area of the gallery. It was such a shame the pieces had to be put back here for safekeeping. Now everyone at the show would miss out on seeing these fine works.

"That's really nice." Rez gestured to a painting of an older woman surrounded by kittens as she tried to feed them.

"I'm afraid that one is sold," Beatrix said.

"How can you tell which ones are sold?" Rez asked.

She moved to a painting beside it. "See the red tag?" When he nodded, she said, "It means the piece is still available for sale. They remove the tag after it's been sold."

He continued moving along the wall, taking in the various painting of people from all walks of life and all ages. When he came to a beach scene, he stopped and stared. This was the piece Beatrix was certain he would like. The painting had a little girl with a bonnet on playing in the sand.

He turned to her. "That could be a painting of Evi at the beach."

She smiled and nodded. "I had a feeling you would say that."

"And it has a red tag." Rez looked quite pleased. "I haven't taken Evi to the beach yet."

"You should do it. She'll love it."

His brow furrowed. "You don't think she's too young?"

Beatrix hesitated. "I think you'd be the best judge of that."

There was so much she didn't know about babies, but there was a part of her that would love to learn. She tamped down that desire. It wouldn't do her well to dwell on things that weren't going to happen.

As they returned to the front of the gallery, Rez let Esme know which paintings he wanted to purchase. Afterward, they made their way slowly around the gallery, taking in all the many pieces of art.

The evening flew by much too quickly. She'd thoroughly enjoyed Rez's company. It was as though something had changed and tonight he was fun and engaging. He was very much like the Rez she used to know.

And then the time came when she needed to go about doing her royal responsibility. "I don't want to, but I should go mingle."

It was her duty to start answering questions about the palace's statement. The sooner they had the correct information out there, the sooner the outlandish rumors would die down.

Rez nodded. "I understand. I enjoyed viewing the gallery with you."

She smiled. "I enjoyed it too."

She didn't say it to him, but this evening hadn't felt like work. Instead it was pleasant to spend time with him. It almost felt like a real date. She reminded herself that he was only putting on a show for the public. The thought dampened her mood.

Beatrix turned and walked away. She was anxious to get home and read the *Duchess Tales* write-up. Thanks to Rez, their evening had gone so much better than the polo match. It had almost fooled her.

CHAPTER EIGHT

HAD IT WORKED?

Had they succeeded in snaring the paparazzi's attention?

Beatrix had been anxious to leave the gallery after spotting Rez walking out the front door with a wrapped package under his arm. She so wanted to leave with him, but she knew she couldn't.

First, she had misinformation to dispel. Second, she didn't want to rush their relationship—in the press, of course. It wasn't like they had a real relationship aside from being old friends.

But she had noticed how the women nearly salivated when he was in their proximity. Of course, she couldn't blame them. He was so handsome—even more so than when they were kids. The years had given him a level of maturity that she found downright sexy.

And so Beatrix stayed at the gallery, making her rounds. There were questions and more questions about Istvan and Indigo. She was floored at some of the more straightforward questions, like was the palace lying to cover up Indigo's arrest record? *What arrest record?* Indigo was never on the wrong side of the law.

Beatrix talked and talked, hoping the information she shared here would be spread among the attendees' friends. It was amazing how the press could take something and twist it until it didn't even represent the truth.

Thankfully, after clarifying matters, most people believed her. And they felt sorry for Indigo and Istvan. Beatrix wondered if perhaps the palace should do a public address to further clarify matters. The King could give a Kingdom-wide address. It'd be like he was coming into people's homes and having a personal chat with them, much like Beatrix had done this evening.

With most people having departed, Beatrix thanked the hosts and made her way back to the palace. On her short ride to the palace, she checked the *Duchess Tales* website. There were still no new posts that day. What were they waiting for?

With a huff, Beatrix stuffed her phone back in her purse. Her feet ached and she was tempted to kick off her new heels. But she knew if she were to do that she would never get the shoes back on. She would have to wait a while longer to go barefoot.

First, she wanted to meet up with Rez and compare notes about the evening. As her driver maneuvered the car up the long drive to the palace, Beatrix pulled out her phone. Her fingers moved rapidly over the screen as she messaged Rez.

Can we meet in the library?

I can't.

We really need to talk.

Come to the nursery.

The nursery? It wasn't exactly the place she wanted to have a serious conversation. But it seemed as though Rez wasn't giving her many options. Still, that didn't stop her from trying again.

We need to talk privately.

Agreed. Let's meet in the nursery.

Fine. Let me change and I'll see you.

We'll be waiting.

She could imagine him with Evi in his arms. When he was with her, it was like his troubles faded away. Instead of frowning, he was always smiling. The baby was good for him. Beatrix just couldn't help but wish he shared some of those smiles with her.

After the car dropped her off, she entered the palace through the back door. As soon as she was inside, she slipped off her heels. She sighed in relief. With them dangling from her fingertips, she rushed up the back stairs.

She changed into a comfortable pair of blue shorts and a white lacy top. She checked her phone again. She was starting to think there wasn't going to be an update from the Duchess that day. She wondered what that meant. She didn't know if it was a good sign or not.

She moved to the guest wing where Rez's set of rooms were located. Once more the nursery door was open. Since she was still in her bare feet, her steps were muffled.

When she reached the doorway, she paused. Rez held

Evi in his arms. His back was to Beatrix. He was singing a lullaby. Beatrix knew she should make her presence known but she couldn't bring herself to ruin this moment.

Who knew that Rez had such a beautifully deep voice? She certainly didn't. In all of the years she'd known him, she'd never heard him sing. And the baby seemed totally entranced with her father's voice.

He danced around. When he spun around, he spotted Beatrix. She expected him to stop singing as soon as he saw her but instead his gaze connected with hers as he continued to softly sing.

In that moment, her heart swooned. There was nothing sweeter than Rez with a baby in his arms. He looked so natural. And the baby was all smiles.

It also reminded her of what she was never going to have. Tears stung the backs of her eyes. She blinked repeatedly. She couldn't stay here and let him see her tears. She turned on her heels and set off down the hallway.

"Bea, wait!" Rez called after her.

She kept going. She swiped at the dampness on her cheeks. Why would he invite her to speak with him in the nursery if all he was planning to do was sing songs? Didn't he understand that they had important things to discuss?

What in the world?

He might have been married and had a daughter, but Rez still didn't understand women. Not really. He thought things were going all right between him and Bea.

He'd even thought they had a good evening. It hadn't started that way for him, but after Bea showed up, he started to relax and to enjoy his time at the gallery. He'd thought she'd enjoyed it too.

But now as Rez stood in the hallway, he watched Bea's stiff shoulders and her ramrod-straight back as she strode away. And he didn't understand what had happened.

Granted his singing wasn't that good, but Evi hadn't complained. Something else must have upset Bea, but he had no idea what was bothering her. Maybe there had been something posted online about them or her brother.

"Bea, wait." He tried once more. "Please."

She didn't so much as give him a backward glance. She turned a corner and disappeared from sight.

"Sir, I heard you. Is everything all right?" Mrs. Wilson approached him with a worried look on her face.

"I, ah, need to speak with the Princess. Would you be able to take Evi?"

"Certainly." The nanny held out her arms for the baby.

"Thank you."

As soon as his daughter was secure in the nanny's arms, Rez took off after Bea. He had to know what had happened to make her take off like that. He was so confused.

The only problem was that he had no idea where she'd gone. Was she upstairs? Downstairs? He opted to check her suite of rooms.

When he reached her door, he rapped his knuckles on the door. She didn't immediately answer. Still, he waited. He needed to fix the problem. She was his only true ally in the palace with Istvan being away.

He knocked again. "Bea, it's me. Open up."

The door swung open and she frowned at him. "What do you want?"

The hostile tone of her voice had him taking a step back. What was wrong with her? Had something happened when she'd left the art gallery alone?

"To check on you. Why did you leave the nursery?" He wanted to ask why she seemed to be mad at him, but he couldn't let himself do it. He couldn't let her know that her feelings toward him mattered.

"You were busy." Her gaze didn't quite meet his.

"You could have joined us. From what I remember, you have a decent voice." She had a beautiful voice, but he wasn't going there either.

She shook her head. "I didn't want to intrude on a family moment."

"Well, there's no family moment now. Should we talk?"

She hesitated, which was not common for her. Something was definitely off with her, but he still didn't have a clue what it was or what it was about.

"Maybe we should talk in the morning."

He didn't understand this sudden change in her attitude. Up until now she was pushing for them to work on their plans—to perfect their ruse with the paparazzi. Now something had suddenly changed.

And then he had the worst thought. "Did Istvan and Indigo call off their wedding?"

"What? No. Why would you think that?"

He sighed as he shifted his weight from one foot to the other and then back again. "Then I don't understand."

"Understand what?"

Really? She was going to play it that way? Then he was going to have to be the one that was direct. "I don't understand why you were the one that pushed me into this ruse and now you are the one backing out of it."

"I am not." Her words were firm and swift.

"Then shouldn't we talk?"

Ding.

Bea moved away from the doorway while leaving the

door cracked open. She picked up her phone. "It's a new post from *Duchess Tales*."

He stepped into the room. "What does it say?"

"Let me pull it up." She started to read to herself.

"Out loud."

Without lifting her gaze from the phone, she said, "The headline reads, A Wedding in Shambles."

This wasn't good. Not good at all. And he wasn't one to worry, but even he had to admit that things were getting worse.

Bea's voice drew his attention as she continued to read.

According to my source, who has access to the palace, Prince Istvan and Indigo are no longer in residence. They have fled Rydiania for parts unknown.

If that doesn't say the wedding is off, I don't know what does. If the palace wasn't covering something up, why run?

Bea stopped reading and looked at him. "How do they know all of this?"

"Is it possible they have a spy within the palace walls?" He didn't like the thought. It was hard enough living a life in the public eye without having to worry about being watched at home—even if your home was a palace.

"I don't know. I never thought of it. I do know that everyone who is hired must sign an ironclad nondisclosure agreement. But I'm not aware of any new hires."

"We can figure that out later. What else does it say?"

While we await the reappearance of the Prince...and perhaps Indigo...we have other royal news. The Duke of Kaspar was once again out and about. This time he was spotted at the Durand Art Gallery...

Rez's body tensed. He hated having the spotlight on him and his life. And if he didn't owe his oldest friend a *huge* debt, he wouldn't take part in this ruse.

It seems as though now that he's reentered society that he isn't going to let any dust settle on his shoes. This evening he was spotted talking to numerous women. Funnily enough, he was so busy with the female guests that he didn't have time to speak with any of the males. Was this intentional, ladies? Or is he on the hunt for a new duchess?

Bea stopped reading and glanced up at him. "I'm sorry."

He brushed off her apology, even though the words poked at the scar upon his heart. "It's not your fault what that horrible woman writes."

"I don't have to read any more."

"Of course you do." He could get through this—even if it killed him to listen to the Duchess go on and on about him being excited to be a bachelor again—as though he were happy to be rid of Enora. The thought sliced into his heart. Nothing could be further from the truth. "We need to know what to do next."

Bea hesitated. And then she continued reading.

Ladies, it's time to get out there. You never know where the Duke is likely to pop up next. And it appears he hasn't set his sights on anyone in particular. Well...

He might have spent most of his time touring the gallery with Princess Beatrix on his arm. But was this the spark of a new romance? Or is it more likely it was just two old friends reconnecting?

Beatrix squealed.

"What's wrong?" He almost regretted asking the question because he didn't want anything else to be wrong. He was so over this whole fiasco.

"Nothing." At last the dark clouds had parted and the sunshine of her smile beamed through. "It's working."

"It is?"

She nodded and then held her phone out for him to see. There was a photo of her and Rez. This time he wasn't frowning and neither was she. Instead they appeared to be discussing a piece of art. It certainly wasn't a scandalous photo, nor was it one of contention. It was a rather neutral photo.

"We have to avoid this going forward," Bea said.

Once more he was confused. That seemed to happen a lot when he was talking to her. "Avoid what? I thought the point of this whole plan was for us to be seen together."

"It is. But this photo is blah. There's nothing here for people to gossip about."

"That's a good thing." People gossiped about the royal family way too much in his opinion.

"Not in this case. Remember, we're supposed to divert attention away from Istvan. However, when I look at this post, most of it is about you." When he arched a brow, she said, "And me. Either way. The more they talk about us, the less they speculate about Istvan's relationship."

"Is there anything else?" He might as well know what was being said about him.

"Not really."

Will there or won't there be a royal wedding? This royal follower would love to know the answer. I'm not even sure whether or not I'm rooting for Prince Istvan and Indigo. Instead of palace statements, this royal follower would rather hear directly from the couple in question because I have questions, many of them.

In the meantime, at least we have the dashing Duke of Kaspar to distract us and tease us as he picks a new duchess. Who shall it be?

Until next time...xox

His hands clenched. His private life wasn't one for public speculation. The truth of the matter was that he was quickly coming to the conclusion that he did need to marry. Evi deserved a loving mother. But he had no idea how to accomplish this when his heart wasn't into the task. It wasn't like he could just take out an advertisement on the internet. Or could he?

As soon as the crazy idea came to him, he dismissed it. There would be no ads. But it might mean he had to pay more attention to the women he crossed paths with than he wanted to. It was the only way to find a suitable mother for Evi.

He wasn't planning to jump into marriage right away. It would take some time to find the right person—someone who loved Evi as much as he did.

She had to keep it together.

Beatrix had never been so happy for the interruption

of a *Duchess Tales* post because it diverted Rez's attention away from her being upset over seeing him with his baby in his arms. But why had it upset her so much?

Sure there was the fact that she couldn't have her own children, but she'd made her peace with that. Her life was good the way it was. She had her life of service—of giving back to the people of Rydiania. And her obligations kept her busy every day. She didn't have room in her life for anything else—certainly not a husband and baby.

Not wanting to think about babies and her solitary life any longer, she said, "Even though our plan is working. I don't have any plans for tomorrow."

"What do you mean?"

"There are no openings, no sporting events or society parties."

"Then we'll make our own event."

She thought he would have been relieved not to have to play pretend for one day. "What do you have in mind?"

"Let me give it some thought and I'll get back to you. I promise it won't involve me singing."

Guilt assailed her. She really did owe him an apology, even if she wasn't ready to discuss the reason for her mood. "I'm sorry about earlier. It wasn't your singing. I promise." And then realizing they were still standing by the doorway, she said, "Come. Sit down."

They moved to her sitting area that had two large white couches flanked by a couple of well-stuffed purple armchairs. She sat on a couch. He sat on one of the chairs.

"Then what had you so upset?" His gaze probed her.

She glanced away. "It was just…" She reached for the first thing that had bothered her that evening. "The way people are so eager to believe the lies about Indigo—to the point of attempting to vandalize her artwork. Who does something like that?"

He leaned back in the chair. The rigid line of his shoulders had eased and the twin lines between his brows had soothed. "I don't know. I was trying to figure that out myself. It's not common in Rydiania."

"That's what I was thinking. We don't have people acting up out in the streets. We don't have people throwing around angry words. So perhaps it's just one or two people trying to stir up trouble." This idea appealed to her so much more than the thought of her country devolving into turmoil.

"What have your parents said about the attempted vandalism?"

"I haven't told them. I thought they had enough to deal with at the moment and with my father's health not being the best, I didn't want to lay this on him."

Rez nodded in understanding. "If it is one or two people, how do you plan to handle it? Tell the Royal Police?"

She shook her head. "Not yet." She held up her finger to have him wait. She moved to the bedroom door and pushed it closed. Then she returned to her seat. "First, I'd like to find out if we really do have a spy in our midst."

His eyes widened. "You're planning to flush out the spy?"

"I am."

"This sounds like an awful idea."

"Why?" She sat up straight. "Would you say the same thing if my brother had suggested it?"

Rez opened his mouth to answer but then wordlessly pressed his lips back together.

"That's what I thought." She didn't like the way her brother and Rez always seemed to think she needed protecting. After the things she'd had to face, identifying a spy wouldn't be so hard.

"And how do you plan to go about this ruse to catch a spy?" He arched a brow as though challenging her to come up with a good idea.

Feeling the pressure, she said, "Give me a moment to think."

"I think you'll need longer than that to come up with a good plan."

She ignored his doubt. The plan had to include a tidbit of gossip that was so interesting the spy would be sure to report it back to *Duchess Tales*. It shouldn't be something about Rez. He seemed very unhappy about the talk of his private life—not that she could blame him.

And she was willing to put herself out there, but she couldn't think of anything that would be interesting enough to make it to print on the Duchess blog.

This left Istvan and Indigo. The thought didn't sit well with her, but maybe the news didn't have to be anything bad. Maybe it could be some good news about the couple. Something to keep the naysayers in check. The more she thought about it, the more she liked the idea.

"Oh, no." Rez softly groaned. "That is not a good look."

"What look?" She didn't realize her thoughts had transferred to her face. The thought of him being able to read her thoughts totally unnerved her. Say it wasn't so.

"The look that says you came up with an idea. And I have a feeling I'm going to hate it."

It wasn't as bad as she'd thought. "*Hate* is such a strong word."

He frowned at her. "Just tell me what it is."

There was a part of her that wanted to keep him guessing, but this was a time-sensitive subject. "We need to share something that is big enough news to rate a post on the Duchess site, but something that is positive for the royal family."

He paused as though thinking it over. "It seems reasonable enough."

"We need to let it slip that Istvan and Indigo have eloped." The more she thought about it, the more she liked the idea.

"What? Do you really think that's a good idea considering the circumstances?"

She shrugged. "I don't see how it can hurt anyone when the truth comes out except the believability of the spy and *Duchess Tales*."

"Do you think you should run this past your parents?"

She shook her head. "I don't see the need. If there isn't a spy in the palace, then it's no big deal. Nothing will come of it. *But* if there is one, this will give them away."

"How are you going to know who it is in the palace?"

"That part I haven't figured out. But at least we'll know if there is a leak. Because the only way they could have gotten the information was from us."

"And how do you plan to get this news out there?"

"I guess we'll need to make sure and talk about it around the staff."

"There's a lot of staff here. Like hundreds. How are you going to say this in front of all of them?"

"I don't think that's necessary. I think it's just the staff that are closest to the family we have to worry about." He didn't look convinced so she said, "Don't worry about it. I'll take care of it on my own."

His brows rose. "You're that determined to do this?"

"I am."

"I think it's a mistake."

"That much is apparent." She didn't like that he doubted her. Not at all. "So don't worry about it."

"And what about us…erm, our fake relationship?"

"We're still doing that too. What did you have in mind for tomorrow?"

He got to his feet. "I'll be in contact."

When he started for the door, she followed. "So that's it? You aren't going to tell me your plan?"

He hesitated. "I don't think so."

"Why not?"

"You seem to have enough on your mind at the moment. Let me take care of this. I'll let you know the plans in the morning." And with that he was out the door.

Beatrix was left staring at the open doorway and wondering what Rez was up to. Should she be worried?

As much as she wanted to figure out what Rez was up to, she didn't have the time. She needed to set to work on her own plan. She grabbed her phone and headed out the door.

CHAPTER NINE

His PLAN WAS in motion.

It was much more his speed.

The following day at noon, Rez pushed the baby stroller along the paved walkway through the park on the edge of the village. In his other hand, he held a picnic basket. He was curious to see what goodies the palace kitchen had packed for this outing.

With the sun shining brightly and a gentle breeze, it wasn't too hot, or too cold. This was the perfect day to be outdoors. He didn't like to keep Evi inside all day. He preferred for her to get some fresh air and explore the outdoors each day, weather permitting.

He searched for a spot to have a picnic. At last, he decided upon a grassy area at the top of a small hill. He pushed the stroller off into the grass. *Oh, yes, this would work just fine.* The green field was wide open with a few trees here and there. Best of all, it had a nice view of the rest of the park with a pond in the distance.

"What do you think, Evi?" He glanced down at his daughter. "Is this a good place for a picnic?"

"Looks good to me."

The unexpected answer startled him. He turned around to find Bea standing behind him. "I didn't hear you approach."

"Must be my stealthy skills." She smiled at him.

"You got here quickly."

"It's not far from the palace. And I might have been dropped off."

He arched his brow. "You couldn't walk that far?"

"I could have but I didn't want to be late. I had no idea what you had in mind."

"Would you mind helping me spread out the blanket?" He reached for the red plaid blanket draped over the top of the picnic basket.

As she helped spread out the blanket, she kept glancing around. "I don't see anyone."

He frowned. He didn't want this day to be about creating a buzz on the gossip sites. He just wanted all three of them to have a nice day. "Stop acting like you're expecting people to watch us."

"But I am."

"Just relax and pretend like you're having a good time."

She pursed her glossy lips as she looked at him. "Do you really think I have to pretend in order to have a good time?"

He shrugged. "This is all pretend… Isn't it?"

She didn't immediately reply. "Of course it is."

He finished straightening out the blanket. "Then smile and pretend like you're having a good time."

She smiled, but it didn't reach her eyes. It made him feel bad that she really did have to pretend to have a good time with him. He wanted the easy relationship back that they'd had all those years ago when they were kids. When they would play ball out in the rolling fields behind the palace grounds. When he knew that she was too young for him, but it didn't stop him from wanting to spend time around her because she was fun to be around.

It all seemed so long ago now. It was like he'd lived a couple of lifetimes between then and now. The life of a loving husband, who thought it was just the start of a happy married life. And then the life of a widower and single father, who had to fight through the darkness of grief in order to be a devoted father to his daughter.

And still he felt as though he was lacking in the parent department. He couldn't help but feel his daughter would benefit from having a strong, loving woman in her life. But the thought of remarrying—of putting his heart on the line again—had him hesitating. He couldn't risk going through another devastating loss.

"Can you hand me the basket?" Bea's voice drew him from his thoughts.

"Sure." He bent over and picked up the basket.

He turned to Bea. When she reached out, their fingers touched. Neither pulled away. The connection felt as though his body had been hit with a bolt of static electricity. It zipped up his arm to his chest. His heart felt as though it'd skipped a beat or two.

Was it just him? Or did Bea feel the arc between them? When his gaze met hers, his pulse increased. She'd felt it too.

The craziest desire came over him. His gaze lowered to Bea's glossy lips. He wondered what she'd do if he were to lean forward and press his mouth to hers. The impulse was too great to fight it.

As he leaned toward Bea, Evi started to fuss. The spell they'd been under had lifted as quickly as it'd started. Bea pulled her hand away from his. He immediately noticed the chill where her warm touch had just been.

Evi's fussing grew louder, distracting him from his thoughts of Bea. He leaned down and released the safety straps before lifting his daughter into his arms. She rubbed her eyes. Her rosy-red lips opened wide as she expelled a yawn.

With Evi in one arm, he rummaged through her diaper bag and pulled out some of her toys. He placed them on the blanket and then he set her down next to them.

He turned to Bea, who was unusually quiet as she removed the food from the basket. There was baby food for Evi as well as a large selection of cheeses from Brie to Camembert. A loaf of crusty bread and dipping sauces. Some meats were included, just perfect to make a savory sandwich. And then there was an array of colorful fruits. It all looked so tempting…but not as tempting as the woman seated next to him. His gaze strayed to her lush berry-red lips. They were just ripe for the picking.

As soon as the thought came to him, he glanced away. What was wrong with him? There was no way he was starting something with his best friend's sister, especially when he knew nothing would come of it. But it didn't stop him from wondering what it might be like to hold Bea in his arms.

For a while, they ate quietly. All the while he wondered what Bea was thinking. Was it possible she was having the same errant thoughts as him?

Bea glanced around as though checking to see if anyone was staring at them. "Did you contact someone in the press to let them know we'd be here?"

"No." She definitely wasn't on the same train of thought as him. He cleared his throat. "Didn't you say there was a spy in the palace? If so, wouldn't they know we were here?"

"Shh…" She glanced over at a young couple making their way along the sidewalk. Bea smiled at them. Once the couple had passed on by, she turned to him. "You have to be careful. You never know who's listening."

He was surprised by how seriously she was taking all of this spy stuff. It also made him wonder if she'd acted on her plan to ferret out the leak at the palace...if there was one.

"Did you work on flushing out the leak?"

She nodded. "I started last night."

"And how did you do this?" He wasn't sure he wanted to know the answer. He didn't like the thought of her doing anything the least bit dangerous.

"I had fake phone conversations."

It wasn't the answer he was expecting, but at least it seemed safe enough. "And who were these conversations with?"

"Istvan. During the conversation I learned he and Indigo eloped."

"Really?"

She smiled and nodded. "Now, we have to wait and see if it shows up on the *Duchess Tales* site today."

He had a hard time believing there was a spy in the palace. He knew the review process before being hired was extensive and a strong work history was a requirement. He knew this because he'd used a similar process for his country estate. If he was going to share his home with strangers, he wanted to protect his family's privacy.

"And has anything appeared on the site?" He hoped the answer was no because the royal family already had enough things to worry about.

"Not the last time I checked." She reached for her phone and pulled up the site. She gasped.

Concern filled him. "What is it?"

"It's there. The story of my brother and Indigo eloping." She looked at him. "There's definitely a spy in the palace."

When she went to stand up, he reached out for her hand. Immediately the feel of her soft, warm skin sent a jolt through his body. His thumb, as of its own volition, stroked the back of her hand.

It was a simple touch. It shouldn't have meant anything. And yet it was as though the touch had awakened a part of him that had been dormant for so long.

When his gaze met Bea's, he didn't see his childhood friend. Instead, he saw the grown woman she'd become. He noticed how her eyes had become windows to her soul. He found himself drowning in their blue depths. Her face had thinned out, revealing her high cheekbones. And then there were her full lips that appeared so perfect for kissing.

Bea stood, jarring him from his thoughts.

"Where are you going?" His voice came out deeper than normal.

"I have to inform the King. We have to find out who the spy is and get rid of them."

"Wait. Let's think about this." When she settled back on her spot on the blanket, he regretfully let go of their connection.

"Think about what? This is big. We can't have a spy within the palace."

"But what if you did leave them there?"

"Why?" She frowned at him.

"In order to funnel misinformation directly to the *Duchess Tales*. I mean you have a direct pipeline now to the biggest gossip site in all of Rydiania. Why would you cut that off when you need to get stories to the site as quickly as possible?"

She paused as though giving his idea some legitimate consideration. Her brows drew together. Her tempting lips pursed and every time he looked at them, he could feel a renewed desire swelling within him to pull her close and feel her lips beneath his.

"Maybe you're right." Her voice startled him from his thoughts. "In fact, the more I think about it, the more I like the idea. Rez, did you hear me?"

"Um...yes."

She studied him. "You were frowning at me like I'd done something to bother you—like you were doing at the polo match. What's wrong?"

He shook his head and replaced his supposed frown with a smile, hoping to ease her worry. "Nothing at all."

"You know, you were really good at the polo match. You looked like you were enjoying yourself. You should consider rejoining the team."

The thought was tempting. He had enjoyed himself out there in the sunshine and on the back of his favorite polo pony. And as much as he'd enjoyed it, he knew he didn't even deserve that bit of happiness.

He shook his head. "I can't."

"Can't? Why not?" Her gaze searched his.

He lowered his gaze to the blanket. "It doesn't matter."

"Of course it matters. Especially if it's the reason you've been isolating yourself."

He knew Bea well enough to know she wasn't going to give up until she learned the truth. It was a story he hadn't been willing to share with anyone.

He could feel her expectant gaze on him. He turned to Evi. He picked her up and gave her a toy. All the while, Bea was quiet as she waited for him to answer her.

"It's a nice day." He hoped she'd go with it. "And the food was delicious."

"You aren't getting off that easily. I know you've been through a lot and I want to understand."

He turned to her and saw the caring look in her eyes. Maybe if he told her, she would understand why he didn't deserve to resume his former life—not with his wife no longer alive. But did he have the strength to voice the painful words?

He glanced down at Evi, who had fallen asleep in his arms. He cleared his throat as he struggled to find a starting point. "That day I was supposed to meet Enora and Evi for lunch. You have no idea how much I wish I could redo things that day."

Bea squeezed his arm. He found strength in her touch. He knew it was time he vocalized what had happened that day.

"Enora called me that morning and we made plans to meet up in town for lunch. Evi had been a couple of months old and Enora was anxious to get out of the house." He remembered that day vividly. "Only when it was finally time for lunch, I was tied up with a conference call." Back then he was a full partner at a big law firm. "And I... I put my work over my family."

"Is that why you haven't been back to work since then?"

He nodded. Just the thought of returning to the office reminded him of the worst day of his life. He didn't know if he'd ever be able to return to the same office. Not that he had to work. He'd inherited a fortune from his grandmother's estate. But as he was quickly finding, he had too much time on his hands.

"That day I decided to continue my business call instead of meeting my wife and daughter. If... If I had kept my word to Enora, none of that would have happened."

Bea squeezed his arm again and then slid her hand down to interlock her fingers with his. "You don't know that."

"I do know it. She wouldn't have been crossing the road at that moment. If it wasn't for your brother seeing her, I would have lost both her and Evi." The painful memories made the breath catch in his chest. It took him a moment to be able to speak again. "If your brother hadn't pushed the stroller out of the way..."

He couldn't finish the words. He couldn't think about losing Evi too. When he'd received the call at the office, he felt as though the bottom had totally dropped out of his world.

"I'd raced to the hospital. Enora had come to and I'd spoken to her very briefly before she'd gone into emergency surgery. She'd fought to live, but..." The memory tore at his heart. When he spoke again, it was barely more than a whisper. "She didn't make it."

"That's why you agreed to this crazy scheme to get the press's attention away from Istvan and Indigo?"

He nodded. "I owe your brother more than I can ever repay him."

"You do know he doesn't feel that way. He just wanted to help."

"I know. I couldn't imagine my life now if he hadn't stepped in. Your brother is my very best friend as far back as I can remember. But he shouldn't have had to do anything if I had been where I belonged. Enora's death is on me."

"No, it isn't. It's the fault of that twenty-year-old kid

who was speeding and hit her. None of it is on you. And if Enora was here now, she would tell you that."

He wanted to believe Bea. He really did. But there was still a nagging voice at the back of his mind that said if only... Evi would still have her mother.

"I'm so sorry for all you've been going through." Bea's voice interrupted his thoughts. "I should have tried to see you more. I just didn't know what to say or what to do. I'm sorry for that. I wasn't a good friend." She lowered her head. "I'll do better."

He reached out and placed a finger beneath her chin, lifting until their gazes met. "You are an amazing friend. I don't know if I could have ever left my home and re-entered society if you weren't by my side. You've made it a lot easier for me. How did I get so lucky to have you in my life?"

She smiled at him. "I'm the lucky one."

Is that what she really thought? She enjoyed having him in her life? His heart beat faster.

It felt like forever since an adult enjoyed his company. His gaze lowered to her glossy lips that shimmered in the sunlight. He should look away but he couldn't.

In that moment he needed a physical connection to remind him that he was more than a shell of a human who'd gotten lost in his grief. Bea was like a beacon, guiding him back to the land of the living. He was attracted to her in a way he'd never been drawn to anyone before.

Without thinking about where they were or who might see them, he leaned toward her. His heart beat so loud that it echoed in his ears. He pressed his mouth to hers.

Bea's lips were soft and smooth. His kiss was slow and gentle. He didn't want to rush this tantalizing exploration. He longed to savor this special moment as long as Bea would allow.

As the blood quickly pulsed through his veins and his chest filled with a radiating warmth, he felt fully alive once more. Bea's kiss reminded him of all he'd been missing in life. And now he wanted this moment to go on and on.

Evi shifted in his arm, drawing him out of the spell he was under. He drew back from Bea. He was about to apologize for kissing her, but the words died in the back of his throat. The truth is that he wasn't sorry. Not one little bit.

In fact, he very much wanted to kiss her again. His fingers tingled with the need to reach out and draw her to him. Maybe it wasn't too late to revisit the kiss.

But was it the right thing to do for either of them? He inwardly groaned. In the past, he'd acted in the moment and dealt with the consequences later. Now that he was a father, he found himself thinking before acting.

Bea was saying something but he was so caught up in the push-pull of his thoughts that he couldn't hear her. Soon his desire to feel her lips pressed to his was winning the struggle. It wouldn't take much to lean over to her.

"I should go." Bea went to stand.

Rez reached out to her. At first, he went to touch her hand, but having second thoughts, he rested his hand on her lower arm. "Don't leave."

She pulled her arm away. "That shouldn't have happened."

"You're right." He'd crossed a line. "Can we write it off as us getting caught up in the moment?"

There had to be a way to get things back on track. Now that there was possibly a spy in the palace, he worried if

Bea was left to her own devices that she'd get into trouble. He had to make sure that didn't happen.

She didn't respond.

"It was just a kiss," he said casually as though it was common for him to go around kissing all of the pretty ladies. "We were eventually supposed to do that for the cameras, right?" When she silently nodded, he continued. "Now we've gotten the awkwardness of the first kiss out of the way." Nothing about the kiss had felt awkward—not in the least. "And when we do it in front of the cameras, it'll seem natural."

Her hesitant gaze searched him. Did she believe the bit of fiction he'd concocted? He hoped so. He didn't want to delve into the real reason he'd kissed her.

"And that's the only reason you kissed me?"

"Yes." The lie came out a little too quickly.

Bea settled back on the blanket. She was unusually quiet. It made him wonder what she was thinking. He filled the awkward silence with casual conversation, hoping to draw her back out.

He turned to his daughter, who was now awake and ready to play. He situated her on the blanket with her pink bouncy ball. When she batted the ball away, he rolled it back to her. Evi laughed. The lyrical sound filled his heart with joy.

Evi batted her bouncy ball harder than she'd ever done before. She was getting strong. The ball bounced off the blanket before he could reach it. It continued its journey over the green grass as it continued to make its way downhill.

Evi's bottom lip began to quiver as she watched the ball roll away. He knew what was coming next, her wail of anger. His daughter was not afraid to voice her displeasure. When she was upset, everyone in the vicinity knew.

Before she could let out her first wail, he reached in the diaper bag and produced her favorite stuffed animal. It was a white bear with a pink bow and he'd learned quickly that they couldn't go anywhere without it. Not if he wanted his hearing intact when they returned.

He handed it to her. Evi batted it away. Her gaze strayed to the direction of the ball.

"Could you keep an eye on her?" he asked Bea as he got to his feet.

"What?" Bea's face filled with confusion. "Why?"

"I need to go get her ball." And then he took off with long strides to the bottom of the long sloping hillside.

Behind him he could hear Evi letting out another wail. He didn't have to pause because he immediately heard Bea speaking to his daughter in soft tones. His daughter's cries faded away.

A smile pulled at the corners of his lips. It was all he could do not to stop and look back. He could imagine Evi in Bea's arms. Bea would be totally animated and Evi would be enthralled with her. And he would no longer have to worry that Bea didn't like his child, which was silly. Of course she would like her. Who wouldn't? Evi was bright and fun. Her belly laughs were contagious.

And yet he noticed in the past how Bea had always made excuses not to hold Evi—always backed away. What had that been about? Although it didn't matter now. The problem was fixed because once Bea held Evi, she'd succumb to his daughter's charms.

Of course, he liked to think that Evi got her outgoing personality from him, but you couldn't tell that lately. Ever since Enora passed on, he hadn't been the least bit outgoing. Grief and guilt had entwined, making a super-strong rope that had held him hostage. But Bea with her sunny personality and prodding had freed him from his misery.

This was the first day where he could really feel the sun on his face. Today he didn't feel as though he were slogging through life just trying to make it to the end of the day. Today he was starting to feel like his old self.

And he had Bea and Evi to thank for helping him to make it through the clouds and to find the sun again. That's why he had such high hopes for the afternoon. If Bea and Evi hit it off, this could be the first of many afternoon outings. Who knew where they'd end up next. And the nice thing was that they didn't have to sneak around because this was exactly what Bea wanted—their relationship out in the open. And if the press made more of the relationship than there really was, then all the better.

At last he reached the ball and picked it up. When he turned around he expected to find Evi on Bea's lap as they played and talked. Instead he found Bea still in her same spot and Evi was across from her.

He didn't understand it. Evi was easy to like. Why was Bea keeping her distance? Didn't she like children?

The last thought sent a worrisome chill through his body. The thought of Bea never bonding with his child had never crossed his mind. It left him with a fundamental disappointment.

As he trudged up the hill, he had to know why Bea would prefer leaning the whole way across the blanket to hand Evi her stuffed animal when she tossed it aside, instead of Bea moving closer to her or even picking her up. But when he reached the blanket, Evi whined. He checked the time. It was time for her afternoon snack.

He reached for some food in a pocket of the diaper bag. And then he got an idea.

He turned to Bea. "Why don't you feed her?"

Immediately Bea began shaking her head. "I don't think so."

"It's okay. She'd like it and you'll get to know her better."

She waved off the bottle. "No. I... I can't."

Can't? What did that mean? "I'll show you."

Her gaze met his. Her eyes shimmered. Were those tears in her eyes? She glanced away. "I don't want to. I... I have to go."

Without waiting for a response, she got to her feet and walked away.

He turned and watched her walk away. She didn't so much as glance back. When Evi once more fussed for her food, he turned his attention to his daughter. All the while, he wondered what was going on with Bea. Why was she acting this way? It wasn't the first time. He recalled how Bea was with Evi in the nursery.

Bea really didn't like children. The acknowledgment hit him like a gut punch. And here he was thinking that Bea might be a loving mother to Evi. He had never been so wrong.

CHAPTER TEN

WHAT WAS WRONG with her?

Why had she kissed him back?

Beatrix walked as fast as she could to the palace. When her security detail offered to drive her, she waved them off. She needed the time alone in order to sort her thoughts.

She didn't believe Rez when he said he'd kissed her to get past the awkwardness. There had been more to that kiss than some random, meaningless act. It had been tender and moving. And yet it had been powerful and full of emotion.

But was that emotion linked to the memories of his wife? After all, he'd just confessed the most traumatic moment in his life. His thoughts and emotions had everything to do with Enora. He'd been caught up in the memories of his late wife when he'd kissed her. That's all it was. It wasn't about Beatrix. Not really.

It had been the unexpected kiss that had her making a hasty exit because it couldn't be sweet, little Evi. She was such an adorable baby. Anyone would instantly fall in love with her.

Try as she might, Beatrix couldn't convince herself that it was solely the kiss that had her so upset. She just wasn't that good of a liar. The truth was the sweet baby scared her more than anything else in her life.

Evi reminded her of what she couldn't have—a baby of her own. Before Beatrix's medical crisis, she hadn't given much thought to having a family. She had been young and single. And so after the surgery it hadn't been a big stretch to convince herself that she was fine with not having her own family.

And yet she wouldn't let herself pick up the baby. She was afraid she would know exactly what she was missing by not being able to have children of her own. She was afraid the pain would be too much. She didn't want to get caught up in the grief again. She'd already mourned the children she would never have—the family she wouldn't have.

Instead she needed to stay focused on her life of service. It was a busy, demanding schedule. It would be enough.

It was time to end this fake relationship. She couldn't do it any longer. They'd have to come up with some other sort of diversion.

She stormed through the back doorway of the palace and nearly collided with some staff that she'd never seen before. They were carrying linens in the shade of purple that had been selected for the wedding. It appeared they were working on more wedding preparations. Now they needed the bride and groom to return.

As Beatrix headed for her room, she pulled out her phone. It was so much easier to focus on someone else's problems instead of her own. And so she began messaging her brother.

When are you coming home?

Why?

Because everyone has noticed your absence and the wedding isn't far off.

Can't you hold everyone off just a little longer?

I'll try. But hurry home.

I'm doing my best.

Let me know if there's anything I can do.

It was all she could ask of him. She entered her room. Her great big bed with its soft pillows called to her. She longed to pick up a book and get lost in the pages. And then she realized there was nothing keeping her from doing exactly that.

Her steps quickened as she moved toward the bed where her e-reader rested on the side table. She kicked off her shoes and dived into bed. The soft pillows hugged her like a long-lost friend. It was there she took her first easy breath. She leaned over and picked up the e-reader. If she had her way, she would stay here the rest of the day.

With the cover flipped open, she perused the list of titles. Although she normally read romance because of their happily-ever-afters, she wasn't in the mood for that this afternoon. Instead she selected a thriller. She hoped the high stakes of the story would distract her from the problems in her own life.

She opened the book and read the first page. By the time she reached the end, she had to reread it because her thoughts had strayed back to Rez with his penetrating gaze that made her feel like he could see straight through her. No man had ever gotten to her the way he had. He could make her heart race with just a glance.

And there was his adorable daughter with her contagious laughter and those darling dimples. She would be so easy to love.

Beatrix let out a frustrated sigh. She'd lost her place on the page…again.

Knock-knock.

She wanted to pretend she hadn't heard the door. There wasn't anyone she wanted to talk to at the moment. Maybe if she sat quietly for a moment longer, they would move on.

Knock-knock.

"Your Royal Highness."

She sighed. Duty spurred her into action. She set aside her e-reader and slid out of bed. In her bare feet, she silently padded over to the door. She swung it open to find one of the Queen's ladies-in-waiting.

"Your Highness." The young woman bowed. When she straightened, she said, "The Queen requests your presence in her office."

"Right now?" She really wasn't in the mood to deal with her mother. Their talks were never light-and-easy conversations. Instead they were usually about a problem and this time she was certain the subject would be about the wedding.

"Yes, ma'am. I'll let her know that you're on the way." The woman turned and walked away.

Beatrix noticed how the woman didn't even wait for

her to reply. It was automatically assumed that when the King or Queen wanted to see someone they wouldn't dare consider refusing to make an appearance. It was the story of Beatrix's life.

With a sigh, she closed the door. She moved to her bathroom to check her hair and makeup. Her mother would comment if she didn't look her best. With her long hair brushed down her back and her hair band adjusted, she took a moment to apply some facial powder and repair her eyeliner. With one last inspection, she returned to her bedroom and slipped on her shoes.

As she made her way to the first floor, she passed many palace workers. They were carrying chairs and other furniture as the palace was preparing for the wedding reception next week. Now they had to hope the bride and groom returned before the big day.

When she arrived at the Queen's office, she was requested to wait while Mrs. Moreau checked with the Queen to see if she was ready for her. It wasn't missed by Beatrix that most people didn't have to be announced when they wanted to see their parents, but life within the palace walls was quite different from other places. Rituals were what made the royal family unique. And her parents did their best to stick to the traditions handed down through the generations.

At least they would be alone for this meeting. She wasn't ready to deal with her sister or, worse, Rez. Hopefully this would be a short meeting.

A few moments later, she was ushered into her mother's office. Her mother appeared to be in a pleasant mood even though she wasn't smiling. The Queen wasn't one to go around smiling. Instead the frown lines were erased from her face. And her eyes had a happy sparkle to them.

Beatrix came to a stop in front of her mother's desk. "What's going on?"

The Queen signed a paper and then leaned back in her chair. She glanced up. "I wanted to discuss the arrangement you have with Rez."

Beatrix nodded. "I wanted to discuss that too."

Just then the door behind her opened. Beatrix's back teeth ground together. This wasn't the time for an interruption. She was just about to tell her mother that she was done acting like she was romantically involved with Rez. She just couldn't do it anymore.

Being around him—being around his daughter—it was opening up the door to things she thought she'd finally made peace with and she couldn't have him undoing all of that. Not a chance.

Beatrix clasped her hands together as she waited for the Queen's secretary to announce the reason for the interruption.

"I hope I'm not late." The all-too-familiar male voice came from behind her.

Rez. What was he doing here? She resisted the urge to turn around. She wasn't going to let his presence stop her from what she'd come here to do. This charade had gone on long enough. It was time to end things.

What was Bea doing here?

Rez came to a stop. When he'd called the Queen's personal secretary and requested this meeting, he'd expected it to be private. He'd intended for this to be a brief conversation, but with Bea here, it might change things, depending on what she had to say.

By his way of thinking, he'd be home by Evi's bedtime. And then his life would get back to normal. He paused as he tried to picture what normal would look like now that he'd gotten back out in society. In the process, he realized he would miss seeing his friends. He would miss riding his polo ponies. He would miss doing things that kept him from dwelling on the void in his life and his guilt over his part in Evi no longer having a mother.

He continued into the office. All the while, he attempted to conceal his surprise at finding Bea here. Her shoulders were rigid as she held her head high.

Her presence wouldn't stop him from saying what needed to be said. This charade had gone on long enough. He hated to admit it but if Istvan and Indigo weren't back by now with the wedding next week, there wasn't going to be a wedding.

Rez noticed how Bea didn't even bother to turn and face him. He had no idea what had gone so terribly wrong. The thought that it had something to do with his daughter made him even more certain it was time to end this charade and head home. How could she dislike Evi? The thought was unimaginable.

The Queen's attention turned to him. He obliged her with a quick bow. After all, even in the most strained of circumstances within the palace walls, formalities must be abided to. When he straightened, he was unable to tell if the Queen was in a good mood or not. The royal family were well-practiced in keeping their emotions masked from the world.

"I'm so glad you're both here. I have some news." The Queen's gaze moved to him. "But first, Rez, did you have something to discuss?"

He wasn't sure what the news would be. Perhaps she was about to announce that their fake relationship had failed or, worse, that they'd been found out, especially now that they knew there was a spy in the palace.

The last thing he wanted the Queen to think was that he was running away from trouble. His pride refused to let that happen. He was no coward.

When he hesitated to answer the Queen, Bea turned to him with an expectant gaze. He swallowed hard. It was best to find out the latest development before he told them his decision. "It can wait."

"Very well." The Queen reached for a newspaper on the corner of her desk. "I have been given an advance copy of tomorrow's newspaper. And you'll both be pleased to know that your efforts have been noticed." She turned the paper around so they could see it before she placed it on the desk. "I'm very pleased that you've both taken this job so seriously."

When Bea stepped forward to peer at the paper, he couldn't help but do the same. What exactly was in the paper?

He lowered his head to take in a colorful photo of himself, Bea and Evi. They were sitting on the blanket at the park. How had the paparazzi gotten this photo? He hadn't noticed anyone close enough to get this shot. But then he realized that with the vast vegetation the paparazzi could have been quite a distance away and taken the photo with a high-powered telephoto lens without ever being noticed.

It was only then that he read the headline: *And Baby Makes Three...*

As he turned his attention back to the image, he couldn't help but think they looked like a cute family. Evi was playing with her pink ball. And Bea was smiling as she watched his daughter. Wait. What?

He leaned in closer for a better look. Yes, Bea was

most definitely smiling. So what did that mean? Had he gotten it all wrong? He was so confused.

"As you can see," the Queen said, "the country is captivated with you two. There was only a brief mention of the wedding. And though that normally would be a problem, under the circumstances, it's a blessing. So I want to thank you both and ask that you keep up the good work for just a little longer." The Queen turned her attention back to him. "Now, would you like to say something?"

His mind raced. What should he do? The truth of the matter was that he couldn't leave here until he understood what was going on with Bea. She was giving out conflicting signals and he didn't know what to believe.

"I just wanted to say that while I don't mind helping out, I hope Istvan and Indigo return soon. I don't know how long it will be until we are found out."

"I'd like to say something," Bea said. "This charade is too much to ask of us. It just can't go on."

The Queen nodded. "I understand the burden it puts on both of you. No one wants to court the paparazzi, but it won't be for much longer. I've just gotten off the phone with Istvan. They will be returning tomorrow."

Finally. The tightness in Rez's chest eased. The charade would soon be over. At last they could get on with their lives. Being a guest at the palace was nice but it definitely wasn't relaxing like his place.

His gaze moved to Bea. She was quiet but the rigid line of her shoulders had eased. She didn't have to say anything; it was apparent she was relieved not to have to force a fake relationship with him.

The knowledge knifed into him. The pain was swift and had him struggling for air. Not that many years ago, she'd had the biggest crush on him. He knew. Everyone knew.

And though he'd thought she was cute for a kid, he knew he was too old for her. He'd moved on with Enora. He thought that part of his life was over and he would grow old with Enora. How was he supposed to know just how wrong he'd end up being?

But something had happened with Bea during that time. She didn't like him any longer. But why? What had changed?

And then he realized that it was a stupid question. Everything had changed since those carefree days of their childhoods. He'd grown up and become a husband and then father. And now he was widower and single father.

As for Bea, well, she'd most definitely grown up with her curvy goodness and those full tempting lips. But there were deeper changes that had her putting up walls between them. He wanted to break through those barriers and understand what was truly going on with her.

"That's great." The happiness echoed in Bea's voice. "Does this mean they worked out everything?"

"I hope so," the Queen said. "We didn't talk long."

"So you won't need us any longer," Bea said.

"Actually, we need you and Rez all the more now. With your brother and Indigo returning, we need to keep the focus off of them. We don't want any cold feet."

"But, Mother…"

"We'd be happy to help out." The words were out of his mouth before he realized what he was agreeing to do. Because there was no guarantee once he found out what was going on with Bea that it would improve their relationship.

Bea turned to him with a deep, dark frown. "No, we wouldn't."

"I've had my office come up with some plans for you

two." The Queen continued as though she hadn't overheard the disagreement between them. "And this evening you are both going to the theater in the city."

"Mother, this is too much." Bea crossed her arms as though she were drawing a line in the sand.

He was curious to see who would win this disagreement. He'd had his say; now he was stepping back and letting these two strong women work things out.

One way or the other, he would have an honest conversation with Bea. He would find out what was bothering her. And he wasn't leaving the palace until he knew exactly what was going on.

"Beatrix, I don't know why you're fighting me on this. I thought you were in agreement that we needed to do whatever was necessary to secure your brother's happiness."

"That was before." Bea pressed her lips together as though she hadn't meant to vocalize her thoughts.

The Queen's brows drew together. "Before what?"

Bea hesitated. "Before I knew it was going to take so long."

"If you're worried about your calendar, don't be. My staff has been coordinating with your staff. All of your obligations will be taken care of." As though the Queen felt confident she'd addressed her daughter's concerns, she turned to him. "The play is this evening at seven o'clock. It is a black-tie affair. I presume that won't be a problem."

"No, ma'am." He'd made sure to pack a lot of his formal wear. He had enough experience at the palace to come prepared.

"Good. Then I won't keep you two. You'll have to leave here shortly. I'll have the car waiting for you. Now go. We don't want you to be late." Bea paused as though considering the benefit of being late and then she shook her head. "Definitely don't be late. We want your photo taken as you're stepping out of the car—together."

The Queen lowered her head and pressed a button on her desk. As she read some paperwork on her desk, the double doors behind them opened. They had been dismissed.

Bea turned and took long, quick steps. The rigid line of her shoulders had returned. She didn't have to look at him for him to know she was furious that he'd agreed to continue with this fake relationship. He could handle her anger. What he couldn't handle was not knowing why she kept running hot and cold with him.

Why was Rez siding with the Queen?

Beatrix wasn't happy with either of them. And yet she couldn't deny that their plan was working. Going forward, she was going to have to be extra careful to keep her distance from Rez and his adorable daughter. Because in the end, she didn't want any of them to get hurt.

The more time they spent together, the more confusing things became for both of them. It was obvious that Rez was lonely and missed his wife.

Her thoughts spiraled back to the spontaneous kiss they'd shared. It hadn't been her that he had been kissing. He'd been kissing a ghost—the memory of a woman he was still in love with.

And Beatrix couldn't be some sort of consolation prize. When she was kissed, she wanted to know that in his mind and perhaps his heart that it was her he craved. She didn't think that would ever happen. It'd already been a year and Rez was no closer to moving on with his life.

She gave herself one last glance in the full-length mirror. The navy blue dress with a crystal-studded bodice fit her perfectly. It was the first time she'd worn the gown but it wouldn't be her last. Not only was it comfortable but it also flattered her figure, making her hips not look so large.

And though the dress fell below her knees, there was a slit that led high up to her thigh. When she walked, it gave a glimpse of her whole leg. Is that the reason she'd picked this dress? She told herself no but there was a part of her that wanted to show Rez what he'd missed by not waiting for her—for not picking her.

With a deep calming breath, she reached for her purse, slipped on a pair of glittery navy blue heels and then made her way out the door. With it being the summer, she wore only a sheer shawl over her bare shoulders.

Rez was waiting for her by the front door. He was propped against the wall as though he'd been waiting a while for her. When he spotted her, he straightened up. She noticed he didn't smile, not that she'd given him any reason to smile at her.

As she made her way down the last couple of steps, she felt his gaze on her. A warmth swirled in her chest and then rushed up her neck to settle in her cheeks.

When she reached his side, he leaned in close to her. His breath brushed across her neck, sending a shiver of awareness down her spine. "You look amazing."

"Thank you." Her voice came out deep and breathy.

His gaze met hers. "If you dressed to turn heads, it worked."

His compliment made her heart flutter. "Thank you."

He presented his arm to her. "Shall we?"

She placed her hand in the crook of his arm. "We shall."

The car ride into the city was quiet. She felt Rez looking at her a couple of times. It felt as though there was something he wanted to say but then he changed his mind. Was he planning to apologize for siding with her mother about continuing this charade? If so, it was too late now. All they could do was their best to keep the focus on them and protect the bride and groom, who'd already been through so much in the press.

As the Queen wanted, the paparazzi were in full force outside the Rydiania House of Fine Arts. It was the oldest and largest theater in all of Rydiania. The building was one of architectural history with large columns and lions at the base of the broad stone steps.

The car pulled up in front of a long red carpet that led up to the open doors of the theater. It would appear tonight was a who's who of Rydiania society.

Her door was opened and Beatrix stepped out to a reception of people calling out to her. As was her practice, she placed a well-rehearsed smile on her face and waved to no one in particular. She noticed that Rez gave her a moment alone in the spotlight.

And then he was there by her side. The crowd went crazy with them together. His hand came to rest on the small of her back. Heat emanated from his fingers and seeped through the delicate material of her dress and into her skin. It felt as though his hand was branding her as his. Her mouth grew dry and all she could think about was him touching her. A desire began to burn within her.

After what felt like a million flashes went off in her face, they made their way into the theater. Immediately they were approached by some people she knew; others she couldn't put a name to their faces. She bluffed her way through the whole thing.

Rez's hand returned to the small of her back. The touch was comforting in a way and in another way it stoked the embers of desire. The heat of each fingertip burned through the thin material of her dress. She couldn't help but wonder what would happen if she were to turn in to him. Would he claim her lips with his own? Would he draw her up close to him? Her heart raced at the thought.

She realized someone was speaking to her and she had absolutely no idea what they'd said. She smiled and nodded before her gaze flickered to Rez. He sent her a knowing smile. She glanced away as heat warmed her cheeks. There was no way he could know she was fantasizing about him. None whatsoever. If only she could move away from his touch, she could think clearly.

She did a lot of smiling and nodding instead of speaking. She didn't want anyone to know how distracted she was, especially by the man next to her. Why had she ever thought this fake relationship would be a good idea?

When at last they arrived at their private box, she turned to him. Perhaps she stopped and turned too quickly because she ran straight into his muscular chest that was much like a solid wall. With her palm pressed to his chest, it was as though the connection had short-circuited her mind. And she forgot what she'd been about to say.

When his gaze connected with hers, it felt as though he was actually seeing her and not a ghost from his past. Her heart fluttered in her chest. She should have moved, but her feet refused to cooperate.

His gaze lowered to her lips. She felt an immediate draw to him. It was so strong that it overrode her common sense. It blocked out all of the reasons that this shouldn't happen. And instead all she could think about was how much she longed to feel his kiss.

She didn't know if she moved first or if he had done it. Or maybe they both moved at the same time. There was a roar in her ears. She didn't know if it came from the crowd in the theater or whether it was the rush of blood in her veins. It didn't matter in that moment. The only thing that mattered was the touch of his mouth on hers.

She lifted up on her tiptoes. Her hands slid up over the hard plains of his chest and then wrapped around his neck. She drew him closer.

And then he was there. His soft lips pressing to hers. There was a hunger, a need in his kiss. She met him with a need of her own.

She felt as though she'd been waiting for this all of her life. She should pull away. But she didn't. She should end the most delicious kiss. But she didn't want to.

Instead she let herself lean into his embrace and she kissed him back like they were about to say goodbye for a very long time. She wanted this kiss to carry her through the inevitable lonely nights after he returned to his estate.

The music began to play, startling Beatrix from the spell that had come over her. She pulled away from Rez. What had she been thinking?

She couldn't blame it on their ruse because there weren't any cameras around to photograph them. There weren't any bystanders to take notice. This time it was just the two of them.

Her gaze met his. She couldn't read what he was thinking. It was as though he'd put up a wall between them.

She should say something, but what? *I'm sorry for kissing you.* But she wasn't sorry. It answered an old question she'd had about what it would be like to find herself in his arms with his mouth pressed to hers. And the answer startled her.

No one had ever kissed her quite like him. She felt the seismic waves from his kiss clear down to her toes. And now she knew that one kiss would never be enough. Was she destined to go through life comparing Rez with the other men that would pass through her life?

"Shall we sit down?" He gestured for her to go first.

Without a word, she moved to her seat. It was so close to his that their shoulders brushed. At the same time they both reached for the armrest. They could have shared it, with her arm over his and her fingers entwined with his. It was, oh, so tempting, but she resisted.

She just hoped no one asked her about the play because she didn't think she would be able to concentrate on it with Rez so close. Was he as startled by the intensity of their kiss? Did he want it to happen again?

She'd never know the answer to those questions because there was no way she would ever broach the subject with him. It was best just to pretend it hadn't happened. Oh, yes, that was definitely the way to handle it, even if she couldn't stop reliving the moment.

CHAPTER ELEVEN

HE YEARNED FOR more of her.

More kisses. More touches. More everything that was Bea.

Rez had no idea what had happened during the play. He clapped at the appropriate times and he'd stood at the end while the actors took the stage. And yet he had no idea about the storyline or the ending.

His thoughts were consumed with the scorching kiss he'd shared with Bea. He knew she hadn't planned it because she'd been giving him the cold shoulder ever since their picnic.

He certainly hadn't intended to kiss her. She still owed him answers for the distance she put between herself and Evi. What was it all about?

There was one undeniable thing between them—chemistry. When they were in close proximity to each other it was palpable. The more time they spent together the stronger the attraction became.

On the ride back to the palace, he considered questioning her about the kiss, about Eve, about all of it, but it wasn't the right place. He didn't want their conversation to be overheard. After all, there was a spy afoot and who knew who it was. The very last thing he wanted was for their private business to be splashed across the internet for everyone to read.

He noticed she was even more quiet than normal. Had the kiss caught her off guard too? And where did they go from here?

If he was smart, he'd pack his things, scoop up Evi and head back to the country where he belonged, but his curiosity about this growing thing with Bea overrode all of his common sense.

After the car dropped them off at the palace, he followed Bea inside. Now was their chance to have a private conversation. But where? His room? Or hers?

Definitely hers. He didn't want them to be disturbed by Evi, who always seemed to sense when he was close by. She would put up a fuss until he picked her up. Sometimes she would need a bottle to soothe her. Other times, he would rock her to sleep just as Enora used to do.

They'd just reached the grand staircase when the King approached them. He was using a cane, something Rez hadn't noticed the King using at other times. Rez wondered if the King's symptoms were worse in the evening or if he was hiding the extent of his disease from others.

The King's face lit up when he saw them. "Don't tell the Queen but I was just on my way to the kitchen for a late-night snack."

"Father, all you had to do was ring for one of the staff," Bea said. "They would have brought you whatever you desired."

He leaned on his cane. "They also would report it back to your mother and you know how she and the doctors fuss over my diet."

Right after the diagnosis, Istvan had mentioned the King had been diagnosed with Parkinson's. It appeared the Queen was doing everything in her power to see that he lived a healthy lifestyle.

The King's gaze moved between the two of them. "Am I to assume the plan for you two to fake a relationship is still going on?"

Bea nodded. "We are just returning from the theater."

"How was it?"

When Bea hesitated, Rez spoke up. "It was a decent play. The audience enjoyed it so much that they gave the cast a standing ovation."

"That's good to hear. Would either of you care to join me in the kitchen?" His gaze moved between the two of them.

Bea yawned. "I think I'll just go to bed."

"And I should go tuck Evi in."

"Okay. Remember mum's the word." He headed for the kitchen.

Bea watched her father walk away. There was a guarded look on her face, but Rez couldn't make out whether it was worry or something else. "Is something wrong?"

She shook head. "It's just my father is changing. Ever since his diagnosis, he isn't so serious anymore. It's like he figured out what's important in life and he's not stressing the other stuff."

"I'm sorry to hear that he's sick."

She glanced at him. "I thought you knew."

He nodded. "Your brother mentioned it. I just never had a chance to tell you how bad I feel about the news."

"Thanks." She turned and headed up the stairs.

He followed close behind. When she turned in the direction of her room, he turned that way as well.

A few steps down her wing of the palace, she stopped

and turned to him. "What are you doing? Your room is in the other direction."

"I'm just seeing you to your door."

She arched a skeptical brow. "Is that all?"

He couldn't help but smile. "I don't know. What do you have in mind?"

"Absolutely nothing." Her cheeks pinkened before she turned away. "I can get to my room on my own."

Her words didn't dissuade him. He'd waited long enough to have this conversation. He continued to follow her, even though she'd quickened her steps.

At her doorway, she suddenly stopped and turned to him. He found himself coming up on his tiptoes in order to get stopped before he ran into her. Although he remembered what had happened the last time they'd run into each other, at the theater. The idea appealed to him. Except they needed to talk and clear some things up before he gave in to the temptation of her lips.

"This is my room," she said.

He took a step back. "So it is."

"You can go now."

"I don't think so. We need to talk."

Her eyes briefly widened. "If it's about what happened earlier—"

"It's not." But was that the truth? "Not really."

Confusion clouded her eyes. She opened her door and stepped inside. He wasn't sure if she was going to slam the door in his face or invite him inside. He surmised that he had a fifty-fifty chance.

Then to his relief, she swung the door wide open. "Come inside, if you must."

It wasn't the warm invitation he had hoped for but it

was enough for now. He stepped through the doorway and pushed the door closed behind him.

Bea placed her purse on an end table before kicking off her heels. Then she turned to him. "What did you want to talk about?"

Where did he begin? He'd had his words sorted in the car but now that they were here—now that she was staring about him with those bottomless eyes he could feel himself getting distracted. His carefully chosen words utterly abandoned him.

In that moment, all he wanted to do was take her in his arms and kiss her again. Because one kiss would never be enough.

The thought startled him. Was that wrong of him? Was he betraying the memory of Enora?

He recalled his wife's last words to him before they'd rushed her off to emergency surgery. She'd told him that she loved him and she made him promise he would go on with his life. But it all seemed so unfair with him here with a chance to find happiness again, while Enora was gone from this world.

The thought cooled his heated blood. And once more he recalled why he'd come here with Bea. He struggled to find the words but slowly they were coming back to him.

He cleared his throat. "Why do you dislike Evi?"

"What?" Bea's mouth gaped for a moment before she pressed her lips together.

"Since she's been here, you've avoided her. When I've offered to let you hold her, you always find an excuse to not pick her up. I need to know what that's about. Don't you like children in general? Or is there something specific about Evi you don't care for?"

Bea shook her head. "It's not like that. I swear."

He wasn't sure what she was trying to tell him. He stepped closer. "Then what is it like?"

Her eyes reflected some deep emotion. Was it pain? Perhaps sadness? He wanted to comfort her, but he didn't know what to say until she opened up to him.

When she didn't say anything and instead stood there silently with a look on her face that said something was terribly wrong, he led her over to one of the couches. When she sat down, he took a seat next to her. All the while he wondered what was upsetting her so much.

He wanted to prompt her to speak but he knew he couldn't rush this. Whatever was bothering her would have to come out in her time, not his. The silence between them stretched on.

She turned to him. "It's not your daughter. I swear. She's so adorable with those chubby cheeks and her little laugh. Who couldn't fall in love with her?"

"I know. Every time I think that I'm not good at being a single parent, she has me striving to try harder—to be better."

Bea's gaze met his. "I think you're doing a great job."

"Why do you say that?"

"Because your little girl is so happy. You can tell just by looking at her that she's loved and she knows it."

He wanted to believe her, but there was this part of him that still thought Evi would be so much better off with a loving mother—someone who knew what they were doing. He had no clue from day to day. He did his best to be a good parent, but most of the time he was just faking it.

"She makes it easy to love her," he said with utter sincerity.

"I always thought some day when I got around to it

that I'd have children." She picked a piece of fuzz from her dress.

"Did something happen to change that?"

She looked away at some faraway spot in the bedroom. "I have endometriosis."

He had a feeling he should know what that was, but he was at a loss. "Is it serious?"

She nodded. "When I first got the symptoms, they didn't think it was going to be too bad, just uncomfortable, but then things changed."

He wished he knew more about it so he was better able to offer her some comforting words. Not sure what to say, he reached out, placing his hand over hers and giving a squeeze.

"I ended up needing surgery and now I can't have children."

This information totally floored him. She'd always looked so healthy. "I'm so sorry."

She turned her head and looked at him. Tears shimmered in her eyes. "I thought I'd made peace with it, but then I saw you and Evi and I found myself realizing exactly what I would be missing. I…" A tear splashed onto her cheek. "I…"

Her pain tore through him. He turned his body and drew her to him. Her head came to rest on his shoulder. He ran his hand over her hair while he absorbed what he'd learned.

He felt horrible that he'd accused Bea of not liking his daughter when all along she was dealing with a devastating diagnosis.

When she pulled back, her gaze met his. "I'm sorry you thought I didn't like Evi. She's so precious. I'm obviously still dealing with the fact that I'll never have a child of my own. The funny part is I was never one of those people who dreamed about having children. I didn't even know I wanted a baby until I couldn't have any."

His thumb swept away her tears. "It's still possible. There are other ways of having a family."

He couldn't even imagine how hard this must be for her. Sympathy welled up in him. He felt awful for jumping to the wrong conclusion. Now that he knew the truth, the wall between them had finally come down.

The truth was at last out there.

Beatrix hadn't intended to tell him her painful truth, but the kiss had changed everything. She realized how easy it would be for things to get serious. And it wouldn't be fair to him to let that happen without him knowing that she couldn't give him the family he deserved.

Now that it was all out there, she could breathe easier. At last, she wasn't holding in all of that painful information. And now Rez was looking at her differently. Sympathy shone in his eyes.

"Don't look at me like that." She glanced away.

"Like what?"

"Like you feel sorry for me."

"But I do feel bad." Honesty rang out in his voice. "You didn't ask for any of this. And it's not fair to you. But you could adopt."

Maybe. But there was no guarantee that a baby would be available. The wait could be long and the disappointment could be great. It was nothing she wanted to put Rez through after he'd experienced so much pain when he lost his wife.

"My life is fine the way it is." She hoped her voice sounded convincing.

"You mean you never intend to marry? Or have a family?" His gaze searched hers.

His questions poked in all the wrong spots, making her think about things she'd been avoiding up until then. She didn't want to contemplate them now. The answers were complicated. And she'd much rather concentrate on the here and now.

But as he continued to stare at her expectantly, she knew she had to say something. "Right now, I want to focus on my life as a working royal."

"And in the future will that be enough?"

She inwardly groaned. Why did he have to push this? She couldn't give him any answers because she hadn't figured them out for herself.

"I don't know." She barely hid the frustration in her voice. "I don't know what the future holds." She kept talking, hoping to stave off more questions. "I have a very busy life and I quite enjoy it. I was born into a life of service and I want to dedicate my life to being a working royal."

Rez looked at her differently. "You can't spend all of your time working."

What exactly did he mean? And then his gaze dipped to her mouth. Her heart began to thump-thump.

He leaned forward, pressing his lips to hers. Instead of their heated clench that had happened at the theater, this kiss was soft and gentle.

She enjoyed that he was taking things slow. It proved to her that even though life had thrown her some devastating blows that there was still goodness and gentleness around her. Her stress and worry faded away. She gave herself over to the moment. She returned his kiss with mounting desire. She turned her body to him and wrapped her arms around him, deepening the kiss.

He tasted sweet, like the champagne from the theater. With his arms around her, she forgot about her inability to have children, her feeling of inadequacy, her pain. In that moment, she was a woman that craved this incredibly sexy man, who held her undivided attention. It was as though she'd been waiting for this moment her entire life.

And then suddenly Rez pulled back. Disappointment assailed her. Her breathing was labored as her heart pounded in her chest. Beatrix lifted her head. Her gaze searched his darkened eyes for answers. Why had he pulled away from her? Didn't he desire her?

He continued to hold himself back. "Bea, is this what you want?"

How could he doubt her? Hadn't she shown him with her kiss how much she wanted him? But if he needed to hear the words, she would speak them.

"I want you very much. Do you know how long I've waited for this moment?"

"Waited?"

She nodded. "Don't you know how crazy I was about you when we were kids?"

"But you were too young back then."

"I'm not a kid anymore." She got to her feet and held her hand out to him. He placed his hand in hers as he got to his feet.

She led him over to the bed with way too many pillows. She had a feeling they would soon be heaped on the floor...along with their clothes. And then she turned to him. She lifted up on her tiptoes and pressed her lips to his. As they kissed, he reached behind her and worked the zipper of her dress downward.

CHAPTER TWELVE

It HAD BEEN the most incredible night of her life.

The next morning Beatrix woke up alone. But it was all right because when Rez left before the sun was up, he'd awakened her with a kiss goodbye, which had started things again. It was like she couldn't get enough of him.

He was so gentle and more loving than she'd ever imagined. In the next moment he could be fiery and hot. And though she knew this time with Rez wasn't going to lead to a happily-ever-after, she intended to savor the moment while it lasted. She would make memories that would last her lifetime. Because as sure as the sun would come up the next day, she wouldn't forget her moment in his arms.

The only catch was reminding herself to keep things casual. She refused to allow her heart to become involved. It would lead to nothing but pain because she couldn't give him the family he deserved. But she refused to dwell on any of that now.

Her feet barely touched the floor that morning. She'd slept in late and missed breakfast. Before one of the staff came to check on her, she rushed through the shower. She wasn't one of the royals that liked to be pampered. She preferred to dress herself unless it was for a special occasion like her brother's upcoming wedding.

And then she realized that Istvan and Indigo were returning today. She really hoped they'd worked everything out and that the wedding was back on track. Nothing would make her happier.

She rushed to the door and then realized she'd forgotten her phone in her purse from last night. It was still on the end table next to the couch. She unzipped the silver glittery clutch and retrieved her phone. When she pressed the button, nothing happened. She tried again. And again.

With a sigh, she conceded that the phone was dead. It was getting older and it didn't hold a charge like it used to. She moved to the charging station next to her bed. Once it was in position and the light on the charger lit up, she headed out the door.

She wanted to go straight to Rez's room, but she resisted the urge. She didn't want him to feel overwhelmed or anything. After all, it wasn't like they were in a relationship. Everything was new and had to be figured out.

She also had to get past her fear of getting close to Evi. Somehow she had to enjoy spending time with the little girl and not let herself dwell on not being able to have a baby of her own. Could she do it? She didn't know, but she really wanted to try.

She descended the grand staircase. With it being midmorning, she doubted anyone would be in the dining room. Still, she was hoping there would be some coffee and perhaps a croissant.

As she approached the private dining room, she heard voices. She stepped up to the doorway to find her brother and Indigo. And best of all they were smiling at each other.

"You're back!" Beatrix rushed toward her brother

to give him a hug and then she turned to Indigo and hugged her.

"It's good to see you too." Indigo sent her a genuine smile that made her eyes twinkle.

"Does this mean the wedding is a go?" The breath hitched in her throat as she waited for the answer.

Istvan smiled as he wrapped his arm around his fiancée. "Yes, it does."

Beatrix expelled her pent-up breath. This was the best news she'd had in a long time. She had a feeling this was going to be a most excellent day. Now she had an excuse to be all smiley and no one would suspect that she'd spent the night in Rez's arms. She wasn't ready to share that bit of information with anyone.

"I'm sorry I freaked out." Indigo's voice distracted Beatrix from her thoughts. "I just wasn't expecting the press to be so vicious."

"I understand," Beatrix said. "It's a lot to deal with, even if you've grown up around the paparazzi."

"We wanted to thank you," Istvan said. "You've really gone above and beyond to help us."

"What?" She wasn't sure what he was referring to. And then she realized the Queen must have told him about their plan to distract the press.

Before she could say anything, her brother moved to the table and retrieved the morning's newspaper. "You must not have seen this yet."

"Oh, did they put a photo of Rez and me at the theater?" If it was good enough, she might have her secretary track down a digital copy for her. It would be nice to have a photo of them as a reminder.

"You might say that." Her brother started to laugh.

What was so funny? Was her makeup messed up? Or

worse, did she have a wardrobe malfunction that she'd been unaware of?

Her body tensed as her brother handed her the paper. Once more she'd made the front page just below the fold. The headline read: *A Steamy Scene...*

The image before her caught her utterly and completely off guard. There she was in Rez's arms. In the close-up of them, her lips were all over his, arms wrapped about each other as they shared a passionate kiss. There was definitely no faking the desire in that embrace.

Heat rushed from her chest to her face. It felt as though she'd been standing in front of a sunlamp for much too long. She would swear soon her hair would go up in a puff of smoke.

"Good morning." Rez sauntered into the room. As soon as he looked at her face, the smile fled his face. "What's wrong?"

She shoved the paper at him. If this is what their conservative print paper had published, she wasn't sure she wanted to know what *Duchess Tales* had said about the kiss.

"Let me borrow your phone." She held her hand out to Rez.

His brows scrunched together. "Where's yours?"

"Just let me have it." And then remembering her manners, she said, "Please."

Without another word, he produced his phone. She took it and quickly sought out the *Duchess Tales* site.

"Perhaps we should give them a moment," Indigo said.

"I was hoping to hear more about that photo," Istvan teased.

Beatrix glanced up to see Indigo elbow her brother before taking him by the arm and leading him from the room. On their way out, Indigo pulled the doors shut behind them.

Beatrix glanced back at the phone screen to see the post about them was at the top of the site. Her stomach balled up into a tight knot.

The title of the post read: *Burning Up with Desire*...

She exhaled a groan. This was so much worse than she'd been expecting. It was one thing when they were trying to put on a show for the paparazzi, it was quite another when the press caught a genuine moment of passion. She felt so exposed.

Rez moved to her side. "Surely it can't be worse than what's in the paper."

"It's so much worse." Her gaze settled on a photo of them with her body leaning fully against him as her fingers combed through his thick dark hair. It looked like—well, it looked like they were one step away from making mad passionate love. And the fact they had didn't go unnoticed by her, but it wasn't anyone's business but theirs. "*Duchess Tales* posted a full-length photo of us. It's like..."

"Like what?"

"Like we're making love with our clothes on." She inwardly groaned again.

"It can't be that bad. Let me see."

She turned the phone so he could see the image. He gave up his denial. When she turned the phone back around, she couldn't take her gaze off the image. Was that the way she really looked in his arms? It's like she was totally oblivious to their surroundings—that nothing mattered but feeling his lips against hers.

Rez's voice drew her from her thoughts. "It really is that bad."

"This is terrible. Now everyone is going to know about us."

He turned to her. "Bea, everyone already knows about us. Remember? We've been putting on a show for the paparazzi."

"But it's different now." She lowered her voice. "You know, since we slept together."

A grin came over his face. "Yes, we did. Again and again and again."

"Rez!" Her face grew hot with embarrassment.

"Okay. So what does the post say?"

Fellow royal watchers, I have to admit that every now and then I get it wrong. This is one of those days. It appears two more royals are off the market. That's right. Love is in the summer air.

The Duke of Kaspar has been snatched up by none other than our Princess Beatrix. She stole him away before any of the rest of us had a chance. So sorry, dearies.

But how can anyone deny that passion? It makes me wonder just how long this affair has been going on.

Obviously this wasn't their first kiss. Ooh-la-la. #steamy

Beatrix stopped reading. Her gaze returned to the photo of them. There was a part of her that longed for this casual arrangement to be something real. The thought startled her. Was that really what she wanted?

"What else does it say?" Rez's voice interrupted her troubling thoughts.

She held the phone out to him. "You read it."

She didn't think she could continue. Her empty stomach felt nauseous. Their plan had taken on a life of its own and now she wasn't ready to deal with the consequences.

Rez cleared his throat and then proceeded to continue reading.

Does this now mean there will be two royal weddings this year? Or is the Duke just getting his feet wet, so to speak. Is the Princess just a fling for the newly minted bachelor? And does the Princess know this?

Rez stopped reading.

In that moment, she wished it was true about the two royal weddings. But she couldn't ask Rez to commit himself to someone who couldn't give him what came so easily to so many other women—giving birth to a child.

Maybe they could adopt, but she knew the wait lists were lengthy and the journey was challenging without any guarantee of a baby at the end of it all. Could she put herself through that? Could she ask Rez to go through it after all he'd already lost?

The answer was unequivocally no. He deserved a wife who wasn't damaged and could give him more children in a traditional manner.

Her gaze moved to him. She could see the frown on his face. Was that pity that shone in his eyes? Did he feel bad that she'd read too much into their night together?

He stepped closer. "Bea, stop it."

She blinked repeatedly, refusing to let him see how much the implications of the post had hurt her. "Stop what?"

"Believing those lies."

"I'm fine." It was a little white lie. The truth was that she was anything but fine. "Read what else it says."

"Not before I do this." He lowered his head and pressed his lips to hers.

Even though she knew her family could walk in on them at any moment, it didn't stop her from wrapping her arms around his neck and kissing him back. His kiss was like a balm upon her scarred heart.

And as much as she wanted to continue this, she knew if they kept this up they'd end up back in her bedroom for the rest of the day. And now with the bride and groom back in the palace, there were wedding preparations and a garden party to attend.

Rez glanced at his phone and then back at her. "Are you sure you want me to keep reading?"

There was a push-pull struggle within her. She didn't want to give any more power to *Duchess Tales*, but there was a nagging curiosity to know what else was being said about her—about them. She knew nothing good would come of it, but she ended up nodding her head.

Rez hesitated before turning his attention back to the screen of his phone.

I told you this was going to be an interesting summer. I did not lie. Now on to the rumor of Prince Istvan eloping. I don't think he would do this. I don't think he'd shut out his family that he's always been so close to. However, if there wasn't an elopement, then perhaps he'll come to his senses and return to his position as the heir to the throne. And he'd once more be on the market for a princess. I know you ladies would be lining up. Me included.

And don't give up on the Duke of Kaspar. This thing with the Princess might be fleeting at best. Rumor has it that she doesn't want to get married or have a family. But who wouldn't want to marry that sexy duke? Sigh.

That's all I have for now. I must run. Things are changing within the palace walls quickly. I'll let you know the latest as soon as I learn the truth.

Take care, my lovely royal followers. Until next time...

xox

Beatrix couldn't help but wonder if the Duchess's prediction was true. Would this thing with Rez be fleeting? Did she want it to be?

After all, she wasn't in the market for a serious relationship. At least she hadn't been. Now she didn't know what she wanted.

"Stop." Rez's firm voice drew her from her thoughts.

"What? I'm fine."

"No, you're worrying about that nonsense on the internet. And she knows absolutely nothing. Do you hear me? Nothing about us."

"But we still have a spy in the palace."

"Yes, you do. Are you ready to alert the King and Queen?"

"Alert us about what?" The King stood in the now-open doorway with the Queen next to him. His gaze moved between both of them.

Beatrix was actually grateful for the distraction. She didn't want to explain the photograph in the paper. Would they really believe it was all playacting and that they knew the paparazzi were there all along?

"You should close the door," Rez said. Once they had privacy, he said, "We believe there's a spy in the palace. Actually, it was Bea... Beatrix that figured it out."

Together they went on to explain it all to the King and

Queen. Her parents were floored they had a spy among them. The King insisted he would set his best security men on figuring out who it was and prosecuting them because spying on the King and his family could rank right up there with treason. More investigating would have to be done. The King was already on the phone.

"Well, now that the nasty business has been taken care of," the Queen said, "you two need to get ready for the garden party we're having for Istvan and Indigo."

"I don't know, Mother." The thought of putting herself back out there in front of the public didn't appeal to her. Not now that the headlines were homing in on the truth.

"If you're worried about the press, don't be," the Queen said. "We have arrangements with the *Rydiania Press* to handle the party. No other paparazzi will be in attendance."

"I need to go meet with security." The King exited the room.

"I'll see you both shortly." The Queen followed the King out the door.

Beatrix couldn't believe what had just happened. Her mother hadn't interrogated her about the photo. She hadn't even admonished them about their obvious public display of affection, which most certainly went against protocol.

Beatrix turned to Rez. "Did that just happen?"

"What?" His brows were drawn together in confusion. "You mean talking to your parents?"

"I mean my mother not lecturing us about how royals are to behave in public."

"Maybe she didn't see the photograph."

"Ha. She probably saw it long before anyone else. My mother stays on top of any news that affects the royal family because our reputation is the most important thing."

He stepped closer and rubbed her back. "Relax. Maybe there's just so much going on with the wedding and she's so happy that your brother is back that she forgot about it."

Beatrix shook her head. "My mother doesn't forget anything."

"You know her best, but I wouldn't worry about it. Now come with me." He took her hand and led her out into the hallway.

"But I didn't have a chance to eat."

"Don't worry. We'll have food sent to my suite."

"Your suite? What are we going to do there?" Some very naughty thoughts came to mind.

"We're going to reintroduce you to Evi." He stopped and turned to her. "I'm jumping ahead. First, I need to know if this is something you want."

After her confession of sorts last night, she felt so much better. It wasn't like she could avoid being around babies forever. Her friends were getting married now and soon there would be babies everywhere she looked.

And Evi was so adorable. Beatrix desperately wanted to set aside her own pain and disappointment in order to get to know her. But was it possible? She didn't know the answer, but she was willing to give it a try.

Her hesitant gaze met his. "I'm willing to give it a try, but just don't expect too much from me."

"I have no expectations, but I'm not worried. I think you two will hit it off."

Her gaze lowered to their linked hands. It was with the greatest regret that she said, "Maybe we shouldn't be holding hands in the palace."

His gaze followed hers to their clasped hands. "I suppose you're right."

Once he let go of her hand, she really regretted saying anything, even if it was for the best. Together they climbed the steps and headed for the nursery.

The nanny was there when they arrived. She turned from the crib and her mouth gaped. "Your Royal Highness." She bowed. "It's so nice to meet you."

"It's nice to meet you too."

They made some pleasantries and then the nanny let Rez know that Evi had just wakened from a nap and had her diaper changed. Rez assured the woman she could take a break and they'd look after the baby.

Once the nanny was gone, Rez called the kitchen and requested a couple of croissants and eggs with juice and coffee. There was something special about having a five-star kitchen at your beck and call. And their croissants were out of this world.

Beatrix made her way over to the crib, where Evi was holding herself up and grinning. "Hello, Evi. How are you?"

The girl's blue eyes stared up at her. They were the same shade as her father's. Evi continued to smile as she jumped. Losing her hold on the rail, she began to fall. Beatrix reached for her but she was too late. Evi toppled back on her mattress.

"Oops. Are you okay?" Beatrix didn't know why she'd asked Evi that question when she knew there was no way the little girl could answer her.

"Is everything okay?" Rez moved to her side.

"Evi got to jumping and fell over. I think she's all right."

The baby rolled herself over, crawled over to the rail and stood back up. The smile returned to her face.

"Let's get you out of there." Beatrix reached out and picked up his daughter.

She drew the little girl close, feeling her weight in her arms. As Evi's head came to rest on her chest, she breathed in Evi's baby scent. It filled her with a deep longing to have a child of her own—a child like Evi, who was the sweetest baby.

Tears pricked the back of Beatrix's eyes but she refused to give in to them. She wouldn't fall apart. This moment wasn't about her, it was about Evi and what a wonderful girl she was.

And so they all settled on the floor and rolled the pink ball around. It appeared to be one of Evi's favorite toys. Beatrix found when she focused on the baby and not her problems that she was able to really enjoy herself. But every now and then when she let her mind wander, she realized that she would never get to enjoy these moments with her own child and it saddened her. She didn't let on to Rez. She didn't want to ruin the moment.

CHAPTER THIRTEEN

THINGS WERE GOING surprisingly well.

For the past few days, Rez had spent most of his time with Bea. Things between her and Evi had totally changed. Bea let down her guard with the baby and was really able to enjoy herself. He was happy for both of them, but it reaffirmed his belief that he wasn't enough for Evi. He'd watched how Evi had responded so well to Bea. It was obvious: Evi needed a mother.

But he didn't have time to dwell on it because he had to escort Bea to the garden party without any untimely photos being taken. They somehow managed to keep their hands and lips off each other, though it was utter torture for him.

It wasn't until the night that they were able to make love again...and again.

The following day had been an outing to the park with Evi that went so much better. And when evening rolled around, there was a formal reception for the foreign dignitaries who had arrived for the wedding. There was a lot of handshaking and small talk. And when the party wrapped up, Rez had once again snuck into Bea's room. He knew he shouldn't get too used to this because when the wedding was over, he'd be returning to his country house.

Even though Bea's relationship had dramatically improved with his daughter, he remembered what she'd said about wanting to dedicate her life to being a working royal. Her words had been abundantly clear. And he found them most disappointing.

The next evening had been the wedding rehearsal and all had gone well. At last, the headlines in the paper were positive and the Kingdom appeared to be excited about the royal wedding.

As they were seated for dinner, Rez was placed at the opposite end of the table from Bea. He really missed having her close by. He found that once he let down his guard, she fit so easily into his life.

He glanced down the table to where Bea was conversing with both of her sisters. They were laughing about something and Bea looked as though she didn't have a care in the world. He knew that wasn't the truth. And if there was something he could do to help her with her medical problems, he would in a heartbeat.

Istvan lightly elbowed him. "What has you so distracted?" His gaze moved to the other end of the table. "Or should I say who has you distracted?"

Not willing to discuss Bea with her brother, Rez said, "So are you ready to walk down the aisle?"

"Yes. I've always been ready. But you don't get to change the subject so easily. What's up with you and Bea?"

He shrugged as he tried to find an appropriate answer. "Why do you think anything is up?"

"Because you haven't been able to take your eyes off my sister all evening. And I did see the photo in the paper."

"We were just putting on a show for the paparazzi."

And somehow they'd gotten caught up in their own pretend relationship.

"That wasn't make-believe. It was a real kiss." Istvan arched a brow. "So what are your intentions with my sister?"

Intentions? Really? They were going to have that conversation. "I... I don't have any."

"I know I warned you away from her years ago, but that was different then. We were just kids back then and you were too old for her. But now is different."

What was Istvan trying to tell him? That he should start a real relationship with Bea? No. He couldn't. His thoughts drifted back to Enora and how she'd made him promise to go on with his life. But could he start all over again?

The thoughts weighed on him the rest of the evening until it was time for them to retire for the evening. After all, the next day was the wedding.

But he wasn't the least bit tired. His gaze strayed to Bea and he thought of their nightly rendezvous in her room. The thought definitely appealed to him.

As though she could read his thoughts, Bea leaned over and said ever so softly, "Shall we meet up in my room?"

The answer *yes* hovered on the tip of his tongue. After all, it wasn't like they hadn't made love before—all night long. But it was now becoming a habit and habits led to expectations. And he wasn't in a position to live up to Bea's expectations, was he?

He was utterly confused. "I need to spend some time with Evi."

"Oh. All right. I'll come with you." She fell in step

beside him. "I didn't get to see her earlier because she was napping."

He checked the time. "She should be up now. And I know she'll be happy to see you."

And just as he predicted, Evi was wide awake. The nanny was just about to give her a bottle.

"Could I do that?" Bea asked.

"Certainly." The nanny smiled at Bea as she stood up. "You'll want to sit in the rocker. Evi loves it."

Rez stood back as Bea took a seat. And then with the nanny's help, she held the baby. Evi started to fuss. She was hungry. But once the bottle was in her mouth, she quieted down.

The nanny excused herself, leaving the three of them alone. He couldn't help but notice how well Evi had taken to Bea. He couldn't blame his daughter. Bea was pretty special. She had this warmth about her that drew him to her.

"Why are you so quiet?" Bea said softly.

He glanced down at Evi, whose eyes were now closed. Every once in a while she sucked at the bottle before she would doze off once more. "I was just thinking about how good you are with her."

Bea shook her head. "I have no clue what I'm doing."

"Don't tell Evi that, she thinks you hung the moon."

"Beginner's luck." As her gaze lowered to Evi, a smile lifted her glossy lips.

She looked like a natural with Evi in her arms. In fact, if he didn't know better, he might have mistaken them for mother and daughter.

He couldn't take his gaze off the two of them. When Beatrix looked at Evi there was definitely love in her eyes. They could be the perfect family…

In that moment, he knew that's what he wanted. Evi would have a mother. And Bea would have the baby she longed for. Now could he convince Bea how good they were together?

It was the day of the royal wedding.

The palace was abuzz with staff hustling here and there.

Beatrix couldn't help but wonder which one of them was spying on them. She didn't like the thought of not feeling totally secure at home—of watching what she said for fear it would end up on *Duchess Tales*. The King had his security force working on it, but so far they hadn't come up with anything helpful.

For the past few days, *Duchess Tales* had been running positive posts about the wedding. At last they'd laid off Indigo. Maybe they conceded that nothing they said would break up Istvan and Indigo.

Right now, she needed to go help the bride get ready for her big day. The thought of her brother marrying the love of his life brought a big smile to her face, but it quickly disappeared as an ominous feeling came over her. What if something went wrong on her brother's big day?

She gave herself a mental shake. It wasn't going to happen. The worst was behind them. She just had to relax and enjoy the day.

She headed out the door. She turned a corner and almost ran into Rez. She stopped in time and took a step back. "Hey. What are you doing?" Her gaze took in his casual attire. "And dressed like that."

"I'm off to meet your brother. And what's wrong with the way I'm dressed?"

"It looks like you're about to go riding instead of getting ready for the wedding."

"As a matter of fact, I am going for a ride."

Her mouth gaped. "Now?"

"Your brother insisted."

"Insisted?" That didn't sound good. Not good at all. "Is he having cold feet?"

"No. He's just bored of waiting around." Rez reached out and rubbed her upper arm. "Hey, relax. Everything is going to go smoothly today."

"I hope so." She didn't know why she kept having this nagging feeling that something was going to go awry that day.

"Everything will be fine. I should get going. Your brother is waiting for me."

"Okay. Be careful. We don't need either one of you getting hurt."

His brows drew together. "You're really worried, aren't you?"

"I'm not worried." It was a lie and they both knew it. "I'll just breathe easier once we get them down the aisle."

He nodded. "I understand. It has been a journey not just for them but us too. We weren't exactly planning to portray a couple. But here we are and I have to say that it wasn't as bad as I had imagined."

"As bad?" She was about to let him have it when she saw the teasing smile playing on his lips. "I'll remember that."

He glanced around to make sure they were alone. Confident of their privacy, he leaned forward. "Remember this."

And then his lips pressed to hers. Her heart tripped over itself as it beat in triple time. He made it so easy to forget her worries. She leaned into his arms, deepening the kiss.

She longed to take him back to her room and have her way with him. But before she could put her thought into action, Rez pulled back.

He smiled at her. "Now you have something to think about instead of worrying."

"You're a really good distraction."

"Thanks… I think."

Her gaze moved to his lips that were now smudged with her pink lip gloss. "You might want to clean off your mouth before you see my brother."

Rez ran his fingers over his lips. "Thanks."

As he walked away, she smiled. Maybe he had a point. She had to lighten up. It's just that she'd been so worried about this wedding for so long that it was hard for her to relax—to believe it was going to have a happy ending after all. But she was going to hang on to Rez's kiss and let herself enjoy the day. And it was to start with a mani-pedi appointment in a room on the first floor.

She moved to the front staircase and rushed down the steps. Her sandals were quiet as she made her way across the marble floor and down the hallway. She turned the corner and came to a stop when she found one of the staff standing outside the room where the bridal party was to meet.

What was he doing? He was standing there, not moving. Was he spying on them?

He turned and practically ran into her. In his hands was an empty tray. "Your Royal Highness." He bowed his head. "I'm sorry. I didn't see you."

"What were you doing?"

"I… I was delivering some fresh coffee. Do you, um, need something?"

She crossed her arms and frowned at him. He was acting very nervous. "I need to know why you were lurking in the hallway."

Just then Indigo stepped into the hallway. "Beatrix, there you are. We were wondering what was taking you so long." Her gaze moved to the young man, who gave them both a wide-eyed stare. "Aren't you supposed to get us some gelato?"

"Yes, ma'am." He was eager to escape.

Beatrix's gaze settled on her soon-to-be sister-in-law's smile. She looked so happy, like she had that long-ago morning when they'd been having their final dress fittings. It was reassuring.

"Gelato, huh? Is that good or bad?"

"Good. Very good." Indigo linked her arm with Beatrix's as they entered the room. "We decided to have some gelato with our mani-pedi. I hope you want some."

"Count me in on the sugar rush." She returned Indigo's smile. "Today is going to be a wonderful day."

"Yes, it is."

And yet there was this teeny-tiny niggling worry that something was going to go wrong today and she didn't have a clue what it might be. But for now, she focused on the happy moment.

CHAPTER FOURTEEN

Six white horses led the white carriage.

Thousands of people lined the streets, cheering as the royal carriage made its way from the palace to the nearby village. Beatrix watched out the back window of the dark sedan that escorted her to the church. Indigo waved like the Princess she was about to become.

At the church, the bride and her mother exited the carriage and climbed the steps. The bridal party gathered at the end of the cathedral. Up close, Beatrix noticed that the color had drained from Indigo's face. It was a lot having thousands of people and hundreds of cameras in your face. Not to mention that she was about to marry a prince that came with a very public life.

Beatrix moved to Indigo's side. She lowered her voice. "Are you okay?"

"I'd be lying if I said there wasn't a dozen butterflies fluttering in my stomach."

"It'll be fine. Just a little longer and it'll all be over."

Indigo nodded. "I know."

The music began to play. Everyone lined up as the doors opened. Beatrix looked at Indigo. "I'll meet you at the end of the aisle."

"I'll see you there."

When it was Beatrix's turn to walk down the aisle,

her gaze moved to the end and connected with Rez. Her heart skipped a beat. He looked so dashing with his morning coat on.

Rez continued to stare back at her. Beatrix would swear she had some of Indigo's butterflies in her own stomach. As she continued to stare back at him, she was grateful she didn't trip over her own feet. After what felt like forever, she made it to the end of the aisle. She took her place and turned.

A collective gasp echoed through the cathedral as the bride made her way up the aisle in the most magnificent snow white full-length gown. Her arms were bare as the strapless bodice twinkled from all of the crystals.

The skirt floated around her as she made her way along the red runner with her mother by her side. Indigo wore her hair up with just a few wispy curls that softened her face. But it wasn't the dress that made her look so radiant. It was the big smile on her face that made her eyes sparkle. Every bride should be as happy as her.

As Beatrix focused on the bride, she noticed that some color had returned to Indigo's cheeks as she smiled at her husband-to-be. Beatrix glanced over at her brother. His full attention was on his bride. A smile lifted the corners of his lips too. Beatrix took her first easy breath. There had been nothing to worry about after all. It was all going to work out.

The ceremony went according to plan. Istvan and Indigo exchanged their vows. And as was royal custom, they did not kiss after the ceremony. It was saved for a more private moment. Beatrix couldn't help but feel the royals had it all wrong. The first kiss of a married couple was, oh, so important. They should be able to express their feelings in the moment. If this was her wedding, she'd be kissing Rez for all to see.

She halted her thoughts. Why was she envisioning Rez as the groom? They'd both agreed to keep what they had casual. It was what she wanted, wasn't it?

Her heart pounded at the thought. As much as she'd been fighting her feelings for him, they had grown a fake relationship into what felt like a real relationship. She'd come to care deeply for Rez. Dare she admit it? She loved him.

The realization was huge for her. Her pulse raced as she came to terms with this revelation. She glanced his way. Did he feel the same way for her? She turned away. What was she supposed to do now? Act as though nothing had changed?

As Rez escorted Beatrix down the aisle, he leaned over and whispered, "Why are you frowning?"

"I am?" She hadn't realized her thoughts had translated into her facial expression. "It's nothing."

"I don't believe you."

"Shh…"

At the church steps, Beatrix was drawn away from Rez by the Queen. They were taking the back way to the palace and waiting for the happy couple there. They ended up waiting quite a while as the wedding processional back to the palace was very slow moving as the Prince and Princess's carriage wound its way through many of the village streets.

Once the bride and groom arrived, the pace picked up as there was a receiving line and a formal dinner followed by a large party in the ballroom.

Every time Beatrix spotted Rez from across the room, he was talking to someone. And it wasn't until she was dancing with someone else that Rez was alone. How could two people keep missing each other?

It was getting late into the evening when Beatrix's feet started to ache and she needed to cool off. She moved to the doors leading to the balcony. She moved outside.

The sun had already set and the palace was bathed in moonlight. It was a beautiful night as the stars twinkled overhead like hundreds of diamonds. There was only one thing that would make it better—Rez.

"There you are," came a voice from behind her.

She spun around to find Rez standing there. "How did you do that?"

"What? Follow you out here?"

"No. I mean yes. It's just that I was thinking about you and suddenly you appear."

He approached her. "I hope that's a good thing."

"It's a very good thing."

They moved over to the edge of the balcony and stared out over the spacious gardens that were visible in the bright moonlight. It was such a beautiful evening. A warm breeze rushed over her skin. And she felt all of her stress and worries carried away.

"You must be relieved now that the wedding is over." His voice was deep and soft.

"I definitely am. And they both look so happy."

Creak!

Beatrix turned and stared into the shadows. She didn't see anything move. "Did you hear that?"

"Hear what?"

"The sound of a door opening." She continued to stare into the dark, wondering if they had company.

Rez turned to check things out. "I don't see anyone.

Maybe they glanced out here, saw the balcony was occupied and returned to the party."

"Maybe." She turned back to him. "What did you think
of the wedding?"

"That you were incredibly beautiful."

Immediately heat rushed to her face. Even with being
a princess, she wasn't good with compliments. "Thank
you. But I meant about the bride and groom. They looked
so happy, didn't they?"

"Yes, they were happy, but it was you who held my attention. You were radiant."

She couldn't help but wonder what had come over him.
Maybe it was the moonlight; it took the edges off things
and obscured the details. Did he really think this about
her?

She wasn't tall and slender like her older sister, Gisella.
And she wasn't cute and stylish like her younger sister,
Cecelia. Beatrix was more on the short and curvy side.
But when she looked into Rez's eyes, she felt like the
most beautiful woman in the world.

She glanced away. "You don't have to say that."

"I'm not just saying that. You're amazing. And it starts
on the inside. You're so warm and kind. Evi is crazy about
you. And that's why I wanted to talk to you tonight before we leave in the morning."

"You're leaving? So soon." She should have expected
this but with everything that had been going on, she'd
gotten caught up in the moment.

He nodded. "Yes. Evi has been off her schedule since
we've been at the palace. It's time to get her home."

She struggled with the fact that this tryst that they'd
been enjoying was quickly coming to an end. "I understand."

He took both of her hands into his. "I want you to come with us."

This was the last thing she expected him to say. "Are you serious?"

"I am." He stared into her eyes.

The idea was tempting—so very tempting. "I don't know if I can take the time off. My schedule is really full. But maybe in a few weeks I could visit."

He shook his head. "You're misunderstanding me. I want you to become my wife."

"What?" She couldn't have heard him correctly.

"Think about it. You and I, we're good together. I think that has been proven every night this week."

The heat in her face flared. "That's no reason to get married."

"And you're really good with Evi." He paused. His gaze searched hers. "She needs you. And you need her."

She couldn't argue his point about Evi. They had formed a close bond. Nothing could compare to rocking Evi to sleep. She could just sit and hold the baby for hours.

But there was something missing from his proposal. He'd said nothing about him needing her. There were no words of love and forever. It was like he was forming some sort of business arrangement.

She did love Rez with all of her heart. It wasn't hard to love him. He could be kind, gentle and thoughtful. All she had to do was watch him with Evi and it melted her heart.

However, a one-way love would never work. It would never be strong enough to handle life's tribulations.

In the end, their marriage would crack and disintegrate. It wouldn't be just the two of them that got hurt. Evi would be a casualty of them making a bad decision for all of the right reasons. And that little girl had already lost one mother—she couldn't lose another. Beatrix felt this overwhelming urge to protect Evi at all costs—even at the expense of her own happiness.

Besides, Rez would eventually come to resent her for not being able to give him more of his own children. Tears pricked the backs of her eyes. And if they tried adoption and it didn't work out, he'd resent her even more. It was best he marry someone without complications—someone who could easily give him the family he deserved.

That acknowledgment sliced deep into her heart. Rez was the only man she'd ever truly loved—perhaps the only one she would love. It was with the heaviest heart that she realized she had to turn down his proposal. It's what was best for everyone.

"So what do you say?"

She pulled her hands free of his hold. She couldn't say the difficult words if he was holding on to her. To do the right thing, she had to stand on her own two feet. She steeled herself, hoping when she opened her mouth that she didn't dissolve into a sea of tears.

She drew in a deep breath, hoping it would calm her. And then she blew it out.

"No." There was a slight waver in her voice because turning him down was ripping her apart. "I can't marry you."

Just then there was a flash of light out of the corner of her eye. They weren't alone. Her heart stopped. Who was taking their photo? It had to be the royal photographer because phones had been banned from the reception. They were collected before entering the palace and would be returned at the end.

"Who's there?" Rez's voice was more like a growl.

He wasn't happy. She couldn't blame him. And for

their private conversation to be overheard was dreadful. Seconds ticked by as they stared into the dark.

"I said, who's there?" Rez wore a fierce look on his face. He turned back to her. "Go inside where it's safe."

She wasn't going anywhere without him, but before she could utter her refusal, Rez moved to the far end of the balcony. With the light on his phone, he began searching for the person that had taken their photo.

All the while her heart beat hard in her chest. She followed him and joined the light on her phone with his.

"Go inside," he said.

"Not without you." Her tone was firm and resolute.

Together they searched around the furniture and the multitude of tall, bushy potted plants. They'd worked halfway across the balcony when there was a crash on the other side of the balcony. Rez took off. And then in the shadows she could make out a dark figure before the mystery person took off down the steps into the garden.

"Rez, be careful!" Her insides knotted up with worry.

Who was the person? Certainly not a guest or the photographer. They had an intruder—perhaps the spy. And now Rez was out there in the dark with him. Anything could happen now.

She thought of following them, but she would never be able to keep up in her high heels. Instead she rushed inside the palace. She skirted around the party and headed for the hallway. She contacted security and told them there was an intruder in the garden. And she made sure to warn them that Rez was out there. She didn't want them to mistake him for the intruder.

And then she started to pace. There was no way she could go back to the reception now. She didn't want to ruin things for her brother and Indigo. They deserved to have a reception undisturbed.

Instead she headed for the King's office. She'd noticed that her parents had slipped out of the reception quite early. They claimed that the partying was for the younger crowd. She knew that with her father's health in decline that he didn't do late nights any longer. But she wondered if he was still up. If he was, she wanted to update him.

When she reached the office, there was one lone light on and her father was behind his desk. When he heard her approach, he glanced up. "What are you doing here instead of at the party?"

"There's an intruder." And then she proceeded to tell him how she and Rez were out on the balcony getting a breath of fresh air—she left out the part about the marriage proposal—and how someone took their photo.

"You called security?" The King got to his feet.

"They're on it. I just hope Rez doesn't get hurt."

"Let's go to the security offices and wait for word."

Together they made their way through the quiet halls. All the while, she couldn't help but wonder how such a lovely day had come to such a troubled ending. And now Rez was in danger.

Her heart clenched. He just had to be all right. Even though he didn't feel the same way about her as she did him, she would always care about him.

He refused to stop.

Rez kept putting one foot in front of the other. As he ran through the darkened garden, the only thought on his mind was capturing the person who had intruded on a very private moment—the person who obviously didn't belong at the palace—where his baby daughter lay sleeping upstairs.

Rez would continue his pursuit until he caught the person. All of his morning runs were paying off. He was gaining on the shadow of a person.

They rounded corner after corner until the person made an attempt to run across a clearing at the side of the garden. In the wide-open space, Rez knew this was his chance to catch the darkened figure that was undoubtedly a man.

Rez gave it his all. He expanded his steps and pushed himself to go as fast as he could. One footfall after the next, he grew closer.

When he reached the point where he could reach out and touch the man, Rez threw himself at the man. They collided. Their bodies hit the ground with an *oomph*.

They rolled around and struggled. Punches were thrown. Rez didn't know how much time had passed when he had the man straddled on the ground. The fight was over. The man gave up.

In the distance, he spotted flashlights. "Over here!"

Palace security rushed toward him. Once the man was restrained, Rez stared into the man's face. He recognized him. He was one of the staff that had been helping with the wedding preparations.

"Are you the one that has been feeding information to *Duchess Tales*?"

The man stared at him with anger in his eyes, but he didn't say a word.

Rez wasn't going to leave it like this. He had to know if this man had been spying on them all of this time. "Search him."

The guards produced a small phone. On it were messages between the man and whoever was behind the *Duchess Tales* persona. At last, the palace's spy had been caught and would undoubtedly be prosecuted for his crimes.

On the phone was a photo of him and Beatrix. The image of them together made him pause. He remembered that moment so vividly. He'd been so nervous when he'd proposed to her. His stomach had been tied up in knots. He'd been so certain it was the right thing to do for all of them. And all she had to do was say yes.

He'd struggled to get the words out, certain he'd make a mess of the whole thing. When he finally spoke the words without making a mistake, he'd been proud of himself. Then she'd turned him down. The rejection had been like a giant gut punch.

He hadn't realized until that moment how invested he was in the family he'd envisioned. In his mind, the three of them would have been so happy. Apparently Bea didn't feel the same way.

How had he read the signs so wrong? With the lingering kisses and the repeated lovemaking, he'd thought what they had was something they could build on. So when he'd proposed, he'd been expecting her to be enthusiastic about the idea of making a family with him. He'd never been so wrong in his life.

The memory of her rejection sliced through him like a rusty nail being pounded into his heart. Why had she said no? The question circled round in his mind with only one viable answer—she didn't feel the same way about him.

It had to be the answer because he'd seen her with Evi. There was love reflected in Bea's eyes when she held his daughter. The realization only made her rejection that much more painful.

What was he supposed to say to her now that she'd turned him down? There was nothing to say. Whatever it was they'd shared was over. The best thing he could do for both of them was for him to head home. The sooner, the better.

CHAPTER FIFTEEN

SHE FELT HORRIBLE.

Absolutely awful.

Beatrix told herself that she'd turned down Rez's marriage proposal for all of the right reasons, but it didn't make her feel any better.

A part of her wondered if she should have agreed to marry him. Maybe he would have grown to love her. But it was too big of a risk to take with her heart.

That morning she'd skipped breakfast with the whole family, including some wedding guests. When her mother had stopped by her room, she'd blamed it on a headache. At her mother's insistence, she'd said she would join them later.

As lunch approached, Beatrix was still in bed. She had no desire to leave her room and wear a fake smile. While she was happy for her brother and Indigo, she was miserable for herself.

She had passed up a chance to build a life with the man she loved and help raise the most precious little girl. Who did something like that? So what if he didn't love her. They were compatible in other ways. That could be enough. Couldn't it?

She pulled a pillow over her head and yelled in frustration. It didn't seem like there was a right decision.

No matter how she responded to his marriage proposal, someone was going to get hurt. At least this way it wasn't sweet Evi.

Knock-knock.

"Go away!" She didn't want to see anyone.

The door opened anyway and in walked her eldest sister, Gisella. Her eyes widened when she spotted Beatrix still in bed. She walked over and sat down on the bed.

"So what's going on?"

"I have a headache. Didn't Mother tell you?"

"She mentioned it but no one believes it."

"What's that supposed to mean?" Why wouldn't her family believe her? She really did have a headache as she came to terms with what had happened the night before.

"It means that something happened. First, Rez leaves unexpectedly last night."

Beatrix sat up straighter. "Rez is gone already?"

"Isn't that just what I said?"

"But why?"

"That's what I want to know. He's gone. And you won't get out of bed today. So what gives?"

She wasn't ready to talk about it. "It's nothing."

"If you think you can keep it a secret, it's too late. And though I make it a point not to believe those gossip sites, in this case they might be right."

"Right about what?"

Gisella gestured to Beatrix's phone on her bedside table. "You should see it for yourself."

She didn't want to see it, but she needed to know what was going on. She turned on her phone and went to the most prestigious gossip site in Rydiania, *Duchess Tales.*

She piled up her pillows and then pressed on the link.

A Happily-Ever-After!

Beatrix breathed a sigh of relief. There was a photo of the newly married Prince and Princess. That wasn't so bad. In fact as she read down over the post there wasn't one mean or spiteful thing said about her brother or his wife.

"This isn't so bad. In fact, it's a nice write-up for Istvan and Indigo."

"True. But keep scrolling."

Beatrix didn't want to but with her older sister sitting there watching her, she didn't have much of a choice. Her finger moved over the screen.

REJECTED!

Beatrix read the headline again. Beneath the all-caps headline was a photo of Rez and herself. They were standing out on the balcony. And then she realized this photo was taken last night when Rez had proposed to her.

She gasped. She felt so utterly exposed. This scurrilous rag had taken her most private—most painful—moment and publicized it without care of how the people in the picture might feel.

Royal watchers, I have the most amazing news for you. The Duke of Kaspar has been turned down by the Princess. Yes, you read that right. She turned down his marriage proposal. The poor Duke. He'll probably need a shoulder to lean on. I'll be the first to offer him my own.

She didn't doubt the Duchess would be first in line to comfort Rez. The thought of any woman coming to his aid had jealousy burning in the pit of her gut. Why, oh, why couldn't he have loved her in return?

But she supposed she shouldn't be surprised. When she was crazy about him as a kid, he hadn't even given her a second glance. Why should the passing of time have changed any of that? It obviously hadn't.

You might ask why the Princess would turn down the Duke's proposal. It was the same question I have. And I'm sorry to say I have no answer for you. Maybe she is hoping to marry someone of a higher stature. Or maybe she doesn't want a ready-made family. Either way, it opens up the field for the Duke to search for a new wife.

The heartless words dug at her heart. This Duchess person had absolutely no idea what they were talking about. None whatsoever. If they did, they would know that status meant nothing to Beatrix. Even if Rez wasn't titled, she would have fallen for his charming smile, his caring ways and the way she could talk to him about anything.

Beatrix almost closed the app before she read the final words, but she hesitated. It wasn't like the Duchess could hurt her any worse than she had already.

With a broken heart, the Duke has departed for the country. So it might be a while until we see him again. But keep reading, my lovely watchers, and I will share with you as soon as we have a Duke sighting. Until next time... Duchess xox

"That woman is horrible." Beatrix slammed her phone down on the end table. "I wish we knew who it was and how she gets her information."

"So it is true?"

"No, it's not." Her denial came out too quickly and too vehemently to be believed.

"Do you love him?" Gisella watched her carefully.

Beatrix wanted to deny her feelings for Rez. It would make things so much easier. And yet she heard herself admitting the truth. "Yes. But he doesn't love me."

"Why would he propose if he didn't love you?"

"Because he wants a mother for his daughter."

"He told you this?"

"No. But it's obvious. There was nothing about love or romance in his proposal. It was more like a business arrangement. And as much as I love him, I know that a one-way love isn't enough to make a lasting marriage."

Gisella was quiet for a moment. "He might not have said the right words, but I think you might be wrong about how he feels about you."

Beatrix wanted her sister to be right, but she knew it was just wishful thinking on Gisella's part. "I don't think so."

"Maybe you should look at the photo of you two again. To me that looks like a man in love." And with that her sister got up and walked out of the room.

Beatrix reached for her phone. Her sister wasn't right, was she? Her fingers moved over the touch screen until the photo came up on the screen.

She turned her phone sideways to enlarge the photo. And then she expanded the photo, focusing on Rez's face. There was definitely emotion written all over his face.

Was he in love with her? She had no idea. She just knew without love, she couldn't marry him.

He hadn't been to bed at all last night.

Rez had paced throughout his darkened country home most of the night, while outside a summer storm raged. Bolts of lightning had sliced through the inky-black sky. Thunder rattled the home to its foundation. It was as though nature had mirrored his emotions and they were on display for all of the world to witness.

He couldn't understand how everything had gone so wrong. It was Beatrix who had encouraged him to re-join life. She had been so encouraging that he was able to move past his guilt and let down his guard.

He thought Beatrix was the perfect person to let into his life—into Evi's life. Was it possible he'd let himself get caught up in the fake relationship they'd portrayed for the world to see? Had he only seen what he'd wanted to in Beatrix's eyes?

He raked his fingers through his hair. Even though he was home again, he could find no peace. The questions had tormented him all night. And now in the light of day, he couldn't find any solace.

Maybe it was exhaustion that was making everything feel so much worse. The only sleep he'd gotten was after Evi had awakened in the night wanting a bottle. He'd rocked her back to sleep and he'd fallen asleep in the rocking chair for a couple of hours.

Buzz-buzz.

He didn't want to talk to anyone. He ignored the call. When the phone rang a few minutes later, he ignored it too. Whoever was at the other end of the phone didn't want any part of his foul mood.

And then a message beeped on his phone and showed on his digital watch. He glanced at his wrist. The message was from Istvan:

Answer the phone. Or I'm driving there.

Rez inwardly groaned. He knew his friend well enough to know it wasn't an empty threat. When his phone rang a third time, he expelled a heavy sigh but answered it.

"What?" He didn't bother with any pleasantries. Even if he wanted to, he didn't think he was capable of it.

"How are you?"

"Just great," he said sarcastically. "How do you think?"

"I take it you saw the photo on the internet."

"No." He could only guess that it was the photo from last night on the balcony. He wasn't looking. He was already miserable enough.

"Do you want me to drive out there so we can talk?"

"No." His answer was quick and emphatic. "Aren't you supposed to be off on your honeymoon?"

"We aren't leaving for a few days. Indigo wanted some time to get her mother situated in her new home here in Rydiania. So I have the time."

Rez didn't say anything. He knew the harder he pushed his friend away, the harder Istvan would push back. Some things didn't change over time.

"So you proposed?"

"Yes." Rez rolled his eyes. He didn't want to have this conversation.

"And she turned you down?"

"Obviously." He bit his tongue not to be sarcastic.

"What did you do wrong?"

That question caught him off guard. "Why do you think I did anything wrong?"

"Obviously if you'd have done it right, you wouldn't be a miserable grouch and my sister wouldn't be holed away in her room all morning."

"Really?" He didn't think it would have fazed her to that extent. He didn't know what to make of that information.

"I wouldn't lie about one of my sisters being miserable. So now I have to figure out what you did."

"I didn't do anything except ask her to marry me and she turned me down."

"Did you have a ring?"

"Uh, no. I didn't have time to get one."

"So this was a spur-of-the-moment decision."

"Yes…um…no." He wasn't sure what he meant.

"Did you get down on one knee?"

"Is that a requirement?"

"Of course. Women love a show of romance." Istvan paused as though to let the thought sink in. "Did you tell her how much you love her?" When Rez didn't respond, Istvan asked, "You do love her, don't you?"

Did he love Bea? The answer was a quick and resounding yes. Despite all of the reasons he'd found to propose to Bea, the main reason he'd done it was because he loved her with all of his heart.

Admitting his feelings scared him. And yet as the silence stretched on between him and Istvan, he knew his friend wasn't going to drop the subject until he answered him.

Rez drew in a deep breath and released it. "Yes. I love her."

"Did you tell her?" Istvan asked again.

"No. I didn't." He held back the fact that he'd only now acknowledged the true depth of his feelings for Bea to himself.

"Let me tell you a secret. Love is the greatest risk but it has the biggest payoff. And my sister loves you. I think she's loved you since she was a kid."

"When you swore you'd beat me up if I even looked in her direction."

"That was different. She was a kid then. Now you're both grown up. And I think you love her too. Otherwise I don't think you would have pretended to have a relationship with her and then sneak into her room each night at the palace of all places."

"You knew?"

"Yep. Just be glad it wasn't my father who found out."

Rez was very grateful the King never caught them. He had a feeling if it had been the King they would have been married by now or else he'd been put in the ancient dungeon beneath the palace.

"You need to make this right with Beatrix."

Istvan was right. There was so much more they needed to say to each other. But would she give him another chance? He didn't know the answer, but he knew if he didn't put himself out there and take a risk, he would regret it for the rest of his life.

"I'm going to need your help." Rez had a plan in mind.

CHAPTER SIXTEEN

HE HADN'T CALLED.

And she didn't know what to say to him.

Beatrix couldn't believe her brother and sister-in-law had insisted she join them as well as the rest of the family for dinner in the village. The very last thing she wanted to do was to get dressed up and go out in public. She didn't want people pointing at her and talking about her. They had no idea what the real story was with her and Rez.

After she had spent most of her day in her room, the Queen had stopped to check on her. She let Beatrix know she was expected at dinner. When the Queen put it that way, there was no arguing.

With great reluctance, Beatrix showered and dressed in a midnight blue dress with a plunging neckline. The bodice shimmered while the skirt floated around her legs.

Her lady-in-waiting came and styled her hair. It was all pulled up with just a few curly wisps around her neck. On her ears she wore diamond studs and on her neck she wore a sapphire pendant.

She took time with her makeup. Cover-up hid the dark shadows under her eyes. And a few eye drops helped with the redness. By the time she finished with all of her makeup, she looked almost like herself. She just didn't feel like it.

When she made it downstairs to leave for the restaurant, she found no one there. Where was everyone? Was she late?

She checked the time. She was six minutes late. They couldn't have waited for her? It was tempting to just go upstairs and forget about dinner, but she didn't want to disappoint her brother. After all, he was still celebrating his marriage.

She stepped outside to find a car waiting for her. She climbed inside. The car ride was short as the village was right beyond the palace lands.

It pulled to a stop in front of the restaurant. The driver opened her door and she made her way to the restaurant. The maître d' opened the door for her. She stepped inside and was surprised to find the place empty. She didn't even spot a member of her family. What was going on?

In the background, the song "That's Amore" was playing. It gave the restaurant a cozy feel. As she stepped farther into the restaurant, she noticed the lights had been dimmed. On each of the dozens of tables were a hundred candles. The flames flickered, casting shadows on the walls.

There wasn't another soul in the room. She was alone. Her gaze came to rest on the table in the center of the dining room. It had a white linen tablecloth with a large crystal vase holding dozens of long-stemmed red roses.

Had she misunderstood her family when they told her about dinner? Was this supposed to be a romantic dinner for Istvan and Indigo? Was she supposed to be having dinner with her family at the palace?

She was about to retrace her steps before she ruined someone else's magical evening. A movement caught her attention. Out of the shadows stepped Rez. He was all done up in a dark suit and tie. He looked particularly charming. No, she took that back. He looked hot—sizzling hot.

She swallowed hard. "Rez, what's going on? Where is everybody?"

"All of the invited guests are here."

She glanced around. "But there's just you and me."

"That's right." He approached her. "Your brother helped me get you here so I could explain things."

Her spine stiffened. Her brother and her mother had colluded to get her to meet Rez. She wasn't so sure how she felt about that.

"I don't know what we have to talk about." Her protective walls went up.

"Lots." He stepped closer to her. "I really messed up last night."

It would have been the polite thing to disagree with him and assure him that his proposal was no big deal when in fact it was a *huge* deal. He'd irrevocably changed their relationship and even if they got past it, things between them would never be the same.

"And so you did all of this for me?" Her gaze moved to the candles and roses before returning to him.

"I did. Yesterday, I acted without thinking through everything."

What exactly was he saying? She thought back to the photo in the *Duchess Tales*. Was her sister's interpretation of the photo right? Did he love her? Her heartbeat sped up.

"And you've now thought things through?"

He nodded. "I have. Bea, if it wasn't for you, I'd still be holed up in my house. I'd still be punishing myself for the accident. You helped me see that I can't go on blaming myself. It isn't fair to me and it isn't fair to Evi. I need to start over and I'd like to do it with you."

"I'm glad you got that figured out, but I don't know if I should be a part of it." It was killing her to say it, but she didn't want to be his good friend—she wanted so much more.

"Of course you should. We've known each other all of our lives. We have so many great memories. And I'd love the chance to make more of them with you." He paused. "Up until now, I've been afraid to face my feelings. After the accident, I swore I'd never let myself get too close to anyone because the risk of loss and pain were too great."

"And you've changed your mind?" The breath caught in her lungs as she waited for the answer.

"I have." He gazed deep into her eyes. "The truth is that it's impossible to hide from true love whether you're willing to admit it or not."

Was he saying he loved her? Her heart swelled with hope as she waited for him to say more.

"And to deny such a love is painful and haunting. I don't want to miss this chance to be happy with you and Evi. I don't want to live the rest of my life wondering what might have happened if I'd taken a risk."

Tears of joy blurred her vision. She blinked them away.

"What I'm stumbling all over myself to say is I love you, Beatrix. I don't know when it started. I just know that pretending to be your boyfriend made me realize what was right in front of me—the woman I'm meant to spend my life with."

Happy tears streaked down her cheeks. She didn't think she was ever going to hear those words from him. "I love you too."

He reached out and pulled her to him. His mouth

claimed hers. Her heart pitter-pattered. This kiss… It felt so different… It was full of love. And she never wanted it to end.

Her arms slid up over his broad shoulders and wrapped around the back of his neck. Her body leaned into his. Her soft curves molded to his hard plains.

How did she get so lucky to have him in her life? She didn't know the answer, she just knew she'd found her very own prince charming. And she never wanted to let him go.

When he pulled back, he smiled at her. He reached in his pocket and withdrew a black velvet ring box. Her heart leaped into her throat.

He had given this proposal a lot more thought. He wasn't talking about a fleeting love, but one that would endure. As much as she wanted to let herself get lost in this moment, her fears about expanding their family came rushing forth.

She couldn't pretend that just because they loved each other that everything would work out. She might be a princess but she didn't believe in fairy tales.

She placed her hand on his, pausing him. Her gaze searched his. "Are you willing to accept that I can never carry your baby?"

He nodded. "I understand. The three of us is all I need."

"Maybe for now, but what about in the future? You're such a good and loving father. What if as Evi grows older, you want another baby? You'll resent me for keeping you from experiencing fatherhood again." Her heart ached at the thought of him resenting her.

He took her hands in his. "Expanding our family won't be a decision one of us makes alone. It would be something we decide together and then we'll sign up for adoption."

"But adoption isn't a guarantee. The wait lists are long and even if you get selected, the birth mother can change her mind. I don't want to put you through all of that."

"You wouldn't put me through anything. If that's what we choose to do, we'd do it together and we'd lean on each other through the entire journey."

Her gaze searched his. "You really mean it?"

"I do. I love you and I want to be your partner through it all—the good and the bad. As long as I have you and Evi, I'll be happy."

He was right. And perhaps one day they would explore those options. But right now, she had everything she would ever need to be happy.

"Okay. Proceed."

His smile returned. He got down on one knee and opened the ring box. "Princess Beatrix, you caught my attention as a kid and now I see you as the beautiful woman you are. I love you with all of my heart. I would be honored if you would agree to be my wife. Will you marry me?"

By now the happy tears were flooding down her face. "Yes. Yes, I will."

He withdrew the ring and she held out her hand. It had a slight tremble. She'd never been so excited about anything in her life. And then the ring slid on her finger as though it were made for her.

She lifted her hand and stared down at the diamond-encrusted platinum band with a large oval diamond. It sparkled in the candlelight.

Her gaze lifted to Rez. "I love it, but I love you more."

"I love you too." He leaned forward and kissed her again.

It was the first of a lifetime of kisses—a lifetime of love and devotion. She was the luckiest woman in the world.

"How long until *Duchess Tales* finds out about our engagement?" Beatrix's gaze returned to the ring.

"It doesn't matter to me. I want the whole world to know just how much I love you."

She turned to him. "The whole world, huh?"

"Uh-huh." He wrapped his arms around her waist, pulling her close. "I could shout it from the mountaintop if you'd like."

"I have something else in mind." She lifted up on her tiptoes, pressing her lips to his. She could get very used to this.

EPILOGUE

Four years later...

LIFE WAS FULL of twists and turns.

Beatrix never imagined she could be this happy. She glanced over her shoulder at her loving, adoring husband as he stood near the window of their country home. He'd taken the last week and a half off from his law firm to spend time with the family.

Since he'd returned to his legal work, he'd been careful not to work long hours. They'd both learned to value their family time. It was for that reason that she'd lightened the number of projects she sponsored. Because when Evi returned home from school, Beatrix wanted to be there to spend time with her.

At Rez's insistence, they'd renovated the entire estate making it their home. And lucky for them it had plenty of bedrooms because their families were constantly visiting. Everyone wanted to spend time with their sweet five-year-old daughter, Evi, whom Beatrix had officially adopted. Though she insisted on helping Evi to remember her birth mother through pictures and home movies.

And there was another reason their families were spending a lot of time at the country estate: Evi's new baby brother, Alexander.

Beatrix had never believed in miracles before but she did now. While they'd been on the waiting list to adopt, she'd gone back to her doctor. He'd insisted there was absolutely no way for her to carry a baby.

When she'd inquired about using a surrogate, they'd done tests. She didn't have many eggs. And so at her insistence and Rez's great hesitation, she'd started IVF treatments. And when the time was right, she had surgery for egg retrieval. None of the fertilized eggs had been viable.

While the doctor and Rez had wanted to call it quits, Beatrix insisted on doing another round. This time there were two viable fertilized eggs. They were fortunate to be put in contact with a surrogate, who was willing to have the two eggs implanted. One egg didn't survive but the other thrived.

She stared down at her ten-day-old son, who was asleep in her arms. Just then she felt her husband's hand on her shoulder. She leaned her head against his arm and then kissed the back of his hand.

"Our miracle baby is a good sleeper," she said.

"He's just like his father."

"He's a mini you." She gazed down at her son's full head of dark hair.

"I don't know. I think he has your nose and eyes."

"You do?" She peered at their son, trying to see herself in him. She didn't see it, but it didn't matter whom Alexander looked like. He totally had her wrapped around his tiny finger.

"Can I hold him?" Evi ran into the room. She stopped beside Beatrix and stared at her little brother. "Please."

Beatrix gazed up at Rez, wondering what he thought of their energetic daughter holding a newborn. Rez nodded his approval.

"You have to sit on the couch next to your mother." Rez patted a spot on the couch.

Evi scooted into the spot and held out her arms. Excitement shone in her eyes.

Beatrix stood and turned to Evi. "You have to be super careful with him and watch his head. It needs support."

"I will."

"He's very small and delicate." Beatrix carefully positioned Alexander in his big sister's arms.

Evi sat very still. Beatrix wasn't even sure Evi was breathing as she stared down at Alexander.

"You're doing good," Beatrix said.

"He's so small. How will he do anything?"

"We'll do things for him until he grows up a little. As his big sister, you'll have lots of things to show him." Beatrix wrapped her arm around Rez and leaned into him. She'd never seen such a beautiful scene.

"I can show him how to play hide-and-seek. I get to hide and he has to find me. And I can show him the tree house."

"Slow down," Rez said. "He's got a lot of growing to do before he'll be ready for all of those things."

"Mind if we join you?" Beatrix's mother's voice came from behind her.

Beatrix turned to find her parents standing in the doorway.

"Grannie!" Evi's exuberant voice woke her brother.

Rez took the baby and rocked him back to sleep. "It's okay, buddy." He spoke in soft tones. "You'll get used to your sister's excitement."

Beatrix watched as Evi was enveloped in her mother's arms. Becoming a grandparent had really changed her mother. Beatrix never thought her rule-abiding, proper parents would become doting, laid-back grandparents.

As Evi chattered to her grandfather about her new tree house, Beatrix's mother made her way over to the baby. As Rez handed Alexander over to Beatrix's mother, there was a look of love that came over her face.

Beatrix leaned against her husband. Her head rested against his broad shoulders. "I don't think I've ever been so happy."

"Me either." He turned to her. "I love you, my princess."

"I love you too."

* * * * *

BACK IN THE GREEK TYCOON'S WORLD

JUSTINE LEWIS

MILLS & BOON

For my brainstorming and coffee buddy Samara.

To many more afternoons in a booth at Tilley's. xx

CHAPTER ONE

THERE ARE SOME things one just can't capture on camera, even a high-end DSLR, and the view from the point over the Ionian Sea was one of them. Oh, one could capture the sun sparkling on the azure water, the light bouncing off the white rooftops and even the magnificence of the almost vertical white cliffs that dropped suddenly down to the sea. But one couldn't capture the smell of salt on the breeze or the way the sun warmed the skin.

The camera also couldn't capture the way Rose's heart swelled to be back in Greece, or the anticipation she felt at what she might finally find on this dig. She'd lived a nomadic life since she was a teenager, but Greece kept calling her back—more than Italy, or Sicily, or Turkey. Certainly more than her native Birmingham with its low, grey skies.

It was her passion for Greece—or, to be more accurate, ancient Greece—that had led her to her career in archaeology. One night when she was seven, she'd picked up a book of Greek myths she'd got from school. She'd read it in bed each night as her parents had fought and then, when her father had left, she'd read every other book about ancient Greece she'd been able to find at her school library. Then everything she'd been able to find at the public library.

Ancient Greece was the land of myths, monsters and legends, where history and fiction were almost as one—the land of Trojan Horses, labyrinths, gods and goddesses. Most importantly, a place where a man might be away from his family for twenty years and still return home.

Unlike her own father. She hadn't seen him since the night he'd left Rose and her mother to have a second family with a woman he'd met on a work trip. A year later, Rose and her father had shared their very last conversation. 'It's best if we don't see one another any more. We have different lives now,' her father had said.

'He has a new family—he doesn't need us,' her mother had said, as Rose had lain on her bed and bawled.

Rose had been replaced. She'd not been enough.

She exhaled, wiped the sweat from her brow and put her hat back on. It was good to be back in Greece and finally have the chance to excavate on Paxos. She had never had the opportunity to work on the Ionian Islands, the special, sometimes overlooked, western side of Greece that also had a shared history with the Italians.

The Ionian Sea had been the birthplace of Odysseus, the hero of Homer's *Odyssey*, who returned home to Ithaca after twenty years away. While her colleagues generally believed Homer's poems were entirely fictional, a series of discoveries over the past decade had suggested there were Bronze Age ruins yet to be discovered on these islands.

Recently, a three-thousand-year-old royal palace had been found just over the sea on Ithaca. More Bronze Age ruins had been found nearby on the mainland at Pylos. It remained to be seen whether any of these finds could categorically be linked to Odysseus and Homer's verse, but Rose wanted to be there if they were.

A team from the Athens Museum had been asked to conduct a survey of this particular site on Paxos. A hotel had been planned for it; however, a routine survey for the building permit had revealed some unusual things in the ground. Her old mentor in Athens had called her immediately, knowing her special interest in the Ionian islands. Not only would she have the opportunity to dig at someone else's expense, but they wanted her to lead the excavation. It was the first major dig she'd been asked to lead and a remarkable opportunity to be entrusted with. If she did a good job, she'd earn tenure for life.

She'd left London as soon as she could. A week later, she was on Paxos. She was staying in a small village called Ninos, standing in the late summer sun and hoping that what the surveyors had noticed in the ground would turn out to be something amazing.

The area they were digging was about half the size of a football field. Up the hill from them was an existing hotel. Down the hill were some olive trees and a path that led down to some more houses. To her right, the earth dropped away to the magnificent Ionian Sea. As workplaces went, it didn't get much better than this.

Rose stood for a much-needed stretch and walked over to the bag containing her water bottle. She drank from it gratefully and studied the height of the sun. It was early afternoon; they still had quite a few hours left in the day.

A silhouette on the hill made her heart hit her throat with a surprising thud. There was something so familiar about it...

It couldn't be him.

The man was pacing along the fence line that divided the old hotel from the land for the new one. He was definitely watching the team. His shoulders were tense and his gait rigid, but she couldn't make out his face with the sun behind him.

It's just the smell of the Greek air playing tricks on you. It'd be too much of a coincidence.

The last time she'd seen Alessandro he'd climbed out of her warm bed, slipped on a pair of chino shorts, pressed his lips to hers and told her he'd see her that night in the taverna down the lane. She'd worn her new white linen dress, an extravagance she'd barely been able to afford on her meagre student income, and had waited for him—for three hours! She'd felt worried at first, then foolish. Finally, she had returned to his room in the university dormitory, found it empty and had been furious.

He hadn't just stood her up; he'd cleared out his dorm room and left Athens. That ruled out him having been involved in a horrible accident or somehow having been detained and left only ghosting. It was bad enough that he had broken up with her, after all they had shared over the previous few weeks. Instead he'd made her wait for three hours, all dressed up and alone in the taverna, while he'd packed up his things and left without a word.

She'd called and called for days but he hadn't picked up. Finally, nearly a week later, he'd called her. It had been the strangest, most heart-breaking conversation of her life. Even more awkward than the handful of conversations she'd had with her father after he'd left.

'I'm sorry, I had to leave. I can't see you any more.'

'You said you loved me.'

He hadn't responded and her plea had felt pitiful. 'Our lives are on different paths now and it's best if we don't contact one another.'

He'd sounded exactly like her father.

And, just like her father, Alessandro had found someone else. Or, rather, he'd already been seeing someone else when he'd met Rose. Despite knowing that she ought not to try and find out what Alessandro's excuse was, a few months later she had searched for him and seen the photos. Alessandro had been holding the hand of one toddler and had another in his arms. The caption had been in Greek, but she'd made out the words *Alessandro Andino and his new twins* before she'd shut her laptop. She hadn't needed to know more.

Rose lowered her head, made sure her hat covered her face and went back to work. Whoever this man watching them was, he was no concern of hers. They were still at the stage of using small trowels to systematically remove the earth from the site. But with each trowel's worth she felt herself uncovering older, more ancient ground.

Snatches of other ancient memories came back to her. Alessandro had told her he had grown up in the Ionian, near Corfu, but had never told her where. Corfu was not far to the north, so maybe Paxos was the place. He hadn't told her much about his family; his mother had died when he'd been a baby and his father when he'd been a teenager. He had an older brother, she recalled. He hadn't spoken much about where he'd grown up, except to tell her he had no intention of ever living back on the islands.

He and Rose had been going to work their way around the world together… She scoffed. Everything he'd told her had been a lie.

Rose looked out carefully from under her hat. The man had begun his descent down the hill and had moved out of the path of the sun. As his face came into focus, her stomach began to drop. Thirteen years? Or was it fourteen? He bore an uncanny resemblance to the man she'd fallen in love with all those years ago.

The man approached Gabriel, her second in charge, and his deep, resonant voice drifted to her on the sea breeze and she knew.

Her chest felt tight and she dropped her head. *Nothing* he'd told her had been the truth. Not his plan to be a journalist, not his desire to travel the world and certainly not the passion he'd felt for her.

Foolish…that was what she was. The connection they'd shared had been so intense, so close that at times it had felt as though they could read one another's minds. But that too, had been a lie, just a trick.

Now she was older, she understood his game better than

she had as a naive twenty-year-old: seduce the undergrad exchange student, sleep with her for a few weeks and lie to her about having a family. Get her to share her dreams, thoughts and desires, but reveal nothing about his actual life. Rose knew that he'd loved Shakespeare and had wanted to change the world, but she hadn't known exactly where he'd grown up. Or that he had children.

To be fair to her twenty-year-old self, she'd also thought she'd have more time to ask the mundane questions. She'd thought she'd see him again. She'd trusted him.

She'd never made that mistake again.

And she wasn't about to start now.

She had to brace herself: they were coming towards her. What on earth was he doing here? Writing a story on the dig? Perhaps, but he was dressed reasonably formally, wearing trousers and a collared shirt, albeit no tie. She'd answer some questions for him, tell him the excavation was just a formality, make the dig sound less exciting than she thought it was and he'd be on his way. No way was he getting the scoop about what she hoped would be the greatest find in the Ionian Sea in decades.

Once upon a time she'd had a short speech prepared in case she ever ran into him again. Even if she could remember that speech now, it was far from suitable to deliver it with half a dozen colleagues listening in.

'Rose.' Gabriel called her name and she had no choice but to stand, push back her hat and summon every ounce of her dignity.

Dignity was hard to come by when she met his eyes, as dark and deep as ever, with dark hair and olive skin to match—because he was, of course, your archetypal Adonis. His classic Mediterranean looks had drawn her to him in the first place: a pair of chiselled cheekbones, a perfectly defined jaw, eyelashes so thick they almost obscured his eyes, especially when his lids were half-closed when he was… She took a deep breath and shook away the memory.

'Rose, this is Alessandro Andino.' Gabriel introduced her. 'Mr Andino, Dr Taylor is leading the excavation.'

'Mr Andino.' Her mind left her body as she said his name for the first time in years.

'Dr Taylor,' he replied, and his voice vibrated in her chest. Neither of them added, 'Pleased to meet you.'

Alessandro held out a large hand and she stared at it, her body unwittingly recoiling. She couldn't touch him. Her heart was beating fast enough as it was. Physical contact might just bring back too many memories of summer nights in Athens and tip her over the edge of whatever precipice she was standing on.

She held up her dirt-covered hands. 'I'm sorry, you don't want to touch my dirty hands.'

A glint flickered across his dark eyes but was gone before she could make out its meaning. He placed his own hands behind his back.

'Rose, Mr Andino manages the Aster chain of hotels. He is the one who wishes to build on this site.'

He was a hotel developer—Alessandro Andino? The man who had once spent a whole night reciting Shakespeare's sonnets to her? Whose heroes were Jane Goodall and Rachel Carson? The same Alessandro who had been a term away from finishing his Master's in International Relations? That same Alessandro was a hotel developer?

He really had changed since they'd known one another.

Stupid. Everything he ever told you was a lie. None of it was ever true.

Alessandro shifted from foot to foot. His long-held plans were unravelling before his eyes. When the people from the Athens Museum had arrived two weeks ago, they'd told him it would only take a week at most to investigate the land and certify it as free for development. As far as he was concerned, the survey had only been a legal formality. The area around the village did not have any other known ruins, and besides, this was the Ionian Sea: most of the significant ancient finds were to the east, in the Aegean.

The Ionian Sea, for all its beauty, had not been the epicentre of ancient Greek civilisation. There were myths about everywhere in Greece, but that was all they were—stories. There was no reason to believe that the land they had purchased next to his hotel hid anything of real historical significance.

But today the team of two had tripled. That was good, he told himself; it meant they would finish sooner rather than later. But his gut had niggled with doubt. And the doubt had grown to full-blown worry when he'd looked down at the excavation and seen the woman. She was new, wearing a large sun hat and white shirt, gesturing to the others.

She was too far away for him to make out her face, or hear exactly what she was saying, but he could tell by their body language that the others were all deferring to her.

Deciding he should meet the person leading the survey sooner rather than later, he'd headed down the hill towards the dig. As he'd approached an English accent had reached him through the air and something inside him had twisted. He'd always been a sucker for an English woman, but had learned to give them a wide berth—for everyone's sake.

He looked at the woman again.

What were the chances?

He'd never been a lucky person; his life had been blessed with what one would call more sadness and duty than luck. But did the gods loathe him so much they would send her here? Now?

He studied her as well as he could without looking directly

at her. As if he was trying to study the sun without burning his retina.

A man approached Alessandro and introduced himself as Gabriel, an archaeologist.

'You'll have to meet Rose—I mean, Dr Taylor. She's in charge of the excavation.' When the other man had said her name, Alessandro's heart had plummeted to his knees.

Dr Taylor. The shock he felt at seeing her was mixed with another feeling—pride. The ambitious, passionate student he'd known was now in charge of a survey. Or excavation.

Before he could digest whether this change in term would be significant, Gabriel was leading him over to Rose, who pushed herself up from her kneeling position to meet him. She brushed herself down and adjusted her hat.

She's nervous.

She shouldn't be nervous. He was the one who should expect recriminations; after all, he was the one who'd abandoned her.

You did it to protect her.

Rose's heart had belonged to her work. She would not want to have lived her life on a tiny island helping him take care of two infants.

Gabriel took him to Rose so quickly he didn't have time to prepare his heart rate, much less come up with some sort of explanation for having left her that day in Athens. And, once she took off her hat and he saw her face properly, her beautiful red hair in a messy bun with tendrils escaping around her face, he was completely lost. His head was only full of heat, her soft skin against his and the taste of summer nights.

He made it through the introductions in a daze but, when he offered her his hand and she refused, he was jolted back to reality. Oh, her hands might have been dirty, but she made it very clear she didn't want to touch him. His mouth went dry and he swallowed to get the next words out.

'Dr Taylor,' he repeated, like a fool.

She hadn't acknowledged knowing him, so he wouldn't either. This might be his land, but it was still her workplace. And she was in charge.

At any other time, he'd be delighted for her—running her own projects had been her dream. Right now, it meant she was the one he had to speak to, and that was far from ideal.

'How can we help you, Mr Andino?'

Thank goodness she could get to the point.

'I've come to see how things are going down here. There seems to be a bigger team than yesterday. I've been dealing with a Mr Georgiou.'

'He's still around, but he called the museum in Athens and they called me.'

This wasn't news he wanted to hear, but he pressed on.

'Why? This is just a survey to get the final approvals before we build.'

She pulled a face. 'That may have been so, but we think there's a chance we'll find something.'

This was Paxos. It was hardly Olympia or Delos. 'Every archaeologist hopes to find something.'

'Well, this is more than just a hope. It's an educated guess.'

'How is that?' Really, she was meant to be the expert. But this was Paxos! He wasn't sure any ancient finds had ever been made on the small island he called home.

'Because the surveyors have found midden. And the resistivity metre shows resistance.'

'I'd be grateful if you could say that in a way that makes sense to someone who isn't an expert.' He hated the bitterness in his tone but was helpless to change it. Even his mouth tasted sour.

'Midden is traces of organic material—waste material. It shows that at some point people may have lived here.'

'Of course people have lived here. They live here now!'

She pulled a face and continued, ignoring his remark. 'And

the geophysical scans show that there's something buried here.'
She pointed in the direction she'd been digging. Then she repeated herself in his native Greek. Her Greek was broken, but
her meaning was clear. 'Can you understand that?' she asked.

He crossed his arms. Of course he understood what she was
saying, but that didn't mean he understood *why* they thought
these random facts meant his hotel had to be delayed.

'I don't see how either of those things prove anything at all.'

'They don't. But they do mean we need to check further.
And the Ministry of Culture isn't signing this permit until I
tell them they can.'

Her. The decision for whether his hotel—or rather, his
brother's hotel—went ahead or not was all down to her, the
woman he'd left behind all those years ago? He couldn't decide if it was ironic or simply crazy.

Of course, he hadn't known as he'd kissed her goodbye that
morning that it would be the last time he'd see her. If he had,
he might not have had the courage to leave. It had been hard
enough to unwrap himself from her on a normal day, but that
day had turned out to be anything but normal. That day everything in his world had changed when his grandmother had
called to tell him about his brother's accident. And that his
two-year-old niece and nephew had been orphaned.

On the trip back to Paxos he had made an oath that he wasn't
going to regret the life that he wasn't going to lead. Returning to Paxos to raise his niece and nephew was not what he
would've chosen for himself, but it was a life chosen for him.
He knew then that the only way to allow himself to dedicate
his life to the care of his new family was to give up the dreams
he'd had for himself. Some people might call it repressed, but
he called it common sense and self-preservation. Paxos and
the family hotel empire was going to be his life, so there was
no point wishing for things that could simply never be.

Rose ignored his silent reminiscences and continued, 'If

we don't find anything, it won't take long, probably just a few months.'

'A few months?' The excavators—of the large, mechanical variety—were due to start in three weeks. And after them the builders and everyone else. The new wing of the hotel was due to open nine months from now, by the following early summer.

'This isn't meant to be an excavation, just a survey. I was doing the right thing.'

'Yes, and the right thing in this instance is to let me and my team do a proper excavation. It's actually very exciting.' Her eyes widened and brightened. 'There have been some amazing Bronze Age finds in the Ionians in the past twenty years, and looking at this—'

'Bronze Age?' He wasn't the expert but the Bronze Age had ended more than half a millennium before the age of classical Greece. Finding ruins from classical Greece was unlikely. But finding something from the Bronze Age? Was she serious?

'Yes, the Bronze Age. The *Odyssey*, the *Iliad*. Homer.'

'You think you're going to find another Troy? Here?'

'Of course not, but the Ionian islands were the birthplace of Odysseus; they've found a royal palace on Ithaca and more treasure in Pylos. These islands were important in ancient times. There's every reason to believe we will find something. Odysseus' palace…a temple, for instance.'

Alessandro laughed. He hadn't meant to laugh as loudly as he had but what she was suggesting was plainly ridiculous.

'Odysseus? You want to find the three-thousand-year-old palace of a man who didn't exist?' He didn't add, 'Be my guest,' because her face had already hardened.

He looked over at Gabriel, whose eyes had grown wider during the course of their conversation. Alessandro had to make her see what she suggested was not only futile but that, if she persisted, it would throw his plans for the new hotel into doubt. Not only that, it would also jeopardise so many other businesses on the island. Paxos depended on tourists, and if there was nowhere for them to stay then the bars, restaurants and boat-tour operators would have no customers.

'Can I speak to you in private?' he said.

'Why?'

'To speak about this in a civilised manner.'

'I'm being civil now. So are you. We couldn't be more civil.'

'Let's talk in my office. We'll see if we can come to some sort of arrangement. Apart from anything else, we can get in from the sun. Have a cool drink.'

Her eyes flickered. He had her. It was mid-afternoon; the day was at its hottest and Rose, he remembered, much as she loved the Mediterranean, was still a redhead from England who had a tendency to wilt in the hot sun.

'Iced water, iced tea, *visinada*?'

She narrowed her eyes. He had her.

'All right then, lead on.'

CHAPTER TWO

Now they were alone, her palms were slick with sweat. That promised cold drink had better materialise or she'd have lost her home-ground advantage for nothing. It was difficult enough speaking to a hotel developer who plainly didn't want her to excavate; speaking to an old flame was another thing entirely. It was probably best they didn't have this conversation in front of her team.

She followed him up the hill and towards what she knew was the Aster hotel. It was just the sort of place she loved: a low rise, rambling affair surrounded with lush gardens. It looked more like a small village, rather than one of those multi-storey high-rise glass-and-concrete affairs that had been popping up in some places. She hoped he wasn't going to build one of those monstrosities. Paxos should retain its authentic, traditional charm and atmosphere.

They didn't speak as they walked, but how long could they put this conversation off? Not the conversation about how he didn't want her to dig up his land—the other one. The one about how he'd left her waiting, in the white dress she'd bought especially for him, and left town without telling her.

He didn't lead her to a hotel reception or foyer, but to what looked like a large house with several entrances. He took her to a blue door, unlocked it and showed her in.

Coming out of the bright sun, it took her eyes a moment to adjust, but the cold air washed over her instantly like the touch of a welcome friend. She sighed loudly, instantly regretting how pleased she sounded. The first thing she noticed when she opened her eyes was Alessandro looking down at her, grinning.

It was still difficult to reconcile the man standing before her now with the one she'd known as a student. That man had possessed a mop of curly dark hair, befitting the cash-strapped student she'd thought he was. His features had been half-hidden behind his hair and the stubble on his face. He'd dressed in worn jeans and old T-shirts.

This man was sharply groomed, his hair now short, most of the curls cut away and only the hint of a wave remaining. His face was clean shaven, which exaggerated his strong jaw and full lips. He dressed business-like—at least as business-like as anyone on the islands ever did. He wore trousers that had been recently ironed and a white shirt was tucked into them. The only nod to the location was the top button of his shirt undone and the absence of a tie.

This man was revealed to the world. The other, she now realised, had been hiding behind something.

'Can I get you a water? Or *visinada*? It's a sour cherry drink.'

'I know what it is,' she mumbled. They had drunk it together as they had walked the streets of Monastiraki. He didn't remember anything about their past connection.

Because it wasn't important to him.

'Water would be fine, please.'

She'd expected to find a house behind the pretty blue door but it was a large, modern office, far larger than any found in a university. It looked out over a garden and, in the distance, the blue waters of the sea.

Alessandro walked into an adjoining room and she manoeuvred her body to get a better look. In the next room were more desks, and she heard some voices speaking in Greek. She could tell the people were greeting Alessandro, but couldn't make out his reply. Moments later he returned, caught her looking, grinned again and handed her a cold glass.

Her hands wrapped around it gratefully and she sipped. Alessandro shut the door to the adjoining offices with an audible click.

'Have a seat.' He motioned to a sleek leather couch with a matching chair.

If she sat on the couch, would he sit next to her? Would he feel the same? Did he smell the same? She wanted to touch him. She barely trusted herself not to.

But no. He was a liar, so keeping some physical distance between Alessandro and her was a priority. She might be over him—heck, she had reason to loathe him—but what if her body hadn't got the message? Even now, something was bubbling up inside her, a need she had to suppress. She chose the chair and he raised an eyebrow.

Right.

The chair was probably where he sat. Good.

She sat, back upright, clutching the cool drink, which was now noticeably warmer in her hot hands.

'So, you want to excavate the site?' he began.

'I *am* excavating the site.'

'But this is a survey only, to finalise the approvals.'

'It may have started out like that, but the Ministry isn't going to certify it as clear to build on now.'

'Why not?'

'I told you. The surveyors have found midden. That's traces of organic material.'

'There's organic material everywhere. People live here.'

'But we can tell this is older. It suggests some sort of waste dump. It means we need to check further. And the resistivity meter—it's a geophysical scanner the surveyor uses—has shown something under the ground that isn't soil.'

'But that could be from any time.'

'Yes, of course. It could be some bricks from a couple of hundred years ago. It could be a slab of concrete from the war. But it also could be an Iron Age dwelling. A Bronze Age temple.'

He shook his head. 'That's just so unlikely.'

'Maybe. But…' She thought of a way to explain it. 'Car accidents are not very likely, but the consequences are terrible, which is why we wear seatbelts.'

His face changed. From open and argumentative, it shut down. His entire body froze and the air in the room shifted.

Figuring he understood her analogy, she continued. 'So we're starting where the meter shows resistance.'

Alessandro stood then, turned and walked to his desk. He kept his back to her and looked at the back wall of his office for a long time.

He's thinking, that's all. He's probably been planning this new hotel for a while. Stay professional.

Finally, he turned back to her, his eyes looking slightly red. 'You cannot be serious.'

His scepticism was starting to get annoying. Or was it simply him? Him and his strong jaw, immovable shoulders and general air of entitlement.

A developer? Alessandro Andino, a hotel developer, destroyer of ancient ruins?

She had been even more deceived by him than she'd thought.

'I am serious. You don't have a choice.'

'They said the survey would take two weeks at most.'

'Yes, two weeks to determine whether a more thorough investigation is needed. They've determined that a further investigation is needed and that's why I'm here.'

He began to pace but did not look at her. She couldn't help wondering if his indignant reaction was because of the situation in general or because it was her sitting here, telling him the bad news.

'The expansion is to support the island. Everyone here depends on tourism in some way for their livelihoods.'

'I appreciate that, I do, but—'

'It isn't just about me,' he said. 'My family's depending on this development for their futures.'

Family.

The word hit her with the force of a sledgehammer.

The kids she'd seen him with... The children who'd already been born when he'd first walked up to Rose in that bar in Athens.

How many kids did he have now? Who was their mother? Was she still around? Had he been cheating on her when he'd been with Rose? These were the questions she'd once asked over and over until she'd realised none of it mattered. Because he'd left her.

She felt slightly faint. Hopefully that was just the heat. She downed her water and it almost came straight back up again. It was ridiculous that her body was reacting like this; her self-imposed physical-distance rule was now more important than ever.

It wasn't important that Alessandro had a wife, a family; not in the scheme of things. She was fighting for three-thousand-year-old history. She had to stay focused.

'Like I said, I do appreciate your difficulties,' she said at last. 'But we have to excavate this site.'

He sighed and scraped his dark hair off his high forehead. Were cheek bones like that even legal? He had dark hair and eyes so intense they could slice through every last ounce of common sense and self-preservation she possessed. 'How long will it take?'

'It depends. If we don't find anything, a few months. If we do, five to ten years. If we're fully funded.'

Alessandro stood. 'Five to ten years! Fully funded! I can't wait five to ten years, and I certainly can't fund a team of archaeologists.'

He'd deceived her and now he was going to get in the way of what could be the greatest achievement of her career. She loathed him—she shouldn't be wondering how he smelt or thinking about running a fingertip along his now bare jawline.

'No one's asking you to fund it. Try and see it from a broader perspective—we might find something that's been hidden for thousands of years.'

He placed his face in his palms, and for a brief moment she felt some sympathy for someone who had made such an investment and was having his plans thrown into chaos.

'We might not find anything.'

'But if you do I can pretty much kiss goodbye to my plans. The children's futures, the island's future.'

Children. The family he'd left Rose for. Just as her father had.

She pushed the feelings of rejection deeper down, to where even she couldn't see them. She had a job to do here and it couldn't matter that the man now standing before her was the one who had once broken her heart.

'It's important,' she said. 'It's very important to preserve the past and learn from it.'

'The future's important too, you know. The people living now. Tourism's the biggest industry on Paxos. The hotel wouldn't only support my family, it would support the entire island. You live in the past but I'm concerned about the present—the people who need to feed and clothe their children, the people who need to buy medicine for their parents.'

'I understand that.'

'But do you? History is important. I know we need to preserve our culture. But we also need to eat.'

'When we find the ruins, it will bring tourists.'

'This isn't Troy. You can't honestly think you'll find something with a connection to Homer.'

Most people accepted that Homer's hero, Odysseus, had never existed, and the hope of finding something definitively related to him was next to impossible. But finding traces of Bronze Age civilisation in this area from the time of the Trojan war was a real possibility. It would change conventional thinking about Greek history and would be a career-defining discovery for Rose. Alessandro's patronising doubt was more than irritating. It was hurtful.

'One more month—four weeks. That's all I can offer. And then the builders will have to start.'

'That's silly.'

'Why is it silly?'

'Because when we find some ruins you'll just have to knock it all down again.'

'You won't find any ruins.'

She laughed. 'You know, I remember your tenacity, but I don't remember your condescension.'

He stopped pacing mid-stride.

This was the first time either had acknowledged their past. Until now it had simply rippled, unseen, beneath the surface.

'I'm not being condescending; I've lived here most of my life, and I promise you will not find anything. And certainly not anything from the Bronze Age.'

She scoffed, shook her head and paused, doubtful. 'What makes you so sure?'

'Because my family has lived in this village for over a hundred years, our ancestors for a millennium. If anything to do with Homer or Odysseus was on this island, we'd know about it. My family would know, the locals would know. There would be rumours, stories about it. And there are none!'

Oh, this man was the limit. Abandoning her in Athens, lying

about having children and now being the one person trying to get in the way of her and a career-critical discovery.

Even if they didn't find something as old as the Bronze Age, the experts who had surveyed this site believed there was something here. Something worthy of further investigation. And how long would it take? If they found something, then it could take years to properly search the whole site. But she knew, as much as Alessandro did, that the museum was not going to lend her this team for ever. That eventually they would certify the site as free to build on if they didn't find anything. She didn't have years, she had a couple of months at most. Probably less.

'Three months. If we don't find anything in three months, then we'll leave.' That would give her plenty of time to investigate the area of interest.

'Three months! Impossible. You have six weeks.'

In all likelihood the museum would recall the team before then anyway. But she wasn't about to tell Alessandro that. Six weeks would probably be sufficient to check what the survey team had identified but, no matter what, she could control whether the permit was signed.

'Six weeks—fine. From today.' She thought she saw him wince. 'And if, when, we find something, then as long as it takes.'

'Fine,' he said through gritted teeth.

She put down her glass and stood. He held out a broad hand to seal their deal. Again, she hesitated. Even the thought of skin-to-skin contact made her body tingle. What would happen if they did actually touch?

He was taken, a family man. Probably a married man. So what if a handshake stirred something inside her? There was no possibility of anything more than a handshake happening between them. So she held out her hand and he wrapped his around hers.

Oh, no. It was a mistake. When his large hand enveloped hers she felt it in her belly. After the obligatory second, she pulled her hand out of his and stepped back.

While she didn't feel as though she'd won, this was the best deal she was going to get. And, more importantly, she could get out of this blasted office.

It was so unlike the life she'd imagined for him. There were bookcases full of books about management. Several large, shiny computer screens. And yet there were still traces of the man she had known just the same—a beautiful globe of the earth, modern painting, an African sculpture.

She should turn and leave, but she hesitated. She'd moved on with her life and, until an hour ago, she would have told anyone who asked that her life was just fine, thank you very much. She knew she should have let this lie; it would only aggravate Alessandro's and her already tense professional relationship.

Was there any point asking? His answer wouldn't change anything. Bringing it up would only inflame an old wound. She'd already wasted too many hours trying to use logic to come up with a reason that could possibly excuse Alessandro's behaviour. There were plenty of explanations—but none that would ever be enough. If he'd really loved her as he'd claimed, he would've told her that he had children. He wouldn't have lied.

What if it's your only chance?

The question came out in a rush, not dignified, not even calm. 'Why didn't you tell me about your children?'

He rubbed his face with his palm. 'I couldn't.'

'Why not? It's easy—"I have kids". People say that all the time.'

He looked down at nothing in particular on his black boot. 'I thought it was best.'

'Best for you, you mean.' Her tone was bitter, but she didn't care. All the hurt, the pain and the confusion of that time was resurfacing and she was powerless to stop it. It was mortifying. She should have been over him years ago.

'No. I didn't tell you because I thought it was best you didn't know.'

She scoffed. 'Yes, it's much easier to seduce someone if you lie about having a family.'

'No, Rose, it wasn't like that. I didn't want to ruin your life too.'

'What are you even talking about? You did hurt me.' Her heart was racing in her throat and her hands were shaking. This wasn't how this had been meant to go. She hadn't meant to let him know how much he had hurt her. She should leave before she said anything else.

'I didn't mean to, honestly. If there had been any other way... Please believe me.'

'If you weren't free to have a relationship, you should have told me from the beginning.'

'I was free. When we met.'

'You expect me to believe you didn't know about your children?'

'Yes, I knew about them. But, Rose, they aren't mine.'

CHAPTER THREE

ROSE LAUGHED, a sad, cynical laugh. 'You just called them your children; I saw pictures… I can't believe a single thing you say, can I?'

'They are my children, for all intents and purposes. But by blood they are my niece and nephew.'

His answer knocked the breath out of her. He'd had an older brother… Alessandro hadn't told her much about him, nor about the rest of his family.

'Your brother's children?'

Alessandro nodded.

'What happened to your brother?'

'He was killed with his wife in a car crash.'

The pieces clicked into place.

'The day you left Athens.' It was a statement not a question. She was as sure of that as she was sure she would find ancient ruins beneath this island.

He stared at her for an age, jaw set, eyes hard, before he finally, slowly, lowered his dark head in a quiet nod.

She exhaled several breaths loudly.

'That's why you came back here? That's why you really left Athens so suddenly?'

He nodded again.

'Oh, Alessandro, why didn't you just tell me?'

'I had to leave quickly.'

That was plausible and yet…

'The twins. They were two years old,' he continued.

'When their parents were killed?'

He nodded as though he didn't trust himself to speak. She didn't blame him. She was finding it hard to speak herself.

'Oh, Alessandro, I don't know what to say.'

He waved her attempt at sympathy away and her heart broke a little more. She felt helpless. She wanted to reach out and touch him, hug him, but no—touch was impossible.

In all the scenarios she'd imagined, all the reasons she'd dreamt up for him leaving, none of them had involved a family tragedy that necessitated him rushing back home.

In almost every scenario he had simply chosen to leave her. Had rejected her.

She'd assumed the worst of him.

Did that say as much about her insecurities as it did about him? She knew that her father's abandonment had scarred her, but had it affected her to the point that she couldn't believe someone might have a different, even innocent, explanation for leaving?

No. Alessandro had told her, point blank, their lives were on different paths. He hadn't told her about his brother. And she'd seen the photos of him and the kids.

It wasn't her fault she hadn't known the truth.

'You still could have told me.'

He was still studying his shoe, looking out of the window, looking at anything but her.

'There was no need to tell you.'

'Yeah, I get it. I was just a fling. There was no need to tell me anything about you.'

'No, Rose, no.' He went to her now, his eyes urgent. He wrapped his hand around her elbow and the world shrank to just the two of them. Warmth spread up her arm, to her shoulder and her chest.

'No. I didn't tell you because I knew you, I knew your

dreams for the future. I knew you didn't want to be stuck on a tiny island with me raising two kids who weren't your own. I didn't *want* to lie to you.'

'Where are the twins now? They must be...' She did a quick calculation. 'Fourteen or fifteen years old.'

'They turn sixteen next week. They live here, with me and my grandmother.'

'You raised them?'

'With my *yiayia*, yes.'

It was a lot to take in.

It sounded noble, but he still could have told her. 'All these years I believed you'd just rejected me, walked out on me. I assumed there was another woman. I assumed...' She couldn't even say it aloud.

I assumed that everything you'd told me was a lie. I assumed I wasn't good enough.

'I would have understood; it would have...'

It would have eased the pain.

She shook her head; she wasn't ready to admit the pain he'd caused her.

'I did what I thought was best. For you.'

'It's pretty presumptuous for you to decide what's best for me.'

'We were so close, it was so hard for me to leave you. It would've been harder if you'd had to leave me too.'

'I don't understand what you mean.'

He ran his hands through his dark hair, the gesture making it stick up and look slightly wild.

'Because you didn't want the life that I was destined for. You wanted to travel, be a free spirt, explore the world. You didn't want to be the wife of a businessman, stuck in the one place.'

He was right. They'd spoken about this in Athens when they'd discussed their dreams and wishes for the future. Her dream had never included comfortable domesticity.

'I couldn't bear to hear you tell me that you didn't want to spend your life with me.'

'You still could have asked.' Her voice was quiet.

He placed his hands on his hips. 'And what would you have said?'

'I would have…' *I would have wanted to be with you.* One question they had never asked one another—indeed, one question she had never asked herself—was, what would she have given up to be with him?

And she didn't know the answer.

'I would have had a difficult decision to make. But we could have made it together. Unless…' The chill slipped down her spine despite the summer heat. 'Unless you simply didn't want to be with me.'

Alessandro looked down.

Right. She had been right all along. He might have had a better excuse for not contacting her than she had ever believed, but the reason he'd left was still the same.

He didn't want a future with her.

Not then.

Not now.

CHAPTER FOUR

ROSE KICKED THE ground as she made her way back to the dig. The dig that would, hopefully, jeopardise his new plans. And put the livelihoods of half the island at risk. Ruin his niece's and nephew's future.

Gah! He was trying to guilt her into abandoning the search and that was not going to work. She would not feel guilty about it; there was a possibility of a world-changing historical find.

Admittedly, the chance wasn't great, but the rewards if she did find something would be remarkable. Not material wealth—she didn't care much for that—but the thrill of discovering something, figuring out what it was and learning from it. The chance to shape what everyone knew about the history of ancient Greece? That was priceless.

Gabriel looked up when she arrived back. 'Is everything okay?'

'I sorted it,' Rose replied. 'He's not happy we're here, but he doesn't have much of a choice. He's given us six weeks.'

'Six weeks? And what if we're not finished?' Gabriel gave her a doubting look.

'Look, let's cross that bridge when we come to it.'

She didn't tell him about her suspicion that the museum might cut off their funding well before that if they hadn't made any progress. But if they found something, even something small, then the museum might have more influence with Alessandro. She wouldn't get too far ahead of herself and concentrate on the present.

They had divided the area into portions and were concentrating on one section at a time, removing each layer of sediment carefully. So far, she estimated they had removed about nearly a quarter of a ton of dirt and this might just be the beginning. But with every trowel-full, every scrape, every bucket load, there was a little hope.

Rose worked until the light faded and she could work no more, as she tended to do when she was in the middle of a project. She found it hard to stop when she was in the flow. She'd have to look into getting some lights rigged up to extend her working hours. Particularly as she was running against the clock.

When the light and her team had gone, she walked back to the room where she was staying. She was sharing it with two younger women, students who were part of the team. They were lying on their bunks chatting about some men they'd met the night before.

Good luck to them. She wanted to stop them and warn them against a summer romance, lest the subject of that romance turn up in their lives over a decade later and throw them into a spin.

But she didn't.

She took a quick shower to wash the dust of the day away. Clean but hungry, she took her laptop down to the taverna her landlady, Myra, had recommended. She ordered a glass of white wine and a plate of stuffed grape leaves, fried aubergine and tzatziki and looked up Alessandro Andino online.

And this time she didn't close her laptop lid at the first photo of Alessandro with the two children but read everything carefully.

It was all true.

Alessandro Andino was the Managing Director of Aster

Hotels, a hotel chain stretching over the Ionian Islands and down the west coast of Greece. The brand was famous for its luxury eco-friendly hotels and boutique resorts that gave the guests the full Greek island experience without the partying and the crowds. It was a family business, established by Alessandro's grandfather and run in turn by his father and then his brother.

She'd heard of Aster Hotels—she'd even stayed in one in Santorini once—but she'd never realised they were owned by Alessandro's family.

Why would she know? He hadn't mentioned it. All he'd told her was that his parents were dead.

There seemed to be a lot of things Alessandro hadn't mentioned about his family.

She found a recent feature on him in a glossy magazine. It related the story of the tragic death of his brother and sister-in-law. A semi-trailer had crossed to the wrong side of the road, killing them both instantly and leaving their two-year-old twins orphaned in an instant. Alessandro had dedicated himself to raising the twins and running the hotel empire. The article spoke about his game-changing ideas and how his practices were influencing other operators to rethink the hospitality business in a sustainable way, not just in Greece but all over the world.

He had been successful and influential.

But it was not the life she had imagined for him.

It was not the life he'd imagined for himself.

He hadn't lied to her about his passions. The relief she felt at that was still marred by the fact that he hadn't been completely open with her either. He still could have told her about his brother. She didn't know what she would have done, but he shouldn't have left her without an explanation.

The customers in the taverna came and went around her. The wooden table was covered in a checked blue-and-white cloth. She sat inside, but next to a window that opened out onto the small square and other tables. The place was lit up with lanterns and smelt of candles and seafood. She bit into her fried aubergine with a satisfying crunch and her mouth filled with soft goodness.

Would it have made any difference, knowing what had happened to him? It would've saved her all the speculation, all the hurt. Yes, the pain would have been less acute if he'd told her he was leaving her to raise his niece and nephew, and not two children of his own he hadn't told her about.

You might have followed him.

Maybe. She was so in love with him, consumed by him. In the crazy storm of new love, who knew what she might have given up to be with him?

Maybe *he* was right. That by leaving without a word he'd been doing her a favour and saving her from having to make the decision. He knew she wasn't looking to settle down, help him raise twins on a small Greek island and run a hotel chain. But, with him knowing what he knew about her, she might have felt obliged to. And then there was that comment he'd made that even now she couldn't quite understand.

It was so hard for me to leave you. It would've been harder if you'd had to leave me too.

What on earth had he meant by that? Had he meant that by sparing her the decision, he had spared her having to break up with him? He'd also spared himself having to be dumped by her. That wasn't a real excuse; he must have known he was hurting her. No matter how noble he thought he was being, he should have discussed the matter with her. He could dress it up however he wanted, but he'd still been untruthful.

She groaned quietly to herself.

Thinking about him, her limbs tingled even now. The sensation of his voice was like the best chocolate melting on her tongue, sliding through her body. The last vestiges of his youthful roundness had slipped away over the years, leaving his jaw lean, his cheekbones defined and his eyes steely. Responsibility had made his back straighter, his shoulders squared and his demeanour determined. And yet…for a few brief moments, when he'd laughed or when he'd grinned and shrugged, she'd caught a glimpse of the Alessandro she had known. And loved.

No matter his reason, he'd still made the decision without her and that was not what couples did, was it? If he had truly and properly loved her he would have told her he was leaving and why.

He'd left her, abandoned her for another family. Just as her father had.

Knowing that he had a good reason for leaving didn't change anything; they still didn't have a future. Alessandro's life was here, raising his niece and nephew and running a string of hotels. Further, he had plans to extend one of those hotels.

On the same ground where her ruins might lie.

Their lives were still heading in opposite directions. He was determined to build this hotel, no matter what she might find. And he was determined she would not get in his way.

'What's the matter, Ali?' Alessandro's grandmother asked him that evening at dinner.

He made a point of joining his grandmother, Lucas and Ana every evening when he was at home. Business often took him elsewhere but he looked forward to these evenings with just the four of them. Yiayia didn't cook a lot any more, and he'd hired a housekeeper, Angelina, to help them all out during the day, but in the evenings it was just family.

'Nothing's the matter,' he replied.

'You're quiet this evening. And Ana said you looked furious this afternoon when you brought a pretty redhead into your office. The one who is staying in the village at Myra's.'

Alessandro looked at his niece. She was smirking.

'The redhead…' He didn't repeat 'pretty'. Apart from anything, 'pretty' didn't accurately describe her. Rose was more than pretty—she was beautiful. Heart-in-the-throat, jaw-to-the-ground beautiful. 'Is an archaeologist who wants to fully excavate the site we're building on.'

'But she is pretty?' his grandmother said.

'Yiayia, it doesn't matter what she looks like, she's trying to stop the new build.'

'Ah, so she is, then. But they have to do a survey. It's the law.'

'Yes, but it was just meant to be a survey. A formality.' Theo wouldn't have waited until the last minute to get the survey. Theo would have been onto it earlier. Theo, the brilliant businessman. Theo, the favourite son. Theo had never been the disappointment Alessandro always was. 'And now she wants to dig deeper. She wants to hold up the build with a full excavation. She thinks she's going to find ruins from the Bronze Age. She thinks she's going to find something from Homer.'

'Wow! That would be amazing,' Ana said, and he shot her a glare.

'First, she's not going to find anything. That's patently absurd, for so many reasons. The main one being that Homer's stories are fictional. Odysseus, Helen of Troy…none of them existed.'

'You're a bit worked up,' Lucas added.

His pulse had been unpredictable since he'd seen Rose that afternoon. It was now punching out a loud nightclub beat in his temples. It didn't help that his family, the very people he was doing all this for, were not on his side. He rubbed his forehead but found no relief.

'Of course I'm worked up. The whole project is being delayed by this nonsense.'

His family looked at him silently. His heart sometimes

caught in his throat when he looked at the children. He didn't know how a real parent could have loved two kids more. The two toddlers he'd found on his return to Paxos were now young adults, tall, long-limbed and unaware of how beautiful youth looked on them. He was doing this for them to protect their inheritance, to give them everything their parents should have given them. To prove that, even though he'd made mistakes, he wasn't a complete disappointment to the family.

'Don't you all care? I'm doing this all for you. For the island. So you children have a future here.'

He didn't add, *It was your father's dream to extend this hotel, the first Aster Hotel.*

Alessandro had waited years for a chance to buy the land that bordered the existing hotel. Theo had always dreamed of extending the Andino offering on Paxos. Alessandro owed this to the village, to the people who had supported his family and him when tragedy had struck them. The people of Ninos had rallied round and helped Yiayia and him raise the twins.

'We care, we care,' they mumbled and looked at their plates.

'We know what you do for us.' Yiayia rubbed his arm. 'You just seem... I don't know. You've handled stress before, but you don't usually look like this.'

'Like what?' he snapped.

'Like you might bite our heads off.'

He looked at his niece and nephew properly. Ana was watching him, questions filling her beautiful dark eyes. Lucas's focus was firmly on his plate and his food.

He loved these children with all his heart. While taking on his brother's kids had certainly not been part of his grand plan, it had been the greatest privilege and pleasure of his life to get to raise them and love them.

They were bright, dynamic and funny, even when they were challenging; he loved them with all his heart. These children had soothed his heart and reminded him why he had made the right decision all those years ago in not telling Rose that he was leaving.

Despite what she thought, he *had* wanted a future with her. For several glorious weeks in a balmy Athens summer he had thought of nothing but being with Rose, loving Rose, spending his life with her.

But it wasn't to be. And he had saved her from a choice that would have ended up hurting one of them, one way or another. She might not have known it then, and she might not realise it now, but by leaving her he'd ensured she had the life she wanted, the career she loved. He wasn't responsible for ruining her dreams or her life. She hadn't had to give up the career she wanted to fulfil a duty. They way he had.

'There is nothing more important than your family.' His father's last words to him still echoed in Alessandro's ears, even after all this time.

He pushed back his chair and picked up his plate.

'I just need some air. I'm going for a walk.'

While he would never admit that Rose was his destination, he wasn't surprised when his feet led him to Myra's B&B. Myra smiled and said, 'Oh yes, she's very pretty. She's gone to Joe's. You can probably find her there most evenings.'

Alessandro thanked her and she waved after him, yelling at him to, 'Have a good evening. Don't do anything I wouldn't do!' before dissolving into laughter.

These people… It was not just his own family but the others in the village who were fixated on the fact that Rose was pretty. Very pretty. Couldn't they see she was out to destroy the plans for the island? If Rose got her way, the site for his new hotel would be a muddy dirt pit for the next decade. Myra's B&B might do a fine trade, but his hotel would bring even more opportunities for everyone. More tourists would

mean more restaurants, cafés and tavernas; more boat operators, more shops.

And more shops, restaurants and boat operators would mean
more customers for Myra too.

Ana's words had shaken him the most. She was excited
about the prospect of Rose finding some ruins on their land,
even knowing it would halt the plans to build the hotel. And, if
his own family were seduced by the idea, others would be too.

He had to do more than just sit on his hands and wait out the
next six weeks. Even if finding anything remotely connected to
Homer was impossible, she might find something else. Greece
was littered with ancient ruins, and someone doing the survey
had clearly thought there was something interesting lurking
down there. Discovery of anything more than a couple of hundred years' old could put an end to the whole project.

The land had not been cheap. The build itself was going
to be expensive as well; architecturally designed for energy
efficiency, using recycled, repurposed material. The money
wasn't the only thing: he would lose a significant portion of
the children's inheritance, but he might be able to use some
of his money to make it up. But expanding the hotel had been
his father's plan and Theo's dream. The plan he'd talked about
since Arianna had first become pregnant with the twins.

*We must leave them a legacy on Paxos. They must have a
home here always.*

He had a family legacy to protect and he needed a plan.

The plan hadn't come to him by the time he entered Joe's,
but no doubt it would when he saw her.

No such luck.

Rose was sitting in a booth near a window, laptop in front
of her. Unlike this afternoon, when her hair had been tied
back in a loose bun, it was now loose and flowed around her
shoulders in thick, amber waves that caught the candlelight.

Beautiful.

Even that word didn't do her justice.

He remembered the first time he'd seen her. He'd literally frozen on the spot mid-turn on his way out of a lecture theatre.

'Alessandro!' Joe called, regrettably alerting Rose to his presence. She shut her laptop lid as soon as she saw him.

Interesting.

There was something on her screen she didn't want him to see. No doubt she had been checking out his story about his dead brother, his orphaned family.

She hadn't known before today, he realised with a pang that felt a bit like guilt. No, he had nothing to feel guilty about! He had raised his brother's orphaned twins. He had run the hotel chain to hand over to them one day.

The Andino family, while successful, liked to keep a reasonably low profile and he was particularly careful about keeping the children out of the press as much as he could. A recent interview he'd given to a magazine was the first time he'd openly discussed his brother's death. But maybe, he allowed, he had assumed that at some point Rose would have figured out the truth, almost as though he'd been expecting her to turn up one day.

You've been waiting for her.

Yes, maybe at the beginning he had wondered if she would turn up on his doorstep, angry at him for not telling her why he had left, having figured it out.

But no. The plan had been for her not to figure it out. The plan had been for her to be able to get on with her life. Not have it interrupted, like his had been.

You were not honest with her. You can hardly blame her. Maybe you just aren't as famous as you think you are.

He had looked her up, many times, on those days he was feeling particularly low. On the anniversary. When an important deal fell through. When Yiayia was unwell. He knew that she'd earned her doctorate, been involved in several significant discoveries and published well-received papers. She was living the life she had always planned.

He hadn't been able to learn much about her personal life; she'd kept that very private. But photos he had seen of her with other men—maybe colleagues, maybe lovers—had made his stomach churn.

Alessandro asked Joe for a drink for himself and another for Rose. He walked to her table. 'May I join you?'

She slipped her laptop into her bag and motioned to the spare chair.

'You were working late,' he said.

'I've got a lot to do. I've only got six weeks.' She smiled at him and he felt it warm his bones. 'I'm going to order some lights in, which will give us more time. We're lucky it's summer, so we have more daylight, but it would be good to get in a few extra hours at each end of the day.'

She was seriously determined. For a moment he wondered if her ambition would be too much for him.

Joe brought over the drinks. Rose picked up her glass and touched it gently to his.

'To old times.'

'Old times,' he repeated, and the memory of those times flooded back: hot nights, sweaty sheets, entangled fingers; promises.

'Your niece and nephew, what are their names?'

Her question shook him back to the present. 'Lucas and Ana.'

'Lovely. Tell me about them.'

The muscles in his shoulders unclenched a little. They weren't going argue, they were just going to talk, like old friends catching up.

'Well, they're teenagers. Full of hormones and angst and belief they're ready to run the world.'

She smiled. 'That sounds about right. Has it been terribly hard, raising them on your own?'

'I haven't been on my own completely. My grandmother's always been there. And everyone in the village—everyone on the island, really. My family's lived here for generations; everyone knew my brother and his wife. Everyone wanted to help me.'

This was true, and yet the financial and emotional burden had fallen primarily to him. He'd always known his grandmother wouldn't be around for ever and then Lucas and Ana would only have him. Another reason why it was so important that he left them comfortably set up for the future.

Not that he had any intention of leaving them, but he did have other family businesses, other hotels, to manage.

'And you? Tell me about you. I thought you wanted to travel. Write.'

He shrugged. He'd almost forgotten those ambitions. He'd buried them deep when his life had abruptly changed direction.

It wasn't all bad; he was healthy and raising two delightful children with his grandmother. As far as life sentences went, he could have done a lot worse. And it turned out he was good at running a business. He might not have been as good as his brother, but he'd done all right. He even, as it turned out, enjoyed it. Who would have known? Not his father, that was for sure.

You're a disappointment, why can't you be as responsible as your brother?

Instead of fading with the years, his father's criticisms were as loud in Alessandro's head as ever. Probably because the hotel extension was at risk. The family's legacy on Paxos was at risk.

'I'm boring,' he said. 'I've been living here raising two kids, keeping a hotel business running. I'm sure you've been doing much more interesting things. Tell me what you've been up to.'

Tell me if you have a boyfriend. Tell me if you're married. Tell me if you have children. He wasn't going ask those questions outright. He wasn't sure he wanted to know the answer.

'Are you still based in Birmingham?'

'I'm in London, actually, but I don't spend a lot of time there.'

That sounded about right. Rose never wanted to be tied down; she always wanted to be ready to find the next discovery.

'After I finished my PhD, I spent some time in Istanbul. Since then I've been travelling wherever opportunities arise—Sicily and then southern Spain.'

'It sounds amazing,' he said, regretting the wistfulness in his voice.

The day he'd received the phone call from his grandmother to tell him about the accident, he'd made the decision not to dwell on a life he wouldn't lead. He hadn't contacted Rose because he hadn't wanted her to feel as though she had to join him. He hadn't wanted two careers to be destroyed that day. Two sets of dreams.

But also because talking to her might just have caused him to break the oath he'd made to dedicate himself to his family. To look after his niece and nephew and to prove to his father that he wasn't selfish. Or disloyal. That he loved his family as much as anyone.

He could feel the memory reaching back into his thoughts again. But now was not the time. He took a deep breath, but it wouldn't leave. He'd been ten, foolish, and had wanted to see how far into the ocean he could swim. Only, he hadn't figured that he'd have to swim back. It was Theo who had come to his rescue, dragging him back to the beach. He'd been freezing, close to unconsciousness, but still alert enough to feel his father shaking him and to hear his words: 'You fool, you nearly got your brother killed.'

Which was why now, after keeping that promise for all these years, he had to be strong. The reasons that kept him from Rose fifteen ago were just as strong now. He had his duty to his family, she had her career. So, even though the need to pick up her hand and press it to his lips might be so overwhelming it was causing his vision to blur, he clenched his hands under the table and simply smiled.

They finished their drink and he followed her out of the warm taverna into the night air, cooled by a fresh breeze off the sea. They stood facing one another, waiting to leave in their opposite directions. A string of coloured lights lit the square and danced across their faces.

He stood only a foot away from her and she felt her body sway towards him. His eyes were so serious and dark, but now she fancied he was smiling. Which didn't make sense.

'Goodnight,' she said, stepping back and needing to put back the distance between them. She needed to get to her room to process the events of the day.

'You should come and stay at the hotel,' he said.

She scoffed. 'I can't afford the hotel.' The Aster might appear low-key but she bet that inside was boutique luxury that earned every one of its five stars.

'I meant, stay as my guest.'

She shook her head. 'I can't do that.'

'You can and you should. For starters, you'd have your own room.'

How did he know she was bunking with the others? While she was used to sharing rooms when she travelled to places to excavate, the other two women were students and good friends. Rose felt like their sensible older sister. Or, worse, their mother.

'And you'll be closer to the site.'

'I can't impose like that. And I really can't afford to pay you for a room.' Her salary from the university was not great but sufficient for her needs. The room she had rented was basic but adequate.

'I'm inviting you as my guest. I don't expect you to pay.'

'Why?' She crossed her arms. The kids might be his niece and nephew, but she still didn't know if there was a Mrs Andino in the picture. Not that it mattered.

'All right, I do have an ulterior motive.'

Her stomach leapt and her body flushed.

'You'll be closer to the site and, with less of a commute, you'll be able to work more. Faster work means you'll be finished quicker.'

A strangely disappointing answer.

'And if you are eating all your meals at the hotel…'

'You're offering to pay for my meals too? No, Alessandro, I couldn't.'

'You keep saying "can't". But you really mean you *won't*.'

'That's true.'

She wanted to dig deeper, probe his true motivation for the invitation. Did he want to be closer to her? How much would she see of him? How far apart would their rooms be? She searched his face for answers and his dark gaze met hers.

Her stomach flipped. Could she stand to sleep so close to him every night or would it drive her to distraction?

'It's less than a five-minute walk from the hotel down to the site. It's nearly twenty minutes to up here. You'd have an extra half-hour a day at least.' His eyes didn't leave hers.

'What do you get out of it?'

'The pleasure of seeing more of you, of course.' His tone was flirtatious, but not serious.

She tore her gaze from his and pretended to laugh. 'Let's not go there.' She was serious. Alessandro was a man you only wanted to get over once and she had used up her turn.

He held up his hands. 'I don't know what you mean.'

'It'll be best for both of us, and our work, if we lay off the flirting, don't you think?'

'If that will make you more comfortable.'

She nodded.

'So is that a yes to the hotel?'

'I still don't understand why you want to help me.'

'Oh, I don't. You've misunderstood—I want you to clear that site and get out of here as soon as possible.' Despite his earlier promise, his flirtatious grin was back. 'Seriously, Rose, I'm trying to make amends for everything. I honestly didn't mean to hurt you and I honestly thought I was doing the right thing by you when I left.'

That was a good reason, she supposed. And she'd save some time each day. And have her own space. But she'd also be closer to Alessandro and she was still undecided about whether that was a good thing or not.

She nodded.

'Great. Pack up your bags and I'll have someone pick them up and bring them to the hotel tomorrow while you're working. And tomorrow evening I'd like to show you around Paxos.'

Doubt stirred in her belly along with something else— danger.

'But why?'

He looked down at her and this time his eyes were serious. 'I am truly, truly sorry for leaving without a word. And despite everything we are old friends. And hospitality is my business. I would like to extend the hospitality to you. You can't work twenty-four hours a day.'

'Maybe I can,' she said, still unsure about whether seeing Alessandro was the best way to spend her spare time.

'You love to eat. You can't have changed that much.'

His reference to his knowledge of her from the past threw her off-guard. She did love food. And she loved Greek food. She salivated, despite having only eaten an hour earlier.

'I do have to eat,' she admitted.

'Tomorrow night, then. Seven.'

'It's still light at seven.'

'Exactly. How can I show you around in the dark? I'll see

you tomorrow evening.' He nodded and turned before she could say anything else.

Had she just agreed to move into his hotel? And go on a date?

Her heart was beating in her throat and her body felt strange, full of nervous energy. Or something else. He'd invited her to stay at his hotel. *That's because you're working on his land and he's extending his hospitality.* His motive was probably what he said it was: to save her time and let her leave the island as soon as possible.

But what if he was motivated by something else? By the very thing that had brought them together in the first place—a deep, irresistible connection? An overwhelming attraction. No, that could never be. He'd lied to her. Maybe not in the way she'd originally thought, but she certainly couldn't trust him with her body again. Let alone her heart.

A hotel room of her own would be more comfortable than the bottom bunk she was currently sleeping on. It would also give her some space from the others working on the site.

But you'll be closer to him. You might meet his family.

And his wanting to take her to dinner and show her around the island—what could possibly be his motivation for that?

CHAPTER FIVE

ALESSANDRO SLEPT BADLY, waking every hour with some other snippet of the previous night's conversation replaying in his head. Images of Rose flashed across his mind, making his heart race and his body sweat. Her light-brown eyes were penetrating, challenging, furious.

He'd fallen asleep again and this time had seen her laughing, her mouth full and wide, her golden eyes bright. But that memory wasn't from yesterday, it was from fourteen years ago in Athens. Before he'd broken her heart.

He'd told himself she would have got over him pretty quickly. It was difficult to imagine that many good men would not have crossed her path, desperate to spend their lives with her. And he, himself, was far from perfect.

But yesterday he'd begun to doubt. Despite her best efforts, the hurt and confusion had been apparent on her face. She'd really never known why he'd left, and for the first time he'd questioned his decision to break up with her without giving her the full story.

It had been the hardest conversation of his life. It had taken him days to work up the courage to call her and say what had needed to be said. *We're on different paths, we need to go in our own directions...* His chest still ached remembering that day.

Her words from the day before gnawed at him. He hated to admit it, but she had a point: it had been easier to hide behind the excuse that he'd made a noble choice by leaving without a word. But, really, he hadn't wanted to hear her say, 'No, I won't come to you.'

Or, worse, he hadn't wanted her to come to live with them, regret it and change her mind, not only leaving him but the twins as well.

He'd never had a serious girlfriend for that very reason: the risk that the twins would become attached to her and then break their hearts if she left. The children's cries for their parents who would never return still rang in his ears. They'd been old enough to know their parents were gone, too young to understand why. He wasn't going to do that to them again. So his relationships had remained light, casual and commitment-free.

Maybe he was mad to have invited Rose to stay at the hotel. Maybe she was right to be suspicious. He did have an ulterior motive for wanting her close. But it wasn't what she thought. It wasn't to ingratiate his way back into her bed.

He would show her how important his business was. He would show her how important his family was and why he'd had to break up with her. It wasn't because he was disloyal, but just the opposite. He'd left her because he'd had to protect his family.

Two sets of eyes looked up at him when he walked into the kitchen, Yiayia's and Ana's. It was as though they knew he had something to tell them.

'I'll let Angelina know, but I've asked Rose to come and stay while she's here.'

'Here?' Yiayia asked.

'Yes, in the flat.'

'Not the hotel?'

'She's an old friend.'

His grandmother and niece exchanged looks. Their silent conversation, communicated with eyebrows and head tilts, went something like, *See, I told you he knew her.*

No, you told me he liked her.
Same difference.
Not at all!

'We will make her very comfortable,' Yiayia said aloud.

'Thank you.' Then, as an afterthought he wasn't sure how to explain, 'And you will…?'

'We'll behave,' Ana said and they both laughed.

After breakfast, he went to his office for a few teleconferences. Mid-morning his phone rang and, noticing the number was from, Demetri, his builder, his heart rate accelerated.

'So I hear you're having some difficulty getting the final approvals.'

Good news travelled fast. 'Not difficulty. There's simply been a slight delay, that's all.'

'How slight?'

'A couple of weeks. At most.' Demetri didn't need to know about the deal he'd made with Rose. He'd convince her to take her pointless search for Odysseus elsewhere in the Ionian Sea.

'You know it will throw all the suppliers out. We've got deliveries starting in two weeks. We're due to break ground in a month.'

The man's impertinence annoyed him. Who did he think he was? Alessandro was the one whose project was on the line.

'I know that,' he said through a jaw clenched as tightly as the deadline he was facing.

'So what do I tell them?'

'Who?'

'The suppliers. Should they still deliver in two weeks?'

Alessandro let out a long sigh. The steel beams might sit on the site longer than planned. Payment would be due on them. The astronomical mortgage he'd taken over the land would increase, as would the repayments. But if he didn't give the go-ahead he'd loose his window with the suppliers. Getting building material shipped from the mainland was already a nightmare. And if the build was delayed? He'd be stuck with a pile of steel frames for a few extra weeks.

'Yes, they should still deliver.'

'Can I get that in writing?'

'What? No, you cannot. My word will suffice.'

Alessandro hit 'end call' with a satisfying jab and threw the phone on his desk.

In writing? *In writing?* His word as a businessman had never been questioned. Nor had his brother's, his father's or his father's father's.

Why would this man question his?

Because you're not your father. And you're not Theo. You're the replacement. Second best. You're just the back-up, the great disappointment. The irresponsible one.

He just had to hope that Rose would finish her search sooner rather than later.

A knock at the door nudged him out of his reverie. His grandmother entered his office bearing a cup of steaming black coffee. His heart rate hadn't returned to healthy levels since his conversation with Demetri, but it was good to see her.

'Thank you, Yiayia, are you having one?'

She waved her hand dismissively. 'I've had three already. That's probably enough.'

He laughed. Three cups of her strong black coffee probably was enough for anyone, but particularly an eighty-four-year-old. As a rule, he tried not to notice that she was getting older, frailer. In the usual course of events it was easy; he stuck his head in the proverbial sand. But some days, such as if he'd just returned from a trip away, her frailty hit him like a gut punch.

She still has years to go.

Yet the rest of his family had all died young. His own mother had passed way after a short fight with cancer when he'd only been four—barely older than Ana and Lucas had

been when their mother had died. And his father had suffered
a stroke when Alessandro had been fifteen. Genetics were not
on his family's side.

You will build this hotel… You will make them all proud.

'Busy morning?' she asked.

'Have a seat,' he said, and she pulled out the chair.

'What's going on?'

'The delay in the certification is having flow-on effects.'

She nodded. 'But it shouldn't take long, should it?'

'No…but…' She was right. It was a delay, that was all. Just
a slight one.

'But what if she finds something?' she asked.

'Yeah,' he admitted.

'Is that likely?'

'I don't think for a second she's going to find Odysseus' palace. But their scans showed something. Whether that's from
the nineteenth century AD or the nineteenth century BC, we
won't know until they dig further.'

'And if they do find something important?'

'Then we won't be able to build on the land for years. Decades, probably.'

'So, we build somewhere else.'

'Yiayia, you know there's nowhere else. Not so close to the
hotel. A lot of money is tied up in this project.' He waved his
hand in the direction of the site.

'You have other money.'

He did. He could use some of his own money to make up
the losses. But that was a technicality only—he saw his own
money also as the twins' money, the family money. He wanted
to leave the family business in a better state than he found it.
It was his duty.

'Besides, you know it isn't just the money. This was Theo's
plan. It was Father's plan. They always wanted the family to
have this connection to Paxos. And their kids as well.'

'What about your kids, *kamari mou*?'

His kids? The thought had never occurred to him. He was never going to bring girlfriends in and out of the twins' lives—he wasn't going to let them become attached to someone they might lose again.

'Lucas and Ana are my kids, Yiayia. You know that.'

'They'll be grown and flown before long, you know. Then what for you? Thirty-eight is still young.'

'They're going to need me a while yet. It'll be years before they can take over the business. Particularly with nonsense like searches for artefacts that don't exist. What would you do, Yiayia?'

'First, I wouldn't worry so much. It will all work out.'

'How?'

'You'll find a way.' She gave him a wide smile.

Her confidence was that of a loving grandmother—blind and not reassuring at all.

That evening, it was with not a small amount of trepidation that Rose climbed up the small hill from the dig to the hotel. The Aster was not obviously a hotel but looked like a collection of villas, even a small village, spread out over the crest of the hill. The single-storey buildings were painted white, with terracotta roofs. Bougainvillea bushes hung over the paved pathways and the air smelt of the oregano and mint plants that filled the garden beds.

She wandered around, looking for a reception area, and stumbled across the building he had taken her to yesterday. Alessandro was nowhere to be seen, but an elderly lady was sitting in a chair in the shade and two teenagers were sitting with her. The boy was looking at his phone and the girl was reading a book.

The twins.

They looked to be the right age. If they were the twins, she had found his home, but she needed to be at the hotel proper. She turned.

'Excuse me,' said the woman, in heavily accented but perfect English. 'Are you Miss Rose?'

She stopped. 'Yes, I was looking for Alessan… I mean, Mr Andino.'

'We call him Uncle Ali,' the girl said.

'Or Boofhead,' said the boy, and they both laughed.

The woman, presumably their grandmother, waved at them to stop and stood slowly and with effort.

Rose moved towards her. 'Don't get up; just tell me where I might find him.'

'He's out, but I'll show you your room.'

'I really don't want to impose.'

'No, not at all. We're glad you've come to stay. Come on. Your bags are here already. I am Anastasia; these are my great-grandchildren, Lucas and Ana.'

Anastasia and Ana. They must have followed the Greek tradition of naming children after their maternal grandmothers, but, sadly, there were two generations missing between these two women.

She followed them through a large wooden door and into a courtyard paved with cobblestones. A few bright-blue doors led off the courtyard.

'This is you,' Anastasia said, pushing one open and revealing a small, comfortable room. 'You have a bathroom and your own terrace. Our kitchen and living area are through there.' She pointed across the courtyard to a small garden, and a patio covered by a trellis that was in turn covered with more bougainvillea. 'Please, make yourself at home.'

'And our pool is through there, but be careful, because Lucas pees in it,' Ana said.

Lucas hit his sister. She screamed and Alessandro approached, red-faced and furious 'What's going on?'

'Nothing, Ali'

'You're yelling and punching one another in front of our guest.'

'Come, come.' Anastasia ushered the teenagers away, leaving Rose alone with Alessandro.

'I'm sorry about them. They behave most of the time.'

'It's fine, they're just kids.'

'But old enough to know better.'

His anxiousness at the twins' behaviour was strangely endearing. She wanted to reach out and reassure him by touching his arm, or wrapping her arms around him. She stepped towards him and looked into his eyes. She saw shock and surprise and pushed her arms firmly down by her side.

He led her into a bright, beautiful room. Bay windows faced out onto a garden and fresh flowers sat on table next to the king-sized bed.

'Will this be comfortable?' he asked, with a slight but still perceptible tremor in his voice. The room was lovely, but it was not exactly what she'd expected. It was not in the hotel, but a room that was part of the family home.

'This is your home, not the hotel.'

'It's attached to the hotel.'

'But this…' *It's beautiful, what are complaining about?* 'It's your home.'

She would be closer to Alessandro than he'd led her to believe. She'd hardly be able to avoid him. And how far away was his bedroom? Not that she would ask that. And, besides, she didn't know if he shared his bedroom with anyone.

'Are you worried about privacy?'

Heavens, no. She didn't need privacy beyond her own room and bathroom. This was already more luxurious than most digs. 'I've got more privacy here than at Myra's with the others.'

'Then it's my family. I am so sorry, I will speak to them.'

'No, not at all.' His grandmother seemed lovely and the kids active and precocious, as teenagers should be.

'Who else lives here?' she asked.

He considered her through narrowed eyes.

'Just me, my grandmother and the twins. Our rooms are across the courtyard, in the main building.'

Just his family and him. He did not appear to have a partner. Or children of his own.

Alessandro hadn't been sleeping his way around the world, as she'd assumed.

Strangely, the truth was painful, but in a different, bittersweet way. He hadn't left her for other women, he'd left her to be a father for these children who were not his own. He hadn't left because he was a scoundrel, he'd left her to be a good man.

And the ache that left in her chest somehow hurt more.

'Sorry, I… That is, thank you, Alessandro. It's very generous of you to let me stay.'

He nodded. 'I'll let you freshen up.' They both looked down at her loose beige trousers and white shirt, now dusty with dirt. 'And then, if you like, I would like to take you for dinner.'

CHAPTER SIX

ROSE WASHED THE dirt of the day away with a quick shower and put on a long, flowing dress that was covered in a pretty blue-and-white pattern. The colours had reminded her of Greece, so she'd packed it. When she had, she hadn't had the slightest inkling that its first outing would be on a dinner date with her old flame.

Date? No. This was not a date. It was a business matter. She was here for work and he owned the land on which she was digging.

A purely professional outing.

Hair brushed, lipstick on, she took a last look in the mirror and a deep breath before walking out of her room, uncertain where she should go to meet him.

She didn't need to worry. He was standing in the courtyard, under the bougainvillea, looking at the sky. Not at his phone or watch, but the sky.

He turned at the sound of her door clicking closed. Their eyes met and she felt it in her throat. She wanted to be immune to these reactions, but her body had other ideas.

Alessandro wore white trousers and a blue shirt, the same cornflower-blue of her dress. He had rolled up his sleeves, exposing his smooth, tanned arms. The top two buttons of his shirt were open and his sunglasses were slipped down the neck of it. Their outfits matched as though they had planned it.

Blast. Looks like a date, walks like a date, quacks like a date.

It was only a date if they intended to kiss at the end of it. In a flash, she thought about his lips on hers, her arms around him, how his hard body would feel against hers. No, she had to be careful. She didn't really know the man who was standing before her. She didn't know what else he was hiding. He might be more honourable than she had believed, but that didn't mean she could trust him.

She was not going to kiss him. Ergo, it was not a *date*.

He walked her to a car, a convertible, and opened the passenger-side door for her. She raised an eyebrow. 'Nice car.' When they'd been students, she'd assumed he was as cash-strapped as she'd been.

'May as well enjoy the sunshine.'

She couldn't argue with that.

They drove north, away from the village, and he explained, 'I've made a booking at a place in Gaios, but we have time for a drive around the island.'

'The whole island?'

He laughed. 'Yes, it isn't very big. You can walk most places, but Gaios is about five miles away, so I thought we'd drive.'

He drove her along winding cliff roads that took in the west coast of the island and the setting sun. They drove past beaches and another village. As the road turned at the tip of the island, he pointed across the sea.

'Corfu is over there.' He pointed and his arm crossed her body. He didn't touch her but her skin still tingled.

'Yes, I'd love to visit,' she replied.

'You've never been?'

She shook her head.

'I'll have to take you.'

'Trying to distract me from work?'

'Not at all. I'm merely trying to show you around. Besides, I'm pretty sure Odysseus spent some time there.'

'Now you're making fun of me.'

He clutched his heart. 'I would never. Besides, I'm also pretty sure he's fictional.'

'That isn't very patriotic of you.'

'While I'm pretty sure he did not exist, he is still very important to the Greeks. And to Ionians, in particular. There are some sites in Corfu there that would interest you. We have a hotel there as well, and I do often visit for work. Next time, maybe you could come with me.'

She was determined to find something on her site, but she also didn't want to pass up a chance to discover Corfu.

'We'll see,' was all she could concede.

They drove down the coast and the air blowing over the car was like balm after a day in the sun. He smiled across the console at her but, when he saw she'd seen him, he looked back quickly at the road.

It was beautiful.

He pulled over to the shoulder of the road. 'Look.' He nodded to the ocean. The sun was resting just on top of the horizon. The sky glowed yellow and orange, and the water was bathed in pink. They took a moment to watch it and take in the magnificent view.

'Down there are the blue caves. And the Tripitos Arch. We can't see them from here, only from the water. If you like, I could take you some time.'

She wanted to laugh. 'Don't you have a job? Or is your job distracting me from mine?'

'I do have a job, but I consider it my duty to show all visitors around the island.'

'Oh, you offer all your guests private tours?' Her mouth was dry as she spoke.

'Only the special ones. Hospitality is my business.'

'So, you aren't trying to distract me from my work?'

'No! I can't believe you would suggest such a thing.'

There were two possibilities, she reasoned. Either he was trying to distract her from her work, or he wanted to spend time with her. The second possibility sent a shiver up her spine, despite the warm evening air.

'Let's go,' he said, once the sun had all but disappeared and the horizon seemed to glow from below.

Rose was looking to her right, over the ocean, when the car stopped suddenly and her head hit the head rest with a thump.

'Oof.' She rubbed her head.

A brown goat stood on the road before them. Alessandro honked the horn. The goat looked at the car and she could have sworn it shrugged. Alessandro honked again, but the goat walked in a circle and then sat, resolutely, in the middle of the road. He honked again.

'Do you know the definition of insanity?'

'I'm sure you're about to tell me.'

'Doing the same thing over and over again and expecting a different result.'

He switched the engine off and pushed open the door. He walked over to the goat, waved at it and said something in Greek she didn't understand but was probably, 'Get out of the way.' The goat sat where it was. He pushed the goat's bottom with his foot but the goat just looked annoyed and didn't budge.

Rose opened her door and walked over. 'Shoo,' she said. 'Get out of the way!'

'You think it's an English-speaking goat?'

'It might be. Get off the road, off the road, shoo!' she tried again.

He laughed. 'What was that bit about insanity again?'

She gave him a wry grin.

'Okay, smarty-pants, what do we do?'

'I don't know.'

'You don't?'

'No, I don't.'

'But there are heaps of goats here.'

'And honking usually works.'

He met her eyes and they both laughed.

'We'll just have to stay here,' he said.

'Fine by me,' she replied. Because, truly, there was nowhere else in the world she'd rather be than here, in this stunning place, with Alessandro giving her a smile that was flipping her stomach and her whole world upside down.

Rose tried pushing the goat's bottom with her shoe but it just turned its head and glared at her, then let out an annoyed bleat.

'Maybe it's sick,' he said.

'We should call a vet.'

'There's no vet on the island.'

'Really?'

'There are only a couple of thousand permanent residents here.'

That explained the calm, relaxed, friendly lifestyle. Everyone acted as if they knew one another because they actually all did.

'The island is that small?'

He nodded. 'When the tourists come in summer, it seems like there are many people, but they only stay for a few weeks at a time at most. Or they just come for the day from Corfu. We don't have a vet. We depend on Corfu for a lot of our services.'

That was why the hotel was so important. It wasn't just about his own family, it was about his island family too. The hotel would be a big employer and would fill restaurants and shops besides.

Still, that was unfortunate, but finding ancient ruins was important too.

'Should we turn around? Go back?' she said.

'What if it is sick?'

Alessandro approached slowly, patted the goat's back,

worked his way up to its ears and petted it like he would a dog or cat. He was tender and careful.

'And?'

'It does feel hot. And a bit out of it.'

The goat's eyes were closed slightly, but it might only have looked that way because it was happy to be petted. She imagined Alessandro rubbing the soft skin behind her ears and gulped.

'Do you think it belongs to someone? It seems happy for you to pet it.'

'Maybe, but I don't know who. Not many people live on this side of the island.'

'Are there that many domesticated goats on the island?'

He shrugged. 'Probably.'

They looked at one another and laughed. 'Goats, dogs, cats. You've seen them all.'

He was right; there were cats and dogs everywhere. They looked healthy enough, they were being fed, but they wandered from place to place as if they belonged to everyone and no one.

'I think we should get it to a vet,' he said and, even though her stomach was starting to feel hungry, she agreed.

'How?'

'I'm going to try and pick it up. Open the boot.'

'You can't be serious.'

'Do you have another suggestion?'

'Um…' No. She didn't.

'There should be a blanket in the boot.'

She went to the car, opened the small boot and found a picnic blanket.

He probably uses it for romantic picnics…

She shook the thought away. So what if he did? She would probably return to London in a few weeks and get on with her life without looking back at Alessandro or Paxos.

She passed Alessandro the blanket and he walked round the goat, looking for the best angle.

'Are you sure?' she asked, but he didn't respond.

After studying the goat a moment longer, he threw the blanket over it and grabbed it. The goat squealed but Alessandro had it. He took two steps towards the car and the goat grunted, leapt from his arms and ran off into the olive grove. The momentum of the goat's kick pushed Alessandro back and he landed bottom-down on the road.

She rushed to him and knelt. 'Are you okay?' He wasn't bleeding, but he wasn't talking either. Before she could overthink her actions, she slid her arm around his shoulders. Their faces were next to one another, only a breath away. 'Alessandro, are you hurt?' His shoulders were warm and firm beneath her palm.

His lips were parted, his breath coming fast. He looked into her eyes, pupils dilated. Was he hurt? Or was he, like her, wondering if he should move that inch closer and press his lips to hers? She licked her lips and saw his eyes glance down and notice. His chest rose and fell, and with the exhale he closed his eyes and nodded. 'I'm fine, just winded.'

She leant back, feeling disappointed and foolish. He was just winded, not thinking about kissing her at all.

'You were really worried about it, weren't you?'

He shrugged.

'Are you really okay?'

He rubbed his stomach and arm. 'I think I'll have a bruise or two tomorrow.'

She stood and held out a hand to help him up. He looked at her offered hand and studied it for a moment before he accepted it. Just like their handshake the other day.

His arm was strong and their opposing weights balanced one another out. He released her hand as soon as he was upright and steady. She stretched her fingers out, hands tingling after his touch. Alessandro brushed himself down, took a final look towards the olive grove and said, 'Let's get going.'

Gaios was clustered around a sheltered emerald bay. Brightly coloured buildings lined the waterfront and sailing boats bobbed in the calm blue water.

She had arrived in Gaios by ferry a few days earlier but had not had time to explore before catching the bus to Ninos.

She was glad to return to look around, but she wasn't about to admit that to Alessandro. He was definitely up to something. If that something included a tour of Gaios, and a dinner as good as the restaurants they passed smelt, then she'd go along with it but she was not going to be distracted from her work.

He parked and they walked along the paved streets before stopping at a waterfront restaurant. It was modern and sleek, rather than traditional and rustic. 'It has the best seafood in Paxos.'

He was probably right. She could tell just by the smell that surrounded them and the delicious-looking dishes she saw being delivered to other patrons.

Their table was next to the water, and once they were seated, Alessandro ordered a bottle of champagne.

'Is that all right?' he asked once the waiter had left.

She nodded. She'd never been able to resist champagne and was touched that he remembered.

Looks like a date, walks like a date, quacks like a date.

She breathed in and took a proper look at her surroundings. This place felt a million miles away from her real life; it was even far removed from the site she was digging on. Whatever his motivation for asking her here, there was no doubt that Alessandro had designed a perfect evening.

Apart from the goat.

'How's your arm?' she asked.

He rubbed his shoulder. 'I think I'll live.'

'I'm glad,' she replied, and before she could stop herself she smiled at him warmly.

He met her gaze and returned a smile equally as warm, eyes deep and soulful with enough gravity to pull her in and under.

No!

She dragged her gaze and thoughts away from him and picked up her menu. She thumbed its corner. 'Do you come here often?' The question was lame but it was far better than getting lost in the spell of Alessandro's dark eyes.

'I've been here a few times. The calamari is good.'

'Great, let's have that.' She shut her menu, unsure if she would be able to eat anything, given the way her stomach was twisting itself in knots.

A waiter lit the candles on their table and they sipped their champagne. Sitting across from him, Rose felt memories from their time together in Athens flooding back. She looked over the harbour and tried to push them away.

Perhaps Alessandro was thinking the same thing when he asked, 'Why do you like to dig up the past?'

This was a question she occasionally asked herself. A love of ancient history had led her to archaeology. But Alessandro's question was more abstract than that. He was asking something more fundamental—about her. When they had been together for those brief weeks in Athens, she had told him how her father had left to start a new family when she'd been seven. But she hadn't had the chance to explain to him the gnawing sense of rejection that had followed her through her childhood and teens. The knowledge that she wasn't enough. That she wasn't worthy of love.

As an adult she'd tried to rationalise his behaviour. She'd learnt to understand that people fell out of love. That people did betray their lovers. And that people could also be cowards when it came to ending relationships. That some people simply found it easier to walk away and start a new life without looking back.

But she'd never been able to understand why her father had cut her from his life so completely. The one thing she knew for sure was that she hadn't been enough to get him to stay. She hadn't been important enough for him to want to keep her in his life.

But his question wasn't about her past, it was about her work.

'To understand how we got here. To make sense of the past.' She looked at him for a long time, but not studying his features. Heaven knew they were easy to look at, but looking into his eyes was risky. 'I thought you were interested in that too.'

The smile dropped from his face.

'Maybe; I don't know. Now I don't have that luxury. These days I have to look after the future.'

His comment struck her as condescending. 'Ouch.'

'What?'

'That was a bit harsh.'

'It wasn't mean to be,'

'It sounded like you were suggesting I haven't grown up. Implied that I lack responsibility. I may not have a family, but I have responsibility. To my colleagues, for one. To my profession.'

He narrowed his eyes. 'I'm sorry, Rose, I was under the impression that you didn't want to be tied down.'

'I don't. That is, not with the usual things—mortgage, pets...'

'Boyfriend?'

Had he just asked that? Were they going down *this* conversational route?

'A good relationship shouldn't tie you down, stop you from living the life you want to live,' she said.

'And have you found that?' His tone wasn't demanding,

but soft and hesitant. The question made his voice crack, and her resolve to keep her personal life or lack thereof to herself broke.

'Not at present.' She could have volunteered the fact that, since him, all her relationships had been short-lived. Commenced on the basis that she would soon be leaving to go off somewhere. It felt far too sensitive to admit that. Instead, she asked, 'And you? Are you seeing someone?'

He shook his head and her stomach swooped again.

'No. The twins have already lost enough. I've never wanted to bring someone into the twins' lives.'

She nearly spat out her drink. 'Seriously? You've been celibate since…me?'

The look he gave her made her insides warm. 'I didn't say celibate. I meant there hasn't been anyone serious, long-term.'

He hadn't been in love since her? No, he hadn't said that exactly, just that he hadn't had a serious relationship. Rose was momentarily short of breath, her chest heavy. There hadn't been anyone else since her. Her thoughts were a tangled mess, her emotions more so. On one hand, she was happy that he hadn't loved anyone since her.

Except, she reminded herself, he had. His niece and nephew. He'd left Rose for them in the past and they would be his only priority in the future. It sounded as if he had no intention of starting a serious relationship with any woman, including Rose.

Luckily their food arrived at that point and the delicious smells of the dishes placed on their table totally distracted her from worrying about how she felt about him.

'Riddle me this,' she said once the crispy, tender calamari had satiated her taste buds and the champagne taken the edge off her confusion and heartache. 'According to the Internet…'

'The Internet? That great oracle?'

'According to the Internet, the chain of hotels you own is

very successful, very profitable.' *You're loaded*, she wanted to say. 'Why don't you just buy another block of land?'

He laughed. 'Suitable blocks of land don't just come up all the time. Besides, if you look around, the hotel is on the crest of the hill and overlooks the ocean. The other side is already built up and on the other side is a road. My father tried to buy this block for years. My brother also. It was always their plan and hope to extend the first Aster Hotel.'

She didn't want to say she was sure his father and brother would have understood. Because, even if his dead relatives wouldn't have minded, it was clear that Alessandro very much did. The situation was tricky and sad, but surely ancient ruins trumped the wishes of his deceased brother?

She stopped herself from opening her mouth to say as much. She considered ancient artefacts priceless, but living, breathing people were also important. As an archaeologist, her perspective of what was and wasn't important was often different from that of other people. She knew she wouldn't be on the earth for ever—only the things she did would live on.

'Building on Paxos is expensive—everything has to be shipped in. Literally. And I'll let you in on a secret. I don't own the chain, not entirely. It's split three ways, between the twins and me. I consider myself holding the business on trust for them, for until they're old enough to take it over.'

'You'd be leaving Lucas and Ana in a less advantageous position.'

'If it was just about the money, I would throw my own at it. But it isn't. It's about my father's wishes. And Theo's. It's about the legacy I pass on to the twins. The debt I owe to the village. To the island.'

'What debt?'

'When my brother died, the village rallied around. I couldn't have done it—raised them to be such happy, bright kids—were it not for them. I owe everyone this.'

'But you...you're a great businessman.'

She fancied his face turned red, but that might just have been the candlelight flickering off the table.

'Is that what Google told you?'

'Maybe.'

'Yes, I could make something else work, but not there, in the village. This extension isn't just important to the kids, it's important to everyone who lives in Ninos. Everyone on Paxos. But...'

Alessandro put down his fork and looked out at the water. It was dark now, but the lights reflected across it. 'I have a duty to my family to do this.'

Familial duty. She only understood the absence of it.

When Rose had been twelve she'd found her father's address in her mother's beside drawer. She'd caught a bus and arrived on his doorstep, not knowing what she was going to say. The neighbourhood had been clean and still, the house much larger than the small bungalow where she'd lived with her mother. Before she could knock, she'd seen them—his other family. Two boys: five or six years old, she guessed. And his new wife, who was dark and glamorous, and had put the two boys into a flashy-looking car. Rose had run around the corner and vomited. She still saw the look of disgust on the bystanders' faces.

Duty was something directed at other people. Just like love.

'But you've raised Lucas and Ana, was that not enough?'

He screwed up his face. 'I will never fully discharge my duty to them, to my family.'

It was honourable, but didn't sound at all like the Alessandro she'd once known. The one who'd hardly ever spoken of his family. 'I don't understand.'

'When I was ten, I wanted to see how far I could swim.'

She nodded, unsure where the story was going, but let him speak.

'We were at the beach, near Ninos. I'd recently become a confident swimmer, and I wanted to test how far I could swim, so I swam out and I kept going. When I was spent, I stopped. I could hardly see the beach and hadn't left myself energy to get back.'

'Oh, no. What happened?'

'Theo. Theo found me and dragged me back. I was hardly conscious and he was wrecked. My father was furious.'

'Wasn't he worried?'

'If he was, he showed it by berating me for risking Theo's life. He yelled at me for being irresponsible.'

'That's awful.'

Alessandro shrugged. 'I was never as responsible as Theo, never as smart, never as fast. Never as good.'

'But you were younger. Much younger. Five years?'

'Eight. I don't think it mattered. Theo was just better at everything.'

Rose took a moment to digest all this. It seemed so unfair, so unjust, for a parent to favour one child over another.

That's what your father did, though, isn't it?

Rose played with the stem of her wine glass. 'And you feel a debt to Theo? That's why you want to build the hotel—because he saved you?'

'Yes, but not just for that day. For everything. For looking after me when my father died, supporting my studies. Because he's my family.'

Her heart cracked in two. He'd been carrying this guilt all this time. No wonder he was so determined to pursue this project. She couldn't tell him it was ridiculous that he felt he owed a debt to his brother, because she would have done anything to win her father's love.

'We probably won't find anything,' she said, but it was an attempt at a peace offering, and she hoped she was wrong.

He laughed. 'Then stop looking!'

'You know I can't,' she said.

He nodded. 'I know.'

* * *

They drove back in relative silence, Alessandro occasionally pointing out a sight. Rose occasionally asking what things were. He pulled up to the hotel, which was in darkness.

He walked her to her room, which was across a small courtyard from his own.

If this was a real date, this was where they would kiss.

Looks like a date, walks like a date, quacks like a date.

Her limbs were light, her lips tingling from the kiss they hadn't even shared earlier. But, no, they couldn't kiss. She couldn't let herself fall for him again.

'Thank you very much again.'

'It was a pleasure.'

She raised an eyebrow. 'Even the goat? How's your arm, by the way?'

He smiled wryly and rubbed his chest and arm. 'It'll be fine. This reminds me of our first kiss,' he said. 'Do you remember?'

His question knocked the air out of her. Of course she remembered. She didn't remember many kisses with perfect clarity—the taste, the pressure, the temperature, the look in the eyes—but that first kiss with Alessandro would always be one of them.

She could only nod. Athens... A summer evening, much like now.

'You were wearing blue, just like you are now.'

That was a detail she hadn't retained.

'You wore a black T-shirt. Your hair was...'

He lifted a hand and ruffled the neat cut he wore now, curls tamed. 'Yeah, it was a bit wilder.'

'I like the new cut.'

'You do?' The hope in his voice made her stomach swoop again. *Damn.*

'We'd been walking around the Plaka all night.'

'We'd been talking and walking for hours.' After dinner they had explored empty streets for hours and hours, talking, laughing. It had been one of the most memorable nights of her life. It had been close to dawn when he'd walked her back to her dorm. Even there they'd stood for an hour talking before he'd finally taken her hand.

What had taken them so long? She'd known, and suspected he had too, that they would kiss—and more. She'd even believed, in those pre-dawn hours, that this was the man she with whom would spend her life. So there was no rush. No urgency.

She looked at him now, fully prepared to be pulled into his eyes and under. But the look in his eyes wasn't open and hopeful. It was hard. Closed.

'Good night, Rose,' he said without looking at her.

She expected to feel relief, but was only disappointed. Why bring up their first kiss if he was only going to close her off like that?

Suddenly, she wasn't sure if was worth digging some things up.

CHAPTER SEVEN

ALESSANDRO HADN'T SEEN Rose since they had had dinner that evening in Gaios. He'd travelled to Corfu to attend some meetings and had then flown over to Crete to visit the properties he owned there.

Back on Paxos, after checking in with the kids and his grandmother, his feet led him down the hill and to the dig. To his untrained eye, it appeared that more ground had been levelled, and a few additional trenches were evident. In the hot afternoon sun, most of the team was sitting under a grove of olive trees, sipping water and fanning themselves.

Someone had strung up a green tarpaulin between an olive tree and a post up the hill to offer some protection from the sun. He proceeded down the hill and spotted Rose under the tarp. Her white hat bobbed up and down as she scraped away intently at years of sediment, focused, determined.

Single-minded.

He knew he had to let it play out, let her search for what wasn't there. She wouldn't stop until she was satisfied there was nothing to be found. Ordinarily he'd find that sort of determination impressive. It was just a pity she was exercising it here, on his land. His family's land.

Her sweeping motions were fluid and repetitive and easily hypnotised him into a trance. He could watch her for hours, and he had—on lazy afternoons when they'd sat in the National Gardens, she reading, he pretending to. In the early hours of the morning as her chest had risen and fallen with each sweet breath.

And now.

The sound of a truck pulling up on the road behind him alerted her; she turned and looked up the hill in his direction.

Damn. Caught.

She looked at him but didn't wave. If he walked away without at least speaking to her, she'd know that his sole mission had been to spy on her. He sighed and made his way down the hill.

'Hey,' she greeted him. 'When did you get back?'

'Just this morning.'

The rest of the team stayed where they were under the trees, but fell silent and still, watching and listening.

'Come to spy?'

He needed a purpose for coming down here. Fast.

'No, I just came to see how you are.'

'I'm well. And, no, we haven't struck gold. Or bronze, for that matter.'

He smiled, supposing it was some sort of archaeology joke.

The truck that had arrived moments ago was now reversing loudly and manoeuvring itself into place.

'What's that?' she asked.

The steel: he'd forgotten it was being delivered today.

'I'm not sure,' he lied.

'It looks like it's making a big delivery.'

She wouldn't find anything here, but it did feel insensitive to be flaunting the new building in front of her.

'You know, there are other islands that may have what you're looking for.'

'I've been researching Odysseus for years. There's a lot of evidence suggesting he came here when he left Ithaca.'

'But there are plenty of other islands. Antipaxos. Kefallinia. Trust me, I'm familiar with the area. In fact, I know a special

place that hasn't been explored. I could take you—show you.'
His island. Well, not his exactly, but the place he and Theo
had explored as kids: Erimitírio.

She narrowed her eyes. 'You just want me to waste a day.'

'No, I just want you to have the best chance of finding something.' And taking a day away from the dig would be a bonus.
As would be spending the day with her.

'I can't, I need to stay here.'

'What about tomorrow or Sunday?'

She didn't answer him but he noticed her glance over at the
olive trees and her team.

'You even work on a Sunday?'

'Yes.'

'Is anyone else working Sunday?' he said a little loudly so
her team would hear.

'No!' they shouted happily.

'So you'd be here all by yourself.'

'Someone has to watch it.'

'Do they? You haven't found anything, or have you?'

She clenched her jaw. If she had found something, she'd
have been jubilant; she wouldn't have been able to resist telling him, rubbing it in his face.

'If there's something to be found here you and your team
will find it. But what if there's something somewhere else
and you miss it?'

She shook her head.

'It's a very special place. There are things left by the Venetians, but things older than that. You should let me show you.'

'Couldn't I just get a ferry?'

'Ah, no. Not to this island. No one lives on this island. It's
the sort of place where, if there is treasure to be found, it has
been hidden for millennia.'

Rose's eyes widened.

He had her.

'Is there any other way I can get you to stop asking me?'

He scratched his head. 'Nothing I can think of.'

'Well, okay, maybe. Thank you.'

He hid his smile the best he could.

The island didn't have any Bronze Age ruins, but it was special. It was special to him. It was where his father had taught him to sail, where he'd played and explored with Theo as a kid. He'd even once thought of asking Rose to go there with him. If Theo hadn't died, then he probably would have. They could have camped, spent a romantic night by the fire, made love on the beach.

But, as he reached the top of the hill, his smile faded. This wouldn't be like that. This trip wouldn't be to show Rose the island because he wanted to show her where he'd spent some of the happiest memories of his childhood; he was taking her there to show her a Venetian citadel and a Roman harbour. That was all.

He and Rose were still on two different paths—she had her career and he had his duty to his family. They had no more chance of a future together than they'd had fifteen years ago.

Leaving the site that evening, Rose passed the mountain of steel that had been delivered by the truck that had arrived with Alessandro that afternoon.

As if he hadn't known what they were. Heck, he probably knew exactly how many of them there were and where he planned to put them all.

Never mind, she was getting closer. The ground was getting harder, older. She could just tell. She would show him and he'd have to send those steel frames back to wherever they had come from.

When she arrived back at her room just after dusk, Ana was sitting in the courtyard and jumped up. She looked as though she had been waiting for her. It had become a habit of Ana's

over the past few days, waiting for Rose to get home, stopping
her for a chat. It had started with Ana asking Rose about her
work, and somehow Rose's questions about what Ana liked
best about school had turned into several hours of career ad-
vice. Rose didn't mind one bit; Ana was bright and interested
in everything. It sounded as if she was an excellent student.

'Hi!' Ana said.

'Hello, how are you doing?'

'I'm great,' Ana said, beaming. 'Would you like to come
and have dinner with us?'

'Oh, I... I don't want to intrude.' But the teenager looked so
eager, Rose didn't know if—or how—she could decline. She
didn't have any other plans, her body ached from crouching
in the dirt all day and she didn't feel like walking back up to
the village taverna tonight...

'You aren't. Yiayia said you should. Besides, I don't think
Uncle Ali will be there.'

Her disappointment at that news was tinged with relief; she
didn't want to spend more time with Alessandro than she absolutely had to. The desire to touch him, smell him and taste
him sometimes came close to overwhelming the need to protect her heart.

'Okay, that would be lovely. Thank you.'

'Great, I'll tell the others.' Ana bounced off inside and Rose
went to change.

She'd been had.

Fifteen minutes later, Rose knocked on the door to the family's main house. Ana slid the glass door open and the first
thing Rose noticed was Alessandro, in the kitchen, taking a
steaming dish out of the oven.

'Ali's back! Isn't that great?' Ana said, convincing neither
Alessandro nor Rose that she hadn't tricked them.

'Yes, it's great,' Rose said as sincerely as she could manage. Alessandro turned but she could see the smile on his face.

They sat outside in the courtyard, under the trellis with the bougainvillea that was strung with hundreds of tiny lights. If Alessandro hadn't been there looking gorgeous and happy, then it might have been a restful evening. But every moment she spent with him was tinged with pain; either she was reminded that he didn't want her to find her ruins, or he reminded her of her youth, her heart and everything that had been lost when he'd left Athens.

'Tell me how the dig is going,' Ana said just as Rose's mouth was full.

Rose looked at Alessandro, knowing that talking about the dig in front of him was hardly the most sensitive thing to do.

Ana noticed the look they shared. 'Please just tell me. Why do you think there's something here? Tell me what you hope it will be—in your wildest dreams!'

Rose chewed her mouthful slowly and thoughtfully.

'Go ahead, please tell her,' Alessandro said.

'Oh, I hope it's a palace. Or a temple, maybe. I hope that it is something as old as the Bronze Age.'

'The Bronze Age...that was before the classical age,' Ana said to her brother, who then rolled his eyes.

'I'm not an idiot,' he said.

'Something like Pompeii?'

'Nothing as well preserved as that, given that there's been nowhere near as much volcanic activity here than in the Tyrrhenian Sea.'

'You say that like it's a bad thing,' Lucas said between mouthfuls.

'It's a very good thing for the Ionians, but it means that the chances of finding anything as well-preserved as Pompeii are not high. But that doesn't mean we won't find something of interest.'

Ana was full of questions about how they knew where to dig and how long it would take, which Rose answered politely.

Alessandro glowered, but even Lucas looked as though he was paying attention.

Once everyone had finished their meals, and when Ana took a break between questions, Rose thanked them all very much and pushed back her chair.

'Oh, and it's my birthday on Saturday.'

'And mine,' Lucas grumbled.

'Oh, I completely forgot,' Ana said to her twin brother and laughed.

Alessandro looked at the twins through narrowed eyes, and Rose could tell he was itching to tell them to be polite, but she found the bickering siblings endearing. She didn't have any siblings and, for all their arguing, she could tell they were close and loving.

'You should come to my birthday party,' Ana said.

'*Our* birthday party,' Lucas corrected.

'I'm organising the party,' Ana said.

'It's still my party.'

'Oh, yeah? What have you done for it?'

Alessandro stepped in between his niece and nephew. 'Please don't feel as though you have to come,' he said to Rose.

He didn't want her there.

'It's not just going to be kids, but other old people too,' Ana said. Alessandro buried his face in his hands and his grandmother laughed.

'Oh, I didn't mean that you're old, just that everyone from the village will be there. Please come.'

Maybe it was Alessandro's discomfort, or maybe just how earnest Ana looked, but Rose nodded. 'I'd love to come. Thank you all very much for dinner.'

'I'll walk you out,' Alessandro said.

She was about to tell him that wasn't necessary, but the

other members of the Andino family exchanged complicit smiles, and she judged it was simply easier to let him. They walked together in silence back through the house and to the courtyard.

'That wasn't my idea, you know—to trick you into coming to dinner.'

'Oh, I know. That scheme had fifteen-year-old fingers all over it.'

'I'm sorry.'

'Don't be. *I'm* sorry that she wanted me to talk about my work all night. I'm sure that was just about the last thing you wanted to listen to.'

Before she knew it, they were back to where they'd been the other night, standing in front of her door, wishing one another goodnight. It would have been better if he'd simply let her walk by herself. It was ten metres across an internal courtyard; she would have been safe.

'You don't have to come to the party—I can make up an excuse for you, if you like.'

Ahh, that was it. His real reason for coming out here.

'You don't want me to come?'

'No, I didn't mean that. I only mean that you shouldn't feel obliged to come.'

'I don't. I like Ana. And Lucas. And your grandmother.'

He lifted the corners of his lip. 'They like you too.' He stepped towards her and her body swayed to his. They held each other's gaze. One more step and they would be in each other's arms.

He shook his head. 'I'm sorry, that was wrong. But sometimes I forget myself.'

Her heart dropped. *What's really the problem?* she wanted to ask. *The twins are older now, they aren't babies. In a few years, they'll have finished school.*

But she knew the answer.

The problem, as always, was her.

She wasn't enough. She wasn't enough for him.

Rose could easily work seven days a week, particularly when a deadline was looming. She wasn't sure how serious Alessandro was about his six-week deal. If they found a trace of something before that date, she figured she would be able to get enough people from the museum or even from the village to support the work continuing.

She was more worried about the email from the museum that had dropped into her inbox that morning, notifying her that they would stop funding her at the end of the month. She wasn't so worried about herself; she had some money of her own and enough leave to stay longer if required. But her colleagues would have to leave. They were all dedicated workers, but not so dedicated that they would be happy to work for free. And most of them did, understandably, want to enjoy some of the pleasures Greece had to offer while they were here.

It was four p.m. on a Saturday afternoon and everyone, except for Gabriel and her, had already left for the taverna. They had been focusing on the site where the resistivity meters had been showing shadow. Whatever they were going to find, it would happen soon. Rose's trowel hit something hard. She scraped further and cleared more dirt.

'Look at this,' she said, but Gabriel was already over her shoulder.

'Stone,' he replied.

'Yes, but what sort? Let's clear from here.'

Gabriel knew what he was doing and the pair of them soon had an area about a foot long uncovered. It was all the same piece of smooth rock. And rock that had been smoothed away or cut by someone at some stage. Her heart was racing. This was it.

'What are we going to do?' Gabriel asked.

'Keep going?'

'Don't you have a party to get to?' he reminded her.

It was a relief to have found whatever this was, even though she'd never doubted there would be something here. But it still might prove to be nothing significant. A couple of abandoned slabs. A statue, if they were really lucky.

'You're right.' If Rose was late to the party, Alessandro would no doubt come looking for her. And not for any amorous reasons, but to check up on her.

And once he saw this? There was no need to alert anyone to this unnecessarily when it still might turn out to be nothing.

'So you'll leave now? Promise?' Gabriel asked.

'Yes, but please don't tell anyone just yet. Let's wait until we're sure it's not just a rock.'

He grinned and saluted.

'See you tomorrow,' Rose said.

'No, you won't. Tomorrow's Sunday.'

'Oh.' That was right—Sunday usually followed Saturday.

'And aren't you touring the islands?'

'Yes.' Rose sighed. And she had promised Ana she would go to her birthday party that evening as well. Two doses of Alessandro. One dose might not hurt, two in a row might prove dangerous.

'We can swap if you want to,' Gabriel teased.

She did want to…and yet, she didn't. She had to go sailing with Alessandro now or he'd really get suspicious. And she wasn't ready to tell him about what they had found that afternoon. Not just yet.

And maybe a little part of her was a bit curious about his secret island. It would probably turn out to be nothing and she could tease him about it at her leisure.

'But, hey, let's use one of the tarps to cover the ground.'

'So no one sees?'

'No, in case it rains,' she replied. Gabriel knew as well as she did that the brilliant blue skies above them were not about to release a torrent; it was best if no one got wind of the fact that they had hit their slab. When she knew more, then she would break the news to Alessandro.

Where was she?

The party was in full swing, the band was playing, people were eating and drinking. Half the village was here.

But not Rose.

Ana seemed occupied enough, chatting to her friends, but every now and then she'd look over to him and frown. He couldn't believe Rose would let his niece down.

She'll be here, he told himself. Something must have come up.

Alessandro stood near his grandmother, keeping watch over the comings and goings. Making sure he was on hand to welcome all the guests.

'Where's the lovely Rose?' Yiayia asked.

He ignored the fact that Rose was now known as 'the lovely Rose' and said, 'I don't know, but I'm sure she'll come.'

'Oh, yes, she will. She asked me what gifts she should buy for the twins.'

'She did?' He hoped she didn't feel obliged to. It was awkward enough that she had felt obliged to come to the party at all.

'Yes. Is that surprising?'

'She doesn't know them very well.' His plan to get Rose to know his family had had another effect he stupidly hadn't anticipated—that they might become attached to her.

'But she has been invited to their party—it's polite to bring a gift. I don't understand you sometimes, *kamari mou*.'

'Why not? You've known me since I was born. You understand me better than anyone.'

'Yes, even better than you understand yourself.'

'Then?'

'I don't understand why you're so strange around her.'

He was not awkward around Rose; his grandmother was just digging for information. 'I'm not.'

'You are. You fidget.'

'I what?'

'You fidget. And sway. Like you don't know if you're going forward or backward.'

Her answer surprised him and he didn't know how to respond.

'Well, if I don't know whether I'm going forward or backward, it's because she's thrown a big spanner in my plans. In all our plans. My life is in a holding pattern until her time on the island is up.'

She laughed, 'Oh, Ali, it isn't that. You think you're focusing on the future, but you can't until you deal with the past.'

Deal with the past? He wasn't the one whose head was focused on what was lying under metres of dirt. His head wasn't caught up in ancient times.

'That's ridiculous, I don't have anything to deal with.'

'Don't you? You're different when she's around.'

'Of course I am! I'm on tenterhooks. I'm worried that the whole plan for the kids is going to be ruined. I don't understand why no one else seems to be. This was father's dream. Theo's as well. It's not nothing.' He owed it to his family.

She touched his arm gently. 'No, it isn't nothing. But you won't fail them if it can't happen.'

Alessandro crossed his arms. He didn't know how she could be so flippant about Theo. It was as though she was forgetting him. He was Lucas's and Ana's father, his brother, her other grandson. Theo had been brilliant—a gifted student, a talented sailor, a natural businessman. And a loving father. Every day Alessandro strove to be half the man that Theo had been.

He had to prove that he wasn't the irresponsible son they all thought he was.

It was about time he got himself a drink. At the very least he should stop listening to his grandmother and her theories. He should go to Rose's room, knock on her door and demand her explanation for standing up an impressionable sixteen-year-old.

Yiayia continued. 'You could never fail them. Look at how you've raised these kids.'

'I didn't do it on my own.'

'No, but I could not have done it without you. And I think you have made the bigger sacrifice.'

He didn't need to turn to know that, at that moment, she was looking across the room at Rose.

'I don't think I realised it, until now. Until I met her. I figured she was just a summer fling. But now I see otherwise,' Yiayia said.

He took a deep breath and turned to look where his grandmother was looking.

The room fell silent or maybe his heart just stopped beating. She took his breath away—literally. Her long hair was plaited and wrapped around her head like a Hellenic goddess. Her dress hung just below her bare shoulders in silken folds. He knew of no statue as perfect.

'She looks lovely, doesn't she?'

Alessandro was too distracted by Rose to lie to his grandmother. And what would've been the point? Denying that Rose looked beautiful would have been like trying to convince her that the sun wouldn't rise. 'Yes, she is.'

'Classical. That's what her beauty is. Which is fitting, don't you think?'

'Why?'

'Because her job is studying the past. But, when something is precious, it is precious for ever.'

He frowned. She didn't know him as well as she thought she did.

'What are you standing here talking to your old *yiayia* for?' She gave him a gentle shove. 'Go get her a drink.'

Arrive late, leave early. She didn't mean to be rude but she needed to keep her distance. For his sake as much as hers.

Alessandro had come over to her with a glass of wine when she'd first arrived, but had disappeared soon afterwards, leaving Rose with Anastasia and some of her friends. When her friends were chatting with one another animatedly in Greek, Anastasia turned to Rose and said, 'I understand you knew one another. Years ago. Before.'

There was no point denying it. She nodded.

'He was different, wasn't he?' the older woman said.

'Yes, he looks different now.'

'More handsome?'

Rose laughed. 'He was handsome then too. Just in a different way.'

'He's still the same man.'

'No, I don't think he is.' Rose hoped that she wasn't being rude by contradicting his grandmother, who no doubt knew him better than anyone, but he was different now. He had changed. He used to love reading and long conversations. The Alessandro of fourteen years ago would have loved her search for ancient treasure. He'd wanted to travel the world. He'd wanted to change it. Rose sensed he'd suppressed a part of himself when he'd moved back here to take over the business.

'He always had this in him. He was always loyal and dedicated.'

Once Rose would have agreed. But by showing loyalty to his family he had let her down.

'It isn't the path he would have chosen for himself, but that doesn't make it bad,' Anastasia continued.

'No.'

'He's always held a torch for you.'

Rose nearly choked on her drink. Really? She was going there? She and Alessandro had mostly avoided talking about their past as much as possible. It was as if they had both agreed it was a no-go topic. That suited them both just fine. 'What?'

Anastasia nodded. 'There's never been anyone else.'

Rose was hungry for information but the more she asked, the harder she pressed, the more she would give away, and Anastasia was clearly not one for keeping confidences.

'Me?'

'You're the woman he met in Athens?'

Was she? She had no idea he had told his grandmother about Athens. It surprised her that he had.

Rose nodded.

'He was different when he came home.'

'His brother and sister-in-law had just died; he'd just become guardian to two kids.'

Anastasia studied Rose closely and for longer than was usually considered polite. Rose tried to remain calm and unwavering under the older woman's gaze. She had nothing to hide and would stand by her comment: if Alessandro was different when he'd come home from Athens, it hadn't been due to her. He had just suffered an enormous tragedy and his life had changed for ever. Rose had been completely forgotten.

Anastasia squeezed Rose's arm and didn't say anything else. She understood, which was somehow worse. She reached for a carafe of wine on a nearby table and poured Rose another glass.

Anastasia turned to talk to one of her friends in fast Greek. Rose tried to follow the conversation for a moment then nodded and moved away. While it had been lovely of Ana to invite her, she was not going to interrupt the sixteen-year-old's evening with her friends.

And that left, of all the people she knew here, Alessandro. He was standing in a group of men, talking, and they were all watching him. She was too far away and the music was too loud to hear what he was saying, and she wasn't sure she'd be able to understand it in any event. But, even though she couldn't hear, she could understand body language and these men were all listening intently to Alessandro, deferring to him and laughing at his jokes. One of the men—who was shorter, wider and at least twenty years older—nudged Alessandro's arm and started a one-on-one conversation. Alessandro shook his head at the man, who was insisting on something.

Then to her mortification they both turned and looked in her direction. More words were exchanged between them and they began to move in her direction. Alessandro grabbed the man's arm and pulled him back, but the man shook off Alessandro's grip and approached her.

Oh, no.

As the man headed towards her, his stare was focused on her. Alessandro followed quickly behind.

'You're the archaeologist?' the man said when he reached her.

She nodded. She resisted the urge to reply, *one of them*. That would only anger him further, and she had no wish to do that. Particularly when she had no idea what she'd done to upset him in the first place.

Charm was her best defence so she offered him her hand. He looked at it as though he'd been offered a dead fish. From behind, Alessandro cleared his throat and the man accepted Rose's hand limply.

'I'm Dr Rose Taylor.'

'Demetri.'

'Pleased to meet you,' she said in Greek. Her Greek was

purely conversational and she hoped their discussion would stay at that level. She already felt at enough of a disadvantage.

'Demetri is our builder,' Alessandro explained.

'Oh, I see.'

'You've delayed me. I've had to lay off my team and now I've lost them to another project.'

That was not her fault.

'I'm sorry to hear that, but it's out of my hands,' she said.

'You could just walk away. Sign the permit. Leave us to it.'

'It might look like that, but I really can't. My team know we're not done here. They'll tell the museum, the Ministry of Culture.'

Why didn't these people see that a significant archaeological find would help their island?

You're going to have to discover something pretty special. A couple of broken bricks isn't going to satisfy them.

'If you were a good boss they'd be too scared to tell anyone,' the man said, and Rose froze.

For crying out loud! This man was actually suggesting she lie to the authorities and threaten her employees. He was the limit.

'I'm not going to lie and I'm not going to threaten anyone,' she said, hoping her Greek was as firm as her tone.

The man stared at her and seemed to loom over her, even though they were the same height. She had no doubt he could flatten her with a simple shove.

Alessandro stepped around the man and put himself in between the pair of them.

'Four more weeks. I told you. Your team will be back from Ithaca by then and you can start.'

The man snorted, but at this point another man joined them, a younger version of Demetri. He took the older man's arm and said, 'What's going on, Papa?'

'He's a little frustrated about the delay,' Alessandro said.

The younger man sighed. 'We've talked about this Papa... it's just a delay; the project isn't cancelled.'

Alessandro took Rose's hand, led her away from the men and back to his grandmother. As if a tiny eighty-something-year-old woman would provide her with an appropriate shield. Though she probably would, Rose thought. No one in this room would touch Anastasia and to get to Rose they'd have to go through her.

Alessandro kept his hand on her arm. It was warm, secure. She was annoyed by how good it felt. 'I knew it was inconveniencing you. I'm sorry I didn't appreciate how much it was putting others out,' Rose said.

'Don't worry about him.'

'I... He seemed...'

'He's angry he's had to lay off some staff; he won't do anything. He's all hot air.'

'Why do you use him?'

'He's not a bad man, he's just stressed.'

Rose rolled her eyes.

'And this is a small island. If I want to use someone local—and I do—there isn't anyone else. Look, he won't bother you again.'

Rose wasn't worried the man would hurt her, but she was worried about any feelings of ill will the islanders might harbour against her or her team. Most people had not only been friendly but welcoming and helpful. But what if the ones that weren't got to them? She didn't want to upset the locals or put them out. She truly believed that finding something would be good for Paxos.

As long as you find something good.

Alessandro squeezed her arm and lifted his hand. 'Will you be okay?'

She nodded. 'Of course.'

He turned and walked towards the band. The drummer gave a drum roll and someone yelled, 'Speech!'

The crowd gradually fell silent. Alessandro cleared his throat and began to speak.

'Thank you everyone for coming here tonight. Thank you particularly to the teenagers for putting up with the old people.'

He looked in Rose's direction and winked. Her chest warmed; no one else in the crowd understood the joke and that somehow made it even more special.

'We're here to celebrate the birthdays of these two amazing children. If you've joined us tonight, then you understand why I'm the one standing here now and not their parents.

'To Lucas and Ana—I tell you this every night, but I'm telling you again—your mother and father loved you more than life itself. I know they're watching over you from somewhere. We all miss them every day, but we are so glad that you're both in our lives. I know I could never replace your parents, but being your uncle and raising you has been the biggest privilege of my life. I love you both so very much and wish you both a very happy birthday. Please raise your glasses. Happy Birthday, Lucas and Ana!'

The crowd lifted their glasses, or at least Rose thought they did; her eyes were full and she couldn't see properly. She took a gulp of her drink and wiped the tears away.

Her vision cleared in time to allow her to watch Alessandro hug his nephew then take his niece by the hand and lead her to the dance floor. The band began to play again.

He'd left her to become a parent to these remarkable children. She couldn't resent him for that, not one little bit. The kids both adored him and, seeing them tonight, getting to know them over the past few weeks, she knew that he had done a remarkable job providing a happy, safe and loving home for them.

The thought soothed her.

Yes, circumstances had meant she hadn't enjoyed the life with Alessandro that she'd once hoped for, but who was to say they would have lasted the distance anyway?

Lost in her thoughts, Rose didn't realise that Alessandro and Ana had danced their way in her direction. Ana grabbed Rose's hand and pulled her out with them. The song was fast and the three of them danced with one another for a minute or so until the song changed. With more confidence than Rose could have mustered as a sixteen-year-old, Ana picked up Alessandro's hand and placed it in Rose's. Then, to make sure, she nudged them together.

'You two have to dance,' she said.

Rose couldn't refuse a birthday wish, but she looked at Alessandro. 'You don't have to, if you don't want to.'

'What if I want to?' He slid his arms around her and she did the same. She felt warm, secure, safe. They swayed together, though she was careful to leave an inch between them. Their arms might be holding each other's but they didn't need to press their bodies against one another's. She had to maintain her self-control somehow.

Even with a breath of air between their bodies his arms still embraced her waist, warm and secure. Her arms were draped around him and she could feel his strong shoulders beneath the thin fabric of his shirt. The urge to slip her hands under the shirt was almost overpowering…

Small talk! That was the solution.

'It's a great party.'

'We do it every year.'

'That's lovely.' Despite her best attempts, she still couldn't steady her heart rate.

'I like to make a fuss.' He paused, cast his eyes down and explained, 'It stops me feeling guilty.'

He was unable to meet her eyes but she studied him. The guilt he felt about his brother was crushing him. 'You have nothing to feel guilty about. You've done an amazing job with these kids,' she said.

'I'm not done, though, am I? I still have to keep building the family business to pass on to them.'

No wonder he was so determined to build this hotel; it was about guilt. Not just about his father, but about Theo too. And, no matter how misplaced or misguided it was, guilt could be a powerful force.

'Is money what they really need?'

'No, but they need their family legacy. And it's more important for them to have it because their parents aren't here.'

Oh, she wanted to sigh. These kids knew they were loved. But, equally, nothing could really compensate for an absent parent. The pain she felt from her father's abandonment had never left her. But it was different with these kids—their parents had been taken from them. Rose's father just hadn't loved her.

Then, as if someone had whispered them a special request, the band struck the opening bars to a familiar song. But Ana was nowhere near the band, and besides, no one else could have known the significance of this song.

In Alessandro's embrace, breathing in his scent, Rose was already reminiscing about Athens. When the music began, she was transported back there.

'Songs, smells…they are like a time machine, aren't they?' Oh, no, had she said that out loud?

'Do you ever think about Athens?' he asked.

In the past week, she'd done nothing else. She'd thought about their walks, their conversations, leaning towards one another over small, rickety, candlelit tables.

And also this—dancing. Bodies pressed against one another, swaying, moving against one another. Sharing the same space, the same air, the same breath.

His embrace tightened and she longed to lean into it. Surrender to it.

But, no, there was no point; that would only make the next few weeks harder.

'I remember,' he prompted, whispering into her ear, his breath sliding down her neck like a kiss.

The silent agreement they'd had not to revisit the past was now close to being ripped up. Ground into the dust.

No.

They had to focus on something else.

But what? If they couldn't talk about the past, they could only talk about the future. She was desperate to say something about what she had found that afternoon, the stone, but he was the last person she could tell.

What had happened to him? The Alessandro she had known in Athens would have been overjoyed by such news. He would have been deeply interested, would have theorised with her about what it could be.

Tragedy… That was what had happened to him. She'd never had a sibling, so couldn't say how hard it would hit her, but his brother's death had altered Alessandro.

Before she could stop herself, she pressed her face into his strong shoulder. Hugging him, being this close to him, was fraught with risk, but it wasn't as risky as looking him in the eye. He smelt of soap and jasmine. She could smell him for ever.

His arms tightened around her. They had danced to this song in Athens. They had held each other in bed while this song had played. She had played this song over and over to herself when he'd left. She had cried herself to sleep singing this song. And now he was holding her again. Her mind and body couldn't reconcile it.

And then the song ended and the spell was broken. The next song was new, unrecognisable, and it jolted her back to the present. They both pulled back at the same moment, but somehow her hand ended up wrapped in his and he lead her away from the dance floor without looking at her.

'I'm sorry,' she said.

He looked perplexed. 'What for?'

'Your brother and sister-in-law. It changed you.'

He shook his head. 'I'm still the same person, aren't I?'

'You used to believe in mythology and lost treasure,' she said sadly.

They were standing too close to the band. He looked around the courtyard, took her hand and led her to a nearby doorway and away from the party.

Once they had rounded a corner, he dropped her hand. She flexed her fingers, her skin still tingling from his touch.

'I didn't mean to be rude. It's just a shame, that's all.'

'Losing precious people makes you think differently about the past. My focus is now the future.'

The future. Always irreconcilable with the past.

She looked away from him and surveyed her surroundings.

The hotel was on one side of the hill, facing south. The view from the other side, where her dig was, faced north. She was very familiar with that view, but this one was new. From here, she could see south down the coast. The lights from the other settlements twinkled in a festive string.

'It's beautiful, I've never seen the island from this angle.'

'I should have shown you the other night when we went to dinner.'

She shook her head. 'You've been a wonderful host. Thank you again for being so hospitable, so welcoming.'

He tilted his head to one side. 'Why wouldn't I be?'

'I don't know. I guess I figured…'

I figured you didn't want to see me again.

He lifted his hand to her upper arm again and turned her gently to face him. 'What is it?'

'When you left, I thought it must have been because of me.'

'I thought I explained, I left because of my brother, because of the kids.'

'Yes, you did. But it's hard to shake that feeling of rejection. I spent fourteen years believing you'd left because of me.'

People often leave because of me.

'Oh, I see.' He drew in a deep breath and expelled it just as forcefully.

She'd said it, loud and clear. *You rejected me. You broke my heart into a million tiny pieces that no one has ever been able to put back together again.*

She had to back track. Quickly. 'I'm okay. I'm fine, but it hurt. A lot. And even though you've explained, well, it still hurts.'

Why shouldn't he know how much he'd hurt her? She continued, 'It hurt a lot. I felt rejected. I felt betrayed. And confused. So confused. I know you did it because you wanted to save me, but… I didn't have that knowledge or perspective until just the other week.'

'I'm sorry.' He looked down, vulnerable, apologetic. 'I didn't know what else to do. I didn't want your life to be turned upside down like mine was.'

'Didn't I matter?' She could hardly speak without her voice cracking.

He pulled her back to him. For the second time that night, he turned her to face him, looked up and faced her, and her stomach swooped.

'No, I did not get over you quickly. Not at all. But you, I figured… Rose, you're remarkable, beautiful, exceptional. I figured it was only a matter of time before you moved on. Before someone came along to take your mind off me.'

It sounded like a compliment but maybe he didn't understand the insult buried within it.

'Rose, when I was young I didn't appreciate my family.

I took them for granted. But then my father died, and then Theo. And when he passed away I swore to make up for it all. I didn't want my obligations to ruin your life'

'You really think that's an excuse for leaving me?'

'Yes, I do. I owe this debt, not you.'

'Debt?' she asked.

'To my family. I'm sorry if you don't understand…'

Rose turned away. *You don't have a father, how could you possibly understand?* That was what he was saying. Maybe he was right.

Now they were talking about it openly, it was as though they were tearing the wound apart. She'd thought that cut had healed over with barely visible scars, but it was now as fresh as it had been when it was new.

'I'm so sorry I hurt you. It won't change anything, or make you feel better, but the truth is I longed for you. Sometimes it hurt so much I couldn't breathe. Or move,' he said.

She turned back to him. 'Same,' she admitted.

He pulled her into his chest and wrapped his arms around her. She buried her face in his chest and surrendered to the feeling. Wrapped in his arms like this felt so…right.

The other night he'd said that there had been no one else special in his life. But that was because he didn't want to hurt the twins by bringing someone else that they might lose into their lives. To save them heart ache. He'd said nothing about his own heart.

Knowing about his own pain didn't give her any comfort at all, but if she'd known he had a reason for leaving it would have helped her. It would have saved her all those years of not knowing. All the hours spent wondering. And it might have helped her move on.

It wasn't that she hadn't moved on; she'd seen other men. But there'd always been some part of her that she'd held back. She'd always been the first to run.

Now she couldn't run. Her feet were stuck here as if they were in concrete. She had to face him. She had to deal with him for the next few weeks, at least.

He's always held a torch for you.

Alessandro still held her close and she slowly became aware that his fingers were sliding through her hair. She felt her chest rise and fall with his. Oh, to say here, just like this, for ever.

But they couldn't. They had to move on, move forward. She lifted her face from his chest, not sure what she would see, but surprised to see him looking intently down at her. As if he'd been waiting for her to be ready.

Was she? She wouldn't know until whatever was about to happen happened. She held his gaze as his lids lowered. Her eyelids followed automatically. His lips brushed against hers. Then pulled back. A taste? A test?

A test she suddenly wanted to pass.

Her body tingled, long-forgotten sensations stirring. He looked into her eyes. The sparkle in the deep-brown depths of his eyes told her that, far from being dragged under, she would be safe. She pressed her lips back to his.

Oh, yes.

This wasn't the past and it wasn't the future. It was now. Only now, and here, with the smell of the ocean, the sounds of the party behind them and the crashing waves in front.

It was her lips as they were now, his body as it was today, older but strong, his kisses more tender yet more hesitant, sweeter. Her body fizzed and ached. The longing she felt for him was about to tip over into something she'd be incapable of stopping.

A shriek from the party made her pull back. The shriek was followed by laughter that shook her firmly back into reality.

The kiss was an aberration; that was all it could be.

'Can we…?' He shot her his most handsome smile, so suggestive she felt her knees slipping. He tugged her to him. The instant before she fell inexorably back into his arms, she extracted her hand from his.

'No.'

'But…'

'Alessandro, I don't think we should torture one another.'

He laughed. 'I think our definitions of torture are very different. If that kiss was torture for you, I apologise. I thought my kisses were adequate. I can assure you, yours are wonderful.'

He'd always been able to disarm her with his smile, to knock the breath out of her and tilt her world on its axis.

'The kiss would not be torture, but what follows would be—saying goodbye.'

'We don't have to say goodbye just yet.'

'But we would in a few weeks. Or do you want me to extend my work here?' She tilted her head; her question was cheeky, but she held her breath for his answer.

The grin he returned was wry and sad at the same time. He shook his head. 'That was unfair.'

Now he was throwing fairness into the mix. Nothing about this situation was fair.

She stepped away from him. She should go back to her room and draw a line under the kiss, but the tie to him was hard to sever. She walked to the end of the patio, the wall that overlooked the sea. Drawing in a deep breath, she tried to centre herself. This was the Ionian Sea. A place that had fascinated her for years. The myths had given her hope and comfort almost all her life.

'Alessandro, the problem is you don't want me to succeed.'

'I do, but…'

'You either do or you don't.'

'Do you want me to abandon my father's dream? My brother's dream?'

'No, but you're asking me to abandon mine. I've dreamt

of making a big discovery since I was a child. I can't let my dream go either.'

This wasn't like their previous arguments, which had been combative and tense. This conversation was simply sad. Yet again, their lives were on opposing paths.

'I don't know what to do, Alessandro. I can't give this excavation up. Apart from the fact that I want to know if anything is here, signing off the permit now and walking away would be professional suicide. My reputation would be ruined.'

'I know you can't, and believe me, I'm not asking you to. I don't know what to do either.'

'Then what do we do?' He couldn't think she was happy about this situation. She wanted to return to the warmth of his arms as much as he wanted to have her. 'How do we fix this?'

'I'm not sure it can be fixed.' Was he talking about the dig and the hotel or them? 'I need to stay in Greece and look after the family business, at least until the twins are ready to take it over. Your life is wherever the next big discovery is going to be.'

He wanted to stay and build his business, prove his loyalty to his father and family. Her life was where her job took her. It almost didn't matter what she did or didn't find, the same thing that had kept them apart fourteen years ago still lay between them.

'I love it here, but I can't stay.'

'I understand. And it's too soon for me to hand the business to the children. I don't know when that would be.'

Rose suspected that Alessandro's attachment to the business was so strong he'd never be able to let go of it. His need to prove his loyalty was so powerful.

He looked out over the sea as well. The evening breeze was picking up and ruffled his hair. Her arms shivered. He slipped one arm around her and pulled her close. The gesture was more platonic and practical, but she leant into it just the same. Together they watched the dark water swirling beneath them.

'Then what?'

'We wait and see. If there's something there, I'm sure you will find it.'

'And if there isn't anything?'

'Then…?'

'It's fate, isn't it?' he said.

'Fate?' A surprisingly romantic word for the man who seemed to have given up on love and happy endings.

'If you were meant to find something, it was decided thousands of years ago. If I was meant to build the hotel, then that was also determined years ago. Our fates were sealed in the Age of Heroes.'

She pondered this for a moment then laughed. 'Yes, I suppose so.'

The thought was terrifying…and freeing at the same time.

Whatever would be would be. In the meantime, if she could just keep her distance from Alessandro, protect her heart, then everything would be all right.

She faked a yawn and pulled her body away from his. 'It's getting late.'

'Yes, and we have a big day tomorrow.'

The sailing trip. A whole day in Alessandro's company. One part pleasure, two parts pain.

CHAPTER EIGHT

THE NEXT MORNING Alessandro readied the things he'd need for the day ahead and tried to keep his emotions in check. Angelina had put together a picnic basket for them and he was gathering a bag of things for the boat.

'It's a beautiful day,' Yiayia said when she walked into the kitchen. She eyed his casual shorts and T-shirt. 'What are you up to?'

'I'm taking Rose sailing.'

She tried to hide her smile, without much success.

He couldn't shake last night's events from his mind. The kiss still thrummed in his veins. His lips remembered it every time he opened them to speak. Each time he closed his eyes, Rose flashed beneath his lids.

But it was the conversation afterwards that was going around his head in a never-ending loop. He carried the bags out to his car. The day was already warm and humid. It would be much cooler on the water.

You don't want me to succeed.

Perhaps, but he didn't want her to fail either. What he wanted, what he really wanted, was to take her in his arms, sweep her up and take her to his bed. That was what he wanted more than anything.

He paused, hand in the air, before he brought the boot lid down on the car.

He wanted her.

Life had stopped being about what he wanted years ago. What he wanted was irrelevant. He'd buried his wishes and desires successfully up until now and it hadn't been a problem.

It wasn't a problem because the children, your family, the business, were always the most important. No other woman you ever met was like Rose.

But now Rose was back in his life—even for a short time— and he wanted her in his arms.

She was standing outside her room, shifting from one foot to the other, when he walked out.

'Hi,' she said. She wore a loose pink sundress that fell to her knees and a big straw hat. She looked edible. He imagined brushing his thumb along the soft skin of her bare arms. He shook the thought away.

'Do you have a swimsuit?'

'Will I need one?'

'Better to be prepared. Of course, if you want to go without...'

Her face turned beetroot. 'I'll go get it.'

He had to push these thoughts of Rose away just as he had over a decade ago. But this was different from fourteen years ago. Last time she had been remote; the kids had been small and had needed him night and day. He'd been exhausted with grief.

Now she was here, near him. His grief had dulled and the two children who had once needed him so much were now, mid-morning, still fast asleep. Maybe, like Yiayia had suggested, there was time for him? Maybe he didn't have to put the kids first?

Except... Rose still had her work. He still had the family business to run. At least for the foreseeable future they were unlikely to be able to be in the same country for any length of time. Which was why it was imperative he kept guarding his heart.

Rose's dig being on his land was an almost laughable coincidence, as though the gods were laughing at his expense. What had been the chances of her turning up on Paxos, on his land?

If it was odds he wanted to bet on, what were the chances of her actually finding anything on his land? Slim to non-existent.

But if she was right, and there were Bronze Age ruins to find in the Ionian, then might she find them somewhere else on Paxos or somewhere else nearby? It was no good just showing her the village, he had to show her the island. His island—Erimitírio.

Taking her there might help her understand him, his family and the connection he felt to them. The debt he owed them, even if his heart half-broke to go there. Even if was one of the places in the world where he felt closest to Theo and their father. A place that bought so many memories flooding back. If there was anywhere near by that was ancient, brimming with history, it was the island.

It was the place where his father had taught them both to sail, the place where he had taken them all for adventures, where they'd pretended to be explorers, warriors.

He hadn't been for years, not since the kids had been younger. They'd preferred to see their friends or play video games. If he'd been their real father, maybe it would have been different. But he wasn't Theo and, as much as he loved them, he always knew he was never quite enough.

Rose re-emerged from her room, glowing. His throat went dry. He was fooling himself if he thought he'd be able to keep his distance from her today. But he had to try. 'Lead on,' she said as she closed the door behind her.

* * *

Alessandro drove them down to the port at Gaios and led her out along the marina, where the sailing boats were lined up in a proud row. They proceeded to a boat he appeared to be very familiar with, stepping onto it as though he was simply crossing his threshold.

Once on the boat, he turned back and offered her his hand. She accepted and stepped onto the boat but, as she lifted her second foot and transferred her weight to the first, the unsteadiness of the boat and the water surprised her and she fell forward, almost landing on top of him, saved only by his quick thinking and strong arms.

The sensations from the night before returned: warmth; security; excitement.

'Are you all right?' he asked once she was steadied. 'Did you slip?'

'No, I'm just not very familiar with yachts.'

He grinned like a professor sensing a foolish student. 'Well, for starters, this is a sailing boat.'

That sounded a lot less solid than a yacht. It was also smaller. It was only as long as a couple of cars, had a small cabin and one tall mast. And Alessandro knew exactly how to drive or sail it—whatever the correct terminology was. She supposed she could bother to learn but that would give him a little bit too much satisfaction. And right now, with the muscles in his arms rippling as he pulled on some ropes and wound a winch to lift the sail, a slight breeze ruffling his hair, he looked pretty satisfied with himself.

And why wouldn't he? He looked as if he'd just stepped out of a commercial for a luxury watch or some space-age razor.

'I'm sorry, I'm no help. I don't know anything about sailing,' she said, sitting back and admiring the beautiful view of Gaios port and the turquoise sea beyond...not the man on the boat.

'Don't worry, I could sail her blindfolded.'

'Please don't.'

Alessandro twisted the rope around something, secured it in place then jumped down onto the deck beside her.

'You're not worried, are you?' he asked.

Any time in the past she'd been on a vessel this small, her stomach had not been happy about it. But, if pressed, the thing that worried her most was simply spending more time in close quarters with Alessandro.

'No, not worried.'

'Ah, queasy, then?'

She winced. 'Sometimes, maybe.'

He laughed. 'This is Greece! You can't get seasick.'

'I'm sure some Greeks get seasick,' she retorted.

He shook his head. 'No, I don't think so. It would be most unpatriotic.'

'I don't believe that for a second.'

He rummaged in a cavity near the front of the boat and then tossed her a plastic sick bag. 'Just in case,' he said.

She didn't know whether to be mortified or grateful.

'So that's why you didn't want to come today is it?' he asked.

She hadn't wanted to come because she had work to be doing. A stone to be uncovered. She hadn't wanted to come because every moment she was alone with Alessandro was both wonderful and awful. But she'd let him believe it was seasickness.

'Stand up here with me.' He was at the helm behind a large wheel. 'Look out at the water and enjoy your personal tour of the islands.'

She walked towards him, still getting accustomed to the way the boat shifted under her.

'If you're looking straight ahead, the less likely it is you'll feel seasick.' He held his hand out to her again to encourage her to join him. She lifted her hand to his, knowing even before the skin touched it would be risky. As his large, warm hand circled hers, she was sorry to be right. Sparks spread from her fingers through her hand. How she wanted him to slide his hand up her arm and envelop more than just her hand...

She snatched her tingling fingers away and held onto a bar at the front of the boat, looking steadfastly ahead at the sights they were passing.

As they sailed out of the port, they passed through a channel bounded on one side by Gaios and the other by a green, lush island. 'That's Agios Nikolaos, with the historic monastery. Built by the Venetians. You might even see parts of the walls of the observatory.' He pointed.

As they left the calmness of the harbour and entered the open water, Alessandro switched off the motor that had propelled them out of the port and began adjusting the sails.

'Now you might feel best if you're sitting here. The wind will pick up as we start to move.'

And it did. Alessandro manipulated the sails and the boat began to slice through the water. The breeze did make her feel good and, as long as she was focused outside the boat and on the scenery, she felt fine.

It was not a hardship. The view from the boat was spectacular. Green olive trees covered the slopes that wound gently down to the glistening emerald waters. They passed numerous secluded coves and bays. 'Most of these can only be reached by boat,' he explained.

They sailed up the coast in the direction of Ninos and another island came into view. He turned the boat towards it. When he changed direction, the sails no longer caught the wind and the boat slowed.

'And this is Erimitírio. It means "home of the hermit". It's been uninhabited for centuries. There's no jetty or marina, so tourists don't come. But I think you might find it interesting.'

She agreed. It was small but beautiful. She could make out

the hint of a white pebbled beach, but otherwise the island rose steeply out of the water into a rocky peek.

Uninhabited was good; unexplored was better. Myth said that, when Odysseus had left Ithaca for the final time, he'd travelled to a smaller island, where he had died. Paxos was smaller than Ithaca. But this island was smaller still. Maybe Alessandro wasn't trying to interrupt her work after all, but giving her the chance to be the one to explore this place.

Once the dig was finished near the hotel, there'd be no reason for Alessandro to keep helping her. No reason for the museum to keep funding her. If she wanted to find anything proving the legend of Odysseus, she would have to do it on her own.

'Tell me about it.'

'This is the island where Dad took us to learn to sail. Over there is the bay where my brother and I would come with a little dinghy and explore.'

'On your own?'

'Of course.'

'And do Lucas and Ana come here too?'

His smile was sad. 'We used to come here all the time together, but now they're older...' He ended the sentence with a shrug.

There was such weight and sadness in that shrug. She'd thought he might be relieved now the twins were older, but no. He had clearly loved sharing their childhood with them. The feelings of pride he'd spoken of last night were mixed with feelings of nostalgia and happy memories of their childhood.

'But speaking of Odysseus...' He changed the subject.

'Which we weren't.'

'Speaking of Odysseus, they say he was nearly shipwrecked here.'

'Let's face it, most Greek islands make that claim,' she said.

He smiled. 'No, but this was real,' he said jokingly.

He was teasing her and she nudged him playfully. When he looked down at her, his eyes were serious and she felt her body falling towards him.

No.

It was just the waves, the boat bobbing gently on the sparkling water. She had to keep her distance. Last night had taught her several lessons. First: Alessandro's kisses tasted even better than they had fourteen years ago. Second, how little self-control she had when alone in his company.

'Seriously, apart from Odysseus, the Romans came here. They built a fort.'

'Really?'

'Truly, but that fort was mostly demolished by the Venetians to build their own. It's called the Citadel. But traces of the Romans still remain. I'm sure if someone had appropriate qualifications they could study the area and write about the history of it.'

'I'm sure they could. And, maybe once that person has found the Bronze Age ruins on your land, they could turn their attention here.'

He raised an eyebrow but she couldn't make out his expression—doubting…or worried.

'Why is it called the Island of the Hermit?'

'Because of the hermit.'

'So I assumed.'

'It was centuries ago. Maybe millennia. He was a stranger from across the seas and came to live on the island.'

'Is there fresh water there? What did he eat?'

'That's a good question, and no. There's no fresh water.'

'So how did he survive?'

'Every week, a man called Leonidas would take him some fresh fruit, bread and water. The hermit paid in gold coins. Apart from that, he lived on fish.'

'He must have really wanted some peace and quiet.'

Alessandro grinned. 'And Leonidas kept bringing him his supplies and he kept paying for them. Eventually, Leonidas died, so his son took over. But eventually his son died and *his* son took over, and then his.'

'And so on?'

'And so on. For over three hundred years the hermit kept paying them.'

'That sounds suspiciously like myth, Alessandro.'

'Of course.'

'I thought you didn't believe in myths and legends.'

'I don't believe in digging up my land for them. That doesn't mean I can't tell the stories. I'm Greek. Of course I tell these stories.'

He said it with a pride that was infectious. But for once it wasn't ancient history she wanted to know about, it was Alessandro's.

'How often would you come here with your father and brother?'

'Whenever my father had time.'

'Was that a lot?'

'He made time. Like I've tried to do.'

A lump formed in Rose's throat and expanded to block it. Alessandro had been such a devoted father to these children, maybe even more devoted since they were not his natural children. Why were some men like that, and yet others couldn't even be bothered to look after their own? Like her own father.

Because he didn't love you. You weren't enough.

Her mother had tried to tell her that he'd left *her*, not Rose. But he had left Rose—he could have asked to see her. He could have contacted her. He could have returned her calls. But he never had.

Her mother's words bounced off her, unheard, because he had abandoned Rose every bit as much as her mother. Because, when it came down to it, she wasn't enough. He loved his new family more.

Alessandro had a habit of being able to read her mind at moments like this. 'Tell me about your family.'

'There's nothing much to tell. My father left when I was young, my mother worked hard to support us both. It wasn't bad. But she did not teach me to sail around a Greek island.'

'Your father, yes, I'm sorry. You did tell me about him. Has he ever…?'

She shook her head. 'No, he never contacted me. A couple of years ago my mother heard that he had died.'

'I'm so sorry.'

'It's fine. I hadn't seen him since I was seven.'

It wasn't fine, but she didn't want to speak about it.

Her father had been dead for six months before her mother had found out. She'd passed the news on gently, but it had still stunned Rose. Now there was no hope of a reconciliation, no hope of an explanation.

To avoid discussing her own family, she said, 'Your family's much more interesting. You never told me much about them, you know.'

'We weren't together very long,' he replied.

No, they hadn't been. She looked away from him and over the water, into the distance.

'I'm sorry, that came out wrong. I didn't mean to down-play what we had. I only meant that I didn't have time.'

'I know.' She nodded. 'We talked about a lot of things in those weeks. Our hopes, dreams, plans for the future. You just told me your family was from the Ionian Islands. And, now I'm here, I see how incredibly important they are to you. I'm also sorry because I didn't think to ask.'

He reached over, took her hand and squeezed it. 'Don't apologise. I don't think I realised how important they were to me until they were gone. I was a selfish young idiot.'

She touched his arm, 'Don't say that.'

'It's true. I took them for granted. Until it was too late.'

'And, besides, I was just a summer fling,' she said.

He turned to face her and gave her his full attention. His gaze held her and her stomach swooped, even before he spoke. 'Just to be clear—I never thought we were just a summer fling. I wanted to spend my life with you.'

CHAPTER NINE

His declaration stunned her speechless. Once upon a time him telling her he'd wanted to spend his life with her would have made her heart sing, now his words just squeezed her heart with pain. They reminded her of a life she'd never lead.

'I think I hoped the same,' she admitted. 'For a few weeks.'

His mouth dropped and something like pain gathered behind his eyes.

Fourteen years ago she would have grabbed a declaration like that with both hands. Now, it just made her wistful for what might have been.

'You were going to travel the world searching for history and I was going to follow you writing about the present. It was going to be an amazing life,' he said.

She couldn't help but smile. 'It would've been wonderful.' And, because something she didn't want Alessandro to see was brewing inside her, she quickly added, 'But we've both still done amazing things. You've grown a hotel empire, raised two kids.'

She needed him to know that those things were important too. Most of all, she needed to believe it herself. There was no point dwelling on what he had just said; it had been a comment about the past, that was all. It certainly wasn't what he currently felt.

Without telling her what he was doing, Alessandro manoeuvred the yacht closer to the island.

'What are we doing?' Her skin was warm, maybe from the sun. Or perhaps because of what Alessandro had just confessed and the conflicting feelings thrashing around inside her.

'Now, we've got some choices here. We can sail around to the other side of the island where there's a better beach to bring in the boat. Or I can leave her here. It's only about fifty metres; do you think you can swim?'

She'd swum fifty metres many times before; she could make it. She studied the shore, the narrow white beach glistening between the turquoise water and the deep green of the island. Most importantly, the water looked cold enough to cool her down.

'Or we can just stay here, but I thought you might like to explore,' he prompted.

'Swim, I guess,' she said. 'Last one in's a rotten egg.' She kicked off her flip flops and dived into the sparkling water, dress and all.

The coldness of the water shocked her at first but after a few strokes her body adjusted. Once away from the boat, she stopped, treaded water and looked back up. He was on the boat shaking his head. She turned and made even strokes through the water. The salt water felt amazing on her skin.

After a while she stopped and turned to make sure he was actually following her. He was now in the water and following behind her. Before she knew it, the sandy sea bed appeared beneath her and she could touch the bottom. Now she was here on the island, she wished she'd brought a towel somehow.

Shortly afterwards Alessandro also emerged from the sea, salt water dripping from his bare torso. Her mouth went dry and her body instantly felt warm again. His chest was broad and his stomach as taut as it had been all those years ago. A memory of trailing her fingers across his naked skin crept annoyingly into her mind and her muscles clenched. Heaven help her.

He shook something from his back.

'What's that?' she asked.

'A dry bag,' he said, unzipping it. He took out two towels and two pairs of sand shoes.

He handed a pair to her. 'You'll need these; we're going for a walk.'

'Where to?'

'You're full of questions, aren't you?'

'But of course. I want to know where we're going.'

He laughed again. 'Just come with me and see. The island's only a hundred metres across, so it won't take long.'

With mixed feelings, she watched Alessandro pull a T-shirt over his head. They made their way across the small beach and into the scrub beyond. He led her to a narrow, mostly over-grown, path that led up the hill. Alessandro had been here many times because he knew exactly where to find the path. While the island wasn't currently inhabited, it might have been at one point.

'Are you going to show me where the hermit lived? Or is he still here?'

'Ha-ha-ha.'

She followed him in silence after that, concentrating on not slipping on the almost non-existent path. It was a long time since it had been regularly used.

They rounded a bend and she sucked in a deep breath. 'Gorgeous.'

He turned back to her and grinned. 'Isn't it?'

Before them, close to the summit of the island, was a pile of ruins. It had clearly once been a small building. A temple, maybe. A castle. It was hard to say.

'Is this the hermitage?'

'Unlikely. This was a citadel, built first by the Romans, re-stored by the Venetians. Come and see.'

He couldn't have stopped her rushing over and stepping over the first stones to get a better look.

'Yes, it's not ancient. At least, not that I can see. The foundations might be...but, oh, look!' After she'd stepped over what had probably once been the threshold, she could see that part of the building was still intact. Four walls and part of a wooden roof remained. The rest was covered by a tree that had grown in the corner, making the space half-ruin, half-treehouse. 'It's lovely.'

She was suddenly aware that he was watching her, not the ruins. Watching as she leapt from place to place, exclaiming to no one in particular what she saw. His gaze was a heavy weight on her heart. It was full of admiration, but also loss. It simply reminded her of what could never be.

I never thought we were just a summer fling. I wanted to spend my life with you.

What a thing to confess. And now—now when there was no hope of them having a life together. The stolen kiss they had shared last night had even been too much of a risk. If she wasn't vigilant, the carefully constructed wall she had built around her heart to protect it from falling for Alessandro again would start to crumble. Just like the ancient fortress she was standing in now.

'It's mediaeval,' she said, running her fingertip along some etchings on the wall, a long-faded painting. 'When did you say it was built?'

The pink dress she wore over her swimsuit was slowly drying, though her red swimsuit was still visible through the thin fabric, which clung to her curves, leaving little to his overactive imagination. *Beautiful.* She was standing in front of him like an untouchable goddess, a sea nymph. Turned out bringing her here and encouraging her to jump into the sea hadn't been the smartest idea he'd ever had.

'This was built by the Venetians in the thirteenth century. But they weren't the only ones who lived here. The Ionian Islands have been occupied by everyone from the Romans to the Ottomans to the Italians.'

He had a feeling he'd already told her this. And it was something she was bound to know herself, but right now he was clinging to small talk to keep himself focused on something other than the thin dress clinging to her gorgeous body.

She turned and gave him a Mona Lisa smile. He had no idea what she was thinking.

Once upon a time he'd known exactly what was going on in her brilliant mind. Now, she was giving nothing away. Including how she felt about what he had confessed to her on the boat.

I wanted to spend my life with you.

She was right to treat his statement lightly; it didn't matter what he'd wanted all those years ago. Right now their wishes and dreams were completely opposed to one another's. He wanted a hotel, she wanted to dig up his land.

Rose walked around the ruins, stroking the walls.

I wish she were looking at me the same way she's looking at these ruins.

'Has anyone ever done a proper survey of this place?'

'I have.'

She turned and grinned. 'While I'm sure you did a great job, I meant a professional.'

'Ah, no. Would you like to?' He knew this would just remind her of the job she was meant to be doing, but he suggested it anyway.

She rolled her eyes.

He held up his hands in surrender. 'Seriously, it's all here—you'd hardly have to dig and you'd be sure to find something.'

'It isn't my era.'

'But it could be. Honestly, I thought you should see this place.'

The smile on her face was wide and dreamy. 'It is amazing. Thank you for bringing me here. I would love to have more of a look around.' She sighed.

'Feel free.'

He'd forgotten what being with Rose was like. It had been a conscious decision to push his memories of her down deep and to throw away the key. Watching her now, he remembered why. If he'd remembered this for the past decade, he would've lost his mind by now. He wouldn't have had the resolve to do what he had to do for the twins.

Now that he remembered, now that the knowledge of her touch, the sensation of her kisses, was at the forefront of his mind, what would he do? He didn't know how he could move on. He only knew he couldn't go back.

You don't know if you're going forward or backwards.

'It's gorgeous. Oh, Alessandro.'

He wanted to believe she was talking as much about him as the island.

'Look how the vines have nearly swallowed it. I think they're the only things holding the stones up in some places.'

He remembered coming here as a kid and experiencing the same sense of wonder as she was now. This had been some back yard for him to explore. He'd probably taken it for granted, but not many kids got to sail to their own private island and pretend they were pirates or kings or warriors.

'It goes on for ages!' she exclaimed. She must have noticed the ruins that led down to the other side of the island and the small harbour.

'Are you hungry?' he yelled out to her. 'There's some lunch on the yacht.'

She didn't reply and he shook his head. She was immersed in the ruins and would be for ages.

He watched her walk away. She disappeared over the ridge and he thought he would go to her in a moment. But in the meantime he decided to go back to the boat and get some water and a hat for Rose. The day was a little cloudy, but he knew her skin was sensitive to the bright Greek sun.

He set off back down the hill. He hadn't been here for a while, but his feet remembered the path well, each rise, fall and corner. Once he emerged from the scrub onto the narrow beach, he saw the colour of the sky was different on this side of the island—grey, close and cold.

Damn. It looked as though a storm would be here within the hour. The boat was exposed where it was now; he should have brought it in to the cove to begin with. They might be stuck here for some time. His phone was on the boat and he should get that to check the forecast.

He strode straight into the water. When it was deep enough, he dived in and then with long, even strokes made his way out to the boat.

Rose walked through the ruins of the citadel and out the other side. The view of the other side made her draw in a sharp breath. This side of the island dropped away, steep and rocky, down to a sandy, sheltered cove surrounded in green.

They'd probably once had three-hundred-and-sixty-degree views of the sea from the top of the fortress. No wonder they'd built it where they had.

'Where did this hermit of yours live, then?' she called out to Alessandro. There was no answer. She thought he'd followed her, but clearly not. She'd become carried away, exploring. The place was amazing. It wasn't her usual bag; the small fortress had been built some time in the Middle Ages. It was in ruins, not half-buried like the things she usually looked at. But it was magical.

And the connection to Alessandro made it even more special. She scrambled back over the ridge of the hill to the citadel and called out again for Alessandro.

No answer.

The bag with the towels was lying where he'd left it. She picked it up and followed the path back the way they had come, expecting to see him around each corner, past each tree. She didn't expect to see him in the water, swimming back to the boat.

Surely he wasn't leaving her here? *No, he wouldn't leave you.*

He did once.

She stood and watched, mouth open, as he made his way through the water with bold, strong strokes. He reached the boat and pulled himself up onto it. She waved. He didn't wave back.

He just hasn't seen you.

'Alessandro!' she yelled as loudly as she could but still he didn't turn.

He just hadn't heard.

Or he's pretending not to.

In the distance it looked as though he was winching up the anchor. She waved again, yelled. The wind blew her hair back off her face. The wind wasn't on her side, either. Alessandro went to the controls. Water churned at the back of the boat and it began to move.

He's really leaving.

He's leaving me here.

The wind wasn't only stronger but cooler than it had been when, foolishly, she'd dived into the water. Back towards Paxos, clouds were gathering on the other side of that island. The clouds were moving at quite a pace and rain would come in the next few hours.

She watched, frozen on the spot, as the boat moved from where it was anchored around the tip of the island and out of sight. Back south, in the direction of Gaios.

It was one thing to leave her in a bar in Athens without an

explanation. It was quite another to leave her on a tiny island in the middle of the Ionian Sea with rain coming. She paced back and forth to expel the excess adrenaline that was currently flying through her veins.

She walked back up to the fortress, scrambling to the highest point to get a better view of the water and see if she could still catch a glimpse of Alessandro and his boat. But even the best vantage point, one that let her see all the way back down the coast to Gaios, didn't afford her a glimpse of him. It was as if the boat had just disappeared. He'd been in that much of a hurry to get away.

The others would realise she hadn't come back with him. How would he explain the fact that she was no longer with him? How would he explain her disappearance to her team, to his own grandmother? There must be some explanation for what he was doing. But what?

What if it took another fourteen years before she found out what was his reason for leaving her stranded on this rocky outpost? What if, like with her father, she never really found out why?

The wind became colder and the dark clouds closer. The speed at which the storm came upon her was remarkable.

Maybe he's just getting help.

Then why wouldn't he tell you? Or why not just get you to sail with him?

It made no sense.

If it was going to start raining, she needed to find some shelter. The citadel was in ruins but the tress that had inundated it might provide some shelter. She clambered over the rocks back up to it. She took herself into the furthest corner under the stones and green canopy, sat, wrapped her arms around her knees and tried to breathe.

CHAPTER TEN

SHE DIDN'T KNOW how much later it was that she heard some-one call her name.

It sounded like Alessandro, but he was probably back on Paxos by now.

'Rose! Rose, where are you?'

Alessandro was running through the ruins of the citadel be-fore she could get up. Before she could hide the feelings that were painted across her face.

'What are you doing?' he asked.

'It's about to start raining I didn't know where else to go.'

'Yes, I'm sorry about that. We're going to have to stay.'

'Stay?'

'I brought the boat around to the cove down there. It's more sheltered and we can bring it right up to the beach. Though the walk up this side is much steeper. I also got some things.' He held up two bags. 'But we shouldn't stay here. I know a better place.' He turned and made his way back out.

Rose still didn't move. Her body was still weak with fear, still processing what was happening.

He hadn't left.

Noticing she wasn't following, Alessandro turned back. 'Rose, what's the matter? Are you all right?'

The feelings churned through her, just like the waves in the ocean.

He wasn't going to leave you. He was bringing the boat in, fetching things.

'Rose?' This time he dropped the bags and knelt down to her. 'It's just a storm. We could sail in it, but we don't have to. We can just wait it out here.'

She forced herself to get up, despite the weakness in her legs, the confusion in her heart. She didn't want to have to explain her reaction to him.

'It'll be fine. It's not a big storm, but given your queasy stomach I thought we should ride it out here.'

Far from leaving her, he was suggesting they stay here to save her from getting seasick.

It didn't make him a bad person—in fact he was a very good person—but she still hurt. Her limbs were still weak.

Why had her mind instantly jumped to the worst possible conclusion?

It was a perfectly natural reaction, considering he's left you once before. Considering he has no intention of building a life with you. Considering people leave you.

He would leave her at some point. Maybe he wouldn't abandon her on an island in the middle of the sea. But once she found treasure on the land he wanted for his hotel?

He might care for her, and those feelings might even be strong, but when decision time came, when it came to the crunch, he was going to choose his family and his island over her. He'd said as much last night. He needed to stay in Greece to look after the family business; her life was wherever her work took her.

'Did you think I'd left you?' he asked.

'Of course not.' She attempted a laugh, but it came out weak, almost teary.

'Then what's the matter? What happened?'

She felt a small drop of rain on her face. He looked at the sky.

'Tell me,' he said.

'I watched you lift the anchor and move the boat. You disappeared without a word. What did you think I'd think?'

'First, you were so absorbed in looking at the ruins I didn't think you'd notice. And then, if you had noticed, I guess I thought you'd see the storm and figure it out.'

'I did see the storm.'

He pressed lips together. 'You thought I'd leave you in a storm? Alone?'

'No, I mean...' *Yes. Yes, I did.* 'You left me once before.'

'Hey, I thought we'd talked about that.' He picked up her hand. Conflicted feelings crashed inside her—embarrassment, relief, anger. But also pleasure at the way her hand felt as he turned it over in his and studied it.

'We did talk about it, and it's silly. But I couldn't help it.'

More drops of rain hit her face and the wind whipped her hair around her face.

'Come with me.'

'Where?'

'You'll see.'

He stood and offered her his hand again. 'Trust me. Please.'

Her hand was heavy at her side and it took more strength than she seemed to have to lift it.

He's asking you to follow him, he's not asking you to hand over your life. You can do this.

She lifted her hand to his. He helped her up.

It was so easy for him to ask for her trust, so much harder for her to give it. She knew now why he'd left her in Athens, but he'd still kept the real reason from her for fourteen years. He'd thought he knew what was best for her. She couldn't trust him with her heart again.

He led her, hand still in hers, along a path that lead down the other side of the hill. She shivered. She'd come dressed for a warm day but had foolishly jumped into the sea fully clothed to cool her mind and body from thoughts of Alessandro. Now she was under-dressed and over-exposed. She hoped wherever they were going was warm.

She was hoping for a large tree, maybe an overhanging rock. She hadn't allowed herself to hope for this.

'It's a cave.'

'It is.'

'How big?'

'Big enough, but we're lucky the storm is coming from the west. We can light a fire without smoking the place out.'

Alessandro placed two large bags on the ground next to her. 'Do you want a fire first or something to eat?'

'You have food?'

'Of course. What sort of tour guide do you think I am? Food or fire?'

She shivered.

'Fire it is. Why don't you unpack the bags?'

As Alessandro gathered some wood and created some magic with it near the entry to the cave, Rose looked through the two bags he'd placed at her feet, a sports bag and a cool bag. She unzipped the sports bag and found a picnic blanket, a couple of towels and two large sweaters.

'Were you a boy scout in a former life?'

'In this one.' He grinned back at her from the fire that was beginning to smoulder.

She unzipped the cool bag and exclaimed, 'Ah! Food!'

Food, wine and everything besides. She pulled out bread, cheese, dips, grapes and olives. Once the fire was lit, he joined her on the blanket and twisted open the top of the bottle of wine.

She passed him two of the plastic cups she found in the bag. Their fingers brushed and her hands tingled.

The red wine warmed her, as did the fire, and the bread filled the empty space in her stomach. The memory of the horrible moments when she had believed she was stuck on the island began to fade. She began to take in her surroundings more closely. Firelight flicked off the cave walls. It was a natural cave, but humans had made their mark.

The world had shrunk to just the two of them. His hair was still damp, scraped off his high forehead. She could look at him all day.

'What is this place? Is this where the hermit lived?'

'Given that I don't actually believe the story about the hermit, probably not. But I do think there are worse places to get stuck.'

'Were you trying to get us both stranded?' The thought of being here, alone with Alessandro, and not having to think about the rest of the world for a time was not unappealing.

'Of course I wasn't trying to get us stranded. I know you. I'm not powerful enough to bring a storm. You'd need a god for that.'

Her very own Greek god.

She had a vague recollection of describing him that way in her diary. Before he'd left her in Athens, of course. His hair was drying in the heat from the fire and flopped into his eyes. She wanted to brush it back, run her fingers through it. She wanted to touch him freely and openly, as she once had. She took a big gulp of wine instead.

Alessandro stood up. 'Wait here just a moment.' He turned and then added, 'I'm not going far.'

She scooted forward to the cave's entrance, far enough to remain out of the rain but so she could see the instant he returned.

This was silly. She was a grown woman—she never worried about being left alone. She travelled the world by herself, for crying out loud. This island was hardly the middle of nowhere. Someone would have found her if she'd failed to return to Paxos.

Alessandro wouldn't leave you.

Maybe not alone on a deserted island, but she had no doubt that one day, somewhere, he eventually would.

When he returned to the cave moments later with some more firewood, Rose was sitting at the entrance to the cave, looking out expectantly.

His chest constricted.

He had really scared her. How could she possibly believe that he'd leave her here?

You left her once before. And her father did too. You haven't given her a reason to trust you. You kept things from her, made decisions that affected her without talking to her. You let her down.

Next time he'd tell her where he was going. If there was a next time.

He put the armful of firewood down in the cave where it would have a chance to dry before they needed it. If he had possessed the power to summon a storm, he would have used it to do much more besides. He would have used his power to bring his father and brother back—or stop them dying in the first place. And he would have used his powers to keep Rose by his side.

But he wasn't a god. He was just a man. And sometimes not a very good one. Today was a prime example.

He'd managed to forget to check the forecast and had got them both stuck on the island. That was something neither his father nor brother would ever have been foolish enough to do.

Worst of all, he'd managed to scare Rose in the process, and put her in danger, because he'd just been thinking about himself. He was kidding himself if he thought he was as responsible as his brother.

He sat back down on the blanket.

'The rain's settling in, I'm afraid.' He touched his hair. It was wet. Rose passed him a towel.

He should have thought more about how his sudden disappearance might have affected her, but he was being honest when he'd said he'd thought leaving without an explanation had been the right thing to do. But he realised now she'd never understood he'd done it for her. Theo's death had turned her life upside down as well, but she hadn't even known.

He poked the fire. It flashed brighter, like the feeling in his gut.

Guilt…that was the sour sensation in his throat and gut. He'd underestimated the depth of her feelings for him.

If she loved you even a fraction of the way you loved her, then she must have gone through hell…

'I'm sorry again.'

'I know,' she replied.

'You didn't even let me tell you what I'm sorry for.'

'I know you're sorry for leaving me. Both times.'

But had she forgiven him? Even if she thought she had, her reaction to him leaving to move the boat just now showed that he'd affected her deeply. He didn't know how he'd do it, but he had to fix it.

And, since he couldn't come up with any other plan, he poured them both another glass of wine.

'Tell me what it was like,' she said. 'When the kids were little. Was it very hard?'

He drew in a deep, soulful breath. If she wanted to change the subject, who was he to argue? 'Yes, it was hard, and heartbreaking. They were old enough to know that their parents were not there, too young to understand what had happened. The heartbreak was visceral; the tears, the cries for their mama and papa, tore me apart.'

He wasn't looking for sympathy, he wasn't the one who needed it, but Rose placed her hand on his all the same. It felt warm and safe. 'That must have been so hard.'

'Thank goodness Yiayia and I had each other. And everyone from the village too. We didn't cook for months. We didn't clean for months. Everyone rallied round.'

'But after a while the twins bonded with me. Properly. We'd talk about their parents, show them photos and videos. And—I think I've said this before—it was awful, but it's also been a privilege.'

'You said that in your beautiful speech last night. More than one handkerchief was taken out.'

He shook his head. 'I don't feel proud, Rose.'

'But you should.'

'No, looking after the kids was a privilege. I'm not the one who made the biggest sacrifice.'

He stared into her eyes as he said this. The firelight flickered over them, giving her a half-incomplete vision of his face. She didn't understand exactly what he meant and something, an invisible hand, held her back from asking.

She sipped her wine and felt warm. She could hear the rain pattering down outside, but in the cave they were warm. It was only mid-afternoon, yet in the cave, in the storm, it was as dark as early evening.

The fire was not only warm but comforting. An open fire had always inspired conversation since ancient times. She felt the same, in the semi-darkness and, because they weren't going anywhere immediately, the conversation flowed.

'How far does the cave go back?'

'I'm not exactly sure. Theo and I only went as far as we could with torches. He once talked about getting profession-als in, but I don't think he ever did. It was one more thing he didn't get around to doing.'

Theo had been older than Alessandro, but must have been no more than thirty when he'd died. A life not even half lived.

'But we did once find some things left behind from the war.'

'Really? What?' she asked, thinking it might be guns, ammunition…a diary.

'Rubbish mostly.'

She laughed. 'That actually sounds about right.'

'Empty tins, wine bottles—also empty.'

He talked to her about the Second World War and how it had impacted the islands. He talked of modern Ionian history too.

'You always did enjoy modern history and politics.' She moved closer to him.

'I still do. Unlike you.'

She shrugged. 'I'm not uninterested.'

'What time would you go back to?' he asked. 'If you had a time machine.'

'Oh, I love this question.'

'I thought you might.'

'It depends on whether I'm dropping in for a visit or having to live there. It would depend on whether I was a man or a woman. Rich or poor.'

Alessandro smiled at her and for a moment she stopped breathing. She adored this man like no other. 'It sounds like you may have already given this some thought. Okay, if you were going back for one day, to see one moment in time. You don't have to live there or put up with the food, the smells, the sexism or complete lack of medical care.'

It was just like being in Athens—sitting at their table in the taverna, drinking coffee all night and talking about everything under the sun.

'Then, oh…perhaps Cleopatra's death? Or maybe the Ides of March 44 BC. Or maybe…'

Alessandro laughed heartily.

'It's difficult to choose! What about you? Where and when would you go?'

He fell silent and looked thoughtfully at his empty wine

cup. He spun it between his two hands. 'To the night before I got the phone call about Theo.'

Now she did stop breathing.

'And I'd call him up and tell him not to drive that day. And, if he did, I'd at least hang around the next day and make sure to speak to you.'

Her eyes stung…probably just from the smoke. 'We can't go back.' It was a pointless, empty thing to say but all she could think of.

'I know.'

The devastation in his voice was apparent, not just at losing his brother but having his life turned upside down. Putting his own dreams on hold.

Rose's heart thudded in her chest.

'But I'd be kinder, more understanding. I know I can't change the past, but I promise to do things differently in the future. I promise to talk to you, tell you everything.'

He was talking as though they did have a future together. But, after everything they'd said, how could that be?

'Has it been awful?'

'It's been hard, but there have been good moments. But losing you…' He stopped and turned to face her properly. He picked up her hand, a gesture he'd made several times over the past day. One which still made her heart leap each time.

Rose instinctively moved closer to him so they were sitting almost shoulder to shoulder. And, because no words had been invented that could express everything she wanted to tell him, she leant forward and pressed her lips to his.

He stilled for long enough for her to freeze. For time to stop. For their lives to hang suspended between them.

Then his mouth yielded, his arms enveloped her and time sped up. Their tongues met, their lips matched each other's and her hands reached for him, making up for all that lost time.

He tasted of wine and longing, and the world spun around her.

His hand slid over her shoulder and under the strap of her swimsuit. She wanted to lie down and pull him on top of her. She wanted all of him. Now.

No.

She gently pulled her lips away from his and took a deep breath of Alessandro-free air before she was lost completely.

They both caught their breath, but she held his shoulders, and his arms were still wrapped warmly around her waist.

I don't want to let go, but I don't trust myself to fall.

'We never had a goodbye kiss,' he said. 'Maybe if we had, it wouldn't be so hard. I'm so sorry I left without saying a word and I don't know how to make it right.'

He cradled her chin in his palm and stroked her cheekbone with his thumb. The desire to lean into him was almost over-whelming.

'I know you had a good reason to leave. It just maybe wouldn't have hurt as much if I'd known at the time.'

He nodded as he pulled her to him. Instinctively he lay down, pulling her against him, and her head came to rest on his chest, her legs around his. They lay against one another, watching the fire, waiting.

'It's actually very Homeric,' she said after a while.

'What do you mean?'

'Shipwrecks, storms. One of the reasons it took Odysseus twenty years to get home to Ithaca was because he kept run-ning into storms.'

Safe against his chest, she felt Alessandro chuckle. He slipped his body out from under hers and turned to look at her, supporting his head with his bent arm, and she mirrored the gesture.

'Just like us, always running into shipwrecks and obsta-cles,' he said.

'You're worth waiting for.' She leant in and kissed him again.

* * *

The sense of contentment and completeness he felt lying here with Rose in his arms was at odds with the sensations of nervousness and excitement brewing inside him. He was complete, yet burning with want at the same time.

You can't go back but you don't know how to go forward.

He slid his fingers into her hair and his skin shivered at the sensation of her sweet breath on his skin.

'I feel we have unfinished business,' she said. 'Is that strange?'

'Not strange at all,' he said. Her words resonated through him. They definitely had unfinished business. He having left so suddenly, with so much left unsaid between them.

His stroked her cheek and neck with his free hand, curious to see if she would push him away, but she leant into the gesture. Her eyes closed slightly. He loved doing this to her. Loved seeing her body react to his touch.

With her eyes still closed, she murmured, 'I want you.'

His breath came out in a rush. 'Thank God, I want you too.' He brushed his lips against hers. Her curves lay along his and he marvelled at how perfectly their bodies came together.

He trailed kisses down her neck and then found soft pink skin behind her ear and kissed it. She shivered.

'Are you cold?'

'Not at all. That was a different kind of shiver.'

'I'm glad to hear it.' He kissed her neck again, eliciting the same physical response. He pulled her tighter. It had been a long time since he'd been with someone he cared about the way he cared about Rose. He took his time. They had all night, after all.

'I didn't bring you here to seduce you.'

She pulled back and shot him a devastating smile.

'I'd hope not. I'd hope at least you would have taken me

somewhere with a proper bed. But, speaking of which, how unprepared exactly are you?'

He looked around for his backpack, rummaged and retrieved his wallet, which contained a foil packet.

He'd been with other women, but not like this. It hadn't been like this since he and Rose had last been together.

Physically they had both learnt a trick or five but emotionally, mentally, it was as though he was twenty-four again. It was old but new, fresh. They didn't break eye contact as he stroked her or when they fully came together.

The intensity shook him inside and out. He saw her.

And she saw him. All of him.

They moved together instinctively. She was soft and sensuous beneath him, but he felt raw and ragged, trembling. He took care. They took their time and he held her tight as she broke again and again with each stroke until they could shatter no further.

He hadn't meant for that to happen. He'd wanted it to, but knew it would complicate the already complicated mess they found themselves in.

He'd been right all along: with Rose a clean break was best. What had just happened between them had reignited feelings and desires he'd carefully suppressed and locked away when he'd left her in Athens. She was in a dreamy, dozy state beside him, but he was wide awake. His body might be spent but his mind was racing in every direction, at a hundred miles an hour. Everything had changed.

Or had it?

Another summer fling. That was all it could be because in a few weeks, or even less, everything would change again. She would return to her life and leave him to get on with his.

Suddenly it felt as though the walls of the cave were closing in on him. The smoke from the fire, which hadn't bothered him ten minutes ago, was now suffocating.

He had to get out.

He unwrapped himself from Rose as carefully as he could but she pulled him tighter and sighed. His ribcage started to crush his heart.

'I'll be back. I won't be long.'

She opened her eyes and fear flickered across them. 'Where are you going?'

'Just to the boat to get some things we might need before it gets too dark.'

Her grip on him loosened and he rolled away from her. He pulled on his shorts and a shirt. Rose's eyes were closed again. He bent down to give her a soft kiss and whispered, 'I won't be long.'

She'd honestly believed that he had left her earlier. That he had got back on the boat and sailed away. He'd made her feel that way. The shame was made even more suffocating because her fear was not entirely irrational.

He did want to run from her.

But not for the reasons she thought. Not because he could treat her feelings lightly. Not because he didn't care. But because he cared too much.

He'd never felt so close to her than he had in the last few hours. He'd coped with losing Rose last time by ignoring it. By devoting himself to the twins, giving them every ounce of energy and love he had. And then giving everything that he had left to the business. He'd made himself too busy, too distracted, simply too exhausted.

It wasn't healthy—he'd never claimed it was—but it had worked. Except now? Now the kids didn't need him as much. And now Rose knew the truth about why he'd left. They'd crossed a line and he didn't know how he could go back to how things were.

You can't go back, but you can't go forward.

Out of the cave, the fresh air was a relief. It was raining steadily. If had just been him, and if there'd been a little more light, he might have attempted the trip back to the main island. But Rose didn't handle waves and the light had almost faded entirely. The best thing to do would be to make themselves as comfortable as possible in the cave and stay for the night.

He got everything from the boat that would make sleeping here more comfortable—a tarp, two old blankets and some windcheaters kept in the boat for just a situation like this. The ground was level, though hard, but with this extra padding and their body heat...

Rose was sitting up when he returned. She was dressed and warming herself next to the fire. Her auburn hair spilled around her shoulders, catching the firelight. She had been keeping a lookout.

'It's still raining,' he said.

'Yes, I can see.'

He dropped the supplies he'd brought from the boat and added more wood to the fire.

'I've let them know where we are. I'm so sorry.'

'What for?'

'I don't think we should sail back tonight. And I'm not sure how comfortable it's going to be to sleep here. I've got some more things, but it's not going to be as comfortable as my accommodation usually is.'

She smiled up at him and fire spread through him in a whoosh.

'But it is very eco-friendly. I mean, the carbon footprint of this place is nearly neutral.'

He sat back down next to her. 'Well, the wood we're burning counts, I suppose, but I built this place for next to nothing.'

She moved in close to him and slipped her arm around

him. 'And you know the most carbon-neutral way of keeping warm?'

She was going to break him entirely. If he spent the night in her arms, he'd lose his heart for ever.

Without meaning to, his body stiffened.

She recoiled slightly and he heard her murmur a soft, 'Oh.'

'Are you sorry it happened?' she asked and he felt her hold her breath while she waited for his answer. And he took a long while considering it. He'd loved every moment of their lovemaking. But he was terrified of what it meant for the future. Her words from the other night, the ones he had dismissed, now rang true all around him.

We'd only be torturing one another.

Finally, honestly, he answered. 'No. Not at all. I think it complicates things, though.'

'It does.'

'I thought we were saying goodbye.'

'It felt a little more like a hello.' Her voice was soft.

She was right. He'd been a fool to kid himself that making love would help them resolve anything; it had only made everything more difficult. Now the memory of holding Rose wasn't old and distant but her scent was still in his lungs, her taste on his lips. And it was driving him crazy. His heart thrummed with need, his body with want.

'Do you think you can sleep?' he asked. There was little chance he would; his mind and body were too awake, too alive. But it had been a long day and Rose had to work tomorrow.

He did too, for that matter.

'I'm not sure, but I think we should try.'

He located the tarp and laid it out on the floor to try to give a little more insulation from the cold ground. Then he looked at the blankets—two old blankets, the picnic rug and some towels. He wasn't sure how to arrange them.

'You know, we would be warmer if we put them together.'

'It's summer, we won't freeze,' he said without thinking.
Her face fell.

'I didn't mean… Oh, Rose, I just don't want to put any pressure on you. You should join me if you're comfortable.'

In the firelight he could see her shoulders tense. Could see hesitation. Half an hour ago they had been naked, holding on another. Now they were both skittish, pulling back, neither sure where they stood. He'd really messed things up.

'With our clothes on. We'll be warmer that way,' he said. He couldn't stand the thought of her shivering through the night. It was summer, but the air was fresh in the storm. It would get cool overnight. And he needed her to know she was safe, secure, that he wasn't going to leave. And he'd hold her platonically all night to show her that.

How could she have believed he would up and leave her on an uninhabited island? What sort of monster did she think he was?

'It'll be warmer, I promise.'

Was she hesitating because he was only offering her a chaste hug, fully clothed? Or was she reluctant to get close to him at all?

CHAPTER ELEVEN

SHE SHUFFLED AWAY from him. It was clear he thought that making love had been a mistake.

'Do you want some more wine? Something else to eat?'

She nodded and he retrieved the basket and poured them both another glass.

She couldn't meet his eye as he passed it to her, afraid of the pain he'd see in hers. It hurt more than she'd been prepared for: Alessandro loving her one moment, pushing her away the next. They had just made love and now he wanted to lie on the other side of the cave.

He knows you should both keep your distance, and you know it too.

Far from resolving their unfinished business, making love to Alessandro had reminded her of everything they had lost—the playfulness, the way he touched her like no other and could read her body and her emotions. She'd never been more in tune with another person.

Sucking the olives away from the pits was at least distracting. Before long a pile of pits had built up in her palm and she studied them, for no other reason than avoiding Alessandro's eyes.

He regretted it. He'd said he didn't but after they had made love everything had changed. Instead of growing closer, he'd somehow become more distant.

He couldn't wait to get out of the cave immediately afterwards.

If you weren't on an island he would have hot-footed it away as fast as he could. He probably contemplated swimming back to the main island.

If only she could sail, she could be the one to leave. Now it looked as though she was going to be the one abandoned yet again.

'I understand it was just a one-off,' she said.

He stilled. That was what he wanted, wasn't it? They both knew it was for the best. She had no intention of letting this man break her heart a second time and last night they had discussed why a relationship between them was impossible.

'I'm not expecting a repeat performance. I can't have another summer romance with you. And we both know that's all it can be. Some people can have no-strings affairs but I'm not one of them.'

'It's for the best,' he replied, looking at the ground and not at her.

She sat on the tarp and towels. He'd fashioned his bag into a makeshift pillow and pushed it towards her.

He lay down first on his back and patted the ground next to him. The desire to lie next to him was only a fraction greater than the need to walk out of the cave. She lay down next to him, but facing away, and adjusted the bag that was to be her pillow. The ground was firm, but not uncomfortable. She felt Alessandro move behind her and wrap his arms around her. She might be warm, but every muscle in her body was on alert. His body felt tense pressed against hers. She willed the wine, the fire and the exhaustion from the day to overwhelm her. But it didn't.

Behind her he shuffled to get comfortable and every movement raised fresh desire that was quickly replaced by heartache. He was right: it probably would have been better if they had slept separately, instead of like this: together, apart.

'I'm so sorry, Rose.' His warm breath brushed across the top of her head.

'I've told you, it's fine.'

'Not about this. But about leaving the island earlier without telling you. I'm sorry that you thought I'd abandoned you.'

'That was my issue, not yours. I'm okay now…just embarrassed. I thought I was better adjusted.'

If there was any man who should get blame for her insecurities, it was her father, not Alessandro.

Alessandro was not going to leave her again, he was not going to break her heart, because she would be the one to leave first.

Just as soon as she got off this blasted island.

It was mid-morning the following day by the time she was showered, dressed and back at the dig. Gabriel had obviously briefed the team before her arrival and they all looked up at her, smiling but calm. They were scraping away the soil from the top of the slab to reveal its full extent. Others were already working at removing the soil from the sides of it.

'Hey, boss,' Gabriel said to her. 'Everything okay?'

Rose nodded. 'Just an unscheduled stop on a deserted island.'

His eyes opened wide. 'See anything good?'

Rose swallowed hard. 'There are the ruins of a Venetian fort, possibly built on the foundations of a Roman one.'

'Wow! No wonder you stayed.'

Gabriel didn't know the half of it.

Rose and Alessandro had left the island just after sunrise. The water had been calm, the wind light, and they'd been mostly silent on the trip back to Gaios and the drive home. She wasn't sure about him, but she had a lot to think about, digest.

They'd agreed they didn't regret making love but, from the awkwardness afterwards, it was clear to both of them it was a one-off. Last night in the cave had proven it. They had lain together, fully clothed, under the blankets on the makeshift bed. Nothing had happened between them, except a night of wondering, ruminating and very little sleep on her behalf. *He's lying here to keep you warm*, she told herself. *He's being chivalrous; you can't turn around and pull his clothes off.*

She was right: they shouldn't make love again; they shouldn't continue to play with one another's feelings and pretend they somehow had a future together.

He didn't want a relationship; he'd been very clear about that. His life was here, hers was wherever the next important dig was.

Besides, they would never agree on her search and the hotel. His dreams of development and expansion might always clash with her desire to protect the past.

Finding a trace of Homer's world in the Ionian Sea had been her dream for as long as she could remember. Building this hotel was his. It wasn't only about building a future for the kids, it was a thank you to the village that had saved his grandmother and him. They had shared his grief and rallied around in the darkest hour. Most of all, it was his way of honouring his father and brother.

She did feel a little guilty about her role in preventing him from achieving his dream, but what she wanted was important too. It sometimes seemed there were no safe conversation topics; the gulf between them arose even when she least expected it.

The problem was, making love to him didn't feel like a goodbye. It didn't feel as though any business was resolved. She only wanted to do it all again and again. She never wanted to leave him. She could, she decided, have stayed on Erimitírio for ever. Just like the hermit, she wanted to live on the island with Alessandro for hundreds of years.

So they couldn't be together again. She sighed as she picked up her trowel. No matter what, her business with Alessandro would never feel finished.

* * *

As he suspected, the team was all still there, focussing their energies on a small patch of land.

She approached him with a grin on her face, fanning herself with her hat.

She was happy to see him. She wasn't furious about yesterday, about their overnight stay or what had happened on the island. His heart leapt in his chest and his insides glowed.

'Good evening,' he replied happily.

'It is, isn't it?'

'I wasn't sure what kind of mood you'd be in this evening,' he confessed. 'I've come to ask if you want to have a meal with proper tables and chairs.' It was a nod to their impromptu meal the day before. And because he still felt bad about getting them stuck on the island.

She looked puzzled, shook her head quickly and said, 'Oh, maybe. Come and see what we've found.'

His heart landed with a disappointed thud.

Rose moved back towards the others but he stayed where he was. She wasn't happy to see him—she was delighted to have dug something up.

She waved for him to come.

His feet moved as though moving through water and he was afraid of what he was going to see. He was relieved only to see a glimpse of stone about a metre or so long.

'Isn't it great?' she enthused.

'Um…what is it?'

'Some sort of wall, we think.'

'How can you tell?'

'It's smooth, it's been carved. It was placed here deliberately. And there's another one there.' She pointed to the side. He could only see dirt. 'They have been placed at right angles.'

He'd have to take her word for it. 'Why is it significant?'

'Because if it's just a wall, or a fence, then it's unlikely to have right angles. Only structures holding something tend to have right angles.'

'So it could be a house?'

'Some sort of building, yes. But we actually now think it's more likely be a tomb.'

'A tomb?'

Aware the others were listening to their conversation, and equally aware of his own lack of knowledge of all things archaeological, he motioned for her to move away from them and she did. In the shade of the olive grove she explained, 'It may be an abandoned house or anything but, given the size and shape appears to be limited, we don't think it is a palace.'

'That's good news.' Her mouth dropped. 'I mean, good for the hotel, not for you.'

She shook her head. 'No, we still hope we will find something. It seems too small to be a building but it could be some sort of hole. Such as a grave.'

'Wait, one minute you're looking for a palace or a temple, now you say it's a tomb.' He was about ready to call rubbish on this entire project. 'How do you know the stones are even ancient?'

'We don't, you're right. The stones may not even be very old,' she said.

He was right! 'Good.'

'It could just be a cellar, or a hole someone had once dug to hide valuables in the World Wars.'

'That's interesting,' he said, suddenly alert to another possibility: the find might turn out to be valuable or interesting without being old enough to render the whole block of land protected.

'It would be, sure. But these stones—they seem older than that.'

His heart fell.

'Though it's just a hunch,' she added. Neither was ready to admit winning, just as neither was ready to admit defeat.

She placed her hands in her pockets and shifted from foot to foot. 'You came to ask me to dinner.'

'I did,' he confirmed.

'I'm actually going to Joe's with the team, but you're welcome to join us.'

He looked around at the tired red faces of the archaeologists. They would probably be an interesting bunch under any other circumstances. But right now listening to talk of Greek tombs and lost treasures was just about the last thing he felt like doing. Even if it meant being with Rose.

He shook his head. 'Have a good evening,' he said and turned.

It's not your fault he's upset.

It wasn't and Alessandro was going to have to get used to disappointment.

She was silent through dinner with the team, letting them talk and speculate around her, wanting to be drawn into their infectious excitement, yet also wanting to be cautious.

If you do find something significant on his land you are still going to have to deal with him. Your lives will be as closely connected as ever...

As she walked back to the hotel, she resolved to go and speak to him, though she had no idea what she would say beyond apologising for her clumsy and unwelcome invitation to dinner. But he wasn't in his office when she knocked. She sent him a brief message to say she hoped they could talk properly the next day.

Anastasia was sitting out in the courtyard, looking up at the stars. This woman had faced so much sadness, yet she seemed so content sitting here, catching the evening breeze, looking at the stars through the leaves of the over-hanging tree.

How could Rose get some of that contentment? How could she make peace with the world, and Alessandro in particular?

'Do you mind if I join you?' Rose asked.

Anastasia jolted upright, as if she'd actually been dozing all along.

'Yes, yes, my dear. Of course.' She looked around, as though looking for her grandson.

'I've come looking for him, but I don't know where he is.'

'Not in his office?'

'No.'

The older woman raised an eyebrow. 'Then you should sit and wait for him.'

Rose fell gratefully into a chair. Her limbs ached and her shoulders screamed. She hoped she wouldn't have to do too many more fourteen-hour days before they found something.

'Can I ask you a question?' Anastasia asked.

'Of course.'

'Why are you so focused on looking for something that you don't even know exists?'

Rose shrugged. 'I have to look. I want to know, one way or another. Don't we always look for things, never knowing if we may not find them?'

'That's true. But make sure you don't miss what you do have.'

'Ah, subtle,' Rose replied.

Anastasia feigned insult.

'I know that was your less than subtle way of telling me to work things out with Alessandro.'

'I would never do that. I simply want you to see what is in your present, without looking too much into the past.'

'There are so many lessons to learn from the past. In particular, we can learn from mistakes in the past so we don't make them again in our future.'

Anastasia sighed. 'Ah, well. Sometimes it doesn't matter how well we live our lives, whether we are good people or not. Fate has other plans for us.'

Ashamed, Rose looked down. This woman had known more tragedies than anyone deserved to: losing a husband, then a son gone before his time, then a grandson and granddaughter-in-law before their children even knew them.

But Rose was no stranger to misfortune. She had lost people too.

'I get comfort from the past,' Rose admitted quietly.

'Comfort?'

'Yes. From the stories. The myths. I know they are not all real, but I find comfort in them. I know there are tragedies, but the stories are also about overcoming adversity, about bravery. I love the story of Odysseus because he came home. It took him twenty years, and no one believed it was him, but he came home to his still-faithful wife. I don't care if it's true, but I think it's wonderful.'

For years and years after her father had left she had dreamt that he was actually off fighting a war and then had been detained for long years on his journey home—detained by shipwrecks, storms and wars.

Of course, her father hadn't returned, but that hadn't stopped her dreaming.

Anastasia squeezed her knee and said, 'Oh, Engoní.'

Rose knew enough Greek to know that she had just called her 'granddaughter'.

'The lovely Miss Rose came looking for you last night.'

Yiayia pulled him up in the kitchen the next morning.

'She did?'

'Yes. Where did you disappear to anyway?'

He turned and poured a cup of coffee. 'Just out.'

He'd walked and walked. And, before he knew it, he'd reached Gaios. Paxos wasn't large, but still, it wasn't a journey he was in the habit of making. After his strange and awkward conversation with Rose he'd needed to be alone with his thoughts.

Yesterday had started off awkwardly with Rose in the cave. His attempts to protect her feelings had been interpreted as rejection. He'd wanted to hold her all night, as he had that afternoon…stroking her, adoring her, loving her…but she'd made it clear they shouldn't make love again.

He'd hardly slept all night. She was right about describing it as torture—holding her to keep her warm, but not being able to be with her, had been torture.

It had become progressively worse. First with Demetri calling every hour, leaving messages demanding the start date be confirmed. And then Rose's discovery of the stone slabs. So they thought they'd found something? They hadn't yet. And so what if they hadn't had dinner together last night? Maybe they would tonight. And why, when they had both agreed to keep things platonic, was he still desperate to spend time with her?

She'd come looking for him. His grandmother's news shook away the last of his doubts and fears. It would be okay.

'What did she say?'

'Not much, just that she was looking for you.'

If only he hadn't decided to go on such a long walk. If only he'd been home to meet her.

That afternoon, he walked back down to the dig, determined that no matter what he would stay on top of his emotions. Even so, his heart raced and his stomach felt light as he approached. When it came to Rose, staying on top of his emotions was always a challenge.

He spotted her large white hat immediately, his eyes drawn to her like a magnet. Then another movement caught his eye. Ana was standing a few metres to Rose's left, waving to him.

What?

'Ali!' she called. Rose pulled herself up, shielded her eyes from the sun and looked in his direction. The light feeling in his stomach turned to stone and dropped.

He made his way down as Ana rushed to him.

'Isn't this great?' she said breathlessly.

'What are you doing here?'

'Helping with the excavation.'

Rose appeared behind Ana, brushing her hands off on her trousers.

'This was your idea?' he asked her.

'No! It was mine,' Ana said. 'I've been asking her for ages and she finally said yes.'

'Can I talk to you for a minute?' he muttered under his breath.

Ana stepped forward.

'No, not you, I want to speak with Rose.'

Ana rolled her eyes heavenward. A look passed between Rose and his niece, followed by a slight nod from Rose. Ana turned back to the dig and Rose followed him to the tent.

'What's going on?' he said once they were out of earshot of the others.

'Just like she told you, she's been asking me for ages and I said yes. We always need extra hands to dig, carry…'

'Digging? Carrying? You should have asked me. What if she gets hurt?'

'She's not going to get hurt, it's perfectly safe. There's no need to go into over-protective mode.'

Maybe it was just the sun or the heat but his vision blurred. 'Are you suggesting she isn't my responsibility?'

Rose pulled a face he couldn't read.

'Because, for all intents and purposes, I'm her father.'

'I know that.' She touched his arm, but instead of the tingly pleasure he'd felt the other day now her hand was heavy. 'I know you raised her, I know how much you love and care about her. I'm saying she's sixteen and it is perfectly safe for her to be removing dirt from a dig.'

'She's a child.'

'And also a young adult. No one's asking her to push wheel-barrows or carry buckets of rocks.'

'That's beside the point.'

'Hang on, Alessandro, what exactly are you upset about?'

Rose was perfectly right. Ana wasn't doing anything dangerous. She was doing something she actually loved. And this, he hated to admit, was rare. Helping a team of excavators was definitely a better use of her time than looking at goodness knew what on her phone.

'You still should have asked me.'

'Fine, okay. Maybe we should have asked you. But, Alessandro, she's sixteen—she's going to be doing a lot of things without needing your permission soon.'

He was about to storm out of the tent when Rose grabbed a cold bottle of water from a nearby cool box and handed it to him. He wanted to push her hand away but thought better of it. Rose was right—launching into over-protective mode at this point was going to be completely unproductive. He snapped open the water and drank.

She pointed to a camp chair and he sat. She sat next to him. 'And, since we're talking about it, you should probably know that Lucas and a couple of his friends have expressed an interest in helping too.'

This was the limit. After everything he was doing for these kids, everything he had done...

'Don't you have enough people here?'

'Oh, wait, hang on! This isn't about protecting them at all. You just don't want extra bodies here, extra helpers. Oh, this is all about not wanting me to find anything.' She stood and placed her face in her hands.

'What? No.'

'So you want me to find something?'

'Well, I mean, if things were different of course I'd be delighted for you to dig up the Ark. But…'

'But things aren't different.' She finished his sentence. 'This
is where we find ourselves. Here, on this piece of land.'

He shrugged. It was all he could do. They were stuck.

You can't go forward, but you can't go back.

'Ana's genuinely interested.'

He knew that. This was the first thing that had got her enthused in months.

'I'm happy for her to be interested. And, despite how it
looks, I am trying to protect them. This hotel was meant to
be their future. This is what their father wanted for them. I'm
only trying to do what he would have wanted.'

She looked to the dig and sighed, giving him a moment to steal
a glance at her. Her skin was flushed in the heat but not burnt.
Her hair was tied back but messy. Small drops of sweat glistened
on her collar bone and he fought the urge to kiss them away.

She turned back and said, 'But what about you, Alessandro? What do you want?'

You, he wanted to say.

You, forever.

But what would have been the point?

Rose was the only woman he wanted, the only women he'd
ever wanted. His heart's deepest desire. She made everything
else fade into the distance.

Except he couldn't let her. Duty, family, loyalty…he had to
protect those things too. Because, if he didn't look after the
kids, if he didn't do his duty to his family, then how could he
ever offer himself to Rose?

He loved her. He'd always loved her and, he realised now
that everything was hopeless, he always would.

The weather changed. It was Greece, so it was still hot, but
something happened as September became October. The sting

came out of the sun, it took slightly longer for the earth to warm each day and the air was faster to cool. Rose's skin was relieved but her heart was not. October meant the end of her time was coming. With each day she expected a call from the museum. In one week, the six weeks she'd told Alessandro she would need would be up.

The entire team was there that morning, as well as Ana, carrying each bucket to be carefully labelled. They had uncovered the extent of the two stone slabs and were now carefully digging trenches either side. The deeper they got, the closer they were to finding something. Or finding nothing at all.

Late morning, Lucas arrived. Not to help with the digging, but bringing cold water and snacks for the team.

'Does your uncle know you're here?' Rose asked.

Lucas grinned and shrugged. It was the same cheeky expression Alessandro sometimes gave her and Rose didn't know whether to feel happy or sad. His father, Theo, had probably been a lot like Alessandro.

Rose sat with Ana, having a break while she drank and ate.

'Everyone's quiet today.'

Rose agreed. 'It's make or break time. We're going home next week.'

'Even you?' Ana looked crestfallen.

There were no guarantees of anything. 'Probably even me.' It might not be next week but, no matter what happened, Rose would eventually leave.

'But if you find something you'll stay, won't you?' Ana asked.

'Oh, I…for a while, I guess.' Strangely, Rose hadn't spent much time considering what would happen if she did find something.

You don't believe you will, do you?

It wasn't that, she told herself. It was partly so as not to tempt fate, partly because so much depended on what it was they did find. And how upset Alessandro would be…

'But won't there be years of work to do?' Ana asked.

'Maybe, yes, but…'

'You don't actually believe you will find something, do you?' Ana looked at her, her face asking the question Rose had silently asked herself. The teenager was wise beyond her years.

'Of course, there are just lots of variables. If it's something amazing, of course I'll stay a bit longer.'

'Then I hope you find something amazing.'

Rose laughed, 'Thank you, that's nice.'

'And I think Ali would be happy if you stayed.'

'Oh, no, I don't think he'd be happy at all.'

'He'll get over the hotel thing.' Ana waved her hand as though the hotel, Alessandro's duty to his family, was merely a fly to be swatted away.

'I'm not sure he will. He's looking after your future. This hotel is meant for you and Lucas.'

'But we don't want it,' Ana whispered.

'But it's your legacy, your inheritance. It's what your father wanted.'

Rose could practically see the weight on Ana's shoulders as she replied, 'I want to be free, like you.'

Rose laughed. Because she wasn't free. Not really…because leaving here would be the hardest goodbye she'd ever had to make. Her heart was heavy. The rest of the world held no appeal, no excitement. This land, this place, was where she had felt more at home than, well, anywhere.

'Alessandro isn't about to go anywhere. Besides, it seems like Lucas is preparing to take over the hotels, and you're probably going to be able to do anything you want. In building this hotel, he's wanting to give you give you both a family legacy. I don't think he's honestly trying to tell you how to run your life.'

Rose hoped she wasn't wrong about this, for Ana's sake.

'He believes in duty,' Ana said. 'He goes on and on about it.'

'But I think he's mostly referring to his own, not yours.'

She saw the thoughtful look on Ana's face and stood. She had to get back to work.

'And if something happens to Lucas?' Ana asked.

'Nothing's going to happen to him,' Rose said without thinking. She sat back down with Ana and squeezed her arm. Life had taught this young woman to take nothing for granted. 'Seriously, it'll be okay. Alessandro isn't going anywhere for another fifty years, at which point Lucas will be running the business and you'll be happily working in a museum somewhere else in the world. You can make your own decisions. And if he tries to stop you, you tell me. Okay?'

Ana smiled and nodded. 'Okay.'

Rose stood again.

'Do you want kids?' Ana asked and her question hit Rose in the chest. If ever an adult was presumptuous enough to ask her that question, Rose usually declared loudly and strongly that, no, she did not.

She'd usually leave it at that, unless the presumptuous adult challenged her with a remark about how not wanting children was selfish.

'Selfish is having a kid and then abandoning them,' she would reply.

But this was not the answer for a teenager who could not remember her parents, whose parents had left because of tragedy and bad driving, not deliberate choice. It was not the answer for Ana, who was wide-eyed and simply curious, just wanting to know about Rose. And it was not the answer for Ana because, if Rose had ever been lucky enough to have a daughter like her, she knew she could never have left her.

'I don't know,' Rose replied honestly.

Ana stood and walked back to her buckets, seemingly satisfied by Rose's ambiguous answer.

Rose walked slowly back to her position, grateful Ana

hadn't asked more. Because Rose wouldn't have known how to answer. All her life she'd been so sure that the answer to that question was a firm no. Rose intended to work all over the world; she intended to have a base, but not a home. A place where she would keep her books, out of season clothes and an address for her passport. And you didn't bring a child into the world to give them a base rather than a home.

But if she had a home?

Then the answer might be different.

You don't have a home, so keep digging!

And if a daughter happened to come into her life…a daughter like Ana? Then that might also be different.

Rose was crouched with Gabriel on the inside of the corner made by the slabs, sweeping the soil away carefully, when Gabriel cried out. Rose turned, looked over her shoulder and saw it.

A flash of green.

Bronze!

CHAPTER TWELVE

HER HANDS SHOOK as she held the three-thousand-year-old pendant.

It was burnished, but definitely gold. Maybe part of Odysseus' treasure. The link to Homer's hero was uncertain but the age, the significance, was not.

Ten years of work, fifteen years of study, twenty-five years of dreaming about it. And here it was—the discovery of a lifetime.

It was now after sunset and a small crowd was gathering. The atmosphere around the site was charged. They all watched her turn the gold pendant over in her hands.

A few hours after the tip of what had appeared to be a bronze sheet was revealed, the colour of the ground beneath her had changed from brown to gold and there it was: a pendant, intricately engraved with the figure of a griffin.

The bronze appeared to be a sheet and had possibly once covered what lay beneath. At some point, it had cracked and fallen in on what it covered. At that point, while they understood they had found something, the extent of it was unclear.

But the pendant sealed it. They had found treasure. A treasure that had either been hidden on purpose—perhaps to evade an invading army—or, more likely, given the structure and shape of the hole they were digging, from a grave, a tomb. They would need further investigation to know for sure what it was and how long it had been there.

Gabriel held out a plastic bag and Rose reluctantly placed the pendant in it.

She picked up her brush. 'You're still working?' Ana asked.

It hadn't occurred to Rose to stop yet. But perhaps she should. Now they had found gold, the site needed to be secured. They needed to inform the museum. Rose stood and brushed herself off.

'Ana, please don't tell anyone. Least of all your uncle. Not yet. Not until we know more and I've had a chance to call the museum.'

'Um...' Gabriel said. 'I think it's too late for that.'

Rose looked up the hill and saw Alessandro's imposing silhouette coming into view.

They'd found something. Bronze, Lucas had said as he'd passed his office. And then, as if it was being whispered on the breeze from the dig to his office, gold. Gold... Gold?

There were half a dozen people standing around the trenches by the stone slabs. The air buzzed with excitement. He found Rose in the crowd and met her eyes. Her mouth was clearly fighting back a smile, but her brown eyes sparkled.

Don't deny her this. She's excited and she's allowed to be.

'Can we talk?' she asked.

He nodded.

She followed him to where they couldn't be heard by the others aware that, even so, all eyes and ears were on them.

'Rumour has it you've struck gold.'

She nodded. She was trying so hard not to smile. She was probably wanting to jump up and down, but she was being calm. For him.

'We came across a bronze sheet or plate; it's hard to say just yet. But as we brushed the soil away we unearthed a gold pendant. It's beautiful. Engraved with a griffin. It could be a treasure hidden from invaders or robbers. Or it could be from a grave.'

A grave—Odysseus' grave. That was exactly what she'd hoped to find.

'So, what does it mean?'

'We don't know everything. We'll need to do some more precise dating but we are fairly confident that it's at least a thousand years old. Probably more.'

Alessandro knew that any artefacts older than five hundred years were deemed to be the property of the state. The Ministry of Culture would definitely issue a protection order over the site.

He sighed. 'I'm happy for you, I really am.'

'I know you are.' She was watching him for signs of anger, but he wasn't yet sure how he felt. He glanced back down at the dig. At Ana and Lucas talking excitedly with the team, Ana rocking back and forth on her heels. The pleasure of the kids was obvious, even from this distance. Next to him, Rose was vibrating; this was the most exciting moment of her career. No matter how disappointed he was personally, the find had made a lot of people happy. He swallowed hard.

'There are practicalities to discuss,' Rose said.

Were there ever. He had to cancel the builders and tell the bank.

'But first thing is, we can't tell anyone,' she said.

'What? I have to tell people and right away. I have to cancel the builders as soon as possible. Every day I don't, it's costing us thousands of euros.'

'If they find out that we've found something like this, the scavengers will come.'

'Scavengers? Are you suggesting we're all scavengers?'

'Not the Paxiotes, but word spreads. We've already found one gold pendant and there's every reason to believe there

might be more. Even if there isn't, they will want to find something, and could destroy the entire site looking for it.'

'So what do you suggest I do? No, Rose, I can't put it off.
I've already inconvenienced the builders enough.'

'Please, Alessandro. A day or two.' She pressed her palm
to his arm. He froze and looked at it. It was covered in dust
but he still wanted to pick it up and kiss it.

It felt as though they could never agree, that they were always at odds. Always travelling in opposite directions and
trying to pull the rest of the world with them.

'Can you wait until tomorrow or the next day to tell the
builders and the bank? I can make some phone calls and get
some security.'

'Security guards?'

'Alessandro, there's gold. And goodness knows what else.'
She squeezed his arm softly. If only he could give her everything she wanted, he'd happily give her the world.

It was already the evening and there was no point calling
anyone now. Besides, there were quite a few people gathered.

'Are these all your people?' he asked.

She squinted and shook her head.

'Then it seems that word's already got out,' he said. 'What
will you do?'

'I'll have to stay here. Keep watch.'

'All night? By yourself?'

'Gabriel will stay with me.'

Her second-in-command, the eager Frenchman.

'No, I'll stay with you.'

'Alessandro, you don't have to.'

If Rose was going to sit outside all night protecting a buried treasure, he was going to be with her.

'It's my land, my responsibility. I'll keep watch.'

CHAPTER THIRTEEN

THANK GOODNESS IT was a still, dry night.

In the end, they organised shifts. Gabriel and another team member took the first, while Rose and Alessandro ate and tried to sleep. At midnight, predictably just as she'd finally drifted off to sleep, Alessandro woke her with a gentle knock on her door.

Sitting outside alone in the moonlight with Alessandro was probably not the wisest thing for her to do at this point in time. He was keeping his disappointment to himself, but it was clearly written across his beautiful features. She wanted to reach over, rub his arm, hug him, but sensed her touch would be as unwelcome as the gold pendant she'd dug up that afternoon.

On the plus side, he did have a flask of hot, strong coffee.

They sat on camp chairs, watching over the darkness of the site, and sipped in silence until their cups were empty and the silence uncomfortable.

'Thank you again for sitting out here with me,' she said.

'Of course. I don't want someone coming and looting the place any more than you do.'

She wrapped her arms around herself. 'It's good of you. I know this isn't easy for you and I appreciate it.'

'Here, I've got some blankets.' He riffled through the bag at his feet and handed her a blanket.

'Always the boy scout,' she said, pulling it around herself, trying not to remember the night in the cave, the fire or holding him…loving him.

He grinned and shrugged, as he did, giving her a flash of the young Alessandro.

It reminded her of her encounter with Lucas today, the Andino shrug and grin: cheeky; light-hearted. Alessandro used to do it all the time in Athens…not so much now. It was a family gesture. Theo had probably done it too. Theo, who always seemed to come between them.

'Tell me about Theo,' she said.

'Haven't I already?'

'Not directly. You talk about him but you never told me about how you feel about him.'

He sighed deeply, soulfully. 'I don't know. He was my big brother. And he was so good at everything. Lots of people hate their older siblings, but I adored him and worshiped him.'

'How much older was he?'

'Eight years older, but it seemed so much more. He threw himself into the business when he was only a teenager and he'd accomplished so much before he was even thirty. Almost like he knew he didn't have eighty years to live.'

Rose wasn't quite sure what to say. It seemed even more of a tragedy that Theo had died so young and yet had packed so much into his short life: professional success, finding true love and having two beautiful children. 'Anyway, I wanted to be just like him, but I wasn't.'

Rose laughed. 'What do you mean?'

'He was good at sports and sailing.'

'And so are you!'

'He was great at running the business.'

'And so are you. It's gone from strength to strength since you've been running it.'

'Who told you that? Google?'

'Yes, but also everyone here—your grandmother, Ana and Lucas, anyone in Ninos who has spoken about you. Why? Don't you believe it?'

'Because he was so much better at everything. He was a natural. And he understood about family and loyalty without having to go through tragedy to see it,' he said.

'I think you're being way too hard on yourself.' She turned to him and, in the moonlight, saw him resting his forehead on his hands.

'I've tried my best, but father always let me know that I needed to do better. That I should be more like Theo. I didn't even think of going into the family business because he had it all so amazingly under control.'

'Hang on, did you study journalism and politics because you wanted to or because your father made you feel that you weren't good enough to do this?' She spread her arms out at the land before them.

'Maybe a bit of both. If he were still alive, then who knows what he would have done?'

'And who knows what he wouldn't have?'

She couldn't believe he was comparing himself to his late brother and coming up short. 'Alessandro, you're amazing. Theo would be so proud. Proud of the way you've run the business. But, most of all, he'd be so proud and grateful for the way you've raised his children. And you have proven your father completely wrong. You're allowed to think of what you want.'

The only indication he gave that he'd heard her was the quiet hum coming from his direction.

'Even now, even with me ruining your plans, even now they'd been proud. They'd be proud of the hospitality and equanimity you've shown me. They'd be proud of the way you protected me from the storm when we were on the island.'

Now he turned and looked but still didn't speak. She wanted

to get through to him, but it was as if her words were bouncing off him.

This hotel was the family's plan. It was the one thing Alessandro couldn't give them. It had never been just about the money, it had always been about his family's wishes. And the fact that, no matter what he did, Alessandro would still feel as though he didn't measure up to his brother. Which was ridiculous. Alessandro was the most loyal, hard working, loving man she'd ever known.

'You are enough,' she said.

He didn't respond but she thought she saw him shake his head.

They didn't speak for the next while. He looked down at his phone and Rose ruminated on the conversation they'd just had. She watched the moon rise higher, felt the air get ever so slightly cooler. When she stood and stretched, the spell broke and he finally spoke.

'I did get a call from the builders. They'd heard.'

'About the gold?'

He nodded. 'Good news travels fast.'

'What did you tell them?'

'Like you asked, I didn't confirm anything. You were right about needing security.'

Rose knew she wouldn't like what she was about to hear.

'He offered to come down with his excavator in the middle of the night and clear the whole place out.'

'What? Are you serious?'

He grimaced. 'I told him not to even think about it. That we had the world's toughest security guards watching the place.'

She giggled; neither of them could ever be called the 'world's toughest'.

'Thank you. That was good of you.'

'Of course I told him to back off—you don't think I would have agreed with him?'

'No, no, but I do know that this is hard for you. I do know this isn't what you wanted.'

He hunched over in his chair and rubbed his hands. She reached over and rubbed his back. His shoulders were solid and warm. She wanted to wrap her arms around him completely. To reassure him. To love him.

He turned his head and the smile on his soft lips made her insides flip.

'You could try and get a little sleep. You've got another big day ahead tomorrow,' he said.

'What about you?'

'I'll watch.'

'Don't steal the treasure.' She yawned.

He laughed.

'I won't. I'll guard it with my life.' She shivered. And not from the cold but from the desire, the want, brewing inside her.

How could she still want to kiss him when he must despise her? Nothing made sense.

Because, ironically, now that she might be staying on Paxos for a longer stay, she and Alessandro really couldn't be together. The treatment he was giving her this evening was the coolest since she'd arrived on the island, cooler even than the first day when he'd tried to convince her to leave.

With his head bowed, she could study him unconstrained. If only she could hug those shoulders which were carrying too much unnecessary weight. If only she could touch his skin, feel his hands on her body again.

It was strange that, now that any chance of them working through their differences had evaporated completely, she could actually imagine herself staying. It was perverse.

It was the strangest feeling, wanting to stay here. Ana had been right—this find was too big to walk away from. She wanted to see what else they found. She wanted to analyse each piece, study them, see them safely to a museum. There were months, maybe years, of work to be done here.

And there was Alessandro.

Of course you want to stay. You want to be with him. He's the best man you've ever known. The best man you'll ever know.

Yesterday, the thought of finding something wonderful had been so appealing. But now? Now it was real and not just a dream, it was far more complicated then she'd realised. There were so many things to think about.

She couldn't leave Paxos immediately; she had to see this through to the end and find out what else was in this pit or grave. It would take months at least. She was staying for a while, but now she needed her space from Alessandro to guard her heart as much as ever.

It was all such a mess. A list of things to do assembled in her head: she had to let her work know; she had to talk to the museum in Athens about personnel, logistics, money.

She couldn't keep staying at his hotel all this time, could she? It wasn't part of their original deal. It certainly wasn't part of her original plan. She seriously doubted Alessandro wanted her around now that she had destroyed his plans to extend the hotel.

Besides, it was better that she left first. It was always better to leave first.

She stood. Moving away from his gaze was for the best. She began to pace.

'What's wrong? They won't come with the excavators. I told them not to and I'm pretty sure he was just trying me out.'

'It's not that.'

'Then what?'

'I think I should move out.'

'Leave the hotel?' he asked.

'I can't stay now, Alessandro. Not when I ruined every-thing for you.'

He stood as well. 'I don't blame you for this. It isn't your fault. Well, it is your discovery, but I don't blame you. It's just circumstance.'

He lifted his hand, as though to touch her, but dropped it just before their bodies made contact. He knew as well as she did the sparks that would fly through them if they did.

'I feel like I would be taking advantage, and it wouldn't be fair.'

'But it's also about me, isn't it?'

She had to be honest, there was no point being otherwise. 'Alessandro, you know I love being with you, and that's exactly why I have to leave. We can't keep doing this to one another.'

I don't think I could get over you again.

'I really don't mind you staying.' He didn't look at her as he spoke but kicked the ground.

'But I mind. It wouldn't be fair.'

'On you or me?'

'On both of us.' She swallowed hard, wishing she'd had the foresight to have this conversation closer to dawn, when at least one of them could leave. Now they were stuck sitting here with one another for the next five hours. *Awkward much?*

'Okay,' he said and nodded. 'I understand, and you're prob-ably right.'

Even though he had agreed, her heart fell. It was what she wanted, wasn't it? Then why did she feel so awful?

She paced around the site for a while, more to keep awake than to keep watch. When her legs began to ache, she sat down again next to Alessandro, who was still hunched over his phone. She must've dozed off for a while, when a noise in the bushes startled them both at one point, but it turned out just to be a goat.

'I hope it's okay,' she said and she thought she saw a sad smile on his face. They settled back down. It certainly wasn't Demetri and his bulldozer.

Eventually, the sky lightened from black to blue to pink. Her team began to return even before the sun was actually above the horizon, and at that point Alessandro took his leave.

His limbs were heavy when he walked into the kitchen. Ana was poring over three books open on the table in front of her and Yiayia was making coffee.

'Did you know that they actually don't know where Odysseus died?'

He shook his head. Homer and Odysseus were not his favourite people this morning.

Lucas was typing something on his laptop. 'Everyone's talking about this,' he said. 'It's the most exciting thing to happen on Paxos since the Nazis invaded.'

'Oh, Lucas, really,' Yiayia chided.

'Good morning, *kamari mou*, are you going to try and get some sleep?' she asked Alessandro.

He shook his head. 'I've got things to do. Lucas, who is *everyone*? Who knows about Rose's discovery?'

Lucas shrugged. 'Everyone around here. Kids at school.'

So maybe not everyone. The find was certainly exciting for the locals but probably wasn't the first thing on the international news. It was one more thing to look into today. One more thing to deal with.

'Oh, Yiayia, Rose will be moving out of the flat.'

'And moving in with you?' Ana asked, wide-eyed.

'What? No! Ana, how could…?'

He regretted his tone and her face fell.

'No, she's probably moving back to Myra's.'

'Didn't you tell her not to leave?' Ana's eyes, which had been so wide and bright moments ago, now clouded over.

You did that.

'She doesn't want to stay in the flat.'

'Why not? What's wrong with it?'

Its proximity to me, he thought.

'What happened between you?' Ana probed. She was too smart, this one.

'Nothing.'

Not nothing. Something. Everything. But nothing any more.

'Now that she'll be staying a little longer, she doesn't think it would be appropriate to take advantage of my hospitality.'

'I don't understand. Now, more than ever, she should be staying. With you.'

'Shh, Ana,' her great-grandmother admonished.

'I see the way you look at her.' Ana had no intention of heading Yiayia's warning.

He shook his head.

'I know you like her.'

'We're friends,' he said. It was such a loaded word—friends. Were they even friends? In between 'acquaintance' and 'lover' came 'friend', but were they even that?

'I love her!' Ana cried.

'You can't love her—you hardly know her.'

'I love her and I want to be just like her.'

He grimaced. This was not how it had been meant to go. Ana was not meant to become attached to Rose. She was not meant to be upset by her departure.

Just as he wasn't. The whole point of not sleeping together again had been to protect his heart. But that ship had sailed already. That ship had sailed almost a decade and a half ago.

'Don't mind her,' Yiayia said. 'She's young and doesn't understand how complicated real life is.'

Lucas watched on as the scene played out but Ana, standing now, was not going to stop. 'I do understand. I understand that you resent her because you can't build Papa's hotel. But that was Papa's dream, not mine, not Lucas's and I don't think it's yours. I think your dream…'

Yiayia held up a hand in front of her. 'Shh, now, Ana, please stop. Please let your uncle and I talk. Go and get dressed.'

Alessandro's heart pounded but his skin felt cold. Ana, for all her precocity, had never spoken to him so bluntly. He wasn't angry, just stunned.

'She's not leaving, she's going back to Myra's. You can still see her.'

She just doesn't want to see me. I've been a fool. I've tried to stop something that couldn't be stopped.

Our fates were sealed three thousand years ago.

Ana looked at him for a long while, but still didn't leave. He didn't have the strength to tell her to leave, waiting for her next onslaught of teenaged wisdom.

'They were our parents, but we don't remember them. You're the only parent we remember,' Lucas said.

'I know,' Alessandro said.

'And we want you to be happy. It's not that we don't care about the hotel, but we care more about you.'

'The hotel is for you. It was your father's dream. It's what we all want.'

Ana and Lucas exchanged glances. Not for the first time he felt ganged up on by a pair of kids.

'We do want the hotel, but not at all costs. Don't you see?' Ana asked.

See? He saw two confused and upset teens. One day, when the excitement of Rose's find wore off, they would regret not having their father's legacy on the island. They would regret that Paxos hadn't got the development it so desperately needed. They were too young to see it now, but one day this discovery would be in the past and what about their future?

'I'm sorry that Rose is moving out, but it is for the best.'

'Best for who?'
This time it wasn't one of the twins asking.
It was his grandmother.

CHAPTER FOURTEEN

ROSE'S DAY PASSED in a sleep-deprived blur, but eventually the adrenaline and caffeine kicked in. The team was delighted to unearth more treasures—two silver cups. The mood was buoyant. This really was turning out to be the once-in-a-lifetime find she had dreamed of.

She'd also managed to get in contact with the museum, and two security guards from the Ministry of Culture arrived late afternoon. By the time she dragged herself up the hill to the hotel that afternoon, she was ready to sleep for a week.

But she couldn't. She had one more thing to do first.

Myra was happy to have Rose back and could offer her a room of her own now that the summer peak had passed. The museum was also more than happy to pay whatever it was going to take to discover the full extent of their dig. Things were looking up.

Rose returned to the hotel that evening to gather her things. She wanted to get out of there, get back to Myra's before she accidentally ran into him again. She could just leave without saying goodbye.

But she couldn't leave without saying goodbye to Ana, Lucas or Anastasia; that would be unforgivable. She had to risk seeing Alessandro again, hope that he too was going to keep his distance from her. It was hard knowing he was out in the world, seeing him but not with her, but not being able to hold him was the hardest of all.

Once she had packed, she wheeled her case to the kitchen door and knocked.

Ana bounded out. 'What did you find today? I'm so bummed it was a school day.' Then she spied the suitcase. 'You're really going? But Alessandro…'

Anastasia touched Ana's arm and she stopped speaking.

'I came to say goodbye.'

'You don't have to go,' Ana said.

'I do.'

'Why? It's much nicer here. And closer.'

Ana made a good point. But it was done.

'It's not right for me to stay.'

'Did my stupid uncle say something stupid?'

Rose smiled at Ana's vehemence. 'No, he didn't do or say anything. But I can't keep relying on his hospitality.'

'Then it must be because of us.' Lucas frowned.

Rose's heart broke at that moment.

'No. Not at all. I've loved staying with you, and you can come and say hello any time. I'll be at the dig. Or at Myra's. I'm not going far.'

They looked at her as though they didn't believe her.

'It isn't about you,' she assured them, as much for herself as the kids.

'Let her go, *agapi mou*,' she said.

The twins gave Rose one last, sad glance then walked inside.

'You understand, don't you?' Rose asked Anastasia.

'I understand. I don't agree, but I do understand.'

Rose hugged her and turned to leave before she burst into tears.

Rose stood at the road and waited for the car to drive her to the village.

Then it must be because of us.

The look on their face had been heart-breaking—and heart-broken. She would have stayed for the twins, were it not for their uncle.

No, she couldn't stay for them, because it wasn't right. It wouldn't be right to take advantage of Alessandro's hospitality now that she was stopping the extension. Putting a halt to his brother's dreams.

And it wouldn't be right for either of them to be so close together, spending so much time with one another. That would be the most unfair of all.

Was this what her father had felt? Had he, in fact, just been too gutless to say goodbye?

Saying goodbye to the twins hurt her physically, and they were not her own; she had only known them for a matter of weeks.

She wasn't leaving the twins, but she was most definitely leaving their uncle. Though it was going to hurt to see them. It was going to hurt to hear them talk about him while not being a real part of their lives.

Her thoughts circled back. Was this how her father had felt—that he couldn't stay in contact with Rose because it would hurt too much?

She shook her head. She still didn't forgive him; a better man would have overcome that fear.

But perhaps now she did finally understand that a reason for his absence might have been that he'd actually loved her.

CHAPTER FIFTEEN

THERE WAS A lot to do—people to call, plans to remake—but this time he wasn't going to make the mistake of fourteen years ago. This time he was going to talk to Rose before he made too many other plans.

His eyes were drawn, as usual, straight to her white hat. She was standing with Gabriel and a woman, hunched over an object she was holding in both hands.

More treasure.

But this time his heart didn't drop. It sang. The find was probably turning out to be bigger than Rose had even hoped. He waved and caught Gabriel's eye. Gabriel nudged Rose and she looked in his direction. He noticed her shoulders drop. She passed the object to Gabriel and walked slowly over to Alessandro, each footstep heavy with reluctance.

She took her hat off and wiped her brow with her long sleeve as she reached him. Her face was pink, flushed and healthy, though some dark circles were under her eyes. Neither of them had got much sleep in the past few days.

'How's the dig going?' he asked.

'We don't have to talk about this, you know.'

'I know, but I want to,' he said honestly. 'I want to hear all about it.'

'Alessandro…' She sighed. 'There's no need to be polite. I know this has hurt you.'

There was genuine pain in her eyes. The greatest moment of her career had been tarnished by him and he hated it.

But fortunately it was within his power to fix it.

The idea had been percolating since the night they had watched over the site. At first, he'd thought her timing couldn't be worse, telling him she wanted to move out of the hotel while they'd still had five hours to sit alone with one another.

But it had been sitting there in silence next to her in the moonlight, looking over the site and wondering what lay beneath the surface, that the idea had come to him. He'd done some research via that great oracle, the Internet.

But the conversation he'd had with his family had sealed it—they loved him regardless of whether he could fulfil Theo's wishes. They'd assured him that this was what they wanted, that there would always be a chance for another hotel but never a chance for this.

He had their full and enthusiastic support—especially Ana's, who'd had to be told many times that it was just an idea and not to announce it to the world.

He still had many, many people to speak to—the builders, architects and the government. There were approvals and all sorts of things. It wasn't going to happen straight away, but that was also okay. Good things, important things, didn't need to be rushed.

Not when he was so sure.

As he was now.

'I'm going to build a museum.' He could feel the tremor in his voice. He was going to build a museum—not a hotel, but a museum! He loved the way that sounded.

'I'm going to build a museum to showcase what you find. To show the history of Paxos and the Ionian Sea.'

She looked at him as though he was mad. He felt a bit crazy, not exactly like himself, and yet more like himself than he'd felt in years.

'I haven't figured out all the details yet, and there's obviously a lot to sort out, but I wanted you to know that that's what I'm going to do.'

He waited, knowing the grin on his face looked foolish and not caring. Rose's jaw dropped and her face seemed redder.

Her voice was soft. 'But I don't understand how. You can't just build something here, even if it is a museum. We're still digging. We're going to have to survey the whole area.' She closed her eyes and drew in a deep breath. Finally, she reached over and touched his elbow. 'It's a lovely, lovely thought, but I don't see how it could work.'

Luckily, he was several steps ahead of her and he just smiled. 'Yes, I've thought of all that. See that land over there?' He pointed at the hill and across the road to the same block of land he'd once told her was unsuitable for the hotel. It wasn't large enough for the hotel, and didn't have the ocean view, but for the early stages of the museum, it was perfect. 'Assuming a survey doesn't find anything there, the government will agree to lease it to us. The building could start as soon as the survey is done.'

She shook her head. 'They take time to plan; you can't just build one.'

'This wouldn't be the completed museum. It would just be the beginning. It would be a place for you to store the things you find, a place if you want to have offices. I think we could design that reasonably quickly. I've been in touch with an architect friend—'

'You've—you've spoken to an architect?' she spluttered.

'I've spoken to a few people, just to see what can be achieved. But I haven't made any decisions. I wanted to know if it was even possible before I spoke with you.'

Her mouth fell. 'You're really serious.'

'I'm very serious,' he said. 'I've never been more serious about anything in my life.' He picked up her hand. It was trembling. Or maybe that was his.

'Why?' she asked. Her voice was small, but her eyes were big.

'Because I've been too focused on one thing for too long. I've been worried so much about Theo's dreams for the children's future that I didn't think of their own wishes. I thought I was doing the best by them by doing what their father wanted, but the best thing for them is what they want, what they're interested in.'

Rose bit her lip and turned round to look back at her colleagues and the dig. 'I never met Theo or his wife but, given that he was your brother, I think he must've been a very good man. And I think that, if Theo and Arianna had known about this, he wouldn't want to be building a hotel here.'

His heart swelled. A very good man? That was what she'd called him. A very good man...but was that going be enough?

'It's funny, the kids told me the same thing when I suggested the plan to them.'

She turned back to face him, her golden eyes bright with excitement. 'You've talked to them too?'

'I asked them before I made any calls. I wanted to ask them before I came to you.'

She nodded. He wished he knew what she was thinking. He knew the plan had holes, he knew that a million things would have to go right to make this work, but he had to try.

'They adore you, you know.'

She kicked the ground. 'I adore them too.'

He looked into the distance, closed his eyes and drew a deep breath, but he needed courage more than air.

Now.

'Rose, there's something else.'

'Something else?'

'I want you to help me with the museum.'

'Help? How? I don't know anything about planning or building.'

'Run it, once it's built. Or whatever you like. I want you to stay.'

'Here?'

'Here with me. I've been a fool, not realising this all along. Your discovery is fantastic for the island. It will bring tourists in more than any hotel. I was hoping you would run the museum—after you've finished excavating, that is. I know it's not a major museum, but you'd be the director. You'd have total control. And you would be able to run the excavation for as long as it takes.'

'Oh.' She turned and looked at the dig as though the answer was there. He fought the urge to spin her back to him. *Me. The answer is behind you.* Why was she taking so long to answer? He was the one who had been so slow to figure this out.

'And if I don't stay?' she asked. 'What about the museum?'

'I'll do it anyway. But I want you to be the one to set it up.'

'Why?'

Tell her.

'I love you. I want you to stay with me.'

She was still, unnervingly so. Almost as though she hadn't heard. Finally, she turned. 'It's a lot to take in. I'd have to leave London. The university.'

'I know, I'd be asking a lot, but hopefully giving you a lot. Everything I can. No one else has ever come close to making me feel what I do when I'm with you.' Maybe all this time he'd been subconsciously waiting for her. 'I love you, Rose. I've always loved you and I want to be with you. I don't have any intention of ever letting you go again.'

She covered her face with her hands. Was she hiding her joy or her distress?

'I don't know,' she said.

'You don't know if you love me? Or you don't know if you will stay?'

'I need time, please. I need some time to think. To process this.'

Shouldn't she be able to answer a question like that right away?

You took weeks to figure this out.

Not just weeks—it had taken him well over a decade to realise that he didn't have to block out what he wanted in his life in order to do the right thing by his brother. He's been trying to be his brother, to replace him. And Theo wouldn't have expected or even wanted that. Alessandro hadn't had to sacrifice his own life entirely to do the right thing by the kids and he saw that now.

Rose had her own worries and he needed to respect that.

'I'm not going to leave you. Never. I'm never leaving Paxos for good, so I'll never be able to leave you.'

She half-sighed, half-grimaced.

'I just need time. This is…big. Can I sleep on it?'

Sleep? A whole day? Could he wait that long?

He'd have to.

Rose turned and walked back down the hill, hardly feeling her feet. Was she floating? She certainly felt strange; her limbs tingled, her heart raced. He loved her. He wanted her to stay. He was building a *museum*. It was too much to process.

She reached the dig and looked down to the place where she'd been sitting prior to his arrival, but suddenly didn't know what to do. He'd just offered her his life and she had sent him away. She spun and looked back up the hill. Should she call him back? He'd disappeared from the horizon. Should she chase after him?

But if she did, what would she say? Could she stay? Could she be with him—for ever?

Her hands picked up a brush and she knelt, on automatic pilot.

'Did he come to try and persuade us to leave again?' Gabriel asked.

Rose shook her head. Thank heavens Gabriel didn't ask any more questions. She wasn't ready to tell them about the museum—they'd all be delighted. She'd lose all sense of rational thought.

Her heart was telling her—yelling at her—to race back up the hill to Alessandro and throw herself into his arms.

But that would be foolish, like walking off a cliff and straight into heartbreak.

If you walk off the cliff, he might catch you...

Could the museum really happen? Was it just a pie-in-the-sky plan?

No. She knew Alessandro better than that. He wasn't one for making fanciful plans that were easily abandoned. He saw things through. For the last six weeks he'd been trying to achieve the plans his dead brother had made years ago. No, Alessandro was not one to change course quickly, or on a whim. He believed in this museum.

And he believes in you.

She wanted to laugh and cry at the same time. Could she stay on Paxos, keep working on the site? That part of his question was easy—yes, she could. She'd love nothing more than to see this excavation through to the end.

It was the second part of the question that was the real problem. She kept working, the smooth, monotonous motion of brushing the dirt away soothing her body, and after a while her mind. *Sleep on it.* What was she thinking? How on earth was she possibly going to sleep while she was thinking about this?

She could stay on Paxos and be with Alessandro. Have the life they'd planned when she'd been twenty.

And a family.

Staying with him on Paxos would mean staying with the

children. It would mean not letting them down, and that was another thing entirely.

She could never let Ana and Lucas down, she realised with a certainty that took her completely by surprise. She also knew with certainty that she'd never let Alessandro down either. His happiness was inextricably linked to hers. That had become so apparent over the last day, when her joy at the discovery had been tempered by his sadness.

No, her reservations were not about her feelings for the children.

'Oh, no. What am I doing?' she muttered and stood.

Gabriel looked up. 'What's wrong?'

'I'm an idiot, that's what's wrong.' She put down her brush. 'I've got to go.'

She was sweating, panting so hard she could hardly make herself heard when she called out to him. He kept getting further and further away.

She stopped, drew in some hard, deep breaths and yelled as loudly as she could, 'Alessandro!'

He stopped but didn't turn. Her heart plummeted.

She called again, 'Alessandro.'

This time he turned and moved slowly back down the hill to her. Was he upset? She couldn't tell; his face was expressionless, his step heavy.

She ran up the hill as fast as she could, and thankfully he met her halfway.

She tried to talk but her throat was dry and there was no air in her lungs.

'I've thought about it,' she gasped.

'That was quick.' He was uncertain, so she reached for his arm and squeezed it while she caught a few more breaths.

'I'm sorry it took me that long.' She couldn't hold back a smile. She was going to spend her life with Alessandro on Paxos.

He lifted his head and a smile began to grow on his lips.

She took the last step towards him and he threw his arms around her. She was home.

He held her close, still panting, his heart racing against her cheek. Her gaze found his, but just for long enough for her to nod and let him know that her answer was yes. Then she closed her eyes and her lips met his. The kiss was sweet, tender and promising for ever.

When they pulled apart, he asked, 'Really? You will stay?'

'I will stay for ever. I love you, Alessandro.'

She felt the tension escape from his body in a rush.

'Oh, thank God. I just need to hear you say it.' He pulled her tighter and kissed her again.

But she wasn't done and pulled back.

'I love you, Alessandro Andino.'

'I love you too, Dr Rose Taylor.'

He squeezed her hand. 'Do you want to get back to work?'

She laughed. 'Not just yet. Whatever's buried there has waited thousands of years. It can wait a little longer.' She took his hand and led him back to the hotel.

EPILOGUE

IT WAS A glorious Greek day. The sky was the colour of the flag and the sun bright, but a gentle spring breeze kept the air fresh. Rose was nervous but excited. The island was packed with visitors this weekend, but not the usual tourists but academics from the museum in Athens, Rose's colleagues from London—or, ex-colleagues now—and some representatives from the Ministry of Culture. They were all here for the opening of the small museum that had been built to showcase the Tomb of the Bronze Age Warrior.

The things they had found were even more remarkable then she'd ever let herself hope. Since the initial discovery, Rose and her team had uncovered bronze basins, weapons and armour. They had uncovered beads made of amethyst, amber and silver and more than thirty stone seals, intricately carved with images of goddesses, lions and bulls. This was one of the most remarkable finds made anywhere in Greece in the last decade.

Several months after they'd first found the items, they'd finally reached the bottom and confirmed what they had suspected—a largely intact skeleton confirmed they had found a tomb. The scientific dating had confirmed Rose's greatest hopes—the tomb did, in fact, date back to the Bronze Age.

Even if she hadn't found Odysseus, she had found the final resting place of a Bronze Age warrior king.

The grave was three and a half thousand years old so did

indeed date to the time of the battle of Troy and Odysseus' journey as told in Homer's stories.

The grave was now covered with an impressive roof, protecting the ruins from the elements, with a raised walkway allowing visitors to observe the archaeologists at work. The plan was now to carefully excavate the entire site. Even if they did not find another grave or remnant of buildings, simply analysing the area and the soil might give them further clues about Bronze Age life on Paxos.

They'd found over a thousand objects in all; it was going to take many years to preserve and curate all of them, as well as learning as much as one could from each of them. The objects were beautiful, but they could also tell so much about the past as well—the story of the man they were buried with, but also the story of the world in which he'd lived.

Today was a celebration; a large party had been planned at the hotel afterwards to welcome their visitors and thank the locals for their support.

Rose wore a long, flowing blue-and-white patterned dress, her red hair flowing in graceful waves around her shoulders. Spotting her at the entrance, Alessandro went to her and slipped his arm around her waist. 'I'm so proud of you.' He kissed her cheek.

'What for?' she asked.

'All of this,' he said, gesturing to the crowd around them.

'No.' She laughed. 'I did the easy stuff. You did this. I'm proud and so grateful you used your money and your time to create this.'

'I can't believe I ever wanted to do otherwise,' he replied.

'I can. You were only trying to build the future for this family that your brother had envisaged. And that's not a bad thing. He hadn't counted on any of this. I know, if he were still here, this is exactly what he would have done as well.'

Rose squeezed his arm and her heart flooded with joy. The

past three years had been the most amazing of her life. The museum was a joint project between the Andino family and the National Museum. Some of the items would be on display in Athens, but many would remain on Paxos in the newly built museum.

It had been a busy couple of years on the island. In addition to the museum, they had built more accommodation nearby, long-and short-term stays, because the academics who came to study tended to want to stay for months at a time.

Alessandro sometimes said he found it hard to believe he could ever have objected to the excavation. The prestige and revenue it had brought to the business was remarkable, and beyond any of their expectations. However, the sheer joy and excitement that the discovery had brought to the village and his family was worth so much more.

Ana was obsessed with all things ancient Greek and was now at university in Athens. Lucas was interested in the hotel business, which he hoped to help grow and solidify, and he was intending to study business management in Athens.

Now that the twins were old enough that Alessandro and Rose could think about travelling and exploring the world together, the only place they wanted to be was on Paxos.

'You've made me happier than I've ever been,' she said to Alessandro, and he bent his head to kiss her. Softly at first, then deepening into something that sent ripples out to her toes.

A groan from a pair of teenagers reminded them where they were.

'Ah, leave them be, they deserve this day,' Yiayia said.

Alessandro was no longer just a hotel developer. He was a benefactor, builder of a museum which, even though it was only just officially opening, was already acclaimed around the world. He had been invited to other museum openings, invited to speak at conferences about the way his family had handled the find and how he had worked with the local and national governments to design and build the museum on Paxos.

Somehow, at forty-one years of age, he'd found himself forging a new career, one that drove him with a new passion. He found himself thinking of returning to finish the university degree he'd abandoned, much to the feigned horror of Ana and Lucas. He reassured them all that any study he did would be remote; he had no intention of leaving Rose on Paxos. Or anywhere, for that matter.

Rose no longer mourned the lost years without Alessandro; what they had now was wonderful. The future was too bright to dwell too much on the past. She twisted the wedding ring on her finger, gold and simple. She spent too much time with her hands in dirt for anything too intricate. But to her it was more precious than any of the treasures she'd found in the grave.

Their wedding had been here, at the hotel overlooking the Ionian Sea. Her mother and friends from Britain had made the trip, but they were outnumbered by all the locals. Alessandro had invited almost everyone on Paxos. They had eaten and drunk all day and danced into the night.

And the bride had worn white.

* * * * *

COMING SOON!

We really hope you enjoyed reading this book. If you're looking for more romance be sure to head to the shops when new books are available on

Thursday 3rd August

MILLS & BOON®

Coming next month

WEDDING PLANNER'S DEAL WITH THE CEO
Nina Milne

"It's a bike."

"Well done," he said kindly, and she grinned.

"Ha-ha. But… I can't ride a bike. I told you that."

"I know. So I'm going to teach you." A pause. "If you want, that is?"

"I'd love that." Warmth touched her that he'd registered her comment at breakfast the previous day, must have seen the regret, the emotion she'd tried to hide.

"Good. We can do a lesson a day and by the time we leave you will be able to ride a bike."

She blinked, knew it was ridiculous to feel tearful, but she did. She hauled in breath. "Your farewell gift." A reminder to herself.

Carefully she swung her leg over and sat, couldn't help but smile at him as warmth touched her again at his gesture. And there it was like a bolt sent on the sweet-flower-laden breeze, a sudden awareness of his proximity, his scent a kind of woodsy, clean, masculine smell, and she felt almost dizzy with a longing. A yearning that it could all be different, that somehow she and Nathan could be two people without baggage or a past, two people open to… To what?

Love? A future? Her eyes snapped open as she registered the sheer foolish futility of her thoughts.

Between them she and Nathan had enough baggage to sink the *Titanic* if it hadn't hit an iceberg. More than that, she would never willingly put herself in the deliberate path of probable pain and humiliation again.

But she watched him, crouched now on the ground so she could see the powerful muscles of his thighs flex, and then he stood up, right next to her, his hands on the handlebars so close to her she thought she'd combust.

And it wasn't only her, she realised—it wasn't. She saw his jaw clench, saw his fingers tighten around the handlebars. And she was tempted, oh, so tempted, to simply pretend to wobble, 'lose' her balance and tumble into him and then he'd catch her in his arms and…and he'd kiss her and she'd kiss him and…that way lay disaster. Absolute disaster. He would be horrified—that was what would happen—and that horror would etch his face. Or would it? He wanted to kiss her—she was sure of it.

Continue reading
WEDDING PLANNER'S DEAL WITH THE CEO
Nina Milne

Available next month
www.millsandboon.co.uk

LET'S TALK
Romance

For exclusive extracts, competitions and special offers, find us online:

f MillsandBoon

🐦 @MillsandBoon

📷 @MillsandBoonUK

♪ @MillsandBoonUK

Get in touch on 01413 063 232

MILLS & BOON

THE HEART OF ROMANCE

A ROMANCE FOR EVERY READER

MODERN

Prepare to be swept off your feet by sophisticated, sexy and seductive heroes, in some of the world's most glamourous and romantic locations, where power and passion collide.

HISTORICAL

Escape with historical heroes from time gone by. Whether your passion is for wicked Regency Rakes, muscled Vikings or rugged Highlanders, awaken the romance of the past.

MEDICAL

Set your pulse racing with dedicated, delectable doctors in the high-pressure world of medicine, where emotions run high and passion, comfort and love are the best medicine.

True Love

Celebrate true love with tender stories of heartfelt romance, from the rush of falling in love to the joy a new baby can bring, and a focus on the emotional heart of a relationship.

Desire

Indulge in secrets and scandal, intense drama and sizzling hot action with heroes who have it all: wealth, status, good looks…everything but the right woman.

HEROES

The excitement of a gripping thriller, with intense romance at its heart. Resourceful, true-to-life women and strong, fearless men face danger and desire - a killer combination!

To see which titles are coming soon, please visit

millsandboon.co.uk/nextmonth